BONKIE

The Great Bank Blagger

BONKIE

THE GREAT BANK BLAGGER

Hi Will,

I hope you can read BONKIE in more comfortable circumstances than those in which the book was written.

Best wishes

Seamus O'Mulgreavey 'Adam' 2008

Seamus O'Mulgreavey

National Library of Australia
Cataloguing-in-Publication data:
O'Mulgreavey, Seamus.
Bonkie, the great bank blagger.

ISBN 1 86305 003 5.

1. Title.

A823.3

Produced in Australia by Lotus Publishing House Pty Limited,
Carlingford, NSW 2118

Cover artwork and design by Christine Boyle

Typeset in Australia by Typezone, Carlingford, NSW 2118

Back cover photograph by Paul Hoyne
Big banana by Rohan Wilson

Printed in Australia by Macarthur Press Sales Pty Limited,
Parramatta, NSW 2150

To Christine

Chapter 1

A LATE spring sun shone down from a cloudless blue sky and warmed up the grimy facade of old Dublin. Dear auld Dublin, birthplace, home and livelihood to one George Beak, armed and sometimes unarmed robber. Georgie stood at a bus stop in College Green and watched movements at the Big Grey Jug with professional interest. He was not distracted by the pretty young girls and boys who fluttered past his post, gay butterflies welcoming the sun, floating among the exhaust fumes and the stink floating up from the Liffey. Georgie wore a blue pin-striped suit, brown brogues, a white silk shirt with matching tie and he carried a brolly in case of an unexpected shower. All the clothes he wore had been nicked for Georgie by the dippers. The shoplifters liked a special order. It meant they did not have to go hawking hot gear after a hard day's shoplifting. Even the big bunch of daffodils, behind which Georgie hid his well-known mug, had been purchased with stolen money. It gave Georgie an indescribable feeling of satisfaction to steal. It was bliss to his crooked soul. The first stroke he had pulled was when he whipped a cone from a rich kid parked in a pram next to his own. It had been delicious but not as delectable as the thrill that had run up and down Georgie's little dumpy legs. The screams, the howls of outrage, were the same; coming out of the mouths of babes or bank tellers. It was all the one big Hee-Haw.

Georgie buried his face deep in the fragrant blooms and willed himself to blend into the pavement. He was a concrete lizard, a camouflaged crook.

The Granada, carrying five heavy porkers, had been in the area all morning.

The boot was hopping off the ground and the car looked to Georgie like a huge can of ham with four wheels welded onto it. He peered out, full of hatred, at the passing porkers, from behind the daffodils. Georgie knew the driver well and the moron with the machine gun slung around his neck. The three porkers squashed into the back, each had a briefcase on his lap holding an Uzi and six thirty-round magazines. All five porkers also carried .38 Special revolvers or Walther pistols. They all wore sports jackets and dark glasses and all had big red culchie heads. A person could not miss them, thought Georgie idly as they passed him by. Secret police my bollox. He focused his attention back on the bank.

Georgie was the first part of a smooth tracking operation mounted by his Firm. He was watching for an unescorted van coming to collect, hopefully, a few bags or boxes of cash. The Firm would track it to its destination with a view to snatching the money at its weakest link, usually in some office being counted after delivery. They always tracked down their own strokes and as a golden rule always did all their own leg work. One could be sure then that the porkers were not going to produce some snivelling, whining, 'inside' man in a Garda station. There would not be any mutton-headed porkers, armed to the teeth, wearing bullet-proof jackets, hiding in the strongroom and not a shilling in the place. The Firm did not get spoof from rip-off merchants looking for easy money for worthless information. No Walter Mitties swearing they saw millions in the local sweetie shop. No loose ends before or after.

A Securicor van pulled up by the side door of the bank. Four dickheads got out with a flea-bitten doberman. Georgie reckoned the dog was the boss. At least if it knew it was going to be beaten or shot protecting someone else's money it would take off like a greyhound. He could never understand the dickheads trying to wrestle shotguns off strokers. On one stroke the Firm had had to mangle a dickhead and cut the bag off him with bolt cutters. They had left him in a bad way. Georgie was cover man in the getaway car with a pump-action shotgun hanging out the rear window. The dickhead had crawled out of the jug and tried to hang onto the back bumper of the Granada. Luckily, for the dickhead, he had been shaken off. Georgie reckoned they thought it was their own money or they were kinky in some way people did not know about.

One dickhead ran into the bank. He was out again with two pink canvas bags full of cash. Georgie saw the outlines of the crammed bundles. Clang, clang. Clang, clang. The chute at the side of the van opened twice and swallowed the two bags of cash. The dickhead ran back into the jug. Georgie sniggered as the mouldy doberman lifted up its leg and pissed against the wall of the jug. The dickhead trotted back out with another two bags of poke. Bundles of notes. He could see them trying to burst out of the sack. Poor little things. Georgie will free you. The dickhead went back in for more poke. This was shaping up, thought Georgie, to have the makings of a decent stroke. Something yer could go ter work on.

Directly across from Georgie was the directors' car park. Georgie was astounded to see Bonkie Byrne, a small time stroker, stroll across the car park as if he owned the gaff, and sit in a big silver-grey Merc.

The Granada came prowling back around.

A well-trained flunky in maroon tails and a top hat marched briskly over to the Merc. Georgie's street play came into life. In a few seconds there would be a big scream for Bonkie would surely chin the flunky and tear off around the place. He was probably screwing out the stereo. In a scream, even well-dressed men clutching bunches of daffodils would not be immune from a pull. Georgie was away, getting offside, even as the thoughts hit his brain.

The flunky undid the chain and waved the Merc and Bonkie out into the traffic. The flunky touched its top hat and its hatchet face split into a cold one second whisp of a smile. The Merc was stalled by the pedestrian lights by the jug. Georgie walked across in front of the car and looked in through the windscreen. He stared right into the driver's face.

There was not one bit of doubt. It was Bonkie Byrne alright. Georgie had the pleasure of spending three years with Bonkie at industrial school. He knew Bonkie better, or worse, than his own brothers. The lights changed to green and the Merc pulled away into D'Olier Street.

Georgie doubled back over to the bus-stop. The security van was gone. He stalked over to where he had parked his bike, helmet and gloves, (all nicked) and threw the daffodils onto the ground in disgust. He spat on the flowers and trod them into the ground.

"Bleeding poxy flowers", he snarled and spat on them. Georgie was not in a good frame of mind.

He squeezed on the helmet, snapped down the dark visor and put on his jacket and gloves. The bike, an inconspicuous Yamaha 80, started on the first kick. Georgie crunched into gear and zipped into the traffic heading up by Dublin Castle. He passed the Granada on the way and ignored it with the contempt it deserved.

Georgie drove past the Castle, home of the heavy porkers, and around into Werburgh Street. He parked some distance behind a small blue Fiat and killed the ignition. He left the key in the switch and the motorcycle gear on the seat. The bike was now a criminal liability to Georgie. He had no further use for it. In this area it would be nicked within minutes, taken by the kids, and there would be no heavy suspicion left in the area for him. Nice and clean. The professional touch. He could always get the bugsies to nick him another bike.

He had his hand on the handle of the Fiat when he saw the chick in the driver's seat. Georgie let go of the handle in confusion and started off down the street.

"Georgie", called a sweet voice he knew well, "get inter the jammer. I won't rape yer. I promise".

He looked around at Alfie Ryan leaning out of the driver's window. Alfie was wearing a neat blonde curly wig. As Georgie got closer he saw painted lips and blue eyeshadow. His foul mood deepened. Alfie was smiling coyly at him.

"You're bleeding bent", accused Georgie Beak. He wrenched open the door and sat in, slamming the door behind him. He stared at Alfie in disgust. Alfie was wearing a nurse's uniform. Georgie spluttered. His head was the colour of a tomato. "Bent, bleeding queer, you're as twisted as a corkscrew."

"Now, now, Georgie Porgie", pouted Alfie. He turned serious. "What's the score Georgie?"

"Bonkie Byrne took a director's car", he sighed, "and the flunky with the hat waved him out in the car into the traffic". Georgie rubbed his weary eyes.

Alfie picked up the mike of the CB set. He pressed for transmit and talked into the mike with a pseudo American accent. "Hello Sitting Duck, this here is Bald Eagle in position two. Is that a big four, come on?"

"Bleeding Burt Reynolds", sneered Georgie. He hated CBs. They reminded him of porker radios. He wouldn't even nick them. If he came across them when taking cars he wrenched them out and smashed them up.

"This is Sitting Duck to Bald Eagle. I am receiving you loud and clear. Please send." Even over the air the Belfast accent was thick and heavy.

"Bleeding Michael Collins", began Georgie.

"Shut up will yer?" Alfie spoke into the set. "Bald Eagle to Sitting Duck. Let's all go back to the nest. Come on."

Georgie was looking at Alfie with humorous contempt. He saw in the rearview mirror two kids eyeing up the Yamaha. Thank God there were still thieves growing up uncontaminated by CBs and mushy pop culture.

"Will do", came back the Belfast voice, "am leaving position for nest. Over and out".

Alfie shook his dainty head.

"Who did the codes Alfie?" asked Georgie.

"Mickey." Alfie started up the Fiat and drove off carefully. The kids had the Yamaha started. "Yeah, Mickey done the codes."

"If the CB freaks hear him they'll think the bleeding Brits have re-invaded us." Georgie looked at Alfie's uniform. "Where did you get the gear?"

"It's Cissie's. She loaned me it. Done me up this morning for the business. Do I look the part?" he asked Georgie slyly.

"The only thing your missus ever nursed was a gin and tonic. Done you up for the business", jeered Georgie, "probably had you strapped to the bed. It's no use trying to cod me Alfie. I know, I know you're bleeding bent".

"We like dressing up, Georgie. She likes dressing me up. It's cool Georgie."

"She? She likes dressing up? Every chance you get you're in drag. Why don't you get the operation and get it over with? Eh?" Georgie was outraged. They were driving over Capel Street bridge.

"She can wear what she wants Georgie.."

"I'm not talking about your wife. I'm talking about you. I'd soon stop my bleeding wife dressing me up. I'm telling yer."

"Georgie you pissed off on your missus the day of the wedding. Why did you do that? Why did you do it Georgie?"

"Mind your own business Alfie."

"It's obvious, isn't it? You're gay. It's nothing to be ashamed of." Alfie fluttered his false eyelashes at the astounded Georgie.

"No, no", yelled Georgie, "I'm not bleeding queer. She had a job-and-all lined up for me. In the Corpo. On the bins..." George Beak confessed this dark secret in his haste to prove his manliness. He realised at once he had been tricked. Alfie was bubbling with the giggles. "I'm bleeding warning you Alfie. If I hear this back I'll burst yer."

Alfie held up a well-manicured hand. "Your secret is safe with me, dear", he lisped. He snatched up a magazine and threw it to Georgie. "Porkers", he hissed.

A black Cortina passed them by. Georgie had his face buried in the magazine. There were two CDU men in the porker car watching the financial institutions of Dorset Street lest they be scurrilously blagged.

"They have passed, Georgie", said Alfie.

"Bleeding filth", replied Georgie and flung the magazine on the dash.

"What happened at the bank Georgie?"

"I missed a model. I saw four bags going into the van. Then I saw Bonkie Byrne strolling across the directors' car park. He got into a big Merc and drove it out. It's, it's weird. I'll bleeding kill him. The flunky in the top hat waved him out. Maybe", speculated Georgie, "he's away to clean the jammer".

"He wouldn't get that job if he's a villain."

"A villain? He's a bleeding cretin. He has his own cell up in the Joy. He's known as a wheelman."

"A driver?" enquired Alfie.

"Naw", laughed Georgie, "you come back to your jammer and Bonkie's away with the wheels. He rolls them along the street like a bleeding shepherd with a brush pole. He's deadly".

" It's weird", agreed Alfie

"Yeah, and when I got back the bleeding van was gone. The area was crawling with porkers. Every culchie in the country is up there with a machine gun to stop you earning a shilling. The Task Force, the Branch, the CDU, the Anti-Dipper Squad, dicks from Pearse Street, uniformed porkers and speedies, and I saw a full platoon of Infantry. Jesus Christ I thought I was in a massive pork-pie factory. The street's a bleeding nightmare."

"Sounds bad. The stroke is bolloxed then?" asked Alfie.

"Yeah. I'd say so. Looks like we'll have to go down the sticks and do Mickey's jug." Georgie sank back into the car seat and sighed the stroke goodbye.

"The Belfast men have a point Georgie. There's no heavy porkers down the country. Well none we can't handle. I think", speculated

Alfie, "they like taking over the town and that. It's the guerilla in them".

Georgie hadn't the energy to make a witty comment, or a snide remark, about primates. He merely snorted.

Alfie turned off at Druncondra and drove along a quiet residential street. He parked the Fiat a couple of blocks away from the Firm's offside flat. Alfie locked the car and went around to Georgie. He held out his arm.

"You're bleeding crazy Alfie", said Georgie, but he smiled, and linked his arm.

Georgie walked around to the flat with Alfie tottering on his arm. His high heels went clickety-click, clickety-click and echoed in the silent street whose upright residents were away at their gainful and lawful employment.

The door of the basement flat swung open as they approached it and a voice informed them from behind the door. "My da's waiting on yews." Matt closed the door after Alfie and Georgie and looked up and down the street suspiciously.

Mickey was sitting in the only armchair in the flat, an old pre-war thing tilted awry on a missing castor. Mickey, a short squat Belfast man in his forties, had endeavoured to position the armchair in such a way as to give himself a commanding view of the dingy room. He looked at his watch and then at the two blaggers.

"Take the door Matt", he ordered his son.

"Yes daddy", shouted in Matt from the hallway.

Mickey's dark, almost black eyes, bored into the pair. It was an old trick of his to try and freak people out. To have them believe he knew all about them. He wore a teddy boy suit with drainpipes, a frilly shirt and a bootlace tie. Mickey spoke out from one side of his mouth and dangled a lit Parkdrive from the other. If one did not know him one may have considered him to be a bit of an idiot, an outmoded chancer, but such an impression would be entirely misleading. Mickey was a daring and intelligent operator, although to be truthful, he was considered to be more than a little crazy. He pointed at Georgie and clicked his finger.

"Alright Georgie kid let's have it. What's the problem kid?"

The Cork city man, Bob, who had remained sitting quietly by the window, got up and headed for the small kitchen. He was a very practical and intelligent man. "I think the lads would like a cup of tea

Mickey boy", he said softly in his singing Cork brogue. "I know I would too."

"Tea? Cups of tea?" Mickey stammered. "Yews are on a debriefing for God's sake."

"I want a mug of tea Mickey. I've had nothing all morning", declared Georgie.

"And me", said Alfie in support. He was sitting on the floor by Mickey's armchair on a cushion. Alfie was sitting as a man, his legs wide apart, and his scarlet brief panties above his white thighs and black nylons struck a very erotic pose. It must be said that Alfie was a very pretty person in drag and had many gays eating out of his lap.

"I'll take a cup too, daddy, if there's any going", shouted in young Matt from the hall.

Mickey analysed the requests for refreshments and, as he was outvoted, made a decision.

"OK lads. We will have a ten-minute tea break. Bob you make the tea. Nice and strong kid. OK?" Mickey sat back in the armchair. He was restless and fidgety continually looking out the small window.

Bob put a big pot of tea and six mugs out on the table. He called out to Matt. "Tea's ready Matt."

"He's on guard Bob", pointed out Mickey.

"Mickey stop the bleeding nonsense", put in Georgie sharply, "He's as much right to be in here as any of us. He's over twenty one." Georgie leaned over Mickey. "He robs banks Mickey so he can have a bleeding cup of tea."

"Matt?"

"Yes daddy?"

"Fall out for a tea break."

Alfie was biting his lip to keep himself from laughing. Bob was sniggering into the curtains. Georgie never knew what to make of Mickey. It must be weird to have a General for a da.

Young Matt came in and grabbed a cup of tea. He was famished. When he saw Alfie's smooth, voluptuous thighs and his sizzling underwear, his hunger left him and was replaced with the dull ache of the sex-starved. Matt slid slyly down the wall opposite Alfie to engage in a harmless piece of voyeurism.

Mickey began to organise things again. He flexed his shoulders in the armchair and sat forward. "OK Georgie, let's have your report and", he snapped his fingers, "let's make it snappy. OK?"

Georgie knew Mickey's quirks so he did not beat him over the head with the kitchen chair he was straddling. Mickey had compensations which far outweighed his stormtrooper behaviour. Besides nobody's perfect and blaggers are only human.

Georgie related his report, crisply, clearly and with perfect accuracy. He had perfect memory regarding strokes.

"Right", said Mickey. He was as confused as Georgie. "It's strange. OK Matt", he looked over at the son, "what do you think this hood was doing in the Merc?"

"What Merc is that daddy?" he asked vaguely.

"The Merc, the car this hood was in", said Mickey exasperated.

"What hood was that daddy?"

"The hood..." Mickey followed his son's leery gaze until he was confronted with Alfie's erotic posing. He blew a fuse and dived at the son across the tiny room. He grabbed Matt and hauled him to his feet all the time clapping his ears. "What are yew doing looking up somebody's clothes during a debriefing?" Mickey was outraged.

There was a sharp knock at the hall door.

Mickey left Matt. He whirled around quickly and produced a big heavy revolver from under his coat. "Cover me", he growled to the son. His face had gone dark with aggression, his lips curled back in hatred at the unseen threat. He ran to the door and crouched in front of it with the heavy revolver extended, thrust forward in both hands, the hammer cocked back, finger on the trigger.

Matt moved just as quickly. He darted to the window without showing himself and pulled out a Browning automatic. Matt cocked the weapon and covered the window.

Whoever came through that door or window was dead.

George Beak had no doubt of that. He searched frantically for a back way out. There was none.

Alfie tried to crawl under the armchair.

Bob went quietly over to Mickey. He was frozen stone staring at the door.

"It's alright Mickey. It'll only be MacGregor. He rang to say he'd be over." Bob gently pushed the barrel of the revolver to the ground.

"Open the fucking door", came a voice through the letter box.

Mickey put away his weapon and Bob opened the door.

MacGregor felt the tense atmosphere in the flat as soon as he walked in. There was strained silence. Georgie Beak was livid. Alfie breathed a sigh of relief and stood up. Matt sat by the window as if nothing had happened. Bob glared at Mickey who sat back in the armchair whistling nonchalantly.

"Nice to see you, MacGregor kid", lied Mickey. "Wasn't expecting you."

"What's going on here?" MacGregor asked the Cork man.

"It's sound boy, sound. Mickey thought there was a bit of a hassle when you knocked on the door. Do you want a mug of tea?" Bob was a diplomat.

"He bleeding nearly blew you across the road MacGregor", said Georgie viciously. He pointed at the whistling Mickey. "Michael Collins is carrying a cannon."

MacGregor pulled at his long red whiskers and looked at the ceiling. He sat directly in front of Mickey and spoke softly.

"Are you carrying Mickey?"

"Aye."

Why are you carrying when we are not working Mickey?" MacGregor turned his ear towards Mickey so he would not miss the answer.

"Ach", replied Mickey lightly, "a wee bit of trouble. Nothing much".

"Are you on the run from the law?"

"Well you see, boys, there might be a few people looking for me. It's nothing I can't handle." Mickey patted his revolver and winked at MacGregor.

MacGregor put out one big fist and grabbed Mickey by the shirt. He pulled Mickey close to him. "Mickey you are endangering everyone of us by carrying gear, stop your nonsense and tell us what you are up to. Now. Tell us all now."

The Firm were all in the horrors. If a porker had come to the door Mickey would have blown him away. There was no question of that. And they were all straight. No gloves, no hoods, no getaway cars. Only the likelihood of a capital murder charge looming in front of them.

"Do you remember the gear I bought for us? The two old Thompsons and the M1 carbine?" Mickey lit a Parkdrive.

"Get on with it Mickey", ordered MacGregor.

"The contact I bought it off was found in a field at the back of Ballymurphy. Questioned and then", Mickey put his finger to his temple, “nutted. I think the Movement is looking for me”.

“Jesus Christ, Mickey”, MacGregor stood up, “that’s all we need, isn’t it? Every porker in the country on our back and you bring the Movement down on us.”

“You told us the gear was cool Mickey”, accused Georgie. “It cost enough to be cool.”

“Give back the stuff Mickey. Tell them it was a mistake, OK? Get them off your back”. MacGregor was stunned. He never expected this.

“It doesn’t work like that Mac”, Mickey dragged heavily on his smoke, “they will have written off the gear – and me with it. It’s a bad problem alright. I’m sorry. I didn’t know it was their stuff otherwise I would never have bought it”. He looked around at the cold faces. “Honestly men. Isn’t that right Matt?” He appealed to the son.

“Aye, if me da had knew he wouldn’t have took it off him.”

Mickey pulled out the revolver and unloaded it. He placed the six squat bullets on the table. “What do yews think of that lady?” He handed the weapon to MacGregor. It was a spanking new Luger Magnum .44. Beautiful.

“Matt”, called Mickey, “show the boys your piece”.

Matt took the Browning from his shoulder holster and unloaded the clip. He pulled back the slide and took the round out of the breech. He threw the empty weapon over to Georgie. It too was in mint condition.

The Firms’ eyes lit up at such treasure. These beauties were a long way from sawn-off shotguns and old .45s. They handled the pieces lovingly and, in their admiration for fine tools, their anger against Mickey cooled.

“I’m almost afraid to ask, Mickey. Where did you get the pieces?” asked MacGregor.

“Where I come from they have a saying. You may as well be hung for a sheep as a lamb.”

“So what?” asked Alfie.

“So if I’m going to be nutted for a couple of obsolete pieces I bought in good faith I thought I may as well be shot for something decent. I lifted a dump. Me and the son.”

This news did not disturb the Firm. It did make sense. If one was going to be shot anyway it made sense to get weapons as good as were available. Hunted men have a different sense of values.

"What was in the dump, Mickey boy?" asked Bob. He perked up a bit.

Oh, wait till I tell you", Mickey was like a little boy at Christmas. "You should have been there when I opened the churns lads. I touched lucky. Eight shorts, five Brownings and three Magnums, and six rifles, four M16s and two AR180s, and a rocket launcher and nine rockets."

There was deep silence as the Firm absorbed this information. The vibes in the room got better.

"Mickey", asked Georgie puzzled, "what do you want with a rocket launcher?" He could not think of any stroke where anyone would need a rocket launcher.

"What? What do I want with a rocket launcher? It can penetrate the armour of a main battle tank, that's what", exclaimed Mickey.

"So what?" asked Alfie.

"It'll make minced meat out of them wee Free State Landrovers, that's what. It'll blow them clean off the road and then," Mickey slipped this bit in casually, "we can take the security van".

Everyone in the room knew exactly what he was leading up to. He wanted to attack the Military Escort minding the big shipments of cash that travelled in security vans up and down the country. He was proposing an ambush. Kill first and take the money as the second part of the operation. The Firm envisioned the scene. Rockets exploding, Land Rovers flaming, rifles cracking before a shilling was snatched. It was a nightmare. There were easier ways to earn a living.

"You can't do it, Mickey", concluded MacGregor. He held up his hand to stop Mickey's protests. "I'd like to do it as much as you. But, this is not the North. We want to be able to spend the money we earn. You're not the only one who's operated. I know what you're proposing. It's too heavy".

"It's a one-off boys. By the time they get organised we would be out of the country and the money buried deep. It's the only way we are going to hit the big one. I know a van must be carrying over two million – in old money."

"Mickey", broke in Alfie, "I don't want to leave the country. I'm telling you straight now. Count me out".

"And me", said Georgie. "I don't even want to listen to it Mickey."

"They will put you against the wall for a stroke like that, boy", mused Bob. "They have done it before for far less. Count me out."

"And I'm out of it too Mickey." MacGregor didn't want any sour grapes. "It's feasible alright Mickey but it's too heavy for us. We all have families, ties, we have to live here."

"What are yews going to do? Another wee jug? Get six or seven grand apiece? We are doing military ops as it is and this latest op is fucked up by some hood. Hung for a sheep or a lamb? Which is it to be?"

MacGregor turned to Georgie Beak.

"What happened down at the Big Jug Georgie? Mickey, we will discuss your suggestions after this, OK?"

"I saw Bonkie Byrne getting into a silver-grey Merc and driving it away. I thought there was going to be a scream so I left..."

"Hold on Georgie", interrupted MacGregor, "that's out for a start. Bonkie's up in the Joy doing twelve months".

Georgie became indignant. "I'm telling yer. I bleeding know Bonkie. He drove out of the Central Bank this morning in a silver-grey Merc, registration NDI-230. I know him."

"Give me that number again Georgie", demanded MacGregor.

"NDI-230. The flunky waved..."

"Never mind the flunky, Georgie. I don't know who was driving the car today but I know who it belongs to and who used to drive it."

"Who?" asked Mickey.

"The manager in charge of cash control. He dishes out the money for all the jugs. I have a good bit of information on him. I was tracing the money back to source." MacGregor looked at Bob. "What have we here Bob?"

"It's fairly clear", began the analyst, "you have a new manager, driving the same car who is also a double of Bonkie Byrne".

"Last year Georgie, when you were doing bird, I dug into the system. The manager used to be called Macwell. I was going to scoop him and send him along to fill up and bring out a couple of bags of cash for me but it never filled in." MacGregor's hands were shaking. "I'm telling you lads. If Bonkie is the new man's double we may be able to crack the Big Jug."

The Firm were on tenterhooks. MacGregor never spoofed or exaggerated about business. He looked at Georgie with an unspoken question in his eyes.

"There's no bleeding doubt about it. I know him. It is him. Not a double. An identical. I'll put me reputation on the line." Georgie was intense.

"How would you go about it, Mac? Say you have the double", enquired Mickey.

"I don't know yet. Scoop the real manager and put in our ringer. They sign out millions down there every day. Millions. It's the Big Jug lads. Once we have the ringer in we have the advantage." MacGregor was adamant.

"It'll never work", said Georgie sadly, "I know Bonkie. He'll fuck the whole thing up".

"No he won't", declared Alfie passionately, "because we won't let him. Will we lads?"

The Firm all shook their heads. How could they let him make a mess of it?

"If he is a crook it is his duty to go into the Big Jug and help us rob it", declared MacGregor.

"Otherwise why did God make him the same as the manager? He could just as easily have been the Pope's double, or the Shah's, or Paisley, or Charlie Haughey, or the Duke of Edinburgh but he's not. He's the double of the man who dishes out the money."

MacGregor saw the stroke unfolding as he talked. "Georgie, what are appearances to a stroke?"

"Everything."

"Right Georgie. Look, I know we can get him in if he's a ringer. I accept Georgie's word that he is. Once he's in it's only a matter of working out how to get the money out. Agreed?"

The Firm nodded their heads in agreement. It was only common sense.

"I'm still a bit dubious", said Georgie because this was all down to him.

"Georgie kid", advised Mickey, "all the best ops have a simple theme no matter how complex the details. I can see it. If he is in we will get the money".

"Alright lads", MacGregor got down to business, "we need photographs of this manager when he arrives for work in the morning."

"I'll get them", offered Mickey who wasn't known in the area.

"Georgie and Alfie. Will you find out the legal position about Bonkie? We will need to get him out." MacGregor looked at Matt.

"You go with your da."

Matt nodded. He wouldn't go with anyone else anyway.

"Myself and Bob will go over the old file and see what we can come up with. By the way Mickey, we will have to hit a small jug or two down the sticks. We will need money if this gets off the ground. Have you one in mind?"

"Several", replied Mickey, "the country's full of them".

That was true – and every one of them were fed from the Big Grey Jug.

Chapter 2

A RED house brick came smashing through Patrick O'Mally-Smyth's front window and slithered to a halt at his hearth. It was one of those bricks with holes made through it and tied through one of the holes was a small parcel. O'Mally-Smyth, who was studying Arabic by his fire, ran to the window. There was no one to be seen in the upper middle class street of respectable red bricked semis. He went to phone the Garda but the parcel caught his eye and he stooped and picked up brick and parcel. The parcel was tied to the brick by a ladies black silk stocking. O'Mally-Smyth, suspecting children or students (what was the difference in mentality at times?) broke open the parcel with a frown on his face. There was splintered glass all over his floor.

The parcel contained a tiny pair of ladies knickers and a Dunhill cigarette lighter. It was his wife Delores' lighter which he had bought for her as a present in New York on their honeymoon. Scrawled, in ugly print, with an eyebrow pencil, on the paper wrapping were the words: YOUR WIFE IS A STINKING WHORE.

The parcel stunk of malicious spite.

Patrick's first reaction was disbelief. He held up the knickers. Delores wouldn't wear these. There was no middle to them. But it was her lighter. The inscription was on it. He had it inscribed himself. Patrick poured himself a gin and tonic and thought about the matter. He deduced that if there was any substance to the allegation hurled so dramatically through his window, no doubt by a very irate lady, then his career at the bank would be ruined. He would be shipped back to the provinces far away from the seat of financial power and intrigue. After all his hard plotting.

He rang a private porker he had occasion to use in his business at the bank, and engaged him to spy on his wife. If indeed Delores was a whore (he was certain she was not smelly) he should have all relevant data so that he might exercise some control of the situation. And so Patrick O'Mally-Smyth swept up the glass in the silent house and tried to get back to his Arabic. His concentration was shattered, like the draughty window, his economist's mind in turmoil. He closed the books and put them in their niche.

His marriage had been reasonably happy and successful when he had been an assistant manager in a small branch in Waterford. There was not much to do and he had plenty of time and attention for his wife Delores.

She was beautiful. Some said stunning. He used to be quite pleased when he saw the admiring glances of the clerks when she would call at the branch or at the Christmas parties. Patrick looked up at the oil portrait hanging above his Adams fireplace. It had cost a lot, too much on his salary, but it was, no, she was worth it. Tonight she seemed to be smiling down at him and he thought he detected smugness: No. Scorn?

"And are you enjoying yourself my dear?" asked Patrick to the painting. He used the mid-atlantic accent so favoured by the Irish bourgeois: a green Oxford drawl with a bit of Fifth Avenue thrown in out of respect for the dollar. He raised up his gin and tonic, his seventh, in a mock toast: the gin and tonic was a prop like the phoney accent. Imagine asking, he reflected bitterly, at a meeting for Irish whiskey or heaven forbid a pint of stout. But such images are necessary to an up-and-coming executive. He needs every little flicker he can find to scramble up the ladder of success. And a great deal of luck or money or clout.

Patrick would have to rely on a piece of good fortune coming his way. His degree in economics was fine down the sticks but up in the Central Bank such degrees were thick on the ground and the rat race was an on-going event. That's why he had been at the Arabic. Arabs. Oil. Money. O'Mally-Smyth, oil, money, Arabs, he speaks Arabic quite well. He had it all planned. Leaked it casually at a cocktail party when the boss of Foreign Investment was there. Not much use though if his wife, his adorable wife, was a stinking whore. He threw the stocking, panties and note into the fire in disgust.

He behaved with perfect decorum upon his wife's return from her visit to sick relations and told her a hairy tale of neighbourhood vandalism. She tut, tut, tutted and opened her wonderful green eyes wide with surprise that such a thing could happen in Rathgar. Of course she did not really care if the boring, staid structure was burnt to the ground by a group of lunatics and Patrick O'Mally-Smyth with it. Such is the power of rejection, the revenge of a beautiful, pampered creature who finds she has lost all of her considerable charms to a job.

Patrick O'Mally-Smyth loved his job more than he loved his wife and behind the flawless skin, the cool green eyes, the impeccable manners and good graces, she seethed with a fury much worse than a woman scorned.

Such is the penalty to be paid by those who seek power and prestige and are not well connected or very wealthy. Such is one of the reasons executives are highly paid yet continually crave more money, bigger cars, interest-free loans and interest-free mortgages and why the plain people should work for sweet fuck all.

Yet out of such stress and strain, cut throating and back stabbing, rise the privileged few, from the shark pool, to grow fat and happy in their castles and mansions. Out of the seething cauldron of the nation's wealth rose brave young bankers, like Patrick, who placed their career above all things.

Such is love of money.

What more dedication can a banker show?

It was not uncommon for Patrick to work, or pretend to work, late. One did not bugger off home to watch the O'Riordans if a deal had to be clinched.

Eleven days after the brick through the window affair Patrick arranged to meet the private porker in his office, a poxy affair whose only redeeming feature was that it had one big Georgian window overlooking College Green. As he waited on Crinion, an ex Branchman, to show, Patrick speculated that the rows of squat armoured cars were a sign of the times. He remembered when he was a green bank clerk how one of his chores was to go to the Regional Office twice a week, in an old Morris Minor, depositing and collecting his branch's cash. He often carried it on his own at that time, and left it in the boot while he had a pint and a sandwich, fifty or sixty thousand pounds. And then the system had changed and all the monies, except silver and copper, were sent and collected by the Post Office. The postman used to arrive with a sack of cash and ask someone to sign for it; just as if it were any run-of-the-mill commodity.

Now? The bank spent millions on security. That was not strictly true. The public, the plain people of Ireland, paid millions on bank security via a hike in service charges.

Those were the days when most of the banks in Ireland did not even have an alarm, or bars on the windows, when a man could travel the length and breadth of the country without fear of being held at gunpoint.

He smiled and nodded at the armoured cars. Such days were gone forever. Unfortunately so.

"A Mister Crinion to see you, Mr O'Mally-Smyth", whispered the receptionist out from the intercom in a sly 'shall I tell him to twaddle off' voice.

"Send him up", ordered Patrick.

The speaker crackled and spat then went dead.

Crinion, a big sandy-haired porker (once a porker always a porker) came in without knocking and flopped into a soft chair. He looked tired. The white sick-looking flesh hung on his big face in folds. There were black rings around his eyes though, to be malicious, they could just as easily have been caused by drink and debauchery as by hard work. He had a slim metal briefcase handcuffed to his arm.

"Coffee? Tea?" offered Patrick.

"A drink if you please. Whiskey, if you have it", replied Crinion.

"Gin or brandy is all I have. I can send the porter for . . ."

"Brandy. A stiff one. I've deserved it. Been working flat out on this case."

"Oh?" Patrick poured him a double brandy.

"It's finished", replied Crinion. He dangled the briefcase and tossed down the drink.

"And?" asked Patrick, very cool, very self composed.

"Do you want it straight?"

"Yes."

"She is having an affair. A very serious affair with", he began to play with the combination of the briefcase, "would you be so kind?", he handed Patrick his empty glass. Crinion opened the briefcase and took out a sheaf of photographs. He selected one and handed it to Patrick. "An affair with this gentleman."

Patrick handed Crinion another drink. A small one. He looked at the snap and made himself a gin and tonic to stop the flutters in his stomach. He filled Crinion's glass.

"How serious is this 'serious affair'?" asked Patrick.

"Can I ask you an extremely personal question, Mr O'Mally-Smyth?"

"Please do. I promise not to take offence, I assure you."

"Do you love your wife?" Crinion did not bat an eye.

"I presume you have a reason for such a question?"

Crinion nodded.

"No, Mr Crinion I do not love Delores and, as is quite evident, nor she I. Why do you ask?" Patrick's senses were sharp behind the civilised cool.

"Could you live without her?" and before Patrick could answer he clarified. "I do have a reason to ask."

"What is the reason, Mr Crinion?"

"I can make you, us, extremely rich, if things are as they appear to be. But I have to know and therefore I must ask."

"That is a very good reason Mr Crinion. The answer to your question is: Yes, I can live without my wife. In fact I am living my own life, and she hers, as things stand. Your report, no doubt, will have told you that I presume."

"Not told, indicated. It indicated that but I had to ask, to be sure."

"And now that you are sure?" led the banker.

"The affair is one of great, er, passion. Your wife and the Minister are very much in love with each other. They intend, if necessary, to set up home together regardless of the consequences."

"How can you say that? It's incredible."

"It's fact. I bugged the apartment ..."

"You did what?" shouted Patrick. He went a wishy washy grey and looked around fearfully. "I gave you no such authorisation. That's illegal", he finished lamely.

"Only if you are caught or mug enough to make a statement. Relax. I wired the place on my own initiative. It's clean now. I removed the devices. I did it for my own sake as much as yours."

"Why for God's sake?" asked Patrick.

"I wish to be rich too. Can you understand that?"

"Oh, absolutely. What are you leading up to?"

"You may remove from your head any thoughts that I am going to do anything illegal. Crime is for fools. If your wife and the Minister are so much in love why should you and I spoil their happiness?" asked the private porker cynically.

"I am to let Delores continue this adulterous relationship?"

"Why not? What good can come of driving her and the Minister, to foolish actions? People in love can behave very weird. I know.

I saw enough of them when I was with the force. Young slips of girls who calmly poisoned their spouse for another. People in love are not rational. Why kill the goose that will lay the golden egg?"

"I am not an unreasonable man, Mr Crinion. Please tell me more."

"In my professional opinion, and I have to tell you nearly all my business is of this nature, if you try to stamp out this affair it will end in resignation for the Minister and political ruin, plus, you will have your own scandal to deal with. The affair will not end and your wife will, probably, leave you and never speak to you again."

"Jesus ..."

"I know that's unfair and damn unreasonable but I've seen it time and time again in this religion-riddled republic. You have no kids. Do you want to know why?"

"Shut you damn mouth, Mr Crinion", roared Patrick. This was a sore point with him.

"He knows", retorted Crinion, "and who else knows? And you have the whole damn thing wrong".

"Tell me", snapped O'Mally-Smyth.

"Your delightful wife has been on the pill since you got married. If you wish I'll play you a tape. Not to deny you a child but to preserve her figure."

O'Mally-Smyth began to laugh. A harsh bitter laugh.

"The sly bitch. All that time. I went to doctors. Well fuck her ..."

"My sentiments exactly Mr O'Mally-Smyth, but I suggest you leave it to the Minister, and we shall screw them both so to speak."

"You are an extremely devious man, Mr Crinion." Patrick looked at the private porker in a new light.

"I do try, Mr O'Mally-Smyth. That's the Branch for you. Always bringing out the worst, and the best, in people. Shall I talk to you about making you and I rich?"

"Yes, let's get down to business. What are your proposals? I'm sure you do have quite a few." O'Mally-Smyth smiled. The private porker had lifted a great weight from his mind. He had harboured a fear that he was infertile. He was cold and bitter inside as the private porker had anticipated.

"We, you and I, are now partners in a new company. SS Security. Safe and Sound Security. I have all the facts and figures, all relevant data here", he handed over to Patrick a slim green folder, "We shall secure an interest-free loan, at the Minister's manipulation, to buy the fleet of cars and on the strength that we will be awarded the tender to shift all monies from the Bank".

"How can we be sure he will agree to what we want?"

"It's a very small piece of co-operation we are asking. Why shouldn't we have the contract? It's not a big thing. As to the necessary capital, it's a sound business proposition after we have the contract. If it isn't us, it'll be a brother-in-law, or a loyal party hack, or a hidden business interest."

O'Mally-Smyth waved his hand in understanding.

"Who are you talking to? I see it every day in here. Lucrative contracts and the chosen few. All I want to know from you is – will it work? Will he do it? I don't want to do anything that has a comeback. It all has to be above board."

"There is one other thing. You need to be promoted. To cash control. With you there we will have the entire thing sewn up . . . "

"But Cash Control is a dead end. It's a demotion really. It's the equivalent of a glorified storeman ..."

"Great. Then there will be no ears tuning in, or raised eyebrows, when you go there. We want things to be as quiet as possible when you are promoted."

"Who shall bring the deal to the Minister? I'm telling you now I'm no good at that sort of thing. You, perhaps?" enquired Patrick.

"No. He must not hear of me. No need. But I would imagine your good wife would be the go between. No contact will ensure calmness and confidentiality. The Minister can dupe himself he is acting in the highest interest of the State. It's foolproof. Assure your wife of complete freedom and no pressure whatsoever and ask her can she get you a couple of business favours. She will know how to go about it I am sure."

"Yes. I can see that working very well. We submit in the normal way and our tender wins. We apply for a loan and it is granted. That's all very much above board." Patrick was very pleased with the turn of things.

"It's business", stated Crinion flatly. "Good business."

"How much can I expect to get out of this, if things go as you expect?"

"I know the security business", began Crinion passionately "I tried to get into it before but the big boys, the international firms, have it all sewn up. If you can swing the appointment to Cash

Control that's where we will make the profit, the big profit. We can join, co-ordinate our efforts, towards the success of SS Security. How many men and women work in Cash Control?"

"I'd say, I'm not sure offhand, about seventy five."

"Well, they will all be working for us, so to speak, only of course the Bank will be paying them. We shall have all the choice work of course. We won't need so many security men either. But we won't be robbed because we shall have all the armed protection that is going. It's not the men in the armoured cars that are stopping the blaggers but the armed escorts. The Minister will press his colleagues in the government for more men for armed escorts. We soon get a good name as an efficient security company. An Irish security company. Native enterprise and all that rubbish. If the long-suffering public complain about the cost of security blame it on the subversives."

"Security", finished Crinion, "is big business".

"You didn't answer my question. How much can I expect to get out of this enterprise?" O'Mally-Smyth was asking bankers' questions.

"Oh, yes", Crinion shook his head, "I got carried away. At least one hundred thousand per year, for the rest of the Minister's term in office at least, and you shall have half ownership in a thriving company. I have no doubt you may receive good advice where to invest your money. The figure I mention is the lowest possible if the venture gets off the ground at all".

"We are partners then, John?" asked Patrick.

"Yes, Patrick, partners", agreed Crinion.

Patrick poured out two more drinks. He handed one to the private porker.

"Safe", proposed Patrick and held up his gin and tonic.

"And Sound", proposed Crinion.

They clicked glasses and drank. The darling of Irish companies, the new success story, SS Security, was born in the richest of possible places.

Chapter 3

A CONCERT extempore was drawing to an end in the basement of Mountjoy Prison. It was odd to hear music and song there because the men locked away down there were deprived of everything possible except the bare necessities of jail. They had no mail, no visits, no association, no recreation, no smokes, no sweeties, no radio, no television and no musical instruments. Such was the nature of the punishment that the prisoners in the Base were forbidden to go into the wood yard and saw up huge trees, by hand, into lumber for firewood. It was better to keep a man isolated than have him sweat in the company of his peers according to the powers who determine such grave matters. Morale in the Base was high and time passed just the same as it did in the prison above.

A raspy Dubliner's voice, of great character and determination, floated out from a cell door peephole and filled the dusty Base. The voice was helped along its way by a toilet roll inner which was stuck through the peephole and was being used as a crude megaphone. It was surprisingly effective and all the other men on punishment could hear Bonkie very clearly.

Bonkie was addressing his audience in a number of different voices. He was a natural at picking up accents and used his talent to slag the screws and porkers mercilessly. He adopted an American accent of the deep south.

"And now all you folk the time has come for the star of our show here in Memphis. It's the one and only. It's the King." Bonkie played a couple of the King's well-known hits on his comb using a bit of paper. He broke into a very good imitation of the King's voice, husky and emotional. In the cell Bonkie was twisting and wriggling his leg, gyrating his hips, getting into full swing. He sang his own words, as he had been doing the whole time, to one of the King's songs of praise.

"They caught me piddling in my pisspot
Before the hour of eight o'clock,

The Governor put me in the Base
And tied a reef knot in my cock,
Oh yeah ..."

At this grossly disrespectful singing, with regard to the Governor, Creeping Jesus, a silent, snivelling, snooping, shit of a screw stepped forward and gripped Bonkie's bog roll inner. He had been standing outside Bonkie's cell door waiting for just an incident, having crept up, silent as the grave, with his shoes muffled in polishing rags. Creeping Jesus, or CJ as he was commonly known, shouted into Bonkie.

"Let go ha dat, Byrne." He tugged on the piece of cardboard. "Let go ha dat hime telling ya, hand less ha your bould impertinence too."

Bonkie held onto his bog roll grimly.

"Leave hit go hime telling ya. You'll be hon governor's parade hin da morning Byrne hand you'll be sorry."

The men on punishment began to cheer and hoot.

The bog roll inner snapped and the screw fell back. Just like a Christmas cracker.

"Oh look", jeered Bonkie through the peephole, "look what I found in me cracker. Hoi, CJ it's for you", called out Bonkie.

"What his hit?" asked the screw gruffly.

"I got a ring for a pig in me cracker. It must be for bleeding yourself ..."

"Right. Ha funny man. Well hisle show you who's a funny man. You harr also hon report for gross disrespect to han hofficer hin the course hoff his duty. Gross disrespect."

Bonkie blew a loud raspberry that was echoed in every cell in the Base.

"Hany more nonsense hand the lights harr going hout. So knock hit hoff," shouted CJ angrily. He drew in a big breath and swelled up like a huge dark blue toad. Silence. CJ exhaled with relief that his authority, that sacred thing to the man in uniform, had been established, his will had been imposed.

Bonkie watched the screw through the peephole, an impertinence in itself, and was, as always, fascinated by his actions. Creeping Jesus was to Bonkie something from another planet. He made Bonkie feel ashamed to admit he was Irish knowing that he was in the country. CJ was a six foot blob poured into a screw suit that was crumpled and shiny with grime. He had horsey teeth, a white ghosty face and hanging onto each side of his head were two big grasser's ears. CJ had wee beady eyes set very close together which glinted perpetually with suspicion. On his feet, tied over his regulation shoes with string from the mat shop, CJ had polishing rags. Old pieces of grey prison blankets that had worn thin with the years of constant use. On these penal pads he slithered up and down the landings silently to spy upon the inmates. He floated off, notebook in hand, and went out of Bonkie's limited sight. The Base stayed silent.

No one wanted to do any extra time in the base over an obnoxious bollox such as Creeping Jesus. The night screw would be coming on soon. The crack had been petering out anyway and it was just as well to end it on a sour note. No one really wants to be happy in prison. Bonkie found it easier to do his whack cultivating hatred of the people who locked him up and away. He liked to brood, foster grudges, hatred, malcontent. If a person ever thought he was happy in the nick, believed Bonkie, the next bleeding thing he might get to liking the place and believing all the old shit they feed the screws, such as: crime does not pay. A person might get to believing all the shit handed down by the judiciary about crime and punishment and justice for all. A person might be led to believe that he was in there for his own good and be reformed into a good labourer or a forklift driver or a lavatory attendant or, heaven forbid, an honest Joe. Yer, crime does not pay, until one looks at the screws' paypackets and the contractors who put up the barbed wire fences, the floodlights and the watchtowers. Crime does not pay unless one has a licence to exploit the old, the sick, the lame, the blind, but above all the plain people of Ireland. If you want to get rich get into the rat race and play the game by the established rules. The snag was there was only so much poke to go around and the rich people had the system all sewn up. To get rich legal one had to go to certain schools, speak and act properly, live in the right area, know the right people, and patronise politicians. No one from Bonkie's area had a hope of making it rich unless a new quirk, or oddity, was belched up by the economic system. Some scheme the economists had no interest in because it was a one-off for the slum people. Rag collecting, or a coal-delivery business or trading in second-hand tyres. Usually a little scheme the big boys would turn their noses up at. The competition for any such little number was ferocious in the slums and anyway, all such schemes for making it rich had long since gone. Nowadays the slum world was as stable as it could be accommodating the pool of surplus labour that the rich people did not use.

The only way, as far as Bonkie could see, to get rich was to steal sufficient capital to launch a decent business. If a stroker touched lucky and saved his poke he might get the necessary money but very few ever did.

The rich educated their children into a system, their system, to become heirs to their businesses or professional people. Doctors, dentists, and the solicitors and barristers.

Bonkie hated the solicitors and barristers almost as much as he did porkers and screws. He lay on the bed and began to have himself a little brood. A little bitter hatred, spiced with wry humour, at the world. He always felt better afterwards. Yeah, no one wants to be bleeding happy in the nick.

Bonkie was quite a dedicated crook. He had an unjust reputation for being stupid but he was far from being an idiot or a thick. He did get nicked a lot but this was because he had a gigantic ego bottle. The ego bottle ruled his heart and his head.

If Bonkie, for instance was strolling down Grafton Street with his woman and he, or mostly she, fancied a little item in a window, well Bonkie would kick in the window at once and remove the item. Irrespective of who was in the street at the time. That was his ego bottle. It would not matter the street was crawling with porkers. In would go the window and out would come the article. If Bonkie needed a car he would get into the first one that he fancied. No loitering about to see if the coast was clear, no peeping around corners, no lookouts. In, start it up and away.

This was Bonkie's style of operating. This was his famous ego bottle and, surprisingly, he had quite a lot of success at stealing.

His most famous stroke was when he strolled into an O'Connell Street bank and calmly lifted up the flap and went behind the counter. No one took any notice of him until he was on his way out with ten grand in tenners he lifted quietly from a lady cashier. He walked out as cool as ice into the street around a couple of corners and into a boozer. No hood, no gloves, no getaway car, no shotgun, not even a straight person to take away the poke. This was Bonkie's ego bottle and he revelled in it.

The blaggers, meticulous planners of strokes, shook their heads in amazement, at Bonkie's caper. As far as they were concerned he had earned the ten grand for pure nerve but there was no way they would dream of operating in such a way. They cut all their risks to the bone. To the absolute minimum. Bonkie was in an odd little class of his own.

Unkind prisoners said Bonkie had not enough brains to be afraid and that he had bigger balls than John Wayne.

Bonkie had a burning desire to be a blagger. To have a chance to break into the big time but, as far as he could see, it was just as much a closed shop as the rich man's system of making poke. He had tried a few times to put a little Firm of his own together but it never seemed to come together. But that was gangland for you. Up one day, down the next, in the Joy the day after. At least he had reached the top of his league and Bonkie was President of the Small Time Strokers' Association up in the Joy here. He had respect. He had dreams yet. He had ambitions. He had a feeling, a stroker's gut feeling, that he was going to be rich, but, it was hard doing the whack on dreams locked in a damp concrete cube deep in the bowels of an old Victorian monstrosity.

Bonkie provoked and brooded himself until he was full of malicious spite. The hatred inside him made his teeth ache to bite and his nails yearn to scratch and tear. Yeah, Bonkie didn't want ter be happy in this kip.

He heard the iron gate to the prison above rattling open. The night screws clattered down the winding iron stairs. Their shod boots scraped noisily on the tiles as they marched up the corridor digging in the heels. A crunching paramilitary sound that rasped out. Authority is here and stomping well. The boots came to a halt outside Bonkie's cell beside CJ's little rabbit hutch of an office.

"Good hevening to you, Mr Gripe", said CJ formally, "High ham handing hover to you. Fourteen hawn punishment. Hall present hand correct".

"Right", replied the chief night screw casually, "I'll have a look at them and I'll let you off".

The eye appeared at each peephole to see if its bread and butter were all there.

"Off you go, Enda."

Creeping Jesus came close by Bonkie's cell. He sniggered then shouted for Bonkie's benefit.

"Another day hup de judge's arse. High'm haway fur ha pint handa roll wid de missus."

Bonkie was up off the bed swiftly. Couldn't let CJ go home in a good mood.

"Never mind the drink CJ. Go ter yer home and give the missus the roll. The poor old cow could do with a good servicing."

The night screws in turn sniggered at Creeping Jesus.

CJ was mortified at such slagging. It had a lewd sexual inference. He had meant a bacon roll or a salad roll. His big grasser's ears burned scarlet.

"High'll make your time hard Byrne", he spluttered through the grey orifice. His horsey teeth gnashed furiously. Bonkie could see his many fillings. Bonkie raised up his arms and beat the air with his fists like an excited horse. He whinnied at Creeping Jesus.

Click. The screw put the light out. Click, click, click, click. The clicks grew fainter as CJ put out the prisoners' lights on his way off duty.

Bonkie lay back down on his bed. He was pleased he had managed to upset the screw but one might just as well insult an imbecile in Greek for all the good it would do. He would be back in the morning, replenished, refreshed, ready for more. All in the line of duty.

Bonkie's mouth was dry. He groped his way over to the cheap plywood table, for the moonlight was blocked out by the bars and grill and it was pitch black in the cell, and found his plastic pitcher of water. He drank it down greedily. CJ had known what he was doing winding up Bonkie about having a few pints. Bonkie thirsted for a cool, black pint of stout and a few more, and then to stretch between Sally's thighs and sink, sink, into the warm, living, centre of her soul. Ah' such bliss. Bonkie's cock sprung up at the thought and grated against his rough denim trousers. He tried to ignore it, sitting on the end of the iron bed, on a hard horsehair mattress, but his penis throbbed gently, persistently, and dreams of feminine fragrances and scents came and frustrated him. Bonkie loved women. He sat dejectedly in the dark his head held in his arms ignoring his insistent erection.

The erection, or rather a past erection was the real reason he was now in solitary, or, separate confinement as the liberals chose to call it when it was discovered that maltreatment of prisoners did not get any votes in today's enlightened age.

Bonkie had spent over ten years in every jail in Ireland, on and off, usually in six and twelve month sentences. During his enforced celibate periods he had to make do with masturbation to relieve the unnatural circumstance of being made to live without female companionship. He was an expert masturbator or, in his own words a master wanker. He realised that every dinnertime, after he had eaten his food and lain down to nap, that he always awoke with an erection. This intrigued Bonkie. He set out to see if he could suppress this regular rising of his organ. For a few dinnertimes after he was locked up (the prisoners were locked up for all their meals in the cells) Bonkie did not nap but read a book or wrote a letter to Sally or stood up on the end of his bed and gazed out through the bars at the dirty Dublin he loved so much.

No matter what he did he had an erection each dinnertime.

Although Bonkie was quite pleased at this virile display of his manhood he was determined to bring his wayward penis under control. He got out a book on yoga from the prison library and studied mind over matter.

Armed with his new knowledge Bonkie had sat on his bed, in the nude, and dared his penis to rise. Bonkie thought of the most sexless things imaginable, the electric chair, burning five pound notes, the gallows, lumpy porridge, CJ, being locked in an abandoned fridge, swimming in a school of giant jellyfishes, claymore mines, castrating pigs with a rusty pen knife like he had seen the culchies do, losing his ego bottle, joining the guards, joining the screws, he thought about cold, cold, cold. He was in Antarctica. His penis actually began to retract. There was nothing there but ice, snow and penguins. A thought passed through his mind as to how ridiculous the penguins looked waddling about carrying their eggs. Eggs, procreation, copulation, sex.

His penis gave a great twitch and began to rise.

"Stop, stop", he shouted down to it, "stay as you are".

The penis was deaf to his pleas and rose up as straight and true as a lamp post and he saw the slit of an eye in his bobby's helmet pop open in expectation.

"I'm telling you", he shouted angrily at the erect organ, "you'll only go up when I want you to. Do you hear me? I don't want an erection. Please go down".

The penis heeded him not and began to throb and thicken.

"I'm bleeding warning you, now." Bonkie waved his finger down at the bold penis. "If you don't go down I won't exercise you for a week."

This dire threat scared the penis mightily. It wilted and began to droop.

Bonkie cheered and clapped as it surrendered, curling down dejectedly, to droop limp and beaten between his legs. He bounced up and down on the bed.

"Well, well, well", came a voice heavy with derision, from behind the cell door.

Bonkie looked up and saw CJ's eye peering into the cell. He had creeped up again.

"High have seen men talking to da wall, hand men talking to themselves but dis his da first time hi've hever seen ha man talking to his cock." CJ's voice was full of awe, as if he had just witnessed a great phenomenon or discovered the eighth wonder of the world. "What harr ye hat, Byrne?" he asked anxiously.

Bonkie jumped off the bed, bent over and displayed his hairy bottom. He threw his voice.

"Talk to me CJ and then we'll be on equal terms." Bonkie threw in a few raspberries and began to sing Faith Of Our Fathers.

"Your hon report, Byrne. Henough his henough." The eye sidled off, silently.

Bonkie could not possibly go on report for talking to his cock, even if it did need to be spoken to. It was unthinkable.

When he was opened up at two o'clock he went down to the sink to wash his dishes and met there the ogre, Buttons Dalton.

"How are ya, Bonkie?" asked the ogre friendlily.

"What did you bleeding say?" shouted Bonkie.

"Ah yer, well? Oh I remember. How are ya Bonkie?"

"What bleeding business is it ter you?" snarled Bonkie.

The ogre was very confused. He looked down at Bonkie from his great height and laughed. Bonkie gave him chocolate and nudie books and made the barber cut his hair for free.

Bonkie flung his dishes to the ground and dived on the ogre, Buttons Dalton.

The ogre, Buttons Dalton, lifted Bonkie high up above his head and giggled. He liked horseplay. Bonkie swivelled around and hung onto Buttons' back.

Some vigilant screw pressed the alarm. It started off in a slow whine going up into an ear-splitting crescendo.

Fifty screws charged up the stairs to Bonkie's landing, hats off, batons out, ready to deal with the trouble.

The whole jail saw Bonkie, up on Buttons Dalton's back, charge into the screws and disappear.

It had taken ten screws to hold onto the ogre and carry him down to the Base. Bonkie had gone after a token protest. He had hidden under the ogre's feet as the huge man had wrestled playfully with the screws.

Bonkie was placed on Governor's report for fighting and assaulting an officer. That was a decent charge sheet, a charge sheet people would respect, and he had been fighting with the biggest man in the jail. That was good for his image too. He could just as easily have picked on a softie or some underhanded molester.

"That Bonkie has loads of bleeding bottle", agreed the small-time strokers.

This assessment of Bonkie's character, when conveyed to him on the grapevine, pleased him very much. It concurred with his own opinion of himself.

He had drawn two months on the boards. Two months in the Base. Two months locked up twenty-three hours per day. One month for fighting and one month for pushing officer Muldoon in the fracas.

The charge of talking to his cock was struck out as it did not contravene any known rule in the 1947 Prison Rules, nor did using one's buttocks as a ventriloquist's dummy.

"He was what?" roared the Governor.

"Talking to his penis, sir, which was hin han erect state", blurted out CJ. He was scarlet.

There was silence in the Governor's office.

"What were you doing Byrne?" asked the Governor.

"I was praying to it, Governor. Praying for the help of God to overcome the temptation that is placed before us." Bonkie assumed an innocent expression.

"He was, er, praying Mister Crinkle. What do you say to that?" asked the Governor.

"He was hopping hup han down hon de bed and yahooing wid his ting waving all hover de place. He jumped hoof the bed hat my happroach hand showed me his backside hand, hand . . . " CJ couldn't get it out.

"And what Mr Crinkle? What did he do then?" The Governor was fascinated. He looked at Bonkie in an odd way.

"He blew hout ha few farts, not real ones mind, hand sang faith hoff our fathers." CJ hung his head low with shame at the recollection.

There was another silence in the Governor's office.

"What have you to say about all this, Byrne?" the Governor asked patiently.

"Well. I thought it was the devil at the peephole, you know. And I was wrestling with the trials of the flesh ..."

"Shut up, Byrne", interposed the chief screw.

"Ask him to show you what he has in his pockets", said Bonkie to the Governor. "There", Bonkie pointed to CJ's bulging pockets, "ask him what's in his pockets".

"What are in your pockets, Mr Crinkle? The prisoner wants to know what are in your pockets. You need not reply", stated the Governor.

Creeping Jesus had his pockets open in a flash and dumped his pieces of blanket and string onto the Governor's desk.

"What do you use those for, Mr Winkle?" asked Bonkie.

"Crinkle, Mr Crinkle", corrected the chief screw.

"High ties hem haround me shoes like dis", CJ put his smelly foot, the shoe was full of chicken shit from his farm, up on the Governor's immaculate table, "hand high can get hup to de cells hand", he touched the side of his head cunningly, "dey can't hear me ha coming. Harr ya wid me?"

"Get both of them fucking out of here", roared the Governor. He reached into his drawer for the milk of magnesia.

The chief screw marched out Bonkie and Creeping Jesus together and just for a moment it was very hard to tell who had been on report. As Bonkie was marched off to the Base to start his two months he heard the chief screw bellowing and roaring at Creeping Jesus in an empty cell.

The ogre Buttons Dalton was not even put on report. They just slipped him a dose of largactol in his pudding for a few days. Mr Enda Crinkle was shoved down to the dusty Base to watch the malcontents.

Creeping Jesus had been gone about fifteen minutes when the

light in Bonkie's cell flashed on. A rolled up magazine was pushed through the peephole. It fell on the old knotty boards. Then two packets of ten Major, matches, and two Bounty bars. Bonkie heard all the lights go back on all the way up the corridor. He collected the goodies off the floor and laid them on his bed. Bonkie flicked through the Playboy magazine. The ladies in it almost took away his breath. It was a shock coming from bleak darkness, to sudden light, the warmth of the gifts, the colour and unique shapes of the girls in the magazine. He peeled back the grey blankets, stripped off and began to bang the door.

"What is it?" asked the screw.

"Knock off the light", requested Bonkie. His voice was hoarse.

"You didn't do much reading Bonkie", teased the screw. He turned off the light.

Bonkie jumped into the bed. His penis made a tent pole with the blankets. He unwrapped a Bounty bar and ate it slowly all the time thinking of the vivid sexual images in the magazine. He finished the Bounty bar. Delicious. He pulled his penis until his back ached and he groaned with relief and pleasure. All the jail tension drained from his body. He smoked a cigarette lazily, hid all his contraband in case of an early morning search by CJ, stretched contentedly then fell into a good sleep.

Bonkie lay dreaming his favourite dream. He was far away in a city of fast cars, blaggers, bank robberies and Branchmen. He was cool, famous and rich. He was a man of respect. He was big time. He was Bonkie the Blagger.

Chapter 4

MICKEY, dressed as an American tourist, walked up and down outside the Big Grey Jug. He wore a blue blazer, large green and white check trousers, white golfing shoes and a shirt heavy with waving palm trees. In his mouth he gripped a large cigar and around his neck hung a Pentax fitted out with a telescopic zoom lens. It was a very professional photographic unit, but Mickey and the son Matt were very professional people at stalking people and shooting them be it with a camera or an Armalite.

Matt, dressed as a student, was lurking over at the university area keeping a wary eye on his da: watching to see if the da was being watched.

Despite his colourful clothing Mickey felt as naked and defenceless as a child. The Firm had disarmed himself and the son before letting them come on their bit of work. They were undoubtedly the best pair to gather intelligence on the banker, well trained and wise in the art of stalking people. Georgie however left them a mile behind at sniffing out poke. That's why he had been sent into the town to track down a job and not the two Belfast men.

Mickey and Matt were liable to wander off following soldiers to see where they kept their gear or leave the job and admire the armoured cars just at the crucial moment when the poke moves.

Georgie would stick it out in a blizzard to sniff out a few shillings. Georgie had an intuition for poke, a feeling for the stuff. It was remarked many times that he could smell the ink on the money and this theory was given credence due to the large size of Georgie's beak.

Mickey and Matt had already been on the job before nine o'clock that morning. They had watched, from a distance, O'Mally-Smyth driving the Merc into the car park, get out and walk the twenty-five yards into the bank. It would be best, judged Mickey, to hit the target on its way out when it was face on to the street.

Mickey and Matt had gone off and spent a pleasant morning

touring Dublin. First they had coffee and cakes in Bewleys and had then visited the National Museum. The pair had been fascinated by the large collection of rifles and pistols on display, relics from the Irish War of Independence. Mickey explained proudly to his son the history of such items as the Peter the Painter and the Howth rifles. They gazed in deepest respect at Pearse's personal firearm and at all the old Republican uniforms and military equipment on display. It had been a lovely morning and Mickey and Matt were sorry Martha was no longer with them to enjoy it too. Mickey had always promised her he would bring her to Dublin.

At twelve twenty-five Mickey was strolling up and down outside the Big Grey Jug. O'Mally-Smyth came walking out, towards his car, at twelve thirty exactly. Mickey raised the camera, breathed in, held his breath, framed the target in the middle of his sight and squeezed the button gently. The camera whirred and took six or seven snaps. Mickey lowered the camera.

O'Mally-Smyth walked on unaware he was being photographed. He stopped at his car door and stooped.

Mickey shot again and took another series of snaps of the banker from the side. He lowered his camera again, pleased with his handiwork. The banker was a sitting duck. Mickey had been careful when shooting not to include any details of the Bank. He had blurred the background. If anyone came across a snap all they would have would be a face.

No one, least of all the many porkers, paid any attention to the tourists.

Mickey strolled off in the direction of O'Connell Street bridge, Matt followed him walking about ten yards behind. On the bridge the tourist was besieged by a bedraggle of poor itinerant kids who begged of him noisily. Mickey gave them all his small change and took their photograph when they scrambled for the money. The kids ignored Matt as he threaded his way past them never taking his eyes off his da. Passers-by thought it was a disgrace that knackers should be allowed to beg on the bridge of the Capital City bringing a bad name on them all and tormenting tourists. Sure, isn't it a wonder they ever came back at all? The porkers came swiftly and chased the eyesore away, muttering curses and clipping little black ears.

The travelling kids hid in an alleyway, behind some dustbins, waited for the porkers to go away and then came back to their begging. The big kids sat the babies in front of them, wrapped up in tartan rugs, and whined up at the plain people of Ireland for a copper or two.

Mickey continued up O'Connell Street and turned right at Sean MacDermott Street. He walked down to the car park at the back of the big blocks of slums. He got into the Volvo and waited on Matt. The car park had eight foot chain link-fencing around it and was patrolled by a man with a big ugly doberman on a long leash. Mickey thought for a dreadful moment he was back in the internment cages of Long Kesh. He shook his head and rubbed his eyes. A concentration camp for motor cars. Good Jesus Christ. What next? An asylum for washing machines?

Matt got inside beside him.

"See anything, Matt?" asked the da. He started up the car.

"Not a thing da. You're clean as a whistle but there is an awful lot of peelers in that street."

Mickey drove to the check point and pulled up at the red and white-striped barrier. He gave the guard a pound and waved away the change. He noticed the men on the guardhouse carried pick handles. Outside in the side street knots of youths hung around waiting to dash in the windows of any likely looking car and run off with the property. The men with the pick handles didn't care as long as it happened outside their territory. The youths didn't fancy Mickey and Matt and let them proceed. A wise decision too, for Mickey had a starting handle below his seat and would surely have bent it over any attacker's head. Mickey did not approve of juvenile delinquency and believed that stern measures were needed to stamp it out. In Mickey's area in Belfast, when he had been OC, the Battalion Area, young fellas would never have dared to interfere with the people of the district. They just would not be able to chase cars and put the windows in on top of people. No. One cannot get far without kneecaps.

"Fucking hoods", muttered Mickey looking into his rearview mirror. He turned out on to Parnell Street. "There's an awful lot of peelers. So what, Matt?"

"It will be hard. I don't see how we can pull off an Op there, da." Matt talked with uncertainty in his voice.

"See you wee lad", replied Mickey after some time, "I don't know if you're an imbecile. I don't know what I'm rearing, do I?" He

mimicked the son. "I don't see, I don't see – the point is, the whole point is, they don't see."
"Who don't see, da?" asked the son.
"The fucking pigeons, the crowds of people, the peelers, that's who. None of them sees, none. They don't see what's going on inside the bank. Do they? Now, do you see?"
"No, da."
"Matt, I think Martha dropped you on your head and never told any of us. It doesn't matter a damn they have the Marines marching up and down the street, complete with the Regimental Band, the UDR and the SAS because we will be quietly working away on the inside. Little moles. They won't see what we are up to. Will they? And what the eye does not see the heart does not grieve. Now do you see?"
"Aye da, it's going to be a sneaky job."
"As quiet as a mouse in slippers son."
"Did you get the photos da?"
"Oh aye, no problem. He is not security conscious at all. I did not like walking about there with no gear on me, Matt. I felt too vulnerable." Matt sat to attention in the front seat. He looked at his da, his head high.
"Ach da, there was no need ter worry. I had you covered all the time."
"Oh? Had ye Matt? What with son?" replied Mickey idly. They were driving out along the road to the airport.
Matt produced a small Chez .32 Automatic pistol.
"Where did ..." began Mickey.
"Now, now", said Matt interrupting the da boldly, "what kind of son would I be if I exposed my own daddy ter danger? If I didn't protect him?"
"Ach, ach, well your heart's in the right place son. I have ter say that."
Mickey was secretly thrilled with Matt's initiative. The son was shaping up well. "Aye, I have ter say it. Well done, son. Your mammy, God rest her soul, would have been proud of ye." He reached over and gave the son's hair a tousle.
"It's my pleasure, da."
"Show me that wee lady there, Matt."
Matt handed over the .32. He cautioned the da.

"There's one up the spout but the safety's on. She holds nine", he added.

"Aye", replied Mickey as he hefted the .32 in his left hand and steered with the other. "She has good balance. Is she accurate?"

"Deadly da. I can hit saucers at fifteen yards. No problem."

"Aye. So ye have a bit of spare ammunition, have ye?" asked the da slyly.

"We are nearly there da if you are going to Gills. Are ye?"

"Where did ye get it, Matt?" asked the da sharply.

"He might be shut for lunch, da."

"I asked you a question wee lad. Where did you get this pistol?"

Do you remember when we cleaned out the dump, daddy? Well I found it laying at the side. I thought you would not mind ..."

"You sneaky wee bastard. You disobeyed orders. You stole gear on your own daddy, I don't know what to say." Mickey sounded furious.

Matt was pale as a ghost in the front seat. He stared straight ahead.

Mickey began to laugh. He tossed the weapon back to the boy.

"Keep that weapon clean and dry, volunteer. You can keep it as a personal", barked Mickey.

"Oh thank you da", said Matt pleased as a small boy at Christmas. He had been on the edge of tears. Matt pulled up the leg of his Wranglers and shoved the .32 into a leg holster.

"What's that?" asked the da glancing down.

"A leg holster da. I made it myself."

"Is that what they learned you in the young prisoners? It's a queer looking wallet. When I was interned, the second time, all we did was drill, drill, PT drill, weapon training, Irish language and history and a wee bit of engineering. It was a damn good course, too. I don't know what's going on with all these wee harps and handbags they are making. Maybe they are going to sneak up on the Brits and bash them with the handbags. Ha, ha, ha, or, when they raid come down the stairs playing harps and the Brits will think they are in Heaven and they will fuck off back to hell where they belong. Ha, ha, ha." Mickey loved his wee jokes.

Matt laughed too for he was delighted to get his gun back.

"A leg holster", laughed the da, "ha, ha, ha. That beats a .45 down the knickers any day".

"But da", said Matt seriously, "it's very good for getting close to people. You can wear a sweat shirt and no one suspects you are carrying. You get up close and pretend to tie your shoe lace, whip out the .32, and give him the message". Matt whipped out the .32 from his leg holster and pointed it at the dash of the car. "Bang, bang, bang", he shouted for the da would be very angry if he punched holes in the Volvo.

"I don't know what they are learning wee lads these days." Mickey was still in good form. "You cannot beat a .303 round through the chest or the guts. Very few get up from it. Very few. A .32 is a pea shooter, Matt. It's for wee girls I'm telling you. A leg holster. Jesus Christ. What is the country coming to?"

Matt was not upset. He knew the da was in very good form. When he was upset he never spoke but sat and glared at everyone.

Mickey pulled up the Volvo at a street corner in Whitehall. He let Matt out of the car. "I'm going to develop the film. Keep your eyes skinned, Matt." He drove along the street a way and parked beside a small group of shops.

It was an old-time chemist shop. The sign was hand painted as was the outside of the shop itself. It was a family business. Mr Gill's father had been the chemist before him and the present owner's son was himself a chemist too. The shop was a discreet drop for the Movement for years. Mickey was banking on the fact that old man Gill never asked questions and simply handed over or accepted the parcels or messages left in his shop. It was unlikely he would know Mickey was in trouble. There was nowhere else Mickey could get the film developed and he trusted no one else to have it done. This way the only man to see the developed prints would be Mickey himself. He pushed open the shop door. A little bell dinged his entrance. The shop was empty.

A very old, stooped man hobbled out from the back. If he had been a younger man Mickey would have seen him go white with fear. He was so grey with age it was not noticed.

"Yes? What can I do for you?" asked the old man as he would a customer.

"Cathal sent me", replied Mickey. He knew the old man knew him well.

"I see. And what is your name, sir?" The old man insisted on the passwords.

"Liam Mellows", answered Mickey.

"What is it you want?" asked the old man. He never used real names.

"I have to use your darkroom. It is urgent. Urgent business", lied Mickey.

"When is it anything else? Come on I'll show you. It's all laid out but please be brief, I do have a business to run." He lifted up the flap and Mickey walked around and went into the back of the shop with the old man.

The old man hobbled back out a few minutes later. He leaned on his glass display case and sighed. Malone had been very explicit. If Mickey showed, phone in. He took out the phone from below the counter and lifted it off the hook gently. He phoned the office. It was answered at once.

"This is Gill", whispered the old man. He was looking fearfully at the back of his shop in case Mickey came in on top of him. It was unlikely for he was busy in the darkroom. "Mickey Campbell is here at my shop. He will be here I'd say for the next half hour at least." The old man paused, listening. "No, he is on his own." He paused again. "Yes, I'll wait on you to call." He hung up and sat down behind the counter in an old rocking chair. The old man rocked to and fro calmly in the chair, unconcerned. He had seen mad dogs come and go in his time but the Movement, his life, remained undisturbed by their rabid emotionalism. Like a dog with rabies that endangered the entire community he believed the mavericks, the mad dogs, should be quietly but firmly put to sleep. He hoped the lads would not be long. He usually napped over the lunch break. The old man hobbled out and put the catch on the door. He put up the sign: CLOSED FOR LUNCH.

Matt was puffing an illegal cigarette sitting on the pavement watching the chemist shop. His da did not permit him to smoke, drink, or go out with girls. Matt threw the cigarette into the gutter and treaded it out.

The two men walking down the street had Movement written all over them. One was average size, neatly dressed, a man who would not stand out in a crowd. The other was a Republican midget. He was under five foot tall, swarthy, with long black greasy hair and wore bomber jacket and jeans, with six-inch turn ups and worn at half mast. It was not their dress or appearance that put Matt's senses on full alert but the casual, too casual way, they sauntered down the street. There was an air about them. A gunman's aura. Matt knew they were carrying.

The Republican midget tapped softly on the door of the chemist shop. Tap-ta-tap,tap. It was opened quickly by old man Gill. The old fox muffled the bell and held his finger to his lips as the pair of gunmen stepped into the shop.

Matt smashed the old man in the jaw with the butt of the .32. In the same movement he stepped inside the shop and gripped the Republican midget by the hair. Matt pulled the midget tight to him, using him as a shield, and pressed the .32 into the back of his head. He flicked the door over behind him.

"If any of you breathe out of place I'll nut ye", he threatened. He moved his left hand and grasped the midget's throat. "Put your hands on your head", he ordered the shield. The midget obeyed and Matt then forced him to his knees. He sank down behind the midget but now had both hands free to cover the other gunman. Old man Gill was laying on the floor, his scrawny neck rolling from side to side. "You", ordered Matt. He pointed the pistol at the second gunman, "take off your coat, nice and slow, and lay it on the floor".

The gunman knew he was a dead man if he tried anything foolish. He took off the sports jacket and threw it on the floor. He had a P38 in his waistband.

"Take it out with your finger and thumb."

The gunman went to reach for the weapon.

"Stop", snarled Matt.

He froze.

"Use the left hand."

The gunman lifted out the weapon awkwardly between finger and thumb. He dangled it in front of him.

"Drop it."

He dropped it. The gun made a clatter as it fell. The midget twitched. Matt nudged the back of his head with the pistol.

"You next, Grumpy", he ordered the midget. "Throw it over with the other piece."

The midget plucked out a .38 Special and threw it over beside the other piece.

"Good boys", jeered Matt. He stood up and threatened the second gunman. "You kneel in front of the counter. Hands on head, move."

When the second gunman was up against the counter Matt took

the Republican midget by the ear and made him walk on his knees, the .32 at his head, over to join his comrade in arms. The old man groaned on the floor. Matt walked over and kicked him in the testicles.

"Shut up you old bastard", he warned.

The old man fainted.

Matt turned to the two gunmen. He went close and squatted down within arm's length. He prodded them with the .32. The Republican midget was playing it down waiting on a break but the other man was white and beginning to sway a little. Matt said nothing but squatted behind the pair breathing down their necks.

"There was no need to kick the old man", began the bigger of the pair, "he is only an old fella".

"What is this?" asked the Republican midget in a squeaky voice. "Is it a robbery? There's very little money here."

Matt thought the midget's voice was fascinating. He poked the back of the midget's head again with the .32. He knew the midget resented that. "I'm no hood, Grumpy, and well you know it too. You wicked wee bastard. You nutted some friends of mine."

The midget stiffened. He thought he had walked into a set up, for the midget was indeed very wicked and had killed many mavericks and cowboys. Sweat ran down his little face.

"Naw. You have the wrong man, kid. I never shot anyone in my life. We were just delivering pieces, that's all. My name's not Grumpy either."

"That's right kid", confirmed the second man, "we were only doing a message. You do know who we are working for, do you?"

"No", said Matt.

"You are in big trouble kid", explained the second gunman, "this is a Movement shop. We are delivering gear for the Movement. If I was you I'd cut my losses and get out of here".

"Jesus", said Matt.

"And", butted in the midget, his tiny face screwed up with sincerity, "that man you kicked there fought in the GPO on Easter Sunday".

"He did not", said Matt, his voice cowed.

"He did so, he did so", squeaked the midget who was furious that Matt should deny the living relic.

"Aye", replied Matt, "so did three thousand others when they were giving out the pensions". He paused. "Where is my da?"

"Who?" asked the second man.

"My da. Where is he?" Matt's voice was cold.

"Good God", burst out the midget shrilly, "there are two of them".

The old man stirred on the floor. He cleared his throat. The time had come he believed for the voice of experience to speak.

"Ah, son", he croaked, "so that's it. There is no need to worry lads. He is one of our own. Your father is out in the darkroom".

"He'd better be, and, he better be in one piece. Otherwise I'm going to nutt the three of you, starting with you old man." Matt motioned to the old man. "Get up and go behind the counter."

Gill got stiffly to his feet. His old wrinkled testicles were like balls of fire. He smiled at the vicious thug in front of him. He hobbled behind the counter.

"Bring me out three large paper bags", ordered Matt.

The old man hobbled out, perplexed, with the bags. The sly old fox was hoping he would get a chance to get at the pistol he kept under the counter.

"Put a bag on each of their heads."

The old man did as he was ordered. He stood stooped over looking stupidly at the third bag. He gave the youth a look of pure hatred.

"Put it on and make yourself comfortable by the wall over there."

Gill slid down the wall and pulled on the brown paper bag. He wondered if the young man was going to kill them. He thought not. He was too cool, too professional. Only amateurs killed needlessly. He relaxed. He had lived through worse times and pulled through.

Matt dragged the midget and then the second gunman over to the wall. He picked up the two discarded pieces. The P38 was straight forward enough. A good safe weapon, reliable and it packed a heavy punch. The .38 Special was a small ladies version, stainless steel, and with only five chambers instead of the usual six. It was a precision-made weapon, not a Saturday night special, with good sights. The ivory butt was very small and suited the midget's small hand. Matt pressed the cylinder release and flicked out the cylinder. He ejected the rounds into his hand. He saw the midget's wickedness then. The five special rounds had for heads flat lumps of pure lead and each was deeply cut with a dum-dum cross. A killer's weapon of the first order. Matt loaded the weapon back up and sat it beside him. He checked the P38. It wasn't even cocked. Matt cocked it and laid it by his other side.

At the cocking of the weapon the three men sitting backs against the wall tensed visibly. They looked like three Ku Klux Klan men with the paper bags on their heads.

"Old man?" asked Matt.

"Yes son?"

"I'll let you take off the bag if you promise not to give me any trouble."

"Thank you, lad." He took off the bag gratefully.

Matt had often been hooded by the soldiers for interrogation. He knew what it was like. Now that he was in control of the situation he wanted to calm down everyone until his da came out of the darkroom. He could not go in and get him because he would have to leave the room nor would he risk tying them up on his own.

"Listen to me yews two. When my da comes out we are leaving quietly so just relax and don't give me any trouble. OK?"

"What about a smoke, kid?" asked the midget.

"If you put your hand near your head I'll shoot you with your own gun, Grumpy", retorted Matt. Midgets were all the same. Give them an inch and they think they are six feet tall. Matt looked over at the old man. He seemed to be ok now. "Were you really in the GPO?"

"I was son. I was a runner and ammunition carrier. Oh, I was there all right. I must say though, that due to my young age, I was ordered out of action before the final assault on the building by the British."

"It was a good day's work, Mr Gill", said Matt with respect.

"They were good men, son. Would you mind an old man like me giving you a bit of advice?"

"Not at all."

"You are pushing against a brick wall. I have seen it time and time again. It always ends like this. Comrades at each other's throats. Only the ideals stand above all. Don't you see? If, even once, we have unity among ourselves the enemy will leave our shores on the morning tide. Good or bad, the Movement is there. Leave off what you are at. Go home. Make peace. I'll do whatever I can to smooth things over, lad."

"Mr Gill is right kid", began the midget. "Give back the gear and lay low for a bit. People forget after a bit ..."

"There are some things people cannot forget. And some things are more important than a person's life. First they shot John. Then they butchered my other brother Sean. We accepted their deaths as casualties in the war. What did they do then? Eh? They threw a bomb into the house and killed my mother and sister. You people are all out of touch. Go home? There's only a pile of bricks there now." Matt spoke softly without bitterness or emotion.

"I'm sorry for your family son", said the old man, "but you can make a new life. You can marry and find a new family. Life goes on. It will be a horrible perversity if you are killed by your own people. But I have seen it happen. It's, it's, ..."

"Oh that can never happen."

"Why not, kid? This is above all us", explained the second gunman.

"As far as myself and my da are concerned we are already dead. It's all only a matter of revenge now. To get as many of them as possible. You cannot make peace with dead men Mr Gill, or frighten them, and, they live as if in the grave."

The old man rubbed his eyes. A wave of sadness rolled over him. The young man before him could not be more than twenty he thought yet he was carrying the grief of ten men. Twenty men. One hundred. His grief was incalculable. It had frozen his emotions deeply leaving only revenge. A fanatic. A person who would kill without compunction. Gill closed his eyes and slumped against the wall. He was too old and weary to waste his breath.

Mickey quickly developed the film. He made one set of photographs and hung them up to dry. They were excellent black and white prints. He was whistling the Cliffs of Dooneen. Mickey looked at a print of O'Mally-Smyth. He looked deep into the banker's eyes, scrutinising, trying to get behind the face, trying to get a gut impression of the man. There was nothing unusual about the man. He looked to Mickey average, even a bit nondescript. That was good. It indicated he might have average likes and dislikes. A conservative surely. The Belfast man touched the print with his finger then turned and opened the darkroom door. He needed a smoke.

"Da", called in Matt at the opening of the door, "out here. Trouble. It's alright."

Mickey peeked into the shop around the inner door. Matt held the P38 in his left hand and waved to the da. The da jumpd over the counter and took the weapon from Matt.

"These two came down the street. I followed them in. Gill set you up, da", explained Matt.

"How long are you in here?" asked Mickey. His voice was low and urgent.

"About fifteen minutes ..."

"Keep them covered", shouted Mickey. He dashed into the darkroom and collected the prints and negatives. Mickey ran behind the counter and grabbed a roll of sticking plaster. He bound the three men hand and foot and then pulled the bags off the two gunmen's heads.

"Are we going ter nutt them, da?" asked Matt.

"Only if their friends show up. You don't send a mouse to do a man's work Matt", panted Mickey. "When are they coming?" snarled Mickey. He dug the P38 into the old man's neck.

"I don't know, Mickey. Your guess is as good as mine. Get out of here for God's sake. They are surely on their way man." Gill had no wish to die so ignominiously, at the hands of a man who had fought so long and so hard against the British. It would not make good history.

"Our orders were to hold you until an Active Service Unit came and collected you", said the second gunman softly. "I am only office staff."

"An ASU, here? In Dublin?" Mickey was taken aback at that.

"You are in big trouble Mickey", squeaked the Republican midget. "Mr Gill is right. Leave while you can."

"See anything, Matt?" asked Mickey. Matt was looking out the window.

"Everything is quiet da. If they come they will knock the door. We can get the drop on them."

"Mickey tore off three strips of sticking plaster and gagged the two gunmen.

"Where are your keys, Gill?" he asked the old man.

"In my pocket here", replied the old man. He looked wan and his breathing was becoming shallow.

Mickey found the keys and gagged the old man. He walked over to Matt.

"You go out first Matt with these", he handed Matt the photographs, "and I will come after and get into the car. Walk along the pavement and I'll pull in and pick you up. OK?"

Matt nodded and picked up the bag. He put the midget's .38 between the bag and his body and the .32 in his pocket. Mickey checked which key fitted the mortice lock on the front door. He and Matt carried the three men out into the back of the shop and locked them in a storeroom.

"There's your brand of haircream, da", pointed out Matt in the front of the shop.

"So it is, be God. It's nowhere to be got down here." Mickey took a large tub. He left the price on the counter and then released Matt into the street. He followed a minute or so later walking swiftly to the Volvo and getting in. He picked up Matt a short distance along the way. A VW van carrying six heavily armed men drove past them and pulled up at the chemist shop. Three men got out and started to rap the door and peer through the window.

"We cut that one a bit fine, Matt", said the da casually.

"Aye da", replied Matt absently. He wondered if his da would let him keep the midget's gun. It was a wee beauty he thought.

Chapter 5

SS

Brave young men of good character
and physique – do you have the GO
to become a Security Guard with
SS Security
Let us test you, let us vet you,
Let us launch you on a secure
career.
Mr John Crinion (formerly of
Dublin Castle and the Bridewell)
will interview upright young men,
of not less than six feet in height
and not more than twenty-five
years old at –
The Farmers Rest Hotel,
Ballroclang – from
2.00pm until 6.00pm on the 1st Aug. '89.
Educational qualifications are not
required, or expected.

This ad was inserted in all the rural papers as part of Crinion's recruitment campaign. It brought a staggering response and the ex-branchman came back to Dublin with a bunch of the biggest, thickest, most ignorant mulchies imaginable. All the recruits were willing to work long hours, in a boring job, for bad money, and take unwarranted and very dangerous risks. Why? Because Crinion gave these rejected porkers and screws what they craved. A job in Dublin, a job with a uniform and a peaked cap. Crinion gave them the self respect they craved and a chance to escape whining, disappointed parents who had wanted the mulchies to be a priest, doctor, lawyer, civil servant, vet, garda, Christian Brother, or a screw. Anything but a farmer's labourer skulking about the land that was not to be theirs. Besides, the machinery had taken away the need for hired help. The mulchies were the brawny bitter products of a society that had no land for them. The mulchies were cross with their lot and ripe for exploitation, though, of course, this in no way condones their wicked behaviour or their moralistic righteous ways. The mulchies were the product of a State that did not permit contraception yet allowed its best land to be bought up and exploited by foreigners with excess money.

All the mulchies wanted to do was swagger back home the odd weekend, in uniform, and tell lies about how well they were doing up in Dublin keeping the jackeens under control and hoping the father would give them half an acre to build a bungalow on after they had made their fortune.

SS Security was their last chance to achieve their modest ambitions. They came out from below hayricks, out from the back of barns, from milking parlours and lofts, from farms large and small, with a blessing from a relieved mother and a dour nod from a doubtful father. They marched into Dublin determined to prove themselves at any cost. A small army of strong young men, like the Irishmen of old, no fancy degrees, poor, but decent, with a strong back and two big fists, swinging a holdall bag and carrying a hurl.

Crinion could not believe his good luck in finding so many idiots and quickly began to indoctrinate them into the SS Security company's methods of operation.

The headquarters of SS Security was located in a disused barge house. The big ramshackle structure was renovated, at minimum cost, to accommodate in military-type accommodation, one hundred and fifty mulchies. The mulchies lived in four-tier bunks that ran the length of the old barge house. It was cheap, lousy, draughty, cold, poorly ventilated and unsanitary. The only thing that could be said in its defence was that it came with the job.

The mulchies loved it and willingly permitted Crinion to deduct fifteen pounds billet charge, from their already low wages. It saved them the bother of tramping Dublin looking for digs, and of course, it provided the mulchies with a centre. The old barge house soon acquired a canteen supplying meals and doubling at night as a bar. But more than anything the lumping together of the mulchies in this way created an esprit de corps and at night in the low dark building when they were singing and swilling beer they began to believe they were the true guardians of the nation's wealth, the protectors of the people's monies.

They thought the Irish Congress of Trade Unions was a railway company and the union rate the price of the tickets.

A small bridge running over the canal linked the barge house with the disused cattle pens across the way. In the mornings the mulchies would fling open the doors of the barge house and they would be marched across into the pens to begin their training, or take out the armoured cars to ferry around the poke.

The mulchies felt at home in the old pens. Even though they were long empty, and waited on the whims of the speculator, the smell and the feel of the animals lingered on. Most of the pens had been dismantled leaving a parade ground type of space. Up in one corner were parked the fleet of SS vans and lorries. The rest of the square was used for a bit of drill and demonstrations of the way in which an SS Security officer was to carry out his duties.

At the far end of the pens was a small building that had been a checkhouse. This was known as the bank or the supermarket. An armoured car would drive slowly up and three mulchies would get out to collect the money, or deliver the money. Other mulchies, dressed as blaggers, would run up and try and get the money off the security men. The mock robbery always failed and ended with the blaggers running away or getting nicked. No one liked doing the blaggers.

In their isolation the mulchies believed that this was the way strokes invariably ended, with defeat for the blaggers, and who was to tell them anything different?

The mock robberies were a great treat for the mulchies and they clapped and cheered when the security officers disarmed the five blaggers, using their special training, and held the robbers on the ground until the porkers came in a big black van and took them off to jail.

They were taught to drive the vans and lorries. They were taught to work the radios. They were taught how to encourage half wild dogs to eat trespassers. They were taught always to be on their guard and to treat anyone who was not in the SS as a potential robber. They were taught how to disarm blaggers carrying shotguns, pistols, and machine guns using nothing but their strength and bare hands, and, the money as a bullet proof vest. They were taught above all things never to meekly hand over the money entrusted to them without a fight. They were security officers not sissies.

When the mulchie learned all these things he was given his full uniform and peaked hat and passed out of training as a probationary dickhead. The uniform was in the style of that used by O'Duffy's Blueshirts and was a great success with a great number of the older business community who looked at them and were reminded of their youth when they had banded together to fight communism and decadence whereever it raised its unholy head. It reminded the old fascists and the new ones in their party, or employ, of the efforts of the stalwart band of Blueshirts who had marched off to Spain, to Franco's rescue, and who had distinguished themselves with honour and glory on the field of battle. Yes, these big, healthy young men in uniform, who so obviously took a pride in their work, these were the typical Irish worker. Not the strikebound, grasping, weedy, sly, avaricious, demanding men of today who increasingly asked for more and more and more. Not the idlers who would not work under any circumstances, not even to go in and demand the rest of the boss' money. People were impressed with the men of SS Security and gave them their business. People wished them well. People believed their money was safe with them. People believed they were the best there were.

Crinion's stature in the business community soared. Where, in the name of industrial relations, did he get them? Business poured into the offices above the barge house.

SS Security blossomed as Crinion had predicted to O'Mally-Smyth. The lucrative contract to move all the money to and from the Central Bank had made them wealthy men overnight.

O'Mally-Smyth had dreaded approaching his wife initially about her affair but when he had started it all came out quite naturally and all very civilised in a chic little restaurant where he had taken her for dinner. She had professed her love for the Minister over the entrecote minion chasseur and apologised to Patrick after the chocolate gateau. Patrick was very understanding even though he thought his wife a scheming selfish bitch and did not spring his business propositions to his wife for a month. She grasped the essentials at once and saw that it was very attractive. She saw economic independence for herself in the deal and insisted to

Patrick that she be written into the profits as well as receiving a generous allowance for the house she did not keep. Patrick smiled and agreed even though he wanted to smash his lovely wife into a bleeding, painful pulp, but, as we know, Patrick was a banker and he loved money so he did nothing to jeopardise the Big Deal.

Delores and the Minister thought that Patrick was a fool for asking for so little. As however, legally, Delores was still Patrick's wife it was in the interest of the lovers to ensure that Patrick became very rich especially when he was so generous to Delores. The spin-offs from SS Security paid for the love nests, the holidays in the Greek Islands, the Rolls, the Opera, the cottage in the west, the cruiser on the Shannon, the beautiful clothes, the gourmet meals, the good life. Perks the Minister could never afford on his limited salary and it was all nothing to do with him, legally, for he met no one or received anything from anyone – directly.

The Minister ensured that SS Security continued to flourish and he quietly fed classified information from his department to Delores when it was to Patrick's advantage. He used his influence with other Ministers to smooth things over for the new security company. The Gardai did not bother them, the corporation left them alone, the taxmen did not know them, the finance houses fell over each other to lend them money.

Patrick was promoted and was well installed as cash control manager before Crinion put SS on the road. The whole operation ran like a well-oiled back scratcher and was an example of the finest type of enterprise. It was a fine piece of graft and SS Security was a native Irish company well able to hold its own in any stock exchange.

Deep below College Green Patrick toiled ceaselessly in a large cavern full of money, old and new. To a man of his talent the job was an insult to his intellect. He had a small army of packers and checkers who spent all their day shoving money into bags or pulling money out of bags. To them and to Patrick it was, after a bit, just bags of paper. There was no feeling with the money for the packers. Perhaps there was so much wealth there they put the purchasing power of the paper out of their heads. At any one time there were at least over one thousand million punts, of various denominations, in the poke cavern.

It had never occurred to any of the men and women who worked there to nick any of the money they handled so casually. Not even the millions of old, dirty, unwanted punts that were consigned to the bank furnaces every month. As far back as anyone could remember there had never been any pilfering in the poke cavern. The people who worked in Patrick's department were honest decent citizens and were happy and contented with their week's pay. They were loyal to the bank, loyal to their employer, loyal to the work ethic of the Christian Irishman. A fair day's work for a fair day's pay.

O'Mally-Smyth began at once to organise the cash control department around the requirements of SS Security. The eighty people directly under his control worked, unwittingly, for Patrick and Crinion, loading up the SS vans, always bringing the SS vehicles to the front of the line, unloading the lorries, sorting out the loads of poke, always having it ready to roll. O'Mally-Smyth smoothly integrated his department with SS Security.

The rival security companies began to get the cold shoulder. They became irritated with the bank staff. The bank staff responded by obstructing them in various ways. O'Mally-Smyth noticed all this and did not discourage it. The dickheads were threatened to be nice to the bank staff, which they were anyway, primarily because they all wore shirts and ties. And they had the young girls tortured to go dancing with them.

It was a beautiful stroke. Money begets money.

Security at the Central Bank was thorough and complete. It was utterly professional. Security consultants were of the opinion that the system was as good as any in the world.

In the blaggers' golden years the powers that be were frightened by a report on a report about the security of the Central Bank. The report, from an American security agency, made it very clear that the bank was wide open to an organised armed raid. While security in the bank branches was almost non-existent at that time and anti-blagger remedies a long way off, the government moved to secure the plain people's poke. Security at the Big Grey Jug became as tight as a duck's bottom.

Security was controlled by a tough Irish American, Maxwell Murphy, who had been prior to his appointment, a security consultant in New York. He brought with him to the job a security man's endless suspicions plus all the modern security technology that was available in the States. The old vaults were installed with sensitive alarms and closed circuit TV watched 24 hrs per day. Each employee was issued with an ID card which was placed into a robotic machine upon arrival at work. If the machine thought you were dodgy it retained the card and screamed the walls down. It was extremely paranoid and guarded the Jug with devotion. This was before getting below. Everyone had to use the security elevator to reach their workplace. At the slightest hint of trouble this elevator would be stopped in the shaft trapping anyone in it if they were up to no good. When an employee stepped out of the elevator he or she was obliged to step through another small machine. If they had any money on their person the machine screamed the walls down. If they were smuggling in firearms or explosives the machine would scream the walls down. The employees in the poke cavern were obliged to leave their money along with their clothes up above in a specially designated cloakroom. They wore special bank uniforms and although they did look smart, especially the ladies' ones, the staff in the poke cavern were a little self-conscious that the uniforms did not have pockets of any kind.

Once through the machine at the bottom of the elevator the employee stood in front of a steel door. They had painted it the colour of old wood but the paint had chipped with use and anyway, everyone knew it was bullet-proof and explosive-proof.

"Name please", the door would demand.

"Eileen Brophy", would come the reply.

Inside, the armed policeman at the console would look at Eileen Brophy's photograph on the screen and compare it with the person he could see outside through his two-way wall. If things matched, and he knew all the staff to see as well, he pressed the green button and admitted the employee. The employee stepped into a small passageway between two doors. The porker was behind a screen of bullet-proof glass.

"Good morning, Eileen", he would call.

"Morning, Paddy." She would wave to the porker behind the screen and he would open up the second door for her letting the employee into the poke cavern.

Paddy knew the walk, the sound of the voice, the mannerisms of every person who passed through his gate. In front of him he had another secret two-way panel that zeroed in on the elevator. In his hutch he was equipped with an Uzi and ten thirty-round magazines, a pump shotgun, a .38 special revolver, a tear gas gun with cartridges and a gas mask. Woe betide any blagger storming out from the elevator, because Paddy the Porker would calmly chop them to bits from his concealed firing position.

There were two other entrances to the poke cavern on either side of Porky Paddy and each was similarly equipped to repel blaggers.

The access/fire control points were linked up to Maxwell Murphy's security office in the bank above. The Chief Security Officer, or CSO Maxwell as he liked to be known, had the entire poke cavern in sight up in the office. From his tastefully decorated office, hung with paintings on loan from the National Gallery, and furnished with old Georgian pieces, CSO Maxwell kept a sharp eye on all that money and bullion. Besides the three armed porkers at the last entrances to the poke cavern, the CSO had five more armed porkers inside the cavern on stand-by. They played cards all day long in a small strongroom drinking endless cups of tea, waiting, waiting, waiting for a raid they knew would never come.

Only a group of madmen would try to raid the Central Bank. If anyone did manage to blow his way in, the CSO had a full platoon of Irish Rangers in a billet in the bank grounds. They were equipped as an infantry platoon for war. A group of madmen might, just, conceivably force their way in but there was no way they would be coming back out alive. The rangers could seal the entrances of the poke cavern (there were only two) in less than two minutes. As if all this were not enough to make any blagger take up shoplifting, if CSO Maxwell hit the raid button in his office the entire city centre would be sealed off in minutes and the rest of the city shortly afterwards. From the time the raid button was hit it made priority on all gardai activity and all would converge on the bank.

The orders were, in the event of a siege in the poke cavern, that no one, including hostages, were to be permitted to come out, unless it were to surrender. Officers of the Army and Gardai had orders to open fire and kill any raiders in a swift counter attack should a raid occur. CSO Maxwell very rarely went down into the poke cavern. He preferred to keep the system he had perfected, and each place needs its own security system, running smoothly from the nerve centre above. He didn't like working underground like a mole anyway. The system almost ran itself now and any defect would show up on the computer straight away.

CSO Maxwell was confident. The only way money was coming out of the poke cavern was by order of the bank.

O'Mally-Smyth signed all such orders. He signed for the money taken in, after it had been checked, and he signed the orders directing the staff to despatch the monies out.

CSO Maxwell and O'Mally-Smyth got along very well together. Maxwell loved his job, he liked the people, he loved the country. He was a tall, healthy man, an ex-marine, in his fifties. Short-cropped grey hair and a face, as his many girlfriends told him, ruggedly handsome. He knew his job and did it with a minimum amount of fuss.

Patrick had suggested to him that the SS Security vans be permitted to come down into the vaults in the bullion elevator so that they might be loaded and unloaded. CSO Maxwell agreed, after studying the proposals, but he stipulated that a barrier, two mesh fences six feet apart, be placed between the armoured car crew and the bank staff. The money would be given in and out via a roller that ran through the barrier.

Patrick and Crinion were delighted. Normally the monies were sent up, a bag or box at a time, in a small lift that ran to an office above. This was the office Georgie had watched the security van collect the money out of. Time was reduced drastically when the vans were allowed down into the vaults. Three men could do the work of five and it was much, much safer too. Patrick ensured SS bags and boxes were always ready on time. His staff worked overtime to accommodate the SS men and were happy to get the extra money. Efficiency rose. O'Mally-Smyth ran a happy department. Security tightened with the introduction of the vans and lorries into the vaults. No one could see what they were loading or unloading. This denied the blaggers their most important requisite – accurate information. The SS vans could have been carrying dirty laundry for all they knew. In addition a bag or box could not be snatched, by an armed lunatic, out on the main street in front of the bank.

CSO Maxwell and his security committee welcomed O'Mally-Smyth's request to allow the vans into the vaults and they saw the request as a new department chief plugging a security gap and increasing efficiency.

"You know, Patrick", drawled CSO Maxwell as he and O'Mally-Smyth played a round of golf one Sunday before dinner, "I suggested that whichever company has the Bank contract, that the company be permitted to bring in its vehicles, but", he hit the ball straight and true, "no one listened to me. How'd ya do it buddy?"

"Do what, Maxwell?" asked Patrick.

"Get 'em to agree, of course. And don't bullshit me. I threatened to resign, but, they would not let that goddamn elevator be used. Wanna know why?"

"Yes." O'Mally-Smyth's swing was as good as the American's but his ball played a little to the right.

"They did not want the lift to wear out." He said 'lift' with an Irish accent. "Can you believe that?"

"No, you're pulling my leg." Patrick smiled. He liked this genial man.

"It's true. Brannigan objected to it, at a board meeting, on those grounds. I believe he said it just to have something to say. An objection, just to let other folk know you are alive and using your authority. Now, I told you. You tell me. How'd ya do it?"

"But you did it, I asked you", stated Patrick confused. "You let the vans down. Didn't you?"

CSO Maxwell studied Patrick to see if he was bullshitting him. He wasn't.

"You mean you did not fix it all up before I asked?"

"No", replied Patrick, wary now, in case Maxwell was onto something. "I thought you had approved it. I merely put the request in, on your recommendation. Was there a problem about it?"

"I had Johnston your predecessor put in umpteen similar requests and they were all vetoed by Brannigan and his clique."

"But why?" Patrick was puzzled.

"I don't know. Maybe because I chop up my food before I eat it. Have you seen us Americans do that?"

Patrick laughed at Maxwell. The banker ate regularly at Maxwell's home.

"Once I went to one of Brannigan's do's. All fusty assholes and dry as dust. Jesus I was glad to get away."

"Yes, but what's the problem?" asked Patrick.

"I think, and I make allowances for my natural paranoia, he hates me."

"You're crazy, Maxwell."

"No. He does and being such a big shot all the
too ..."

"Now you are being paranoid, Maxwell. Why should th

"Because I get more money than them. A lot more. And it's a free and inflation proof. I'm going no further than where I'm at. I say what I think and I do not think too much of the financial hierarchy."

"Now you make perfect sense. You get more money than Brannigan?"

Maxwell nodded and smiled smugly.

"Well he must have had a change of heart, Maxwell. I merely forwarded the recommendation."

"No." They started to walk after the balls. Maxwell turned to Patrick. "The Board moved much too quick. I study the politics of the Bank. Someone, someone with an awful lot of clout, Patrick, ordered the Board to endorse the suggestion. Brannigan proposed it, Lynch seconded it. It was passed unanimously."

"How do you know all this?"

"I have the whole damn place bugged, of course. Security, goddamn it."

"Well I can tell you nothing about it Maxwell", he paused, "honestly".

"Bullshit, Patrick. You have friends in high places I think. Someone up there", CSO Maxwell pointed to heaven with his driver, "loves you".

O'Mally-Smyth shook his head and laughed his denial at Maxwell's absurd deductions but it was not lost on both of them that just at that moment the sun chose to peep out from behind a dark threatening rain cloud and send down a golden ray of purest light to shine on the golfers.

"See what I mean, kid?" quipped Maxwell.

Patrick smiled and breathed in deeply. It felt so good to be alive. He marched after the striding American towards the green. He was quite confident the security chief knew nothing of his influence with the Minister. Patrick wondered where Delores and the Minister had gone for the weekend. For the first time he wished them good luck and a bit of happiness. Why not? He knew now, for certain, that he did not, and had never, loved Delores, nor she him. He hoped they stayed together for a long time.

The sunbeam was a prelude to better weather. The rain clouds scurried away with their load of water and dropped it on the Dubliners down below. The sun was unmasked, a golden yellow ball, high up in the sky.

It had turned out to be a beautiful Sunday.

Chapter 6

MR Gill died thirty-four hours after Mickey and Matt had left his shop. The Movement used the old man's death to generate hatred against the two renegades. Movement people the length and breadth of the country, and abroad, were horrified when they were told of the way the old man had been abused. Mr Gill's well attended funeral acted as a catalyst and drew the attention of everyone onto Matt and Mickey. It became a Movement priority that they be dealt with. An order was drawn up. Matt and Mickey were sentenced to death, in their absence, and the order was sent down the chain of command. They were not to be arrested. They were to be shot. Two Active Service Units were put full-time on Matt and Mickey's trail.

In a tiny bedroom, in a flat at the top of a tower block, a man lay on a small single bed. He lay staring at a photograph he had pinned onto a green board. One of those fancy lecturer's boards that the papers adhered to just by pressing them into the green matt. There was no one else in the billet and the man was glad for the stillness. He looked again at the photograph that had been left behind in the darkroom. A photograph of a bunch of itinerant children scrambling around on O'Connell Street bridge. The snap had been found laying on the floor in the darkroom. What was Mickey up to? What was he doing in Dublin taking photographs of itinerants? The man wondered had Mickey finally gone over the thin edge between oddness, eccentricity, and insanity. He had been dressed as an American tourist. It was very queer in the circumstances. Mickey must have known he was for the bullet as soon as he lifted the dump. What did he want the weapons for? Revenge? Alright. But who did he intend to slaughter and what would be the consequences? And why was he walking around Dublin dressed like a Christmas tree? The man rubbed his eyes. There were bad, bitter feelings about the whole business. The old man's funeral had been an occasion of great anger, not sorrow. The man looked at the money Mickey had left behind for the hair cream. That was a calculated insult. An unnecessary piece of bravado. He stared again at the photograph trying to get a clue, to have a bit of inspiration. He lifted up the report filed by the two men who had gone to the shop and the report of the Active Service Unit. He set it down again. He could remember it off by heart. He looked at the photograph again. It was all they had. He sat up on the bed. They had better start with the travelling people. The man hoped someone would come in and tell him the pair had been stiffed but he doubted it would be that simple. No one liked fanatics, no one. It was impossible to predict what they were going to do, or where they were likely to be, next.

"I'd give anything, Matt, to see MacStravick's face when he finds the snap of the travelling kids", Mickey smiled grimly to himself in the Volvo.

"You left it behind?"

"Aye. When I was packing in the snaps. On an impulse. I threw it down on the floor as if I had dropped it. You know son the more I think about it, the more I like it. They will be following every knacker's wagon north and south."

"Da, we are in big trouble now, aren't we?" asked Matt.

"Aye Matt. The biggest there is. You done well at the shop. You saved us both. Well done, Matt." He glanced at the son briefly and then back at the road. "I mean that, Matt."

"Thanks da. What do we do next?" asked Matt.

"We will have to go underground son. We will have to lay very low until we get the money we need. If we kept out of their way for a couple of months the heat will die down. In the meantime don't tell the lads in the flat that we had a bit of bother. OK?"

"It will leak out, da."

"Well let it leak out in its own good time. There is no sense in upsetting the boys. You see Matt", explained the da, "it's not everybody understands politics".

"I think you should tell them, da. They have a right to know."

"You fucking listen to me", snarled the da, "the only right anyone has is to die. Do you hear me? The only thing any one of us are entitled to, that we can depend on, in this stinking world, is the right to die. If we brief them and they are lifted what happens then? Eh? They will get nutted for just knowing about it. If it leaks out we will handle it but otherwise you keep your mouth shut. Do you understand me, wee lad?"

"Aye." Matt was sullen at his father's outburst. He looked out the passenger window so Mickey would not see him blushing.

"Look son, I'm sorry to be shouting. I'll tell you what. We will tell the lads we have to take off because they are on our tail about the gear. Alright, Matt?" asked the da consolingly.

"Alright da, alright." Matt was huffing.

"Tell you what, son. We will go off and work out the routes on a couple of those wee banks and we can do a bit of fishing. How does that sound to you volunteer?"

"Can I keep the midget's .38?" asked Matt seizing his chance.

"Aye, I don't see why not. We will be carrying all the way from now until we get the business over with anyway."

"Why do we need so much money, da? Why don't we just go across and shoot her in the dome?" asked Matt sharply.

"Because we would not get off the boat. Because we would not get near her. Because we are going to blow her and her poxy family clean out of the sky. That's why. And we need a lot of money to buy the SAMs."

"Will you and me be firing them, da? Firing the rockets ourselves?"

"Nobody else will do it. You can count on that, Matt. Nobody else has the guts." Mickey thumped the steering wheel. Tears were rolling down his cheeks. "You will be revenged, Martha, this I swear on my life, they shall know thy name and feel fear."

Matt reached over and touched his da's arm.

"Please, da. Don't be crying. You will only make me cry too", pleaded Matt, but the big tears came rolling down his cheeks and fell onto the paper bag he clutched.

The man and his son wept a couple of minutes, the only sound their racking sobs in the car.

Mickey wiped his eyes with his sleeve. His grief turned to scalding anger. "We will see how they like it, we will see how they like it", he croaked in a voice that was utterly distorted, so intense was the raging hatred inside him.

"Aye, da, we'll see how they like it alright", agreed Matt. He took refuge in his da's hatred. It was strong. It was fierce. It was whole and complete and a comforting place to be.

Mickey and Matt composed themselves, dried their eyes, and

parked the Volvo in a garage at the back of the offside flat the Firm had up in Drumcondra. They went into the flat with the snaps to have a meeting with the rest of the Firm. Neither Matt nor Mickey were in the least embarrassed by their emotional outburst. In fact they had them regularly during which father and son released their tensed-up emotions, spitting out all the frustration of two bereaved people who were fugitives in a strange, hostile land. The Firm were waiting on them.

On the wall in the flat, pinned over the fireplace, were two snaps side by side. The resemblance between the two men in the photographs was uncanny. It was more than the fact that they looked identical – they looked the same man wearing different clothing. The age, the height and the weight were all perfect.

"The photographs are excellent lads", praised MacGregor to the two Belfast men. "Did you have any bother getting them?"

"Naw", replied Mickey with a dismissive wave of his hand, "it was wee buns boys. Wee buns".

Georgie stared at Bonkie in his best suit, at his young brother's wedding, taken only eighteen months ago, and then he stared at the banker.

"He's a dead ringer boys that's for bleeding sure", observed Georgie.

He sat down. "He's doing twelve months at the moment up in the Joy. I was talking to his brother. He has two months done and he expects to be just out for Christmas."

"We have to get him out", said MacGregor, "in case things change. The ringer could get moved, or sacked or ran over by a stolen car. We have to get it together as soon as we can".

The Firm was mortified at the thought that their ringer be run down by a drunken joyrider or the prospect of him getting moved to a Jug where he was not in control of vast amounts of money.

"Jimmy Apple says he can get him out on bail, at the Appeal Court, but that it will cost a lot of money", put in Alfie. He was wearing denim jacket and jeans.

"How much is a lot of money, Alfie?" asked MacGregor.

"As much as he can extort out of us I suppose. He's an awful greedy man Mac. I don't trust the bastard either but he is the only bent solicitor I know."

"Yeah you are right, Alfie. What did you tell him?"

"I told him a bummer about Bonkie having a lot of antique silver buried and that we have a big buyer for it, I mean, that I had a big buyer for it. The asshole was so impressed he bought me a pint."

"Bleeding hell Alfie that's a turn up", put in Georgie, "he's a mean one alright".

"Hold on a minute", Mickey did not know what was going on, "what do you mean you don't trust him? Do you mean to say he is a tout?"

"The guards have him by the scrotum Mickey. They can get his licence taken off him any time they please. He is useful to both sides", explained Bob.

Mickey had gone very red in the face. He was almost speechless. He held up his head. "Hold everything lads. I vote to execute this Jimmy Apple."

"I'll second that", called Matt.

MacGregor went and pulled a bottle of Harp from the fridge. He drank half of it staring all the time at Mickey.

"Mickey we do not want to kill anybody. We are not into that line of work as you know. All we want is the poke with as little fuss as possible. Jimmy Apple will not tell anyone any of our business because we won't tell him what we are up to, will we?"

The Firm all shook their heads gravely.

"I'd feel more sure of that if he was in a wee quiet grave", commented Mickey.

"I'll second that", put in Matt, "informers beware".

"See you bleeding two", said Georgie in amazement, "you are really something else too. Are you his bleeding parrot?" he asked Matt.

"Mickey boy", said Bob quietly, "we need Jimmy Apple to get Bonkie out the legal way. Alfie is very good at deceiving people. Alfie will give him a dose of bullshit to dish up to the porkers ..."

"And may they enjoy it too, amen", joked Alfie.

It brought a laugh from the Firm.

"I suppose we have no choice. Do we Mac?" asked Mickey.

"None. Don't worry Mickey, we know how to handle the Apple. We'll have the porkers running up each other's tails while we work quietly away. More practical matters. We are going to need poke. How much is in the war chest Matt?"

Matt took out his notebook. It was filled with tiny cryptic figures.

He studied them for a moment.

"Seven thousand eight hundred and fifty plus there is a few bags of silver I never counted."

"Will that be enough to spring him, Alfie?" asked MacGregor.

"I'd say so, Mac, but it will leave us with no operating money."

"Well", laughed MacGregor, "we will just have to do a jug or two, won't we?" The Firm greeted this proposal enthusiastically and gave it their heartfelt approval.

"It's agreed then, is it? That we get Bonkie out as soon as we can?"

All said aye.

"And", continued MacGregor, "that we do a couple of jugs, the poke collected to be used to try and crack the Big Grey Jug?"

All said aye.

"I think there is something I have to tell you, boys", said Mickey in his most reasonable voice.

The Firm became suspicious immediately. A hush descended on the flat.

"Myself and Matt are in bad trouble over the gear. We will have to lie very low for a while. The Movement have people looking for us."

"That was only to be expected, Mickey", replied Bob. "You can go down the sticks and do all the routes and dig the dugouts and dumps. I don't think Dublin is too safe for you boy". Bob had been looking for a way to suggest this to the Belfast men anyway.

"That's good thinking, Bob", said Mickey in a very shallow voice of praise. "I was thinking that as we are all the one unit I'm going to hand the gear into common ownership. It's the Unit's gear now, lads. I'm handing it up to us all. Me and Matt will look after it for us all."

"You are too bleeding much, Mickey", laughed Georgie, "does this mean we all get shot now for the common good?"

"Knock if off, Georgie", warned MacGregor, "I think it's very kind of Mickey to make us such an offer. Thank you, Mickey".

"Ah, it's nothing boys", said Mickey shyly, "sure I'll set up a wee camp for us and run yews through the weapons. There is plenty of rounds for the M16s, plenty boys".

The Firm, despite knowing that Mickey was up to something, were delighted at the prospect of going on a training camp with such fine weapons. MacGregor did not believe Mickey's offer to put the gear into the Firm's dump for a moment but, as chairman of the gang, so to speak, he had an obligation to keep matters running smoothly.

"What will we do with Bonkie, if we get him out?" asked Alfie.

MacGregor turned to the photograph of Bonkie up on the wall.

"This man is the most important man ever to hit our lives. He is now one of us. He will be with us twenty-four hours a day from now until we crack the Big Grey Jug. He'll be coming with us, Alfie, on the strokes. There is no other way. He will be safer with us than running around Dublin acting the bollox. He is one of the Firm now. Agreed?"

All said aye.

Alfie collected the few grand from Matt before he and his da headed off down the sticks, and went off to be extorted by Jimmy Apple.

Chapter 7

BONKIE was in the big D though, to look at or to listen to him, a prisoner would conclude he was his usual, happy-go-lucky, irrepressible, 'I don't give a bollox' self. It was part of Bonkie's image that nothing in jail could get through his tough exterior. This image, at times, was very hard to present and Bonkie sometimes wondered if the prestige of being the President of the Small Time Strokers was worth all the aggro he had to endure. He could, he reflected, do his whack easy without any hassle and give the screws a break. Creeping Jesus was taking matters very personal. He waged a relentless campaign against Bonkie in a stubborn, vindictive, silent world of nastiness. There was something sour in his mulchie's head that would not accept the fact that Bonkie hated him, not because he was ugly, not because he was obnoxious, but because he was a screw – and Bonkie hated all screws. Past, present and to come. Bonkie hated them all no matter what religion or nationality. A turnkey did the same thing everywhere. He locked up his fellow human beings for money. What did he want the prisoner to do? Lick his ass for locking him away?

Bonkie marched up and down the cell. He was furious, but he forced himself to sing. Earlier that morning the cell had been turned over by CJ in a snap search. The screw had gone straight to a loose piece of board and levered it up with a screwdriver. He put in his hand and pulled out all Bonkie's smokes, two joints of really good grass he had been saving, and two dirty books. It was the first time that Bonkie had ever seen CJ smile. He looked like an anaemic shark. His hands shook. He was flustered. You'd think he was after discovering uranium. He rooted around a bit more and came out with a biro refill and a blue envelope.

"Hand what have we here?" asked CJ of the wall in front of him. He opened the envelope and pulled out the single sheet of paper. The screw smiled at Bonkie. He cleared his throat in a shallow theatrical gesture. He began to read Bonkie's letter out loud.

"My Daharling Sahally,
Hit his lonely now widhout you hand high miss you hand de baby. Hit seems so long since high ..."

Bonkie rushed forward and snatched the letter from the screw. He tore it into bits in an instant. Bonkie turned to CJ and spat in his face. He leapt forward in a frenzied attack.

The screws beat him into a pulp and left him in a heap on the floor.

It was not the beating, or the degradation, or the loss of his contraband that had Bonkie wound up like a clock spring. He did not care about the loss of his love letter to Sally. He could still love her silently from the cell and she was such a super woman she would understand. It was not the extra two months in the Base or the month's loss of remission. That was all part of doing your whack. What had Bonkie wound up was that he let CJ catch him out. It was obvious that the screw had known about the loose board. It was obvious, in hindsight, that CJ had carefully cultivated his hole in the cell on the chance that Bonkie would put his contraband down there. It was even probable that CJ had loosened the board himself. Bonkie knew the way he had gone straight for it and the look of triumph in his moronic eyes. Victory! Reward! Vengeance!

"I must be getting bleeding institutionalised", muttered Bonkie to himself. How could he let CJ catch him like that? He fretted he was losing his cop-on. Bonkie had been given, for educational purposes, a few pencils by the screws (but no paper) and he used these in a remarkable exhibition of the efforts a prisoner can make to overcome adversity. Bonkie had written down all one wall of his cell, in neat blocks of one thousand, the words, 'I am not depressed, I am not depressed, I am not depressed, I am not depressed, I am not depressed'. He had written that two hundred and thirty-one thousand times. It was very relaxing and Bonkie hoped to have a quarter of a million finished soon. That way, he felt, he was expressing himself very clearly, even if he was a bit repetitive. The blocks of neatly written 'I am not depressed's were an artistic work of great grit and fortitude displaying the prisoner's inner urge not to permit the excess of captivity to bruise or crush his spirit. It took great willpower for Bonkie to get up off the warm bed, to rouse himself from jail apathy, to deny himself the drowsy daydreams of freedom, to rise, sharpen his pencil and start again.

Bonkie shifted his bed, plywood stool, and locker over to the wall he had covered with 'I am not depressed's. He looked at the bare wall that was his penal canvas. A cream coloured monstrosity. A wall. The essence of imprisonment. Filthy. Cracked, the layers of years-gone-past crumbling through here and there. Only the graffiti showed any flicker of humanity. One graffito in particular caught Bonkie's eye. It was a ballpoint sketch, far up the wall, of a porker's head, with an extremely long neck, rising out of a pisspot. The porker was looking down suspiciously at Bonkie. Bonkie gave the graffito a wipe with a damp vest he was using as a wash cloth. The porker sprang to life. Its small beady eyes glinted with paranoia and badness. Written on the pisspot in tiny script were the words – Go straight, the Law are everywhere! Bonkie smiled to himself. Whoever had done the graffito was a good artist. Probably a counterfeiter thought Bonkie. He continued to clean down the wall, making it ready, bringing to light names and sentences, some of whom Bonkie knew, some long since dead, their sentences finished, their bodies nothing but dust with a few bones in a wooden box. Bonkie thumped the wall with his fist. It was an outrage to his mind that this kip could be so permanent. If the country was invaded by aliens this place would still be here he thought. He dragged over the small table and shoved it in flush against the wall and placed two jail bibles (they were stamped 'PRISON SERVICE' in case someone ran away with God's holy books) up on it. Standing on the bibles he could reach the top of the wall where it joined the curved whitewashed ceiling. He contemplated trying to find a way of writing on the ceiling like the great Michelangelo so he could fill all available space with his 'I am not depressed's. Bonkie took a deep breath and started. He wrote in small neat print, the first – 'I am not depressed' of the new day. And, once he had got going, he soon settled into his work, becoming absorbed. Time passed. He heard the screws coming and climbed down off the table. Bonkie had notched up an astonishing number of I am not depressed's in the three hours. He sat on the bed. The door clanged open. In came the assistant governor.

"Ah, there you are, Bonkie", he exclaimed, though it must be said he could hardly have been down in Grogans having a pint, "and how are you?"

"To tell you the truth, governor", said Bonkie, "I have never felt better".

"Oh, good", replied the assistant governor and he was genuinely pleased for it must also be said, in all fairness, that governors of prisons like prisoners to be content with their lot in the jail.

"It's the view", said Bonkie, pointing to the glimmer of light stealing into the dungeon, "and the sea breeze". The cell stunk of stale piss. "I have heard it said", confided Bonkie in a conspiratorial whisper, "that wealthy people are paying five hundred pounds per week to enjoy such conditions as we have here".

The assistant governor was not listening to Bonkie. He never listened to any of the prisoners. There was no point. All they ever did was complain.

"You have no complaints then?"

"Ah, no Mr Turnlock .."

"Mr Turnoch, Byrne", interjected the chief screw. He did not look pleased.

"Good man, Bonkie", stated the assistant governor. "You have a visit." He came down out of his middle-class aloofness and stared at Bonkie sharply. "A legal visit, Byrne. As it is a legal visit the Governor has decided to permit it, even though you are on punishment."

"Oh, thank you kindly sor", said Bonkie and touched his sidelock as the starving peasants did to the priests and the landlords. Bonkie knew they had no power to stop the visit.

For just a second Turnoch's genteel mask slipped and his lip curled up in a sneer. "Let me give you some advice, Byrne. Don't cause trouble in my prison. Do you get me?" The assistant governor turned on his heel and walked out of the cell. His entourage did likewise all passing mysterious looks of warning at Bonkie. Bonkie deduced that as he did not know what was going on then they did not know what was going on and were trying to freak him. The door opened again and the Chatterbox came into the cell. He had Bonkie's civilian clothes in his hands.

"Put 'em on, put 'em on lad. Then you goes for a shower. Governor's orders. Put 'em on now. I suppose you could do with a smoke. Here's ten and a box of strikers but don't say I gave 'em to ye. Sure I know you won't anyway. You're no grass. You'll want to be fresh for the visit I'm sure. Don't press charges and we won't press charges. That's what the word is but don't say I gave it to ye."

"Hold bleeding on will yer?"

The Chatterbox paused for a moment. He put the clothes on the bed. He winked at Bonkie.

"I", Bonkie pointed to himself, "I don't know what is going on, do you?"

The Chatterbox looked around the cell in a bewildered way as if he was looking for a life raft or a bolt hole. He wasn't a bad screw. The lads above had an arrangement with him and it was he who had left in the smokes and books to Bonkie. The prisoners did not have such a bitter opinion of him due to the fact they believed he was not aware of what he was at. Kind of not responsible for his actions. All he seemed to want to do was chatter all the time.

"Well if you don't know, how can I be expected to know? And if you don't know then the governor don't know. It seems to me lad nobody knows nothing in this place but how to make wallets. Have you seen this?" He produced a wallet, then returned it to his pocket swiftly. "There were nine hundred people killed in a train crash in India. There's another two thousand missing. Yes, that's right. The train was on a ferry and the ferry sank. It's very strange isn't it though? You'd think they could build a bridge if they can drive a train and there wouldn't be any life jackets on a train either."

Bonkie let him ramble on. He picked up his civilian clothes, a towel, shampoo and soap. He walked out of the cell, the Chatterbox following and Bonkie leading. Up the iron stairs, through the gate, to the big prison above. The lads were out picking up their grub. When they saw Bonkie they gave him a cheer. Bonkie put the head up, shoulders back and gave a sight swagger.

"Are you going to a wedding Bonkie?" shouted someone.

"Yeah, your mother's", retorted Bonkie and waved his suit.

"I hope you're not the groom Bonkie", yelled someone else, "she bleeding looks like Chisler".

And so the banter and friendly insults flew along the prison landings all designed to show support for the underdog, the man in chains, the man in a prison within a prison.

The hot water was invigorating. Bonkie soaped himself three times. The water stung the bruises on his face but he stayed under the shower with his eyes closed. He didn't even try to think about the strange visit. He had learned a long time ago to take things in jail as they come. He was locked in and all problems were locked out. He turned off the shower reluctantly. The Chatterbox was waffling outside the shower to another screw about the price of building a bungalow. Bonkie stepped out into the dressing cubicle. He dried himself and slipped on his Courthouse suit, a white, three piece, tailor-made piece of clothing in pure new wool. Bonkie combed his hair straight back in the American style of the thirties. An intense face stared back. He carried his forty-odd years well, considering the amount of whack he had done. How long can yer stick it? This question was sneaking into his head at odd unexpected times, when he was not prepared to handle it. He forbade his mind to frame that question. He instructed his brain not to process it. But the insidious question returned, a doubting monster, that grew stronger and more insistent with the passing years. Bonkie spat into the mirror. "I'll bleeding stick it longer than you." He made a face at himself and laughed at the melting doubt. The laughing face that looked at him was somebody else. It was the optimistic Bonkie the Blagger. He made a smile. He had good white teeth. A good-looking chick had once told him he looked a lot like Clark Gable, only kind of tougher.

"That's true kid", he had told her, "I'm the real thing".

He stepped out of the cubicle fresh and clean.

"Are you right Bonkie?" asked the Chatterbox.

Bonkie nodded to the screw. He took out a smoke, put it in the side of his mouth and lit it. He flicked the match to the ground then flicked a piece of dust from his lapel.

The Chatterbox gulped but said nothing. Bonkie was still on punishment.

They marched off. Three blue screws and a man with slicked back hair in a white suit, cigarette dangling from the side of his mouth, walking briskly along a dim, red and black tiled, corridor. Bonkie shone like a star in a clear desert sky.

He looked the part. He was cool.

Bonkie walked up with the escort into the granite circle, the nerve centre of the jail, from which the wings radiated out in an old Victorian pattern. Here in a small office were kept the great books of penal knowledge which contained a permanent record of all who were brought in handcuffs to the house of Mountjoy. He looked up at the huge dome. All that light coming down from the glass roof hurt his eyes. The screw at the corridor to the visiting box unlocked the gate. A principal screw was waiting on them by the small room used for legal visits.

"This way, this way, Byrne", he said in an officious voice. "Legal visit for Byrne."

Bonkie walked to the small room and recoiled back when he looked through the window in the door. It looked like the Supreme Court in there. Nothing but wigs and silk gowns. He thought they were going to hit him with a Capital Murder charge. Bonkie turned to the principal screw.

"I want me bleeding solicitor. I'm not going in there", he snapped at the principal screw.

"What harr ye talking habout? Dat his your solicitor in dare", replied the principal screw. He pointed back at the small room.

"They're hall here to see you", declared another screw in a voice that indicated to Bonkie they thought the whole process as odd as himself.

"Harr you refusing the visit, Byrne?" asked the principal screw slyly.

Before Bonkie could reply the door of the visiting room flew open and a huge man jiggled out. Jimmy Apple had a briefcase, full of nonsense, in each pudgy hand. He wore a grey pin-striped suit and a bow tie around his bulging neck just below the last of his four chins. Jimmy wiggled his spiky eyebrows. At a glance his opportunist's mind took in the scene before him. A hesitant prisoner. Was he going back to his dismal cell before the cause of Justice had been served? Was it possible, due to the prisoner not being aware of his constitutional right to legal advice, that Jimmy Apple was to be denied his fat fee? Intolerable. And therefore, even though Jimmy had never heard of Bonkie before, (ten thousand pounds had been mentioned) and had never seen him before it was paid over, Jimmy stepped forward bravely and gripped Bonkie by the hand.

"Good day to you, Mr Byrne." He dragged Bonkie towards the door of the visiting room. "Counsel", he declared in a voice of great power and resonance, "are waiting on your instructions". He opened the door with his foot and shoved Bonkie into the room. Jimmy nimbly squeezed through, two briefcases in the other hand, and slammed the door with a flick of his elephantine leg. The screws stared boggle-eyed into the visiting room. Jimmy threw his briefcases onto the floor, produced a large red silk handkerchief and wiped the sweat from his brow. He worked hard for his bread did Jimmy Apple.

There was a large table in the room. In front of the large table were two plastic chairs, the inmates of transport cafes and hospital waiting rooms seemed to prefer. Bonkie was settled into one of the chairs by Jimmy Apple. The chair was too small for Jimmy Apple. He sat astride it resting his thick arms on the back.

"Gentlemen", began Jimmy Apple, "this is our Mr Byrne".

The four barristers, two junior counsels and two senior counsels, stared at Bonkie as a flight of vultures do on a staggering dying creature. The eyes below the wigs were bleak and harsh. As if on cue all four gave a curt nod and said, together, "Good day, Mr Byrne".

Bonkie reached for his smokes. He put one in his mouth. A lighter appeared under his nose and clicked alight. Jimmy Apple smiled. He reminded Bonkie of a Halloween Lantern he used to make out of turnips.

"Mr Byrne", started up a voice old and wise in the ways of the law. "It is my opinion, and that of Wattle-Murphy I must add, that in your case there has been a grave miscarriage of justice."

Bonkie stared fascinated at the old leathery face as it spoke from behind parched lips. It had a beak of a nose. If it had a bigger wig and a red gown it was a model for a judge. There was no difference anyway as far as Bonkie was concerned. They were all in the same Firm. Prosecution or defence or up on the bench they were all in the one exclusive gang. They made up rules to play the game but they always won.

"Yer", replied Bonkie, who was possessed of the horrors.

"Accordingly, and having due regard to all, to everything in this case, we have decided to appeal conviction, and severity of sentence, should that prove necessary, and this afternoon a motion shall go before the Appeal Court to release you on bail pending appeal proper." The senior counsel produced a silver snuff box, tapped out a pinch and sucked it up his nostrils. He remained perfectly motionless for a full minute, then erupted, uttering a roaring bellowing bah and spraying Bonkie and Jimmy Apple in a thin brown haze.

"That's a nice snuff box, Bonkie", whispered Jimmy Apple to Bonkie and before Bonkie could reply Jimmy winked at him and placed his finger to his lips. He jerked his eyebrows and said softly, "it's antique".

"Yeah", replied Bonkie wiping the tobacco smog from his face and suit.

The senior counsel erupted once more a huge Bah! He then gave a little hmmmm of satisfaction and settled into his seat.

"Where was I, Bartie?" asked the senior, speaking to a junior to his left.

The junior, a pasty-faced young gentleman with a Bob Hope nose, whose wig was worn at a rakish angle, consulted his notes. He uttered in a servile undertone, "er, bail, for Byrne, pending appeal proper".

"Ah, yes. Thank you Bartie. It is inconceivable to us, Mr Byrne, that ye should remain in prison a moment longer. I'm of a mind – by jove I will, Mr Wattle-Murphy", he looked over at the other senior, "I think I'll take the bail motion into Judge's private chambers. I am not without influence Mr Byrne and I may say their Lordships shall listen to our case".

"Hear, hear", chorused the other counsel.

Jimmy Apple rubbed his hands together.

Bonkie hadn't a clue what was going on. He nodded wisely to the rambling old man.

"And, be damn", cried the old man thumping the table, "If they do not grant bail, why, I shall present a Writ of Habeas Corpus. In my opinion you would then be in illegal detention. You have a constitutional right to bail, Mr Byrne, and the Constitution will not be taken from you".

"Hear, hear", chorused the other counsel.

Jimmy Apple clapped Bonkie on the back and knocked his smoke out of his mouth.

Bonkie coughed his guts up. His eyes were watering and his throat burning.

"Snuff?" offered the senior counsel.

"No, tank you", he almost said your Lordship, "I gave it up".

"I must confess, Mr Byrne, it's something I have been unable to do. The snuff I fear is like claret; it gets into the blood, and, over the years becomes part of the blood, and, if one has lived as long as I, I think it becomes the very blood itself."

The legal people laughed politely at the witty counsel.

Bonkie thought he was going to bore the Appeal Court into granting bail. He had never heard such a boring old bollox.

"I'd like to say something", said Bonkie.

"What?" roared the old senior counsel.

"He wants to talk", explained Bartie into his ear.

“Who?” asked the senior counsel.

“Mr Byrne, our client”, reminded Bartie.

“Oh! Yes, you may speak. Please do.” The old senior counsel took out a huge horn and stuck it in his ear. He turned it in Bonkie’s direction.

“I pleaded guilty”, said Bonkie.

“What?” roared the senior counsel.

“I pleaded guilty”, screamed Bonkie into the horn.

“Silly man”, muttered the senior counsel. He put down the horn and spoke to Wattle-Murphy. “Tell him, in language he shall understand.

“Mr Byrne. You were not legally represented at your trial. Is that correct?” Wattle-Murphy spoke crisply and clearly in green Oxford with a touch of Trinity twang.

“Yeah, that’s right. I sacked me solicitor.” Bonkie liked telling them that.

“But you had no legal representation. I mean that’s what I asked you. Please answer yes or no.”

“No.”

“And you were found guilty. Is that correct?”

“I took a bow. Ye know. I was caught be the bollox, the short and curlies, if yer know what I mean. I pleaded guilty.”

“And you were given the maximum possible sentence that the court could impose. Twelve months. Is that correct?”

“Yeah, but you see I was happ...”

“Mr Byrne. Please. Answer the questions yes or no. OK?” Wattle-Murphy glared at Bonkie.

“Yeah, I mean yes.”

“Good man. You had no legal representation. You pleaded guilty but you did so in a state of legal ignorance. You were given the maximum sentence, which I must say was very severe coming on top of no representation, and you have had no appeal. That is correct, is it not?”

“I did not want to appeal, did I?”

“Of course you wanted to appeal Mr Byrne”, scolded Wattle-Murphy. “It is indicative of your ignorance that you believed that you did not, at that time.”

“At that time”, emphasised Wattle-Murphy’s junior. He wagged his finger at Bonkie.

"You are going to try and get me something off my sentence?" enquired Bonkie.

"As a last resort, perhaps we may make such a plea", began Wattle-Murphy wearily, "but as far as we are concerned, Mr Byrne, we shall be looking for the sentence to be squashed on the grounds that, even though you were induced to plead guilty, and you being ignorant of the law, and had no legal representation, your statutory rights were violated. Your constitutional rights as a citizen of the Irish Republic were taken from you in, I consider, an act of base disrespect for you as a human being and, worse, an act of denigration against the Constitution itself."

"If I", cried out Wattle-Murphy passionately, "or Mr Birdman were upon the bench", the old senior counsel bowed, "and if an ignorant person such as you were to appear before us, why, why, it would be our duty to refuse a plea of guilty in such circumstances".

"The requirements, the rigorous requirements, of Irish justice, I am ashamed to tell you, have not been met. But Mr Byrne, I shall eat my wig, my gown, buttons and all, I swear, if we don't have you treated decently."

The two juniors stood up and began to clap. Jimmy Apple tried to stand but was unable to do so. He clapped from the chair, whose legs were bending with his weight, and Bonkie saw tears in his eyes.

The prisoner had two choices. He could go along with the lawyers or he could jump up and run out to the screws and tell them to lock him up. He looked out into the corridor and saw the boggle-eyed bunch of screws staring in at him. He could see they resented the private consultation. It went against their natural nosey streak. It was something beyond their limited control, like a shit. They could control the supply of toilet paper but they could not restrict or control the shit itself. Bonkie shook his head. Why was he making such absurd observations? The room was full of smoke. The legal heads were waffling away, just like the courthouse where the prisoner could not hear, or understand, what they were talking about. The prisoner was just a thing, an artefact, a necessary thing to have if they wanted to play trials and appeals, pleas and punishments, cops and bleeding robbers.

"Hold on a minute", said Bonkie. "I want to say something and I don't bleeding want to be interrupted, otherwise I'm going back to my cell. OK?"

There was a stunned silence. Was it conceivable that this ignoramus was intent on going back to his dismal cell therein to brood and do his whack? Was it conceivable the seniors were going to lose two grand each for a morning's manipulation, the juniors twelve hundred pounds, and Jimmy Apple over three grand? No, it was inconceivable. It was unthinkable.

Jimmy Apple strained himself to his feet. He blocked the door in case Bonkie did a run for it back to the cell.

"Speak, Bonkie", he waved to the counsels to be quiet, to stop the charade.

"I was bleeding caught by the bolloxs in Capel Street after I done a snatch. The auld one came out with the poke, eight hundred pounds in her handbag for wages or something, and I snatched it nice and clean. I didn't get ten yards up the street. Sullivan from the Bridewell and Thorn were in a shop doorway. Two big bleeding porkers. I ran straight into them. I was knocked clean unconscious by Sullivan with a cosh. I woke in the Bridewell. I bluffed it I was nicking a handbag and they agreed to do me in the District Court if I took a bow and copped for a few other things I had been at and they wanted cleared up. I'm telling yer now. I was well pleased to get the District Court because if I were sent ter the Circuit for trial I would be doing two or three years, wouldn't I? I have a record going back to when I was nine years old. I'm a thief and when I get nicked I get sent to jail. It's an occupational hazard, isn't it? If I'd pleaded not guilty they would have sent me forward for trial. I didn't appeal 'cause they'd laugh at me. Now that yer know my position, what are yer up to?"

"We are getting you out of jail, Bonkie", replied Jimmy Apple smoothly.

"When?"

"This afternoon."

"And can I get more time than I am already doing?"

"No."

"What do yer want me to do?"

"Sign the affidavits that Mr Wattle-Murphy has prepared. That's all we want you to do Bonkie."

"That's it, then?"

"That's all, Bonkie." Jimmy Apple looked at one of the juniors. "Do you have the documents, Nigel?"

The four counsel stared at Bonkie with utter loathing. If he ever came before them when they were on the bench, please God and a new Government, he'd get no twelve months. The crass lout.

Nigel dropped the unsworn affidavits onto the table as if they were dusted with anthrax. The four counsel stood up, together, and glared at Bonkie.

"Goodday to ye, Mr Byrne", they intoned as one, then trooped out of the visiting room, silks swirling, wigs straightened, their noses wrinkling in profound disgust at having to use their legal talents on such an ignoramus.

"What the fuck are you upsetting the barristers for?" asked Jimmy Apple when they had left.

"Because they were talking shit, Jimmy. About the Constitution and Justice and because I wanted to make my position clear. That's bleeding why."

"All the same there was no need to upset them Bonkie. You know how haughty taughty they are about the law. Justice can be a very abstract thing to them. It's the case, the legal points, the procedure, all the very fine legal details laymen may not appreciate. They are the best there is. Between you and I, it is almost certain that Mr Horace Birdman will be soon upon the Bench and, as to Wattle-Murphy's affidavits, they are a work of art. They are ground out in genius." Jimmy Apple went behind the table and retrieved the affidavits. He produced, like a magician, a small black bible.

"Come over here, Bonkie."

Bonkie went over to the table. Jimmy Apple gave him the bible.

"Raise the bible in your right hand, Bonkie."

Bonkie did so. He peeped over his shoulder and saw the screws giggling at him.

"Do you swear Christopher Byrne that you drew up this affidavit and that its contents are true? Say, I do."

"I do."

"Sign here, Bonkie."

Bonkie signed the two affidavits. One lodging grounds for an appeal out of time and the other making an application for bail. He chucked the bible down on the table.

"Now Jimmy who is springing me?" asked Bonkie.

Jimmy Apple looked up from the documents. He signed them in his capacity as a Notary (Public) and jerked his eyebrows at Bonkie.

"I would imagine Bonkie that you would know more about that than I. I am merely carrying out the instructions of an interested party. A Mr Alfie Duggan. Oh, yes, I have a message from him. He says to remember rule two though I can't tell you if it be cricket or hurling. Haw haw haw." Jimmy Apple gathered up his papers and stood up. "I'm off to the Appeal Court. You are not required to attend. If bail is granted", he winked at Bonkie, "a suitable person is ready to go surety for you. In the meantime may I leave you with this thought Bonkie? Every, every cloud has a silver lining". He winked at Bonkie again and wiggled his spiky eyebrows furiously.

Bonkie could see the greed flare up in his eyes.

"If, for any reason, your cloud does not strike lucky for you, I am always available for advice." He handed Bonkie his private telephone number and leaned close to him to whisper in his ear. "Jimmy Apple can get you a good cloud, less ten percent commission and expenses."

But Bonkie, having been given the secret warning of the second rule of gangland – 'In the presence of a grass never open your mouth, not even to breathe' – remained tight-lipped and got his air supply through his two good nostrils.

Jimmy fiddled and fuddled for a bit, to give Bonkie the chance to make an indiscretion and thereby place Jimmy at a financial advantage, but the cunning stroker made no reply to Jimmy's fishing.

"I'm off", said Jimmy cheerfully, and extended his sweaty palm to Bonkie. It was shaken vigorously and Jimmy could not but come to the conclusion that the small-time crook before him must indeed have a great hoard of precious, marketable, silver to afford his services. He hated Bonkie. The very thought that the imbecile was going to get out and sell the lot for a pittance made his ulcer nip his guts. He winced inwardly. If Alfie Duggan was laying out ten grand Bonkie must have at least one hundred grand's worth of stuff and it was cool. There was no scream for it either. It sometimes happened that the small-timers touched for something really good. He wondered for the hundredth time what it was. Jimmy could shift that stuff on the Continent or the States and get at least half of its value, maybe more. Bonkie was not going to tell him that's for sure. He would have to deal with Alfie. Jimmy walked to the door of the visiting room.

"I'll see you this afternoon for a drink, Bonkie. You're buying.

OK?" He smiled and waddled off.

Bonkie sat down on the plastic chair and sighed. He was tired and was developing a headache but inside he was trembling with excitement. Alfie Duggan was a well-known blagger and a good one too. If he was springing Bonkie it could only be for one thing. Business. Bonkie tried to guess what it was he had that Alfie and his Firm wanted. He caught his reflection in the window. He grinned reflectively at his bashed-up countenance.

"Maybe it's my good looks he's after", muttered Bonkie (he had heard of Alfie's sexual perversities) to himself.

"What did you say, Bonkie?" asked the screw taking him out of his speculative lull. The screw was standing before him.

"I was saying me prayers", replied Bonkie piously. He blessed himself.

"Come on, Bonkie."

The escort marched Bonkie through the silent prison, past the rows and rows of cells where the men lay dreaming, weeping, masturbating, plotting, all thirsting for freedom, down into the bowels of the jail, behind the gates, to the last place on earth.

The door slammed behind him. The lock turned once, then twice. An eye looked in, out of habit, to see he was alive. The key was withdrawn. Rattle, jingle, rattle. Footsteps of a hungry screw rushing off to the mess to have his dinner and a couple of pints.

Bonkie sat on his grey bed, his iron bed, his rusty horse, his dream machine and lit a smoke gratefully. He sucked the smoke deep into his lungs. The smoke made him a bit high. The feeling (he had only had it once before) started as a tingle in his toes. It rushed to his head and took away his senses. He had to lay down, so strong was the euphoric wave of good tidings. He remembered the other time it had hit him. In an old house he was screwing. The wave had hit him as soon as he went through the window. It was a spartan place. He went straight upstairs and under the bed he opened the trunk. There in the bottom was a leather bag full of sovereigns, half sovereigns and golden guineas. He still had them buried in his little old-age dump. His own pension scheme. He had often been tempted to sell one or two in tough times but he had always resisted. The thought crossed his mind that maybe Alfie was after his hoard but, no one, not even Sally knew of his bag of gold. No. There was a stroke on and Alfie wanted him for a reason. Bonkie lay back and relaxed. He was stoned on a Major and prospects. He had the feeling. He had the feeling. Bonkie got up and paced the cell. One, two, three, four paces, turn, one, two, three, four paces, turn. He lifted up the white cloth that lay over his tray of steamed wholesome food. Potatoes, in their jackets, a thin slice of dry meat, and steamed green grass. The pudding was a block of stodgy rice speckled with bloated sultanas. Bonkie sneered at the dinner. He covered it over as one does a corpse to hide the obscenity. He walked up and down the cell, up and down, up and down, up and down, treading the penal mill, up and down, up and down, up and down.

At the back of his mind he heard the prison being uncanned after dinner and the sound of shuffling feet, stamping feet, prisoner sounds as they went into workshops and exercise yards, screw sounds, rattling of keys, banging of gates, numbers shouted, checked and accounted for, and then the jail wound down into the afternoon routine. He walked up and down, up and down, up and down. The gate leading into the Base was clanged open (Bonkie knew the sounds of the different gates) and a screw shouted down –

"Byrne is wanted at reception. Bail."

"Whose taking him?"

"I am."

The cell door opened.

"You're wanted at reception Bonkie", said the screw.

"What for?" he asked. He wanted it confirmed. He did not want to be hearing things.

"High don't know, Byrne. Just get hup dere."

Bonkie stepped out of the cell and saw one solitary screw. He blew him a kiss. It was the reception screw, the man who signed you out of the jail. Bonkie walked over to him.

"Bail, Bonkie." The screw turned on his heel, in a casual twirl, that said – cut the bullshit, let's get on with it, you are being released. He walked ahead of Bonkie, up through the prison, through innumerable gates and steel doors and every step they took brought them nearer and nearer the front gate. Bonkie stopped by a cell. He looked in the peephole, a weird experience, then shouted to the man inside the cell.

"I'm away Jimmy. I'm out on bail for appeal. Good luck. Tell the lads I was asking for them."

A small grey-haired man shuffled over to the cell door. He was making tiny cathedrals out of matchsticks and a few Celtic crosses. The man was stooped over under the heavy whack he had endured. His eyes were dead, listless, only reflecting the hopelessness, the whack he still had to do.

"I'm very happy for yer Bonkie", he said softly through the peephole.

"I stopped by to tell yer, Jimmy. I'll need a few of those crosses and that for the auld ones. I'll leave you in the order. Don't be bleeding robbing me now."

The lifer laughed. He was one of Bonkie's friends going back over the years always renewing their friendship when Bonkie arrived back in. He had never left.

"Alright Bonkie, I'll do a good job for yer. Go on with yer. I hope I don't see yer again anyways." The lifer cut the conversation short.

"Good luck, Jimmy."

Bonkie walked over to the screw. He was standing by the door to the reception. It was the nearest Jimmy was going to get to being out for a long time. The poor bastard had thrown a fit and slaughtered his entire family. The screw opened up his store and Bonkie stepped in.

When he had all his property the screw brought Bonkie up into the office. He signed his own recognizance in the sum of five hundred pounds. The independent surety of two thousand pounds had been signed by a Mrs Kelly, publican. The last gate was opened and he stepped out into the prison laneway facing the Mater Hospital. The thrill, the kick of getting released, was always a beautiful thing. Just to be able to walk in a straight line for a hundred yards. To know there was no one watching you. To realise that the world is not made up of tiny spaces separated from each other by steel gates. To get away from the noise of the jail. It was raining slightly. Bonkie wished it would pour and take away his jail stink. He reflected on Jimmy and understood how some poor men were unable to handle release after the long, long, years. It blew their heads like too much smack. He looked up at the sky and the grey scudding clouds that danced across Dublin on their way to the sea. He walked on, undecided to go and have a pint or go straight around to Sally. I'll send her a message – I'm out. It would wreck his head if he went home unexpected and found his Sally with the drummer of some stinking pop group. He hated drummers. He'd go to the local and send up a kid to tell her he was out.

Creeping Jesus walked past him on his way on duty. He sort of done a hop around on one leg and stared at his livelihood walking out onto the main road.

Alfie was there parked in a nice Cortina 2000 GLS. It was a nice motor, metallic green with a black roof, about a year old. He beeped the horn at Bonkie.

Bonkie opened the passenger door and sat in.

"Who is that bleeding shithead?" asked Alfie. He was dressed in a nice sombre navy suit, with matching hat and veil. Alfie pointed at the creeping CJ who had followed Bonkie out onto the road. The screw had his notebook out and was writing, with greatly exaggerated deliberation, the rego of the car.

"It's Creeping Jesus, Alfie. He's an awful bollox."

"Is he?" asked Alfie, and seeing an opportunity to be perverse he got out of the car, walked around to the front and pulled down his knickers.

Well, CJ noted all this with great interest, although he had stopped writing.

Alfie lifted up his skirt daintily and shook his thick hairy cock at the screw.

"That's what you need", roared Alfie in his hand-over-the-money voice.

CJ took off like the hare at Harolds Cross. His pasty face had gone the colour of a bottle of milk.

Alfie pulled up his knickers and got back into the car. He started up and pulled away from the prison.

"Bleeding hell", said Bonkie. He looked at the prison disappearing behind him. Only another memory now, like pain, like ...

"I was at a christening, Bonkie, yer know", explained Alfie. "One of me mates had a little son. He's delighted with him too."

Both of them started laughing at the same time. Bonkie was speechless for a time.

"He'll give your reg to the porkers, Alfie", warned Bonkie.

"So what? It isn't bleeding my car, is it? Anyway it's plated up. I'll change the rego again tonight." Alfie drove on for a bit in silence. "I suppose you are wondering what this is all about? Why we sprang you?"

"Yeah, I am a bit Alfie."

"We want you to operate with us, Bonkie. We want you in our Firm. All I can tell you is that there are a couple of big strokes on. Are yer game?"

Bonkie tried to be cool. He swallowed hard and nipped himself in case he woke in the Base and had to send for the quack.

"Do yer need to ask, Alfie? I'm ready to go to work straight away."

Alfie pulled up at a nondescript house in the North Strand. He took Bonkie into the hallway and opened the door to the right. It was a beautiful room furnished in Eastern style, lots of big fluffy silk cushions low tables. In the middle of the room was a big water pipe and the unmistakable smell of good shit. A slave girl with her face hidden held out the pipe to Bonkie. He took off his jacket and shoes in a trance. He sat opposite the girl. Alfie left the room. Bonkie took a pull of the cool draw and held it deep in his lungs. Quiet perfume wafted across to him from the woman. He reached across and gently touched her bare arm. She did not draw away. Bonkie pulled her close. Her warmth, her touch and smell overwhelmed his senses.

"Master. You are my master", whispered the girl. She wrapped herself around him.

He buried his face in the woman's soft neck. Her voice was reassuring. His heart raced like a sixteen year old virgin. It became important for this woman to want him. Only that way could he touch her. He was afraid she would vanish and he would wake up with CJ at the peephole. His body was hard, urgent, pressing. He slipped off the woman's baggy pants. She lay on the cushions limp and yielding ready to be taken. Bonkie took off her silk mask.

"You dirty louser. Yer a filthy, treacherous, underhanded, sneaky man", spat Sally.

"S-S-Sally", he gave her a peck, "ah sure I bleeding knew it were you all the time".

"Yer a dirty liar", retorted Sally, "did yer think I was one of yer floozies?" She pulled on her pants.

Bonkie heard the giggling at the door. He wrenched it open and the Firm fell into the room, wives and girlfriends too. They hooted and cheered. Someone popped a magnum of champagne.

Sally hugged Bonkie close. "Welcome to the big time, Bonkie", she whispered in his ear.

Chapter 8

MICKEY's training camp could not be seen from the air and the only creatures likely to stumble across it would be disorientated mountain climbers or scavenging goats. The camp was nestled in a small depression between two peaks of the Coomera Mountains. A state forest ran up to the edge of the camp and beyond the small patch of ground was a cliff that fell for over a hundred feet. The men were bivouacked in the forest living in temporary dwellings which Matt and Mickey had fashioned out of the local forest. It was a very professional camp. It could only be approached from one side, up through the forest, and it blended in perfectly with the forest. When Matt had led the Firm up on the long march to the camp they had all failed to see it until they were right in the middle of it. Mickey had a pot of stew ready. He heated it up on the fire and made coffee with a nip of brandy in it. To the weary, green, starving men it was the best meal they had ever tasted. Mutton stew, thick with big chunks of best leg of lamb, chunky carrots and potatoes, all flavoured with paprika and a touch of garlic. Mickey had slaughtered the young sheep the day before and let it hang. He and Matt liked living off the land slipping down from the mountains and raiding the farms. It was good clean, romantic, fun. Mickey had a crude cage containing several stolen chickens. The morning one of them laid an egg he had woken Matt up excitedly. Matt had to get up out of the sleeping bag, even though he had been on guard from four to six, and have a look at this phenomenon. Now Mickey had a sheep, tethered to a stake in the small clearing, the chickens, and was considering stealing a small pig from the pig farm they had discovered the other night on their rambles. When the Firm arrived there were enough rations to keep a platoon in luxury for a couple of weeks. Mickey and Matt could raid within a twenty mile radius of the camp on their Bultaco scramblers. They were ideal machines, light, strong, fast and easy to hide in the forest. There was a track up through the forest that came within a half mile of the camp.

The Firm was obliged, not having Bultaco scramblers, to hike eight miles over some very steep ground. The march was no problem to young Matt but the rest of the Firm, with the exception of the Cork man, were all city slickers. Men of late nights and long sleepy mornings whose most strenuous physical exercise was lifting pints of Guinness. When they arrived at the camp all were cursing that they had agreed to come to Mickey's training camp. They ate, drank, stood watch and fell asleep in their bags on the hard ground, dreaming of wives and feather beds.

The first arms lecture of the next morning changed all their views. All were very glad they had come. Mickey had not been bragging about the amount or the quality of the weapons he had lifted from the dump. He knelt beside a stripped down FN rifle giving a lesson.

"This weapon is made by the Belgian FN company. It's a very good, reliable weapon. If you look after it she will not jam or let you down. It takes 7.62 mm which is a very common round, used by the NATO countries and our darling defence forces. In fact I think that is where this rifle may have originated. There's a shamrock burned into the butt." He showed the mark to the class. "The FN can be used, at a pinch, as a section support weapon, possessing as it does automatic fire capability. But I think I'd rather have a Bren gun myself. For what we want it for it should prove first class for laying down covering fire. It will make mince meat out of any porker car that comes along our way. And any porkers inside. I'll name the guts for you. This here is the gas plug, gas piston, slide, and the breech block. As you can see it is not a complicated weapon. We will practise stripping and assembling the weapon."

Mickey was in his element. He wore a combat jacket with the epaulettes of a French colonel. Around his waist he wore a low slung .45 revolver and on his head was a broad black brimmer. The Firm were afraid to laugh at him in case he shot them. Mickey looked a trifle odd and acted at times in a very peculiar, bizarre manner but, where the weapons were concerned, he was tops. He did not go in for any long boring demands that the Firm should know some tiny part they could not see. If they could not see it then neither could the enemy. Mickey had read up well on the Vietnamese guerrilla's only requirement. How to strip, clean, assemble and shoot, accordingly, his SKS or her AK 47. No jams and a straight shot. Strip, clean, assemble, shoot, strip, clean and oil. Keep your weapon clean and your ammunition dry. Don't tell me about the weapon – use it. Shoot – don't talk.

"Right men. When yews can strip and assemble this weapon, without hitch, I'll let yews fire it."

"I'll do it", said Bob stepping forward.

"Oh aye, didn't I tell yew? Blindfolded. When yews can strip it and assemble it – blindfolded, then yews can fire it."

Bob made a complete bollox of it. He put the gas plug in back to front then tried to put the guts up the barrel instead of the breech. The gas plug flew off into the scrub followed by the gas piston and spring. The Firm were tittering at the blundering Bob.

"It's dark", shouted Mickey, "the Brits are up your ass. You have a stoppage. You've lost half your rifle and now it won't go bang, bang, anymore. It's dark and you're dead". He drew his Webley and fired close to Bob's head. "Yer never even saw it coming, kid." He put back the pistol.

Bob wrenched off the blindfold. The Firm had gone very quiet. They stared at Mickey as if he had two heads.

"I don't want any fucking about on my lectures yews men. No giggling. In fact there will be no more laughing at general lectures. That's an order. Aye, laughing is forbidden until yews can strip and assemble this weapon blindfolded or tell a good joke. Can any of yews tell me a good joke?"

No one replied.

"Can any of yews men strip and assemble this weapon blindfolded? I'm looking for a volunteer."

No one moved.

"I'll have a go at it OC", offered Matt. He stood to attention.

Mickey retrieved the gas plug, piston and spring and assembled the weapon. He gave it to the blindfolded Matt.

Matt did everything possible with the weapon except penetrate the oil well in the butt. In swift, deft, practised movements he stripped and assembled the rifle finishing by standing to attention and sloping arms.

"You will have reached this standard of proficiency by tonight. This I assure you. It's easy. All you have to do is concentrate the mind. To feel, to have a touch for the gun. I'll leave you now with the weapon. Help each other, learn from each other's mistakes. If you go into action, the way you are, the Brits will have you for breakfast." Mickey marched off to feed his chickens and the pet sheep.

Bonkie, who was only out of the Base three days, was in a state of great confusion. He was also scared shitless. What was he in? A Firm or a Flying Column? What money was to be made in attacking the Brits? Not that he liked them or agreed with them or anything – he was a patriotic Irishman and had done time himself for smashing up a chipper in Bristol – but, well, Bonkie just hadn't got the bottle for it. Besides he might get bleeding shot and where would that leave gangland? And what kind of weapons instruction was the General giving? If you did it wrong he fired a bleeding great revolver at you. Bonkie began to think he was sprung by a gang of Irish kamikazes and the price of his freedom was to charge across the Border, FN blazing (by night of course) with a big bomb on his back. He would run into a barracks full of Brits, roar 'up the Republic', and touch two wires together. Bonkie thought about that. No, it was no use. It didn't suit him at all. He didn't even think he had the makings of a one-time hero. He hadn't even got a uniform or a beret only a bleeding balaclava made from an old pullover. Bonkie came to the conclusion he should resign and return to the safety of the small-time. He looked over at Mickey sprinkling dry porridge into the hens. Mickey was cluck clucking at the hens and had his M16 slung on his shoulder. To Bonkie the whole scene reminded him of a still from a jungle warfare film. The sun shone down through the trees mottling everything in browns and greens. Bonkie wondered if he was in El Salvador or Waterford.

"Don't take any notice of him", said MacGregor, bringing Bonkie's attention back to the present. "He goes in a lot for theatrics to catch people's attention. He is very good with the gear."

"Theatrics? I think", whispered Bonkie, "he's a bleeding mooner. He's going to shoot his own men because they are not good enough to shoot the Brits and", Bonkie looked around him suspiciously then turned back to MacGregor, "I haven't a fucking clue what he is talking about. I thought we were going to do a jug".

"We are too, Bonkie. It's just Mickey has odd old ways. Humour him. You know, go along with him. He's going to give over the gear to the Firm but he won't do it unless we can use it. MacGregor winked at Bonkie.

"And we are not going up to fight the Brits?" asked Bonkie.

MacGregor shook his head and whispered. "No way".

"Er, Mac, could I ask yer something?"

"Go ahead, Bonkie."

"Is there", Bonkie took a deep breath and came out with it, "is there any chance, if I shaped up well, that the General would give me a shooter for meself? A little handgun. I've always wanted to have me own shooter ever since I was a tiny robber. Ever since .. well, yer know. Any chance?"

"A personal?"

"Yer, a personal."

"Ah, I don't think that's any problem. Mickey, by the way, is not a General. The thing is you are going to have to learn how to handle the gear and don't be put off by Mickey. He's only testing you. To see if you have the bottle for the job, Bonkie. He's trying to give you the knowledge that may save your life. He's trying to communicate the urgency of the situation to you and, to him, all reason comes out of the barrel of his revolver. If he can use the weapon to communicate he will do so. It's all part of the instruction. You're part of the Firm now, Bonkie. You have to learn to use the gear to survive. You are one of us and we care about you. Do you read me?" MacGregor stared at Bonkie, a light burning in his eyes that Bonkie could not read.

"Ah, yer. I have it all now", replied Bonkie to the madman. He imagined that domestic life would be very trying with the General with him shooting the knobs off the television, the door bell, the insurance man, the milkman – two pints, a bullet in each leg, bang, crash, in goes the neighbour's window, anyone at home? March the kids to school at bayonet point, put the wife in front of the firing squad. Bonkie winked at MacGregor and gave him the thumbs up. "I'm going for a shit, Mac."

"Make sure you bury the turd", advised Mac.

"What?"

"Security. That's the first thing the porkers look for."

"Turds?"

"Turds in out of the way places. And paper. Fingerprints. They can pinpoint the camp and the occupants. Use grass."

"Ah, yeah." Bonkie winked at Mac and gave him the thumbs up. "I'm going for a shit Mac and", he held up his finger, "I'll use grass and bury the turd".

Bonkie walked casually away from the class. He needed to have a radical reappraisal of his position. He needed to think. He was stuck on top of a mountain with a bunch of mooners. There was a big flat rock in a fire break. Bonkie sat in the fire break, beside the rock, and rolled himself a big fat smoke. He lit up. He relaxed and lay on the rock. He had to think this out.

"Hey, give us a smoke of that", asked a tree.

Bonkie started, but, before he could run off screaming the tree jumped into the fire break beside him.

"Me da doesn't let me smoke", confided the tree. It was carrying a pump action shotgun and Bonkie could see through the foliage two criss-crossed bandoliers of cartridges.

"Don't, don't talk", said Bonkie. He handed the tree his smoke.

The tree took the smoke and puffed it greedily. It sat beside Bonkie on the rock. "I'm guarding the fire break", confided the tree, "yew see it's the only logical way anyone would come to the top of the mountain".

"Why wouldn't anyone come through the forest?" asked Bonkie.

"Ach, sure me daddy has the forest booby-trapped." The tree sucked greedily on the smoke.

"Give me back me smoke."

"That's queer stuff. What is it? Virginian?" asked the tree.

"Paki black. It's one hundred notes an ounce."

"I can hear the crickets."

"So what?"

"They're singing 'A Nation Once Again'."

"Here kid", said Bonkie rising up from the flat rock, "finish this off. I'll roll another one." He gave the tree his smoke.

"God bless you Mr Byrne", and anticipating what Bonkie was going to say next the tree explained, "me da doesn't allow me to use nicknames on people, especially people older than me".

Bonkie reflected on the news that the forest was mined or whatever the General had done to it and the tree was guarding the fire break. It seemed to Bonkie a person could not leave the camp without permission. He lit up the second smoke.

"Hey kid what are the crickets singing now?"

"'Roll Out The Barrel', 'The Sash My Father Wore' and 'The Green Grassy Slopes'. It's a Victory party. History is repeating itself before our eyes. The orange crawlies have eaten the native Irish crickets and driven the dispossessed to the bog."

"And we are powerless to intervene", declared Bonkie.

The tree jumped to the ground and snatched a creeping thing from the green grass of Ireland. He broke its tiny legs and held it out to Bonkie. A big bright orange cricket wearing a pith helmet and carrying a club. Its face was a picture of pure outrage. It faced the natives bravely, a sneer below a walrus moustache.

"Yet", said the tree, "a gesture, a symbol can be created".

"What are you going to do?"

"Do unto others as they would, they have done to you." The tree ate the imperialist crawlie and the crawlie went to its death bravely humming God Save the Queen all the way down into the darkness of the native's rancid bowels.

"And how was your crawlie?" asked Bonkie.

"Bitter. Very bitter", replied the tree.

"There is nothing worse than a bad crawlie, kid. It's worse than a bad pint of stout."

"Me da doesn't allow me to drink either", confided the tree. "Or fuck girls."

"What?"

"I'm not allowed to do it. In fact I've never done it before, not the right way anyway. Once, when he was away operating, Lily Martin showed me her pussy. There was a good bit of hair on it too. I didn't know what to do with it so I kind of grabbed it between my finger and thumb and pulled my wire. I thought it was great", the tree began to shake at the recollection, "but it didn't do Lily any good. Ach, she didn't mind but she was as sex-starved as myself. I got her the next night up on her knees. I took down her pants, wee white ones, and kissed her pussy. She shivered and shook. I took it out and was just ready to go in when the door opened and in come me da. I was caught with me pants down. He grabbed Lily and drove her off. He gave her a right fright".

"I'm sure he did."

"He took her up the mountain and gave her a good dose of his mind."

"I'm sure he did."

"Aye, me da is very hard."

"Is she pretty?"

"Aye, she is a lovely wee girl but that's the way it is. And then we have been on the run ever since. I wouldn't like to die without doing it."

"Why did you grab the girl by the pussy?"

"I was afraid it would bite me or something. It seems to me there is a lot to be said for being celibate like the Christian Brothers. If yew knew yew were not going to do it maybe it would not bother yew so much. Maybe it would stay down for a while."

"I have the same problem kid, and I had my cherry plucked when I was thirteen years old. The rising of the penis, the surge of the blood, the tingling testicles, the racing of the heart, the dry throat, are all part of the sexual urge, the drive to reproduce. It is a very powerful thing. People who try to suppress the sexual urge, to frustrate a natural and beautiful process, are behaving in an unnatural way. They are fucking people's heads up about sex. They have the bleeding country in bits. I'll tell you kid, if my cock never stood up in the morning I'd lay in bleeding bed until it did. There used to be a famous Irish clan who had their society built around masturbation and free copulation. They were extremely happy and thrived away until the priests came and put the lot to the sword. Did you know a sword is a cross upside down? I can get you fixed up with a really nice chick."

"Did they dance around the fire pulling it and things like that?"

"They pulled it three times per day by law and there were different classes of pulling. Sometimes like the grades in the tug of war. It was a great bleeding thing in our past. But it will never die while an Irishman possesses his two patriotic testicles and his upright organ."

"You wouldn't tell me da, would you? If he found out he'd be very upset."

"What? About the MacJerker Clan?"

"No, no, about the really nice young chick. If yew get me a girl I'll teach yew the secret of the gear. How to strip, assemble and fire firearms."

"There's no problem there, kid. I know a nice young lady who would be delighted to seduce you. As regards the stripping business forget that. A sawn-off shotgun will do me. Two barrels, one bullet in each and two triggers, one for each bullet. Two squeezes for two porkers. It's only fit for a hole in the ground after that."

Bonkie rolled another smoke. The tree was a very interesting person and he thought it really sad that it was virginal. It was so green.

"A deal is a deal, Bonkie. I'll trade yew the secret of gear if yew get me a nice wee girl. Mind yew now I don't want to meet a horror picture or anyone over twenty and definitely no wives, and if yew could get me an auburn haired girl with big diddies I'd be really grateful to yew. It's a great secret I have to trade."

"Can the lady in question dye her hair to suit?"

"Ach aye, sure I'm not particular. Is it a deal?"

"Alright", said Bonkie reluctantly, "it's a deal".

The tree began to whisper to Bonkie.

"I was given this secret by an old armourer. He's one hundred and eight and still cycles to mass every Sunday but he lies about his age because he doesn't want to be in the Guinness Book of Records and he still thinks they are looking for him over the Manchester Martyrs job. Anyway, it sounds a bit crazy ..."

"Never", thought Bonkie to himself, "it all makes perfect sense to me".

"... but it works. When he dies yew and I will be the only two volunteers that has it. Listen to me carefully now."

Bonkie's senses were acute. Every word that the tree spoke was etched into his head. He had never had a buzz like this before. He lay back on the flat rock and listened to the tree. The tree was telling the pure truth. That was undeniable. The tree spoke with utter conviction, with sincerity, and with the knowledge of expertise.

"The firearm is a stranger to yew. You regard it as a mere piece of machinery, yet you want it to do something that is unique to humans. You want it to kill, in various different ways, but you want it to kill. It isn't a boat, or a tin opener, or a washing machine, or a coloured TV, or a motorcar, or a cruise missile, or a club. It's a firearm, the most personal, widely-used instrument of death we have so far invented. It will kill a rat for you or the Pope, someone you hate or your mother. There was a great deal of human coldness went into the making of a gun. It's in the steel. There is an awareness in a gun and", declared the tree, "it can be brought out and made to work for you".

"Tell me", said Bonkie.

"I'm only repeating what the old man told me. There is a rhyme, sung to the tune of Little Brown Jug, and if yew sing it to a firearm it will strip down for yew and reassemble. First time. I've tried it on all sorts of guns. It has worked every time but – yew have to believe it."

"Yeah, I do believe yer kid, work away."

"My weapon and I are all alone
in an empty world that is our own.
We have shot-up everyone
I'll tell you we had lots of fun.

Bang, bang, bang, rat-a-tat-tat,

we shot the bollox of this and that
Bang, bang, bang, rat-a-tat-tat,
we shot the bollox of this and that.

Now be a good rod for me
strip down and let me see,
all your springs, breech and bolt,
I'm a fan of Samuel Colt.

Bang, bang, bang, rat-a-tat-tat,
I shot the bollox of this and that,
Bang, bang, bang, rat-a-tat-tat,
I shot the bollox of this and that.

My weapon and I are all alone
in an empty world that is our own.
We have shot up everyone
I'll tell you we had lots of fun."

The tree had laid its Browning pistol and its pump shotgun on the grass in the fire break and was singing the rhyme to them. Its branches swayed in time to the beat. Bonkie tapped out time on the flat rock. It was turning out to be a beautiful day and the big nugget of black hash Sally had packed with his sandwiches was superb. He could taste and smell his freedom. He liked the crazy IRA kid. He couldn't decide which was more deadly the tree or the hash.

"And that's it", finished the tree. "I'll run through these two weapons very quickly and then you try them." The tree quickly stripped and put back up the two bits of gear. He gave no instruction.

Bonkie floated over to the gear. He handled the pieces. They were warm and had their own distinct smell. He sang the song to the guns and then stripped and put them back up as if he knew them all his life. He was not surprised in any way.

"It's a deal kid", he held out his hand to the young gun wizard.

"Don't forget", whispered Matt taking his hand, "the big diddies".

"Kid, yer have everything about women mixed up. Women are, women are. I don't know how to tell you. Women are the most perfect thing in existence. I don't bleeding know how anyone can give them such a hard time. I don't bleeding know how, or why, we have organised things to give them such a bad deal. Maybe if women are set free the rest of us will be bleeding happy or everyone on the labour will get a bungalow and a new jammer. Women are the very essence of life. If yer treat a women as an animal, don't be surprised if she bites and scratches your soul. Women, women", Bonkie paused.

"Me da says ..."

"Your da is not a woman, kid."

Bonkie and the tree contemplated this obvious fact.

"Some of the tings we say about women are too much. When I was a kid like yerself I bleeding believed for years and years that a woman's pussy got wider as she grew older. Oh yeah, and after she had a child it was like a 'barn door'. I was told this by a bleeding imbecile of the worst type in a casual conversation. It never occurred to me he was ignorant. Know what I mean? And who was I to contradict him? If I'd asked me auld fella he'd a knocked the shit outta me and then told me it was true in a fit of drink. I'm trying to cram yer something that's straight. Yer know bleeding nothing about women. Take my advice. Question everything yer hear or read about women that's said or written by men and yer can't trust some of the women writers either. Yer auld fella may not be wrong in some of his ways but yer have ter make yer own scene."

"And does it get wider?"

"Of course it doesn't. It's all bullshit. Does your mouth get wider? Or your ass? Or your ear hole? It's a huge great lie the whole bleeding way it's worked agin the women. Imagine walking around and yer arse getting wider year by year, but I'm telling yer there is loads of straight guys believe it. They bleeding believe something as obscene as that about someone they are supposed to love. And that's only the half of it, kid. You're gonna have ter get to meet a few ladies from the Liberation. So drop the diddie talk. Yer want a chick to talk to, to be friends with, just to bleeding be with. Don't boast, don't try to lay on the white man's accomplishments, don't act someone who is not yer, and don't ever do nothing yer don't want ter do. Women are at least half of yer life unless, unless yer gay. Yer not gay are yer?"

"No. I only have it in my head to do it with women. Jesus I'm floating around the sky up there. I'm starving. I could eat a sheep myself. See down the valley about six miles is a big pig farm. Me and the da were in there having a look around. Some of the pigs are pure ugly. I mean some of them are even more ugly than the others and yew can see too, the mean ones, the bullies, the cowards, the heroes. Even though they are just a bunch of pigs yew can still see traits in them. Me da was going to bring up a wee one. I'm sorry now he didn't. I'd love a couple of pork chops and mushrooms."

"Mushrooms?"

"Aye. There are hundreds of them at the edge of the forest. Me da and me picks them for the stew and that but I like them best fresh, fried up with bacon and eggs. Do yew want a bar of chocolate?"

"I'd love a bar kid. Yer have me mouth watering."

The tree produced two bars of wholenut and threw one to Bonkie. They devoured the chocolate greedily.

"Emergency rations", explained the tree.

Bonkie stood up. He stretched and sighed. He had made a friend of the IRA kid. It was incredible his head wasn't completely fucked up coming up to puberty, in the middle of a war, in a repressed sexual state. Bonkie thought the kid was cool and he was certain his outlook on life would change instantly if he met a good woman. Bonkie walked back to the camp humming 'Little Brown Jug'. He was going to strip the FN and anything else – blindfolded.

The tree melted back into the forest. The green crickets counter-attacked.

Bonkie stripped the FN and put it back up – blindfolded. His nonchalance and Mickey's profuse praise settled the other members of the Firm into a learning frame of mind. It was like everything else, easy, once one got the hang of it.

They graduated then from the FN onto the M16s and the AR180s that had been stolen from the Movement. The automatic and semi-automatic rifles were all constructed around the same principles. The Firm stripped them up and down blindfolded without fumbling or dropping bits and pieces. Bonkie handled the weapons like a veteran, secretly singing to himself Matt's rhyme. It worked like a dream.

"Did anybody ever tell yew, Bonkie, that yew are a natural with the gear? Yew must have handled weapons before. Did yew?" asked Mickey.

"I'll tell yer the truth. The only thing I ever handled before was a single barreler sawn-off shotgun. It was one of them ones with the cocker on the side."

"A what?" asked Mickey puzzled.

"He means a hammer", explained Georgie.

"That was an antique, Bonkie", laughed Mickey. "Alright lads. The class is over for the day. Tomorrow at dawn, before the natives are stirring, we will have a shoot off. Let's eat and well done men. Bloody well done". Mickey marched off proud as punch with his class.

Matt came in at last light. He strung a few warning flares across the fire break and a few tin cans on strings. Bonkie was giving a hand in the field kitchen.

"Want a hand Mr Byrne?" asked Matt.

"Yeah", said Bonkie amicably. He threw Matt a couple of tins of fruit pudding. "Open those. I'm in charge of the pudding."

"What's for dinner?" asked Matt.

"Irish stew of course."

"Yews two men there", shouted Mickey, "less of yer lip and more elbow grease. Hurry along with that pudding". Mickey was over at the fire stirring the big stew pot. He was going to make the custard and let it set while the Firm ate the main course. He had the meal laid out like a kindergarten. All the Firm had their own plate and had to wait on Mickey dishing out the grub. No one was allowed to go near the fire.

"Does yer da ever take a day off?" enquired Bonkie.

"What do yew mean?"

"From being a General?"

"No."

"Does he ever get drunk?"

"Only at Christmas. He's deadly when he's pissed. He sings and dances around the place."

"Does he?" said Bonkie with a nasty gleam in his eye. He chopped up the fruit pudding and put the portions in each man's bowl. "Matt do yer think yer auld fella would mind if I put a bit of dis inter the pudding?" He flashed his nugget of hash.

"He might but sure he wouldn't know. Would he? And I wouldn't tell him for he needs a break. Stick it in."

Bonkie crumbled up most of his delicious Paki black and sprinkled it into the fruit pudding. He and Matt brought the dishes over to the fire. Mickey gave each of them a huge mess tin full of stew. They went into the lean-to to eat their meal. The lean-to was fashioned from a large canvas strung between two trees. Inside was a crude lumber table and bench. The lean-to was lit by a hissing Tilly lamp that dangled above the table. Mickey was last man to the table.

"Are yews all fed, lads?"

He received a chorus of ayes. Only then when his men were happy did Mickey take his place – at the head of the table.

"We're like the bleeding twelve apostles", cracked Georgie.

Mickey broke open a brown wholemeal loaf and dug into the stew.

"Whose Judas?" asked Alfie.

"Mickey's sheep", whispered Mac.

"What did yew say, Mac?" said Mickey.

"What is there to drink?"

"Tea or coffee. It's on the fire. Matt bring in the boiling water."

"If I want water I'll get it myself Mickey. I mean what have you to drink, drink? Any whiskey or wine?"

"My camps are dry, Mac, but for medicinal brandy. Yew can have one tot in your drink going on guard. But that's it."

There was a murmer of dissent from the volunteers.

"Change that to the boy scouts, Georgie", said Alfie. "At least they had a drop of wine at the Last Supper."

"No bleeding gargle", roared Georgie. He waved his spoon around and then stood up to shout at Mickey. "We are bank robbers Mickey, not poxy pioneers or bleeding boy scouts".

There was a chorus of hear, hears.

Matt, still stoned, thought the behaviour of the men hilarious. He was full of good humour. The hash had unlocked the laughter that had lain just below his skin. Bonkie knew he was on a good buzz. He felt as if he had accomplished something lasting and worthwhile. The protest grew.

"Now listen men."

"Cut out the bullshit, Mickey ..."

"Where's the nearest village?"

"I have some nice pudding for yew and because yew were so good today at the GLs, I'm issuing out, not one, but two tots of brandy per volunteer."

"I'll get the pudding", said Bonkie to the General.

The General gave him a curt, but appreciative nod, he was shaping up well, and pointed to Matt.

"Give Mr Byrne a helping hand", he barked.

Bonkie and Matt carried in the puddings and the pot of thick creamy sauce.

"Mmmmm", went Mickey to the men, "mmmmm, it's delicious lads, eat up. There is plenty of custard". He devoured the pudding but the Firm sat sullen as workhouse brats and would not eat their treat.

"Where is the brandy, Mickey?" asked Mac.

"I'll go and get it for you", offered Bob.

"I'm sure yew would wee lad", said Mickey who stood up. He licked his plate. "Yummy." He left to get the drink.

"Are yer not going to eat yer pudding?" asked Bonkie of the crossheaded gang.

"What's bleeding wrong with you, eh?" demanded Georgie. "We are on the top of a mountain, in the middle of nowhere, and we can't have a bleeding drink. I'm going back ter Dublin."

"Yer can't leave", stated Bonkie.

"Why not?" enquired Mac.

"The forest is booby trapped. The General mined the forest."

"Good Jesus Christ", said Alfie but a smile played at the corner of his lips.

"Well", stated Bob firmly and not without truculence, "I'm not eating it until I get a drink. It's a matter of principle. He'll be telling us where to piss next and when".

"I'm dreaming of a White Christmas, just like the ones we used to know, tree tops glisten, doo dah dah dah dah da – with every Christmas card I write – hey, in the meadow we can build a snowman", Mickey sang in the Crosby style. He came into the lean-to with two large bottles of best French brandy. "It's a beautiful night boys. The stars are out already and the moon's a wee slice of silver. Matt, son, break open the drink and give the men their rations."

There was a silence in the lean-to while the Firm considered Mickey's behaviour.

"Did yer enjoy the pudding, General?" asked Bonkie.

The Firm, as one, gobbled down the pudding.

Mickey produced a tin whistle and began to play a series of jigs and reels.

"I learnt these in the Kesh."

"Did you, er, make the pudding Bonkie?" asked Georgie, holding up his empty plate.

"I did but it's all gone."

"Pity."

"A great pity", said Alfie and Mac.

"A tragedy", concurred Bob, "however I nominate Bonkie as cook".

All said aye.

"But I, er, could roll yer a few smokes if the General didn't mind."

The General did not mind because his mind was away somewhere else, in the alternative, in the land over the hill, at the bottom of the rainbow. When the smokes were passed around Mickey lingered on his draw the same as everyone else and clean forgot to berate Matt.

Matt saw his father as he had never seen him before. He wondered what kind of control had been exercised upon him to make him hold the attitudes he held. It was weird. Before the latest troubles his father had been a drone, working every day, if he could get it, to provide bare sustenance. He would never have caused a ripple if violent, horrendous, events had not wrenched him into a position where vested interests had demanded he take a side. Of course, his father had taken the side of the underdog and the oppressed. He woke up one smoky morning to find out that he was not free to be a slave any more. If he tried to clock in, a gang at the gatehouse would kill him. So he went and got a rifle and shot the bollox out of them from the top of the street. It was very simple. Then he blew up the factory – four times, but the State kept giving the Boss compensation – from the workers' pockets. And paying out dole to those laid off and the wages of the so called Security Forces. Somebody had to be making an awful lot of money to sustain losses like that. And when security became so tight that he could not blow up or burn the factory anymore, he had gone and nutted two of the Directors. And they paid compensation to their wives and families. They even, at that time, paid his father's dole. 'I suppose' thought Matt, 'that if they ever stop paying out to the dispossessed it will be a de facto recognition that there is a war going on'. But they are trying to constrain it all within the civilian framework for making money. NO WAR – BUSINESS AS USUAL!

Matt saw his da as he really was for a brief moment – a lonely heartbroken man. Bewildered, in a life that held no meaning. At bay, in a homeland full of people trying to kill him. He understood perfectly his father's unconcern with the prospect of a very early death. But now he saw his father in the frame of mind where an alternative could at least be voiced and considered.

"Here Matt." Bonkie handed the kid a new joint.

MacGregor came in and pinned up a street map of a town on one of the tree trunks.

"Alright lads, look this way. This is our next stroke." Mac asked for quiet.

There was an expectant hush.

"We have Mickey and Matt to thank for this one. It's a very prosperous town and only the one little jug."

"Shame, shame", came the cat calls.

"And only one poor overweight, overworked sergeant to protect the town from wrongdoers such as we. But I must warn you that the porker is exceptionally mean and vicious and has the local mulchies terrified. He will give us a bit of trouble I'm sure."

"Fuck him."

"Shoot him."

"Fuck him and then shoot him", roared Mickey.

The Firm erupted in laughter. Matt was astonished, and proud, of his da.

"Alright, calm down", appealed Mac, wiping tears from his eyes, "wait 'till ye see the porker lads. He'd frighten Frankenstein".

"What's the name of the place?" asked Bonkie.

"Ballygojingle", replied Mac, "it's very prosperous. Every house has been made into a wee holy business of some kind. The mulchies themselves don't farm anymore but they milk the pilgrims. A young mulchie claimed to have seen a saint up on a soapbox giving out. The place is booming. Every Monday there are fifty mulchies, at least, standing in line with bags of poke, waiting for the jug to open. There is a lot of poke going into that jug, lads".

"How much do ye reckon?"

"Oh, I'd say we will pull out thirty to forty grand Tuesday before noon."

"Do yer mean this Tuesday, Mac?" enquired Bonkie.

"Yes. We leave from here. The transport is parked two hours away and Alfie and Georgie will collect it. The routes are done. We hit the jug from a Toyota van and then burn it. We transfer into a VW van and drop you, Alfie, Bob, Matt and Mickey at the first bunker. You take the money and gear. Myself and Georgie go on in the VW van and abandon it, in flames, about twenty-five miles from you. We transfer onto bikes and go to another bunker. It's cool. We'll all be below ground before the porkers can get a whirlybird up. It's a nice stroke. Matt and his da take the street and we five clean out the jug."

"We should consider Mac", proposed Mickey, "in order to avoid death, that we go into the porker's pen first thing and lock him out of the way. It'll save a lot of messy business".

"What do you think of Mickey's suggestion lads?"

The Firm debated Mickey's suggestion. It made perfect sense. The best place for the porker was under lock and key. Locked in its own pen. Bonkie was enthralled by the very idea of going in and locking up the law. You couldn't have porkers interfering with robbing jugs. They ruined everything. He sat silently giving these men the respect they were due. Locking up the porker meant they would control the town and could take their time collecting up the poke. He would go on this stroke for nothing.

"Bonkie, just to fill you in. We do all our country work like this. We gather in the woods or mountains. We tool up and leave for the stroke. We discuss the stroke like we are doing now. We relax and everyone has a voice and a vote. Think about nothing but this stroke until it is finished. After it forget about it. No one knows we are going to hit Ballygojingle. No one but us. We don't head back into roadblocks but into holes in the ground in remote areas. We burn everything and never leave evidence. You'll be given a job to do in the jug. Don't talk, unless it's necessary. Don't bash the staff. Just do what you have to do as quickly and as proficiently as you can."

"What will that be Mac?"

"You are to collect the money in the tellers' booths. There are two. Make sure you get the lot. Silver and all. Every penny."

"No problem Mac", said Bonkie. What a delightful job to be given on your first big stroke!

The fine details were fitted together in a very casual way in the smoky lean-to but Bonkie was aware these men had worked out all these plans, done all the leg work, and had told him nothing about them. Even if he was loose tongued, which he was not, it had not been possible for him to break security. The only place he could go now was down and rob the jug. This was a cool Firm. For the first time in his life he was actually looking forward to a stroke. He'd pull five or six grand out of this. Enough, for a start, to bring himself away on a nice relaxing holiday in the sun, somewhere to bake the stinking jail out of his bones.

"... the poke is collected by SS Security around half two on Tuesday so if we go in around twenty past twelve we should get it all. Leave the dickheads an empty jug. That's about all for now lads, I think. Who wants to have a look at Ballygojingle?"

"Do yer mean now Mac?" asked Bonkie.

"Yeah, come on lads. Mickey, have you any booby-traps over by the cliffs?" asked Mac.

"No, no. They are all in the forest. I'll come with yews for the air."

The Firm trooped out with Mickey leading them through the darkness until they all stood at the top of the cliff. Away down in the valley below twinkled the lights of Ballygojingle. The Firm stared at the town silently.

"There is a till in every house", whispered MacGregor.

Chapter 9

SUPERINTENDENT Edward (Ned) O'Stitch was the porker responsible for the locking away of Ireland's blaggers. He was the darling of the Government who adored any security innovation from John Bull's bobbies. Ned brought to Ireland the 'Fit Up'. It was not just a simple matter of planting evidence on people who had committed crimes and left nothing behind. It was a very complex and time-consuming business. The rewards for putting away the blaggers were great but one only had to be caught once and every newspaper in the country would scream the walls down. Evidence had to be planted properly and what no one seemed to appreciate was that the evidence had to be collected, fitted together, planted and be good enough in court to convict the blagger. Shoving revolvers into people's pockets was a waste of time. Everyone knew the blaggers did not walk the streets with revolvers except when they were robbing and no one ever caught them on the actual stroke itself. A good Fit Up man had to bide his time. He needed the right stroke and the right circumstances. A car that did not burn. A coat left behind in haste. An idiot who swears the blaggers wore no gloves. One small slip from a Firm and Ned would be on the scene with his box of hairs, fingerprints, fibres, nail clippings, boot impressions, sprinkling the scene liberally with forensic. Then he would take out his .45 filled with blank rounds and fire it into any clothing to get a good positive reading for the handling of firearms. When the blaggers were picked up Ned would make off with their bits and pieces and throw them off over ditches or alleyways and then order a search of the area.

In a book of evidence a porker would swear he found the gloves, or jacket, or whatever in a field and no one would shake him in evidence because that porker never told a lie. Did he?

In a book of evidence the forensic scientists would put their professional reputations on the line that the items examined were full of hairs and fibres and firearms' residue.

Found at the scene of a crime by an honest porker and, when examined by neutral forensic men, found to be full of evidence.

"I'm afraid the evidence against you is bloody damning, Mr Blagger." And that's your own counsel.

"They are telling lies."

"The Court doesn't think so."

"I'm being stitched up I tell you."

"By whom? Dr Mary White?"

"No, that fly bastard hiding under the stairs over there."

And there he would be at the trial skulking below a stairway to the right of the Bench in the gloom and half murky world of the unscrupulous zealot.

So the Firm burned everything and laid low after a job. When they reappeared it was in clothes purchased after the stroke (with the stolen money of course) and they all had perfect alibis.

Superintendent Edward O'Stitch had his frog's eyes on MacGregor's Firm for over two years. They were a sly bunch of bastards. Hardened and ruthless. No fear of anything. No respect for anything. Parasites stealing people's hard-earned money. In the Super's office was a filing system of all known blaggers. A unique filing system. It contained not data but forensic evidence in the form of little stitch-up kits for all the different Firms that were operating in the Republic.

Ned was humming some ditty down through his flat broken snout (the result of an altercation with his wife over the feeding of greyhounds) engrossed in putting together a new kit for Bonkie. He had his prints and photographs and as Ned lifted the hairs out of the hairbrush and put them into an undated forensic hair container – he had the rat's hair. It was quite easy. He had organised a raid on Sally's flat with a search warrant. There had been no one at home and Ned had taken the hairbrush, a pair of gloves, a map of Ireland, with a lovely set of Bonkie's prints on it, and a ski mask. Ned put a few hairs from the brush (he had examined the brush and established they were Bonkie's hair) into the ski mask and then put the ski mask into an undated forensic bag to preserve the evidence. He did likewise with the map, gloves and hair sample. Ned put the evidence in a folder and placed it in the back of the forensic evidence file he had marked – The MacGregor Gang. Ned watched a lot of American movies.

Ned had enough evidence to lock up the Firm for a long stretch but he was lacking two things: a decent opportunity and he did not know who the heavies were. Who were the Northern Ireland men?

MacGregor's Firm, contrary to their opinion of themselves, did have a modus operandi – they were good, they were tight-lipped and they left no evidence behind them. That, in itself, told Ned what their strokers were. He had travelled too often with his boxes of ready-made convictions only to be confronted with burnt-out wrecks and not a blagger to be seen. It was his stated intention to lock them away. He was more than a little paranoid about them. He dreamt at nights of blazing cars and vans and all his hairs and clippings and masks and gloves all shrivelling up in an inferno. Blazing cars and vanishing blaggers. It had to come to an end. Every two-bit crook in the country was firing the car after he was finished with it even if he took it to drive his woman to a gig.

He wondered about Bonkie Byrne. Why had he been sprung? To dig up a cache of silver for the blaggers? Hmmm. Possible, but unlikely. Why not wait until he got out? That type of market did not vanish. He thought that Jimmy Apple had been fed a load of old-fashioned bull. Jimmy looked at things in a different way to Ned. Our Jimmy was concerned to get as much as possible out of his clientele and would be easily duped with tales of riches and vast profits. That's why he was attracted to gangland. Looking for fools' gold. But Ned worked on the fundamental porker principle never to believe anyone about anything and always think the worst. They sprung him for a stroke.

Ned packed away Bonkie's evidence and the rest of the Firm's in his fireproof, bombproof, earthquake proof, filing cabinet and tumbled the security lock. He set the alarms. If anyone tried to tamper with the cabinet, any subversive or blagger (what's the difference to a porker?) attempting to obstruct or pervert the course of justice, they would bring down the wrath of Ned's highly-trained squad of porkers. They would, and were instructed to, defend the cabinet to the death.

Ned stripped to his long-johns and looked at himself in the long mirror. He almost puked. His belly, even when he sucked it in, hung halfway between his knees and his groin. A squat, hairy man with a good dose of orangutan genes in his make-up. The porker went to a closet in the corner and took out his light-blue dress uniform and his cap with the gold braid on it. He struggled into the uniform, shirt and tie, and crammed the hat onto his porker's head, though it should be pointed out he looked more like a frog than a porker except for his ears which were truly porcine. Ned looked at himself in the mirror once more. The porker uniform improved his appearance greatly. The intercom buzzed.

"O'Stitch", answered Ned sharply. He had once seen a film and saw the actor playing Eisenhower answer the same way. It was the epitome of a powerful man's answer.

"Your car is waiting, sir", snivelled an officer porker.

Ned collected his swagger stick, black gloves and his speech and left his office high up in the Castle of Dublin. Ned, Fitter Extraordinaire, Bogey Man of the Blaggers, walked down the stairs out into the courtyard and into his waiting limousine. The Ban Garda saluted the Superintendent and shut his door. Ned's frog's eyes bored into her plump buttocks as she minced around to the driver's seat. She looked in her rearview mirror and, satisfied that her boss lusted after her, she put the car in drive and pulled smoothly out the castle gates. O'Stitch hated lady policewomen just like he hated his wife. He hated his wife but he could not do without her. She was the best woman he had ever come across at looking after his dogs. She loved them and treated them better than her three sons who were all mini-Neds, thankfully, scurrying around the planet trying to make their fortunes. Now that the mini-Neds and big-Ned were off her hands she was really looking after the dogs. Ned and the wife had not spoken for eight years but they were both good catholics and so divorce was unthinkable. But, if John Bull's bobbies could have a divorce why not Cathleen na Hoolihon's Gardai? Ned rested himself in the plush seats of the big Peugeot, a hand-me-down from a Secretary for State, and contemplated life without his wife. He would get along fine but who would exercise, groom and feed his dogs? Good doggie women could not be bought for love nor money but it was hard at times living in the same house as the bitch. The car was travelling along the canal. It slowed at the gates to the old cattle pens. An SS mulchie, in full dress uniform, black trousers, jack boots, blue shirt and Sam Browne belt and a big peaked hat on his square head, saluted Ned's car and opened the gate of the cattle pens for him. Over the gates hung the SS Security company's motto – They Shall Not Have IT – running in a circle around two black SSs. The SS mulchie waved in the car.

At once the Exiled Mayomens Brass Band (they never got past Dublin) started up with 'Money, Money, Money, It's a Rich Man's World'.

Ned's car drove slowly up between a dickhead guard of honour and stopped at a small dais that had been erected beside the small square. The Ban Garda opened up the door. Ned wriggled out and the Ban Garda saluted with a limp wrist. She stank of female aftershave. He never returned the salute but marched over to the assembled directors up on the dais.

"Gentlemen", boomed a military-type voice over the PA system, "three cheers for the Gardai. Hip, hip."

The ranks of dickheads threw their gestapo hats in the air and shouted as hard as they had been taught, "Hooray".

"Hip, hip"

"Hooray"

"Hip, hip"

"Hooray." The dickheads' caps were lying all over the place.

Superintendent O'Stitch mounted the dais. Crinion shook his hand. The ex-Branchman picked up the mike.

"Men, we have today at our passing-out parade a most distinguished member of An Gardai Siochana. He needs no introduction to us or the heartless criminals who plunder our people. Here he is, the man who has done so much to convict the wrongdoers in our midst, Superintendent Edward O'Stitch."

The dickheads cheered and hooted and farted and stamped their feet.

Ned picked up the mike. The dickheads kept a respectful silence.

"Thank you lads for the welcome. I accept it for all the young men in my own force who, like yourselves, are starting out in a new career. It's hard today to find the dedication, the commitment needed, for a life devoted to the protection of all that is good and wholesome in this tiny island of ours. But as I look around me here today I can see that this company has succeeded in finding young men of integrity, dedication and that elusive quality – honesty!

"You men, in your duties as security officers, will be subject to endless temptation. Scurrilous villains may try to undermine you, to bribe you, to corrupt you, to pull you down into the sinful pit of roguery. Your honesty, the decency instilled in you by parents, Church and State, will be stretched to the fullest extent.

"It is a great pity that we cannot come to grips with the main conspirator who can instill greed into the heart of the staunchest man. I refer to that arch villain – Lucifer himself. Yet you may be sure, gentlemen, if he ever falls down this way again, in the flesh, the gardai will have him behind bars with a very strong objection to bail."

The band started up with – 'You're The Devil In Disguise'.

The mulchies roared with laughter, the directors laughed politely and Ned was suspicious of their mirth. What were they laughing at? That Satan was free to instigate innumerable crimes? That the gardai was unable to arrest the arch villain and bring him to the Bridewell for questioning?

No one, as far as Ned was concerned, was above, or in this case below, the law. He continued: "There are some in our community who believe that when we (he meant the dickheads) are confronted by armed criminals that we should not resist but hand over the sacred property given into our care. They make the case that we should give it up without a fight, we should lay down and let the gunmen have their way. They say that this is a sensible way to behave and that", (he went pale and shivered) "money is not worth getting killed over".

Five dickheads fainted and fell from the ranks. They fell to attention onto their stalwart heads and were saved serious injury.

"They say give it up but we say", Ned raised his hairy pudgy hand in a Roman war salute, "They Shall Not Have It".

At the mention of the company's motto the dickheads let loose a mulchie growl that came from the back of the throat. They snarled and bared their teeth.

"They Shall Not Have It", shouted Ned. He shook his fist and stamped his foot on the dais and wound up the dickheads in no time. The imbeciles would have attacked a tank with their bare hands.

"And let the message go out to gangland from here today. We shall resist you at every turn, on every stroke. We shall chase you on every getaway. And remember this. For everyone of us who fall in the war against crime there are ten more like us back home ready to come up to Dublin and take our brother's job.

"If money is not worth dying for men would not be running the streets of Ireland with guns trying to rob it. If money wasn't worth dying for then we would be missing a great part of our past. Protecting our nation's money is the very same as protecting your own dear mammie's purse. If money is not worth dying for then it's not worth living for and we may as well all burn our wage packets and head back to the half acre and the one cow and a pig."

The dickheads were mortified. The directors clapped politely at the philosophical policeman. Such eloquence from a porker.

"When they say", shouted Ned, "hand over the money, what do we tell them?"

"Thou Shalt Not Have It", chanted the dickheads in unison.

"Drop the box", continued Ned.

"Thou Shalt Not Have It."

"Hand over the bags."

"Thou Shalt Not Have It."

"Bail."

"Thou Shalt Not Have It."

"Trial by jury."

"Thou Shalt Not Have It."

"Justice."

"Thou Shalt Not Have It."

"A small whack."

"Thou Shalt Not Have It."

"What will we give them lads?" urged Ned to the chanting dickheads.

"A hard time and plenty of porridge."

Everyone cheered at the dickheads' performance. It was superb. Flawless. They had a firm grasp of security in such a short time. They were a credit to their instructors and were obviously very competent to drive around the big city minding the people's poke.

"Good men yerselves", said Ned softly. He turned to Crinion. "I must say, John, you are the talk of the Castle. How do you do it? They are first class. It's at times like these I feel proud to be in the Force."

Crinion winced inwardly at Ned's words. He speculated if Ned was giving him a bit of a rub up. The ex-Branchman had left the Castle before he was evicted so to speak but gangland had been unable to find out what dark crime he had been caught out at (and it must have been serious hence – keep it in the castle) due to the porkers' code of honour. He smiled at Ned and replied, "Oh you know, knowing where to look, good advertising. It's a great pity that the qualifications for the Force are so strict these days".

"Changing times, John. The criminal today is mobile, armed and well versed in the law. If our own men were as knowledgeable there would be a lot more of them up there." He pointed in the direction of the jail. This is a peculiar trait of porkers. Put one anywhere in the world, blindfold him and yet it will always be able to point in the direction of the nearest jail or lunatic asylum with unerring ease and accuracy.

"Or", butted in a small, weedy culchie that had a shop that sold horsemeat, "down there boy". He pointed to the ground and screwed up his wicked head. "In the cold clay is de best place for em. Den we would not have ter water and feed em like."

Ned ignored the idiot. If that happened the market would fall right out of blagging. It was a big business. Who is going to destroy his own living? The weedy culchie was wrong. He was ignorant and confused. Time, give them plenty of hard whack. Release them old, grey and bent with the rattle of the keys and the banging of the cell doors forever locked into their minds.

"There's our Columbanus now, Matthew", stated a horsey-type woman to the weedy culchie. She was tall, broad, with a craggy, pitted, equine countenance and wore a little blue silk biteen of a hat on her stiff hair.

The weedy culchie became excited as the dickheads marched past the dais.

Columbanus was in the front rank twirling his long baton and marching at the half goose step. He had his ma's heavy build and his da's small plucked-up head. The dickhead was all out of proportion and Matthew thanked God again and again that the SS had taken him off their hands and they were going to pay him!

This small miracle was, to the dickhead's parents, a reaffirmation of their belief in God's powerfulness, their abhorrence of communism (where the dickhead would have been gassed at birth without any form of baptism) and their dedication to native Irish capitalism.

"Well done, Columbanus boy", shouted the weedy culchie.

The dickhead hearing its name mentioned looked over at the ma and da. It turned in the ranks, its small red head lit up with joy and delight, and it waved vigorously to its parents. The swinging feet and the big pair of polished jackboots came down out of the half goose step. The dickheads were in danger of losing step whereupon the dickhead instructor leaned forward and whacked the moron on its little misshapen head. At the thud discipline was instantly installed. The big boots snapped back into step. The dickhead's neck snapped around to face its front. Order and rhythm were restored.

The horsey woman began to weep.

"It seems, it seems", she sobbed, "only yesterday that he was only a tiny baby. Oh, my little boy is gone..." She pulled out a hanky as big as half a jail sheet and blew her hooter. A noise, not unlike the St Patrick's funnel, issued forth. All the other dickheads' mammies began to hoot and whinge after their sons.

The weedy culchie determined to go and see Dr Suilleman and ask him what he was giving her. Columbanus had never been a boy, he had always been a smaller Columbanus. He had often thought to throw him into a bog hole with an anvil tied around his head. But he didn't have an anvil and nothing else would be heavy enough. Suilleman was giving his wife all sorts of expensive dope and she was prone to making irrational outbursts. It was giving her an insatiable sexual drive. He had been forced to mount her in the toilet on the train on the way up. He had been flung about on her big quivering posterior like a fly on a jelly. The noise she was making was something else. She then ate two full breakfasts, fell asleep and had snored all the way into Huston. His knees were scraped raw and it looked to him as if she had popped some more dope. He dreaded the bed and breakfast.

The dickheads marched twice around the cattle pens, halted and formed three ranks. Ned ceremoniously presented each new security man with his certificate of enrolment in the SS and his company number, collar dogs, cap badge and belt buckle all in EPNS.

The passing-out parade ended with the new dickheads falling-out to join their parents, girlfriends, wives and associates. All went to watch the displays. The dog handlers put the Kerryblues through their paces. The armoured vans and lorries drove past in anti-blagger formation. The highlight of the display was an exhibition of foiling blaggers on a stroke.

Paddy Peg was the dickhead bringing out the bag of poke. He was a dickhead of great tenacity and an over-abundance of guts. Paddy Peg had once routed four fully-armed blaggers who had tried to take away his bag. Paddy Peg had seen red. He put down the head and charged into the blaggers, determined to protect his bag at all costs.

He had lost a leg and one testicle but had, even then, filled with pain and buckshot, fallen onto his bag shielding and protecting it with his body. The blaggers, unable to move him off the poke (he weighed twenty stone) had been obliged to flee empty-handed and distraught.

No bleeding poke and having to shoot a dickhead. Where would yer get it?

Paddy had been fitted with the best artificial leg charity could buy (he was not insured for attacking blaggers) and a wondrous technological device from Japan – a beautiful new plastic testicle. The company had retained him, on half pay, as training instructor. The SS looked after their own.

Paddy Peg hopped out looking this way and that for blaggers but all looked clear and peaceful. He hopped towards his van with the big bag of poke but the sneaky blaggers were hiding in the P&T Van and they burst out upon the dickhead, demanding his bag at gunpoint.

"Drop the bag", demanded a pseudo blagger, kitted out in a duffle coat, balaclava and carrying a replica Schimesier submachine gun.

"Drop hit hor high'll let yew have hit", threatened another dickhead dressed up as an armed robber. He carried an empty sawn-off shotgun.

The third robber pointed a handgun, a Woolworths Luger, at the dickhead hero.

Paddy Peg went into action, swivelling into a well-rehearsed anti-blagger routine on his plastic leg.

"They Shall Not Have It", screamed Paddy Peg to the audience. He flicked out the money bag, which was full of paper and a couple of lead pipes, and caught the blagger with the submachine gun in the guts. He went down with a whoosh and the Schimesier went clattering along the cobblestones.

The dickheads and their visitors let out a cheer and shouted encouragement to Paddy Peg.

He hurled his fifteen stone (he had lost five stone on half pay) through the air and dropped the blagger with the handgun. Paddy Peg forward-rolled onto his feet and advanced on the thug wielding the shotgun, holding the bag as a bullet-proof shield against his body, his right arm extended in a karate attack position. The blagger threw away his shotgun and fled when faced with such resolute determination.

"Why didn't de man wid de gun shoot de man and take de money mammy?" asked a bright little mulchie kid.

Mammy boxed his ears.

The audience cheered Paddy Peg and hooted at the fleeing, cowardly blagger.

But Paddy Peg was not finished yet. He rolled one prostrate blagger over towards the other and began to beat them with a small pickhandle he produced from down his pants.

"What's he doing now?" enquired a potential dickhead.

"He's making ha citizens arrest."

"Be Gob, he might only have the one swinger now, but, he's a quare man just the same."

"No. Yew don't say? No. And is he able to procreate just the same?" The horsey woman was being told of Paddy Peg's stud prospects by a dried-up old lady who was only there to watch the displays. She never missed them.

"Oh, 'tis true alright as sure as yew and meself are standing here today. When he lost the first one the one that was left grew and was as big as a small orange, I'm told."

"Go away. It's a joke I'm sure", declared the horsey woman.

"'tis no joke, not to his poor wife least of all. She's only a small scrap I hear and what with his weight and the growth and the peg leg, ach, sure she had a hell of a time." The old woman lowered her voice to the merest whisper. "They had to take him away to Tokyo in China and the' put in a plastic one. The very same weight and all. 'twas only then the other one stopped growing. As it was it filled the bag to bursting."

"And tell me now", asked the horsey woman slyly, "how is he te go?"

"He's mad fer pussy. Them Chinese are devils. Whatever way the' have it plumbed in he's pure mad fer it. He'd do every woman here standing on his peg leg."

The horsey woman popped a pill and edged closer to Paddy Peg. She was flushed. She was determined to meet this extraordinary man. And he a hero too.

The dickheads had an old ex-gardai Bedford van which they used in their training. It came cranking up to the scene and the bogus porkers (strictly speaking a breaking of the law) took away the unconscious blaggers and their weapons.

Paddy Peg held up his bag and the crowd cheered wildly. Paddy

Peg bowed and put his bag into the SS van. The hatch clanged open and shut. Paddy Peg dusted his hands in a job-well-done gesture. He climbed into the armoured van and drove off into the setting sun going down below the cattle pen wall. The crowd dispersed over to the dickheads' billet across the canal for a good old-fashioned hoolie. Passing-out Parade Day was a day to remember indeed!

Inside the relatives had lain out long tables filled with huge enamelled bins of pigs' feet. The old barge house smelt like a farmhouse kitchen at the end of a hard day on the land. Beside the bins of pigs' feet were tubs of potatoes boiled in their jackets and dark-green tasty Irish cabbage. There was a barrel of stout beside each table. It was tapped into big cool china jugs and drank down gratefully. There was buttermilk for the pioneers. The dickheads and their visitors fell to the feast, savouring familiar tastes, swallowing down the goodness our country is rich in and spitting the crubeen bones at each other. They ate everything, skins and all, and proceeded to get as drunk as possible.

And all this was happening not two miles from O'Connell Street! A small pocket of our rural heritage flourishing in our metropolis.

Paddy Peg limped into the barge house. He sat behind a large plate of pigs' feet and ate every one of them, bones and all. The young dickheads clapped and stamped and encouraged him to eat more, pulling them out from back pockets and from below hats. He broke his own record again.

The Mayomens Brass Band started to play. The dickheads began to sing and yahoo about the place. The horsey woman dropped a hand on Paddy Peg's crutch. The old woman was not a liar.

The mulchies gave vent to their true feelings for a day. Gorging, drinking, singing, fighting, crying, stealing, fornicating, wrecking, pissing and leaving big brown squashy turds in odd, unexpected places.

They gradually fell asleep, full of gristle and Guinness, dreaming of disarming blaggers and eating seventy-four pigs' feet in one go.

The snores of happy and contented men rose up out of the old barge house, a noise not unlike that made by bees when the hive is sweet and full of honey.

Ned O'Stitch dismissed his driver and sat in the back of Crinion's BMW. He had been invited to a private dinner, courtesy of SS Security, in a private room at the rear of an expensive Chinese restaurant in Dame Street. As they drove through the quiet, dark, Dublin streets Ned reflected on the speech he had delivered to the dickheads. He laughed silently, within himself, at the scene confronting any blagger who thought he was getting a handy few grand. He had to make hard decisions. It was better, if it came to it, to have a dead security man than a successful blagger. The blaggers wanted money, not a murder hunt. A killing was always very emotional. Things began to crack. Ned suspected that the plain people of Ireland admired someone with enough bottle and brains to make off with a large amount of cash. After all the years of the banishments, the exiles, the years of weeding out the malcontents from the nation, there was still a very strong strain of lawlessness that bubbled below the illusion of order, behind the mirage of a dutiful people. If they got to thinking robbing banks was morally acceptable, like tax evasion for instance, blagging would become the new national sport.

The blagger had to be belittled and outwitted at every turn.

Ned changed in the washroom. He was given a silk gown and a pair of slippers. Behind the small delicate rosewood table the porker radiated powerful vibes. Freed from the confines of European dress his obesity did not look so grotesque, so sloppy. He was a dark, brooding Buddha. He was a feudal Warlord. Crinion, on the other side of the table, turned on his cushion. He struck the small gong.

The girl who entered wore traditional oriental dress slit up the side but had none of the mock servility of the geisha. She was quietly exuding a very strong sexuality. She sank gracefully to her knees and smiled at Ned.

"Will you drink before meal, sir?" The girl smiled at Ned.

"Do you have a wine list?" asked Ned. He appraised the girl. She was good.

The girl reached to one side and lifted the wine list. Ned noticed she was naked behind the flimsy silk. She leaned forward and gave him the list. He caught her subtle musk. Ned smiled back at her and crinkled up his frog's eyes. If he had her for a driver the blaggers would have every jug plundered from here to Bantry. He looked at the wine list. It too was very good. He ordered two bottles of light Rhine wine in ice. Crinion concurred.

The meal, prepared by the owner of the restaurant himself, was a gourmet's dream. The best of food, carefully considered, superbly cooked and presented. Ned ate and drank with gusto.

"John", he burped, "that was first class. Thank you. I don't know how to return the compliment".

"Good", thought Crinion, "we are down to business". He filled up Ned's glass. "Ah", he spoke heartily, "it's on the expense account, Ned. Er, did you ever get any word back about the escorts for the supermarket and store collection? Blue tape has everyone tied up".

Ned stared at Crinion for a moment. They both knew what the other wanted.

"I did but I've been very busy with the dogs."

"Oh, yes Ned", exclaimed Crinion, "wasn't I only talking to MacMahon two weeks ago".

Ned's piggy ears picked up at the mention of the greyhound trainer. He was the best in the country.

"He would be very pleased to take all your dogs. Take them off the wife."

"How much? How much per dog?"

"Nominal. Just the feed. he'll take them on a percentage of sales and winning basis. He is ready anytime you are."

"Are ye sure of your facts? Will he take all the dogs?"

"Yes, of course I'm sure. I concluded the deal with him myself. There is a really nice bungalow, red brick, one acre of gardens beside MacMahons. It's within easy distance of the Castle."

"So what? Talk straight, John."

"It's up for rent. On a twenty-five year lease at, to the right customer, ten punts per week. It would be ideal if ye wanted to be near the dogs. I know the auctioneer. It's on hold at the moment. You are probably not interested anyway, Ned."

The porker wondered how Crinion knew he dreamt, perpetually, of leaving his wife.

"You wouldn't have a copy of the lease in your pocket, John?" asked Ned.

"I, I ah", they both began to laugh at the absurdity, at the pretence.

"Arrange it John. As soon as possible. Everything must be scrupulously legal. I will not be a party to intrigue or misconduct. Where is the bungalow?"

"Between the city and Swords."

"I'll go and see the agent myself. If he mentions your name to me I'll not take it. Tell him to delegate the renting to a subordinate. I'll see MacMahon as well. That's all in order I take it?"

"Perfectly."

"Good. I have some good news for you. I have managed to convince the powers that be to allot extra men, armed plain-clothes men, to escort SS Security vehicles to and from supermarkets and big stores. It took a lot of convincing. I had to stand on my record."

"It's the best, Super. Everyone knows that."

"Do you realise that there has not been a decent stroke pulled in the city in four months? And, there hasn't been a jug robbed in Dublin in over six?"

"Wasn't there a couple of banks hit down the country some short time ago?"

"Oh there were alright", confirmed Ned, "by MacGregor's Gang. The bastards burn, incinerate, everything. I can't catch blaggers if they haven't got the bottle to go out and rob. Can I? And I can't st- er, collect forensic evidence if the exhibits are burned to a crisp. Can I?"

"Perhaps they have stopped. Perhaps with security so tight they can't work and have taken to other ways of making a living?" offered Crinion in consolation.

"Such as what?" scoffed Ned.

"Well writing, maybe, or, how do I know? I'm more than a bit pissed Ned."

"I'd say so John. I'll get them. I'll get the bastards if it's the last thing I do! I swear this on Taskforce Boy's life. They won't burn evidence up in top security."

Both porkers turned instinctively and looked in the direction of the Joy.

"Who, Ned?" asked Crinion. He had never known Ned to swear on his stud dog's life before.

"MacGregor's gang. I'm coming under fire from the Commissioner, John. The continued existence of this gang is an affront to my clean record. I've put down every gang that raised their heads in this State. They are all up walking the yard. They are all doing their whack. Things are as they should be. It is not in the natural order of things that blaggers should succeed anymore than women should train dogs. I suppose we should shake, John. Everything is as we would wish it. Agreed?" He put out his hand.

Crinion shook it. He got to his feet. "I'm away Ned. Before I go I'll tell you this. You're up for retirement in a few years. If you wanted a position with us we would be very glad to have you as Security Consultant."

"I will give that very serious consideration, John. I am very interested in such a proposition. At the right time of course."

"Of course. Super?"

"Yes?"

"They will make a slip and you will nail them. Long runs the fox but he goes to the well once too often."

Ned brightened at the prospect. MacGregor's Gang had one big surprise to collect in a book of evidence. And Mr Bonkie Byrne whatever he was up to.

"They all do, John. Even the smartest slip up. They all do."

"Goodnight, Super." Crinion was so pissed he thought he was back in the Castle. He staggered out of the private room.

The girl returned with a bowl of hot water and a bundle of fleecy white towels. Ned stared at her silently. She went behind him and kneaded his thick neck. Ned relaxed. The girl expertly slipped off his robe and gently pushed the porker onto his back. She ran her wet tongue up and down Ned's hairy chest, going down until her head bobbed up and down, up and down, between his legs. The porker grunted and stretched out contentedly on the cushions. He wriggled his toes and licked his lips.

Chapter 10

MAJELLA Lynch would most probably have lived a very quiet life in the Ballygojingle backwater, if, that sunny spring morning seven years before, she had not followed the butterfly.

Majella climbed over the five-bar gate and ran after the butterfly through the fresh green grass. She clean forgot she was on her way to school, so imbued was she with the strange insect's beauty. The butterfly led her to the edge of a thicket before settling in a patch of nettles. Majella could scarcely believe her eyes. The clump of nettles was covered with the exotic creatures. The old stingy nettles were a riot of colour. Where had they come from? They had to be visitors. The girl squatted down silently to watch the graceful creatures which became to her the most special things in the world. She had eyes for nothing else. The morning wore on and when she did remember about school it was too late.

The young girl was hungry. She picked the mushrooms that grew around the dark edge of the thicket and began to munch them, all the while keeping her eyes on the butterflies lest they fly off on her. She ate some very odd fungi indeed!

Majella sang and danced the day away with her new-found friends.

It had been a lovely day the girl reflected as she climbed back over the gate late that afternoon. She was aware, in some vague part of her mind, that she was in trouble for not going to school. It all seemed so far away, as if the trouble belonged to someone else. She resolved never to tell anyone about her friends. They had told her confidentially that if she talked, wicked old men, with grey goats' beards carrying nets and wearing plus fours, would come and imprison them in glass cases. No sir. She would tell no one. Not even her da.

Majella skipped happily along the narrow road which curled gently up the hill and down the other side. Her small house was in the valley beyond. Just before the crest of the hill was a rocky bank of brown granite. A small trickle of water ran down this face and fell into a basin scooped out by the locals in time gone past. There was always enough water in it to slake the thirst of an ass or pony and the people who passed by. Only the odd person used it now and the cars and buses sped past it in their rush to nowhere. It was sometimes used as a lay-by if someone wanted to change a tyre or, at night, for courting purposes.

The day was hot. Majella was very thirsty and tired. The girl made a cup of her hands and drank the cool water. It tasted different. How could water have such a taste? Did thirst make such a difference? She drank her fill then splashed the water on her face. She let the water settle and looked into the pool. In the clear pool she saw the reflection of a young bearded man looking down at her from the tall rock above.

"Do not fear me", said the young bearded man gently.

Majella stood up and stepped back to examine the stranger. He was tall and very handsome. His eyes were the gentlest blue imaginable and his long hair, which fell in ringlets down his back, was bleached white with the sun.

"I'm not afraid", replied Majella. "What are you doing up there?"

"I have been sent to deliver a message to the plain people of Ireland, at home or abroad."

"Oh! Is it about the sugar factory? I heard me da say it was being shut down."

"No, no", snapped the messenger. He hated having to deliver orations of global significance to young virgins but, that's the way it seemed to work. "I have been sent to deliver a warning. The end of the world is at hand."

"Oh my God!" exclaimed the child.

"Yes?"

"Are you? Are you God?" asked Majella. Her mouth hung open and her brace showed clearly.

"Well", the stranger hedged, "no..., not exactly God. But I talk to him every day. I know him very well".

"The Father, the Son or the Holy Ghost? Which one?"

Trust the Catholics to make a mystery out of a simple thing like God thought the messenger. He sighed and shook his head.

"The Old Man himself of course! I have to deal direct with the top.

I have to get it straight from source. I cannot be coming down here with hearsay, upsetting and confusing people."

"I know", declared the little girl, "what you are. You are not God, and you have no wings, so – you must be a Saint!" Majella clapped her hands together.

"You're a bright kid, Majella. But I'm only on probation so to speak. I'm on the short list to be canonised."

"Oh, you know my name." The little girl was thrilled.

"Yes, of course", said the stranger looking at his heavenly telegram, "Majella Lynch, Virgin, Ballygojingle. Are you ready for the portents and the message?"

Majella took out a notebook and pencil from her school satchel. "I am doing shorthand at school", she explained. "What are portents? I thought you said you were going to give me a message?"

"Yeah, well the message is from the Boss, but the portents are my own. You see every prospective saint always gives out his portents with a message. And the more he gets correct, why, the more the faithful shall remember him in their prayers. Saintships are very hard to come by and every little thing helps. Like, you know kid, there are no saints passing away up there. A soul has to compete in the saint race. The more people who pray for me or who arrive up asking after me is all to my credit with the Boss. Portents are predictions of events which shall occur in the future. Hopefully."

"Like the horoscopes in the press", said Majella. This was getting to be fun.

"Yeah", agreed the stranger flatly. "Are you ready?"

"Ready."

The stranger cupped his hands to his mouth and began to shout like a bookmaker looking for punters –

"Fifty portents delivered by the prospective saint, Barobus Madden, at his shrine at Ballygojingle." He paused.

Majella scribbled furiously in her exercise book. Barobus continued.

"The Troubles shall continue for another six hundred years.

"Derry City shall be sealed off with barbed wire and an armoured division. It will be used as a jail to hold the wayward populace.

"A time shall soon come to pass when there are more people in jail than there are enjoying the freedom of the Province.

"Britain shall never concede political status to the Province's half million, yet to be born, criminals.

"After six hundred years Ireland will sink below the ocean with the weight of the shrapnel, coffins and empty cases used up in the war that never was.

"Even so, Ulster shall remain part of the United Kingdom.

"Irish prisoners in British jails shall be repatriated.

"Ireland shall be united, posthumously, by the democratic wishes of the Irish living abroad.

"The United Kingdom shall ignore their insufferable whining and claim territorial jurisdiction of the waters above the sunken nation.

"O, hear ye well, true men of Ireland. The faithful shall have warning in which to build a great Ark to carry their livestock and agricultural machinery.

"The Royal Navy shall sink the Ark for drifting into its one-thousand-mile protection zone flung around the sunken nation.

"Even so, many shall still be saved. They shall drift to an island off the west coast and there start the new Irish nation.

"The British shall ring the island with mines and intern the inhabitants indefinitely.

"An Irish-American consortium shall try to reinflate the nation with an advance from the expected income on the movie 'Raise Up The Emerald Isle'.

"The British Secret Service shall poison the consortium.

"The American President, seeking re-election, shall visit the townland of his emigrant Irish ancestors.

"President Poncho Starvos Orlav Luchenko IV shall descend into Armagh in a diving bell and tie a wreath of sympathy on the spire of the Cathedral.

"A monstrous squid, many armed, aye, and of many colours too, shall haunt the watery lobbies of Dail Eireann.

"The Paddies on the last B&I crossing shall get no refund and be refused entry at Hollyhead.

"Towards the end of this century, oil, gas, coal and gold shall be discovered.

"Strangers shall come across the seven seas at the news. They shall dig and suck out all these good things. They shall sell all and pocket the money. The plain people shall be diddled again.

"O, hear ye, men of Ireland. Ye shall have your reward in heaven.

"O, hear ye, men of Ireland. The stinking rich shall become obese and decadent on their ill gotten gains. They shall not fit through the pearly gates and will have to use the back door. Woe unto them and their riches.

"Guinness shall launch a stout from the stars on the Irish market.

"It will crash land in the drinkers' desert.

"Charlie Haughy shall be replaced – no, scratch that one kid." Barobus scratched his chin and explained to Majella. "No one can predict Charlie getting the push. No one. Not even up above. He's too damn stubborn and unpredictable. How many is that, Majella?"

Majella counted up. "Twenty five, with Charlie Haughy scratched."

"Husbands shall beat their wives.

"Wives shall beat their husbands.

"Parents shall beat their children.

"The family shall be venerated.

"Divorce shall remain outlawed to the faithful.

"There shall be a population explosion.

"Unemployment shall continue to rise.

"The labour exchanges shall fail and there shall be another famine.

"Contraception shall remain outlawed to the faithful.

"Abortion shall remain outlawed to the faithful.

"Those of little faith shall turn gay and fornication shall descend like a plague upon the land.

"A strong man shall rise up among the wallowing and enact the Offences Against the Sex Act.

"Still those of little faith shall fornicate among the briars and the brambles, the rocks and the ravines, the bushes and the bogs. On buses and in bars, in barrack rooms and boardrooms, in brothels and building sites, a fever shall grip the nation and send it trembling and shaking.

"The Penis Laws shall be enacted to put the country back on its feet.

"Anyone with more than twelve children shall be compelled to sell half of them to married couples who claim to be barren for a sum not exceeding five punts per babbie.

"Special Sexual Courts shall be established. O hear ye well! Those of immoral habits shall be liable to castration or a fine not exceeding five hundred pounds or both.

"Lord Lucan shall be arrested in the Ballsbridge area disguised as a member of the Fianna Gael Party. His extradition to England shall be refused on the grounds that he is not an Irish citizen and that the killing of his children's nanny is, clearly, an offence connected to a political offence.

"Lord Lucan shall be invited to run for the Dail but shall refuse on the grounds that he believes the Irish to be beastly, uncouth and fundamentally beyond civilising.

"The Lord's words of wisdom shall be serialised in the Sunday Independent and read eagerly by the socially aware among you.

"Fierce, independent, men from the North shall make raids deep into the South and loot the banks.

"The culchies shall be sick of heart.

"Extra-terrestrials will land in West Cork looking for the formulae of Josser X's poteen.

"Apart from general fallout Ireland shall not be attacked in the first nuclear war.

"The British shall regard this as clear evidence of spineless treachery and shall accordingly obliterate Dublin, Belfast and Cork in the second nuclear conflict thereby denying the enemy succour in the event of him winning.

"The body of Shergar and Captain Niarac are buried together, embalmed, in an empty slurry tank in George Colley's back garden."

Barobus wiped his face. He was sweating. He was very satisfied himself with the portents but there was no pleasing some people.

"Did you get all of them, Majella?" he asked the little girl.

"Yes. I think some of them are a bit rude and, if you forgive me for saying so, a bit downright distasteful. I'll get an awful hiding if I give these to anyone, I can tell you."

"It is prophesied, child. Did I not tell you? Parents shall beat their children. Have ye no faith?"

"It's alright for you to say. It's meself who will get the strap offa me da. He is an awful man. He, he will kill me."

"The road to greatness is full of hardships, child. You do not understand the import of the words you have received. Have faith. You must spread the good tidings."

"Good? What's good about them?"

"Oh, dear me. I quite forgot. All these terrible things can be forgone, reduced to naught, prevented."

"Oh, I am so pleased Barobus", said the little girl. It was so nice to have a bit of good news to carry. Who wants to listen to gloom and doom?

"The nastier portents shall not come to pass, if, if, the Paddies heed the message I have here from the Boss."

"Oh goody", enthused the girl, for her tiny heart was full sore at the news her beloved Ireland was to sink beneath the waves.

The potential saint marvelled at the girl's innocence. Since when did the Paddies ever listen to anything that was good for them? They were certain to disregard the Boss' message. Barobus started up in his bookmaker's twang.

"A Message From Above for the Plain People of Ireland. O, heed ye well lest the Banks claim thy farms and the Portents come to pass.

"When ye look at a jail ye look at thy own house. Prisoners must be treated as if they are thy own son and daughter. Listen not to the media bigot. Read not the denunciations of the gutter press. They are but slaves to intolerance.

"To take a woman's or man's freedom is grave punishment. Let that suffice and heap not indignities on the soul under lock and key.

"A prison is but a reflection of thy city. It sits in gloom, in shame, beside the places of worship and the slum. Yet I ask ye – who raised it up? Who pays taxes that it may endure? Who shall look over its high cold walls? My friends I tell ye it is a place of your own making, a place of suffering and torment into which ye fling thy own children. Ye must question the use of prison.

"The parasite, the modern pharisee, has made a vocation of captivity. The architect, the contractor, the administrator, the civil servants, the lowly turnkey have all taken it to their breasts.

"Listen not to the howls of outrage from those who seek thy vote. If any among ye deserve the cold cell and the barred window it is but they. Listen not to their talk of persecution and tough measures for they seek only to inflame thy passions and distort thy sound judgement.

"Listen not to the right wingers for they have greed in their eyes and reaction in their hearts.

"Listen not to the porkers for they are but puppets and know not who pull their tails.

"Give prisoners a fair time. Give them half remission.

"Give them a decent parole system.

"Give them decent visits.
"Give them very small whacks.
"Give them grass instead of valium. Give them hash, not lumpy porridge.
"Give them conjugal rights.
"Do these things and let the name of Ireland be renowned throughout the world as synonymous with true Justice. Go further my friends. Look after the weak, the sick, the depressed, the unwanted, the wino, the junkie, and those trying to get their heads together.
"Be kind, be good, be a genuine Paddy. Thou art not made from Empire plastic.
"And, when ye have done all these things, let the people descend upon the empty jails with shovel, pick, and gelignite (if there be any left) and rend the kips asunder. Use the rubble to fill in the potholes of Ireland. Build palaces of entertainment on the sites that the people may forget what stood there in the dark times.
"Come here to the shrine of Barobus and pray for an enlightened prison policy. Those who drink the well water and beseech Barobus to intervene for a prisoner shall get the prisoner a small and happy whack. Barobus shall be the blaggers' patron in the Great Big Jug in the sky.
"Heed this message well, ye plain people, for if thou do not ye shall surely end thy days as fishbait."
Majella looked up at Barobus. "Finished?" enquired the girl.
"Aye, child. The apparition is at its close. But first I must ask you. Is there anything ye desire?"
"Oh yes. I'd love a date with Bob Geldoff of the Boomtown Rats."
"Jesus", whispered Barobus. Young girls were the same everywhere. Always running after pop stars. The celestial choir were tormented above.
"What is it, Barobus?" whispered the wind.
"Beam me up", demanded the prospective saint. "I've done my bit."
Barobus soared up into the darkening sky on the flimsiest beam of sunshine. He didn't even say goodbye, reflected the little girl. Maybe he didn't like the Rats. She waved to him anyway even though he was just a tiny speck and was like a climbing swallow. She ate another couple of mushrooms, packed away her portents and the Message

and skipped off along the road. Night was falling.

Seven years later, to the very night, Bonkie lay under the stars not five miles away, dreaming of the bank he was going to rob in Ballygojingle the next morning.

Paudge Lynch met his child on the darkening road. He was full of porter and bile. Silently he grabbed the child by her plaits and dragged her along the road to the three scrub acres he stubbornly called a farm. He beat the child with an ash plant and when, in desperation, she screamed out her experience at the well he had renewed his onslaught until he panted with exhaustion. Majella was locked in the cowshed, empty, because Lynch had no livestock, only bills from the local pub. He lifted up the child's satchel and tipped the books into the fire.

The exercise book with the portents and the message would not burn in the glowing turf fire.

Lynch poked it with his ash plant, opening up the pages of gibberish symbols. Still it would not burn, yet, all the other books were but ashes. Lynch poured himself a glass of poteen to calm his nerves. He drank it. There had to be an explanation for this. He peered into the fire, extending his shaking arm until the heat drove him back. The matter ended when the book, quite of its own accord, having quite enough of the fire, hopped out of the fire to land in the frying pan up on the old deal table by the door. Lynch ran to the cowshed and brought the bruised and battered child back into the house.

"What in the name of God is that?" he frothed, and pointed into the pan.

"It's my exercise book. Let go of my arm. Please da. You are going to break it", pleaded the girl.

Lynch's eyes were glazed with ignorance, fear and poteen. He flung his child onto the stone floor. She landed awkwardly and began to wail. Lynch lifted up his heavy ash plant and threatened Majella. His speech was incoherent. He stuttered. Brown frothy spit dribbled down his chin onto his filthy collarless shirt.

"Wa, wa issit? Tell me wa wa issit?" He shook the stick like a witchdoctor. "Won, it won burn." He spoke to himself in a very clear voice. "It will not burn Paudge." He brought the stick down on the child's legs."Devil you are, she devil, I know. Wa, wa, issit? Tell you."

Majella screamed in agony. He was going to kill her. Her cries rang out over the desolate bog land. Nothing. Not even an echo. Only a fox that stopped and raised his ears at the distress call. The fox took a wide detour around that place. Another scream rang out over the bog. Lynch became unhinged. He was totally irrational.

"Oh help, help me", pleaded the girl. She was curled into a ball.

Lynch began to wreck the small house looking for drink he knew was not there. He had drunk the lot and he knew it too. This was the time he was most violent. He threw the old deal dresser onto the floor. The crockery and cutlery spilled and shattered onto the flagstones. He wrenched open the door of the food closet. A three-eyed horned devil stepped out. It was scaley and it stank shocking. A lick of flame flared from each nostril. It raised its claws and screamed, "Paudgeeeee, Paudgeee". The three-eyed devil whacked Lynch in a beautiful one-two. A claw into the solar plexus and a right hook to the jaw.

Lynch didn't even get a chance to scream out his fright.

"It's not often we get a chance to do that", said a familiar voice.

"Barobus, is it really you?" Majella would not turn around.

Barobus took off the dried devil's head mask. He unzipped the devil's suit and sprayed himself with deodorant. He went over and lifted up the trembling girl. She was ice in his arms. So cold and frightened. Barobus set her by the fire and piled it with turf.

"I must ask your forgiveness Majella. I was not to know your father would be so sick. How long has he been like this?"

Ever since he came back from the war. He is crazy. He cannot sleep or rest. I hate him. I hate him."

"No, no", crooned Barobus. He touched the child's head and filled her with peace. "You hate what he has become. But once long ago, when you were tiny, he lifted you high above his head and made you laugh so sweetly, the finches got cross. Do you remember those times?"

"I do. We were all very happy then." Majella's eyes were closed. She rocked to and fro by the fire. "There is something eating away inside him. I know it."

Barobus examined the prostrate Lynch. He looked deep into the man's body. His liver was a small shrivelled green thing. Lynch's heart was so brittle it would crunch. His soul was black as coal. His spirit was just the tiniest of sparks hiding away in Lynch's once happy memory. It was fading fast. He had cancer of the stomach and piles. Barobus sighed and got to work. He replaced everything except the brain. There was no use him fixing up Lynch if he was going to start all over again. Barobus did a miraculous lobotomy and left Lynch with a normal disposition to go with his new body.

Lynch's recovery from his many documented illnesses and the demon drink were cited as proof of Barobus Madden's miraculous powers. It was undoubtedly a miracle of major significance. Majella's exercise book was translated by a church expert who immediately proclaimed the portents and the message as a warning against lack of faith in the Church and that, if the faithful did not buck up, Ireland would sink under the weight of Soviet arms. Barobus Madden's old grave was dug up. His body was in a perfect state of preservation after two hundred years. Unfortunately, it lacked a head, Barobus having lost his on the block for the heinous crime of stagecoach robbing. He was one of the very first blaggers! The lack of a head was tactfully left out of the press releases and Barobus was reburied in a steel coffin under a few tons of concrete. Madden's very old criminal record was whisked out of the files up in the Castle by a very discreet, understanding, pious, porker. History was then disputed. Barobus wandered the hills and dales, preaching peace and a hard day's work for the gentry, God bless him. He was being reviled by atheists and agnostics.

Barobus Madden, patron saint of the blaggers, became Barobus Madden, patron of the drunken house-devils. Paudge Lynch was cited again as proof. A drunk who had risen from the DTs, never to touch a drop, and had never stopped working like a horse since his cure. The well water became renowned as a cure for a hangover. The plain people were advised that if they did not buck up not only would the country sink under the weight of Soviet arms, a clear innuendo to invasion by the Reds, but also people, their sons and daughters will be imprisoned in their own homes. Curfew. Military Law. Communism.

The shrine at Ballygojingle thrived. Ballygojingle became the most prosperous little village in Ireland. Tourists poured in and were relieved of their material possessions. They were to be ripped off. The WASPs thought Barobus Madden was one hell of a guy for a Catholic.

The culchies prospered and stuffed their monies into the small bank every week.

Barobus Madden was disgusted at the way his portents had been twisted and distorted. He resigned from the saint race in dismay. Many fail.

Majella ran away from home and became a Boomtown Rats groupie. Barobus, now that he had a bit of time to himself, visited her and they ate mushrooms and smoked and talked over old times.

Ballygojingle well water (from the public tap), Ballygojingle Irish crosses, Ballygojingle cigarette lighters (made in Hong Kong), Ballygojingle rosary beads, Ballygojingle nick-nacks of every description imaginable were churned out in every little house. Hand-painted statues of Barobus Madden were a great favourite with the pilgrims. These took the form of a very wise, old, grey-headed man, kneeling on the rock, looking mysteriously up at the heavens. Ballygojingle T-shirts – I'M BACKING BAROBUS – on the back and front.

The nick-nacks did generate a great deal of money for the culchies but it was only a secondary spin off. The big money was to be made in the accommodation for the pilgrims.

Most of the pilgrims were house-devils trying desperately to mend their antisocial ways. All were drunks of the first order and came from every strata of society in Ireland and abroad. For the first day or two they would go on the dry and then most would slink into one of the many dark cool bars to quench a raging thirst. There, in the chapel-like gloom, would be hundreds of kindred souls sipping away. All quietly very mellow. All pissed as a bullfrog in a poteen bog. It was a very unique experience for the house-devils. They found out they were not alone. They talked about how many times they wrecked the front room and how about the time they had thrown the TV through the front window and had to explain it to the neighbours. As the nights wore on and more and more confidences were exchanged the house-devils began to boast of their obnoxious domestic exploits. The bars were all 'men only' establishments, the staff all male.

If you gave the mulchie extra money on top of his hiked-up prices he would put 'well water' into your whiskey on the QT.

The shrine at Ballygojingle became a great favourite and its fame spread to the four corners of the globe. It was highly regarded as the best pilgrimage available though a trifle expensive.

The great tragedy was that the prisoners, for whom the good Lord had laid down the shrine and given Barobus Madden as their very own saint, were all doing their full whacks and knew nothing of the great fraud that was being perpetrated upon them by the culchies.

As if it were not sufficient to be incarcerated by them! The culchies' behaviour was intolerable and the Lord was not pleased. His message on behalf of the prisoners was ignored in the culchies' scramble for punts and foreign currency. Woe, woe, woe unto the wicked culchies!

And so, was it the hand of vengeance that sent the VW van speeding into the town that Tuesday at twelve o'clock? A VW van laden down with a Firm of blaggers and their equipment? We may speculate my good friends but only the good Lord and Barobus know for sure and the author was unable to contact either from his cell in Portlaoise Prison for security reasons.

Bonkie had gotten into the van from the edge of the forest which adjoined a small boreen. He wore a navy boiler suit, Wellington boots, gloves and a black balaclava. All six of his comrades were similarly dressed. Slung on his back was a pump action shotgun loaded up with heavy shot and he carried fifty shells for the gun in a bandolier fastened around his waist. In a shoulder holster he carried a .38 revolver. He had proved to be a reasonable shot at the fire-off in the early hours of the previous morning but the pump shotgun had clearly been the weapon for him. It was very simple. Anyone or anything that stood in Bonkie's way was getting blown away. He had felt the barking power of the shotgun and seen the damage it had done to the sheep and the chickens. He did not envisage having to use the pump. That's why it was slung on his back. Hopefully, if things went well, he would not even have to pull out his short – just collect the poke in the drawers and shelves of the tellers' booths.

It was quiet in the van. The Firm was tense before the stroke, each man engrossed in his own private thoughts. Georgie drove the van, disguised, wigged up and wearing a false beard. Everyone carried a short and either an M16 or a submachine gun for close up work. Bonkie sat on a big coal sack he was to collect the money in. He was gagging for a smoke but no smoking. There were five gallons of petrol in the back of the van with them. It was better that it flared up after the stroke, leaving the forensic scientists depressed, than before. He closed his eyes in the stuffy, swaying van. If they even half filled the sack with poke it would be more money than Bonkie had ever seen before. There was one job they had to do before they went and collected their wages.

"Here yews are lads", said Mickey. He handed each of them a pick handle.

Georgie pulled off his wig and beard and pulled down his mask. The Firm in the back all did the same.

"Coming up to the porker's pen, lads." He sounded cool and relaxed. "It looks sound." Georgie pulled in beside the porker's pen (a white, pebble dashed, two-storey house), very gently, with the side door of the van level with the front door of the station. "Hit it", he screamed and was gone out of the driver's seat in a flash.

Timmy Pat Boy O'Shaunassey was the biggest and, reputed to be, the strongest, porker in the thirty-two counties of Ireland. He was six foot eight, nineteen stone nine pounds, and had a scrotum so big the station had to be equipped with extra large lavatories so it would not dangle in the wet when he sat down to perform his natural functions. He shaved twice per day, wore an immaculate uniform and one could see one's face in his boots, especially if he was giving one the hospitality of his one-celled station. Sgt Timmy Pat, as he was known to the locals, kept the most beautiful station record book in the thirty-two counties. He recorded everything in a carefully crafted, scripted, prose. His station book was often brought up to Templemore and shown to the young recruits as an example of gardai craftsmanship. It was compared by some porkers as being of greater cultural significance than the book of Kells. It was work of national significance, a work of art that was practical, and one that the plain people could relate to. As each book filled up it was whisked away up to the Phoenix Park to be placed in the porker archives. Sgt Timmy Pat was very anxious to fill up his station books as quickly as possible. He had no shortage of incidents in Ballygojingle. In any day he had at least five drunk and incapables and at least two drunk and disorderlies at night. He spent all his time keeping the pilgrims in line and it was quite common to see him wandering up the main street of Ballygojingle with an incapable pilgrim under each arm. He brought them back to the station and locked them in his cell to sober up and cool off. The Sergeant himself was a very devout pioneer and would not let strong drink pass his lips. In his cell he had a big statue of Barobus Madden in a little niche up beside the barred-up window. Barobus looked down with compassion upon the snoring pilgrims who lay oblivious in the straw on the floor.

When the drunks awoke and were quickly whisked in front of Ballygojingle's resident judge, peace commissioner Eammon Fleece, they soon found themselves sober and broke. They were fined and put on the next available form of transport out of Ballygojingle.

The porker never got up from behind his desk. His mouth fell open in amazement as the seven pickaxe-handle wielding, screaming men ran into his domain. His mouth snapped shut with a whack of a pickaxe handle. The blaggers beat the porker unconscious and tied him up after stripping him of his uniform.

"Bleeding hell", exclaimed Georgie looking at the naked porker, "what is it lads?"

Although the porker shaved his face and neck twice per day his hairy body had been let grow wild. He was covered with a thick black hairy coat from chest to toe, back and front. He looked like a great gorilla.

MacGregor had found the cell keys. He opened up the cell. There were three people in the cell. Two conscious and one laying sprawled in the corner.

"Wot's going on then, mate?" asked a small friendly Brit.

MacGregor pulled a short on him. He stuck it in the little fella's guts.

"Shut fucking up and lie on the floor. Move." He barked it out. He did not have to tell the other prisoner. He hit the deck before the Brit. "Let's have him in."

Four of the Firm carried the porker into the cell. They threw him against the wall. He grunted. The blaggers walked out and MacGregor locked up the cell. Matt and Mickey were outside covering the Gardai Station.

Bonkie was peering out from his balaclava. He was as high as a kite and not with dope of any kind. This was too much. He had enjoyed bashing the big porker. The porker had been so shocked at the turn of events, men coming into his station and beating him, he had been unable to put up any resistance. The adrenalin surged through his veins. He felt full of bottle, full of blaggers fizz and grab.

The Firm expertly ransacked the porker's shop. They threw up on the big table, the porker's walkie talkie, the keys of his private car, the dog licence and fines money, the porker's uniform and his confidential files. Alfie came in with a .22 rifle and a double barrel shotgun belonging to the porker.

"I think we better take these with us in case he shoots himself."

The Firm tittered at the porker and made lewd remarks about his elongated scrotum.

The porker, who was coming to, peered out of his own cell into hell. Blaggers in his station. Criminals ransacking the station. He closed his eyes and hoped it would all go away. It was a bad nightmare.

Having secured the gardai station the Firm went off to screw the jug, leaving Bob to hold the porker's shop. He went out and started up the porker's Avenger and left the keys in the ignition in case he had to make a quick exit. He came back in and settled in behind the porker's desk. He waved good luck to the lads in the VW van and wished he was going with them but he was sensible about the thing. Someone had to watch the porker. He was exceedingly dangerous looking. Bob made a mental note never, under any circumstances, come near this part of the country again. It would not be prudent to be stopped for tax and insurance by Sgt O'Shaunassey after this escapade. Bob began to examine the porker's station book, He was intrigued with the little bottles of Indian ink and the script pens.

In the cell the porker was threatening the two conscious prisoners with dire penalties if they did not untie him. The prisoners pretended they did not hear him.

Bob ignored the porker's whisperings. He would not get out of his own cell. Bob knew his cells. It was fitted with a Chubb multi-lever security lock set into a solid steel door. Anyway if he did try and get out Bob intended to shoot him with the Armalite. How else was he going to stop such a hairy monster? He turned the pages of the book and hoped the lads would make out alright down at the jug.

The Manager of the bank at Ballygojingle was a reasonable, rational, very courteous human being. As soon as the blaggers came into his bank he calmly raised his hands into the air and ordered his staff to co-operate with the raiders. He walked up to MacGregor, his hands way above his head.

"Good afternoon. I am the Manager here. Will you please tell your men to point their guns in the air and I shall organise my staff to give you the money."

The blaggers loved him and pointed their gear at the ceiling. The Manager collected up various keys and opened up the one big safe.

Bonkie was in the second teller's booth. There had only been a couple of grand in the first but there was plenty of poke in this one. He methodically shoved it into his coal sack.

The customers were lying on the floor in an orderly way and those bank staff not assisting the blaggers stood quietly faces to the wall.

Bonkie finished the two booths and jumped back over the counter. He saw the four men in black suits and white collars clutching briefcases, laying among the dozen or so customers. Bonkie knew they were carrying poke.

"Er, excuse me Father but I'll take the briefcase", says Bonkie.

"What", snarled the first guy in a black suit, "this money belongs to the Church".

"Yeah, well I'm the bleeding Prodigal Son." Bonkie whacked the man's knuckles with his .38 and snatched the briefcase. It was heavy but not copper or silver heavy. Bonkie flicked it open. It was bursting with bundles of fivers and tenners.

Outside in the street everything was cool. Mickey and Matt had stopped the first couple of cars and blocked the road. They lay behind them with the M16s covering the road and the bank. The citizens gathered outside to watch the bank being robbed. Mickey and Matt didn't mind so long as they did not interfere.

"Over here", shouted Bonkie.

Alfie leapt back over the counter ready for trouble. He took one look at the briefcase Bonkie held and his eyes lit up in his hood.

"There", pointed Bonkie at the other three men in the black suits.

Alfie soon robbed them.

"Do you know whose money you are taking?" asked one of the men.

"I don't give a bollox", replied Alfie, "I'd rob anyone. If yer hadn't got the poke yer wouldn't be getting blagged, now fuck up. It's yer own bleeding fault".

Alfie tipped the contents of the four briefcases into Bonkie's coal sack. It was filling out nicely. Georgie and Mac came over the counter with the safe money and put it into the coal sack.

It was a beautiful big sack of poke. It was a blagger's dream. Something to sleep on in jail. The Firm thought this was their lucky day.

The first shotgun blast drove in the windows of the bank and sprayed the bank staff with broken glass and pellets.

"Down", screamed someone, "everybody down".

Bank girls began to scream. Customers began to shiver and shake. The blaggers took the safety catches off their heavy weapons and crawled towards the windows and front door. The men in the black suits began to pray.

Outside in the street Mickey and Matt were as surprised at the first shot as the lads in the jug. The firing was coming from a hardware-cum-grocery, a culchie haberdashery, across the road from the jug and slightly to the left. Mickey and Matt were not in the line of fire but the lads coming out of the bank were running right into it. Mickey got on the walkie talkie to the Firm in the jug.

"Enemy fire from position directly to your front. Hardware store." Two more shotgun blasts peppered the face of the jug.

"Receiving you. How many?"

"Seems to be only one. Is there a back way out?"

"Negative, we are coming through the front door."

"We are going to dislodge enemy now. Over."

"Roger. Take care."

Mickey and Matt edged their way to the hardware shop. A shotgun blast drove Mickey back. Matt pumped ten rounds from the M16 into the hardware shop. The windows shattered in. Mickey crept closer. The sightseers had all vanished. The shotgunner drove Mickey back every time he came within line of fire.

The phone rang up in the Garda Station.

"They are robbing the bank, Sgt Timmy Pat", came a secretive voice over the line. "'tis Councillor Clutch speaking. I have dem boxed in".

Bob was in the horrors. So that's what the firing was all about.

"Dis his a bad line." He muffled his speech. "Har ye on your own?"

"I am but I'm telling ye I has em trapped like."

"You are acting illegally. Cease fire at once and let the law deal wid dis", bluffed Bob.

"I always knew you were a big bag of wind O'Shaunassey." The phone went dead.

Councillor Clutch, a crazy old man full of odd notions, the town's only Protestant, peered over the top of his barricade of peat brickettes. It was a very good firing position. The brickettes were stacked four feet high and over three feet deep. It was as effective as a sandbagged position. Clutch had a brace of Holland and Holland shotguns which he used for his hobby of clay pigeon shooting. The guns were a legacy of his planter past, when he would not have been expected to sell goods to the natives to earn his living, and he knew well how to use them. His natural law and order mind had reacted at once when he had seen the van pull up and the Firm get out. He had no intention of letting anyone get out of the bank – alive. If they wanted to surrender he would disarm them. Ever since the withdrawal of Crown forces in his father's time the place had gone to wrack and ruin. It was good to make a stand. He lifted up his second gun and fired two quick, and accurate, shots at the remaining windows of the bank. They shattered.

Matt and Mickey tried to creep closer when he let go with both barrels. Matt poured fire into the hardware shop. The high velocity rounds tore into the haberdashery ripping and gouging, smashing and scarring. Mickey had made it under cover to one of the windows.

If the Councillor had not been so anxious he would have caught Mickey flatfooted. Clutch sprang up as Matt finished firing and let loose a blast. The shot came through the shattered window and missed Mickey by an inch. He had just been about to run into the shop.

"Fuck you", screamed Mickey. He pulled the pin off a grenade and lobbed it into the shop. He hit the deck.

The Councillor curled up behind the bales of peat.

The explosion was heard all over the town. Fire, blast, glass and splinters of every kind flew out from the hardware shop. The blast frightened an old woman. She ran with her dog to get out of the area of the bank and hardware shop. Clutch rose up from behind his barricade. His ears were ringing but he was unhurt. He saw movement across the street and fired off both barrels. He shot the old woman dead. The dog was grievously wounded and ran yelping up the street trailing its entrails along the pavement.

The Firm in the jug unleashed a torrent of fire in at the hardware shop. They were dealing with a headcase. He would shoot hostages, priests and all.

Mickey summed the situation up quickly. He crawled to the van and got into the back.

Two shots came from the hardware shop. This time they were fired directly through the windows.

Mickey fired the first rocket through the front door of the shop. It went in, ploughed through the back walls and went on to hit the shrine at the back of the hardware shop, on the other side of the street, (the townsfolk had moved the shrine so the pilgrims could be closer to Barobus). The rocket detonated at the base of the old man Barobus statue and hurled it high into the sky. The fountain disintegrated, exposing the municipal water supply pipe that fed it.

Mickey loaded up the second rocket. He hoped he did not have to use it on a nutcase. Two shots came from the hardware shop and went in through the bank windows. Mickey fired the RPG7 at the base of the front wall where he judged the gunman to be. It was a masonry shell and, after it had breached the shop wall, it exploded inside the shop. The primary explosion from the warhead detonated camping gas supplies, kerosene, paint thinners and all the other inflammables in a hardware shop. The shop collapsed. The roof fell in on top of it.

The lads over in the bank, and a few locals, began to cheer. Bonkie was tense with amazement. He could not believe this was taking place. The shop was a mass of rubble and a cloud of white dust.

Something stirred in the dust. It staggered forward. A burnt, blackened, matchstick figure, clothes blasted off it, half blind, still clutching a shotgun limped forward against the bank.

The Firm fired as one and Councillor Clutch went down to his death with great fortitude. Here was a quiet example of the heroism of the man in the street. As he fell he managed to fire one barrel into the air before a soft-nosed round from a .306 hunting rifle hit him between the eyes and took away the back of his skull. His brains, what there were of them, gushed out of the huge hole. The shotgun fell from his hands and he lay still.

The Firm breathed a collective sigh of relief. Mickey ran up to the stiff that had cost two of his rockets. He kicked it in temper. The Firm came out of the bank on the double and piled into the van. Mickey and Matt were the last ones in. They drove past the dead old lady. Passed the wrecked shop. The van squashed what was left of the dead poodle lying on the road. They pulled in at the porker shop and collected Bob.

"Alright now. Listen to me", said MacGregor to the porker. "We are leaving a bomb nailed to your desk. This bomb is being left here because we hate the law. That's all. It is an excellent bomb. If yer try and drag it out or fiddle with it, it will go off. Do yer have that? It will go off if yer fiddle with it. I know", he explained to the porker, "I made it. I'm putting the key in the cell door and one of the prisoners will untie you and yer can get out". He gave the porker his fingers. "It was nice knowing yer, Chi Chi."

Inside the cell the porker strained at his bonds and went purple in the face with rage.

MacGregor checked that everything was alright. They had the porker's stuff in the van. Mickey carried in a wooden box marked BOMB and gently nailed it onto the table. He lifted off the lid and did something to the inside of it. He replaced the lid and locked it onto the box.

"She is primed to go in one hour, sir." He saluted MacGregor. "All anti-handlers to activate in twenty seconds."

MacGregor put the key in the cell door and both blaggers fled out to the van. It tore off at high speed with Alfie, in the porker's Avenger, following.

The van and Avenger passed the statue of the bogus Barobus which had landed in a field on the way out from the town and which had landed the right way up. It appeared to be thumbing a lift. The Firm hooted their horns at him and made the full up sign. When they passed Barobus toppled over into the ditch.

A huge, hairy, angry man ran along the road after the van. His scrotum swung to and fro, to and fro, to and fro, swish, swish, swish, swish but he cared not about his nakedness or the high growing nettles. At the first cross along the road he found his Avenger blazing uncontrollably. He turned and ran all the way back to his station. He prayed the bomb would not go off.

In Ballygojingle the culchies came out from their nooks and crannies and walked about the rubble of Clutch's Haberdashery in a dazed and shocked condition. Sure and wasn't he a great man all the same, advanced the councillor's staff who had fled instantly at his warlike behaviour. The old woman and the dog were lifted off the street.

The pilgrims in the bar had a few to settle their nerves. People said they were bad and they only wrecked the house. The events of the day made for good manly drink talk.

At the first change the Firm got out of the VW van and jumped into a Toyota van. The VW was examined to ensure there was nothing left behind. The number plates were taken off it and thrown into the pile of newspapers, boiler suits and Wellington boots in the body of the van. This was all doused with petrol and five gallons were left in the middle of the pile. Mickey lit a petrol soaked boilersuit and flung it into the van. It whooshed alight. The Firm waited until it was blazing then pulled off in the second van. The five gallons exploded in the van and incinerated the vehicle. The heat was so intense the body twisted and buckled, the paintwork blazed, the tyres belched foul black smoke.

The Firm pulled away and left the blazing piece of scrap behind them.

Chapter 11

THE Hee-Haw that was raised after the Ballygojingle blag was the worst that gangland could remember. The porker shops of Dublin were bursting open there were so many gangland people being interrogated. The underworld was dug up, dusted down and released. The sum total of all this activity was absolute zero. There were no leads, only the usual nutters claiming that they had done it or it was the man up the road. Murder on the streets. A holy shrine devastated. Priests robbed of the collections. Gardai station overran. The robbers were nowhere to be seen and the gardai were continuing with their enquiries. To be sure. The press were not impressed and said so in their editorials. The gardai chiefs were not impressed. The Government was not impressed. Gangland was not impressed either: they were delighted that someone had made off with one hundred and fifty-odd grand.

Superintendent Edward O'Stitch was carpeted and asked when did he expect to have these dangerous criminals under lock and key?

"You do not appreciate the problem, Minister. I have just come from Ballygojingle. This gang has left no trace of its criminal activity. None whatever. All we found were the remains, the incinerated remains of two vans we believe, but cannot prove, may have been used in the raid. We are dealing with a gang of people who have the foresight and intelligence to counteract any, er, measures we might be obliged to take to, er, bring them to justice."

"Do you have any ideas as to who these people are?"

"I have an idea, Minister. A hunch that's all."

"Who?"

"MacGregor's Gang. I have been on their tail, so to speak, for some time. I have been waiting for an opportunity, waiting for them to slip. There is a subversive element to this gang. We do not have the names of the Northern men. That makes things difficult you see."

"Yes. I can see that but you must realise this. Ballygojingle is in my constituency. I want results Superintendent and I want them soon. Is that clear? You have full resources. Call me anytime but I want them. That's all."

O'Stitch left in a state of great agitation. He could not possibly produce evidence against men he did not even know, never mind a case that would stick against them in court. He decided to go and have a few drinks. There was no use going through all the usual gardai routine enquiries in this case. The bastards were holed up somewhere and would show up, in their own good time, clean as a whistle. Red hot pincers, or the ball crackers, would not get a confession out of them. Besides, as the Minister kept telling them all, brutality against suspects in gardai custody would not be tolerated. In fact it was illegal. O'Stitch smiled to himself. One could end up doing time for maltreating our own dear blaggers. He sat in the snug of Mulligan's pub brooding deep into his pint of stout. The writing was on the cell door. He could see that. The Commissioner, the Minister, they all knew what he was at. They turned deaf ears, saw nothing and did not answer questions in the Dail. A bunch of political monkeys. It was time he got out. Thought about taking the pension. SS Security would give him a good position and with the bungalow, the trainer for the dogs and his pension, he would be well boxed off. Leaving his wife had been the best thing he had ever done.

It was very clear to O'Stitch that he was obliged to lock up MacGregor's gang. This would be the crowning achievement of his illustrious career. He thought again of the way the local gardai had handled the scene after the robbery in Ballygojingle and ordered a large whiskey. He was tired of dealing with fucking idiots. He had to outwit his own men, his superiors, and the blaggers. And, if he slipped up? They would throw him to the dogs. O'Stitch liked the metaphor. He made the decision. After this one he was quitting.

Bonkie switched off the radio. The news had been the same for the last three days. A massive concerted campaign by the media to whip up public revulsion and outrage at the Ballygojingle murders. No one had so far mentioned that the crazy bastard from the hardware shop had shot the old woman. Or, that it was also he who had wounded the bank staff. There was a bit of a silence in the bunker. It was still a murder hunt and no one liked that. The thing was it was just the same as any other stroke if one did not let the porkers freak one out. They were trying to flush people out with hysteria. Bonkie relaxed and lay back on the big bag of poke. It was the richest mattress in Ireland, maybe even the world. They had lifted one hundred and fifty-seven grand out of the jug. That was incredible good luck. No one had ever dreamed there would be that much poke in such a small bank. Bonkie's whack would be twenty grand clear. Seventeen thousand went back into the kitty for future strokes. He had enough to buy a small gaff for him and Sally and maybe enough for a decent second-hand jammer. He lay drowsy in the bunker planning away his poke. The air was stale below ground and the burning candles made the air acrid. He looked at his watch. It was eight forty-five, another one hour and fifteen minutes before they could get up into the fresh air. They stayed up most of the night in the fresh air and went back below ground during daylight hours. Bonkie marvelled at the bunker.

It was dug in the middle of a patch of dense thorn and brambles in a very wild and remote part of the country. When they had been dropped off out of the second van with the poke and weapons they had waited until nightfall and made their way to the bunker. They kept to the forests and hedge rows. A few sheep were all they had ever seen and those far off in the distance. A long crawl through the brambles and thorns to a small clearing hacked out of the almost jungle. The entrance to the bunker was cunningly concealed. No one knew where the bunker was located, not even the two blaggers who had driven away the second van. They had burnt their van about forty miles away and travelled to their own bunker twenty miles further along. The Firm would make contact by radio at prearranged times. No one was going to move until the heat was lifted. All they could do was stick it out and then filter back to Dublin clean. By that time the papers would have found some other lurid news items to titilate the plain peoples' sense of morality.

Matt began to titter in the bunker. It was about half as big again as a cell and big enough to stand up in. Big enough for the five of them to lie stretched out side by side in comfort and still take all the gear and grub.

"What are yer laughing at?" asked Bonkie.

"Thon peeler, Bonkie. I wonder how he got on with the bomb?"

All five blaggers burst into a kink of laughing.

Sgt Timmy Pat Boy O'Shaunassey, on his return to the porker shop, had dashed upstairs and put on his second uniform. He ignored the pleas of the prisoners to be released. The Sergeant eyed the BOMB warily. He contemplated trying to throw it out into the street. The prisoners began to wail and scream and create a terrible racket.

"Who will look after the people if it goes off, Sergeant?" shouted the small Brit.

This made perfect sense to the Sergeant. Who indeed? Ballygojingle needed Sgt Timmy Pat. He opened the cell and took his three prisoners outside and chained them hand and foot to a tractor that was parked nearby. Never were men more pleased to be manacled to an agricultural machine. The Sergeant then went into his town and began to organise the people. His first mistake was calling in the Irish bomb disposal experts.

The bomb disposal men arrived before the Regional Task Force, Ned O'Stitch and his forensic bloodhounds, and promptly cordoned off the porker's shop. They ascertained at once that the BOMB was ticking merrily away. This was done by sending in Private (Jug Lugs) Muldoon to listen to the BOMB. It was decided to defuse the BOMB by way of a controlled explosion. This was done by sending Private Muldoon back into the porker's shop with a two pound plastic explosive charge (it was a very strong looking box) and ordering him to place it on the side of the box and then light the fuse. He was further ordered to evacuate the building at speed and report to his CO who had made his HQ in an Armoured Personnel Carrier parked up the road some distance.

Sgt Timmy Pat's second mistake was remaining too close to his station while the controlled explosion was taking place. Had he looked around him he would have seen that the Army were all lying in various holes wearing steel helmets. The two pound charge blew the pig's head that was in the box through the window of the porker's shop. The heavy pig's head, complete with garda cap, struck Sgt Timmy Pat and, among other injuries, it broke his big square jaw. He went down poleaxed. The chemicals in the box poured out thick dense smoke coating the porker's shop in anti-stitch. The pig's head rolled up the street of Ballygojingle and people believed that the sergeant had been decapitated.

The culchies spread a rumour that Barobus had appeared saying 'enough is enough' and put the sergeant back together again.

The Firm had shot the pig and sawn its head off and put it in the box. They were aware that the porker shop was the only place they could be stitched up. If the Bomb Disposal had not blown the box, it would have belched out the thick smoke anyway after the hour was up. MacGregor had glued the garda cap onto the pig's head. It took a size eight and a half.

The pig's head was now up in the forensic laboratories. All they could say was that it had been shot at close range with a .45 revolver, within the last two days, it was male, and it had been beheaded with a bow saw. It had died instantly. It was exhibit A. Useless for prints. It was covered in the thick tarry substance.

As if all this were not sufficient aberration, it was discovered by Sgt Timmy Pat on his return to consciousness and his heroic dash to save his station book, that Black Bob the Blagger had poured the bottles of Indian Ink all over the pages. As a last gesture of contempt he had defecated on the page containing that day's entries and closed the book on the fetid faeces. When Sgt Timmy Pat had discovered this he ate his baton and had started on the other boot before a quack could get close enough to give him a jab.

The residents of Ballygojingle stopped each other, shook their heads, and asked each other, "Sure and what his de auld place coming 'till?"

And some replied in the barest whisper, "Wouldn't we be better off under de Russians dan dis unholy mess?"

Superintendent O'Stitch had come upon the scene a short time after the controlled explosion. He had been driven down from Dublin at high speed and all for what? There was nothing here for him to work with. He had given the gang of heavy porkers instructions to look for two or three burnt vehicles and he circulated the descriptions of Bonkie, Alfie, MacGregor, Bob and Georgie. He had a gut feeling this was not a political job. Other porkers disagreed. Where would robbers get M16s and an RPG7? Where indeed thought Ned. In gangland's arms market? No. Stolen? Yes. From who? There was only one group of people who would have such stuff. Ned gave instructions to lift every known political activist in the county and all bordering counties and give them all a hard time. Squeeze and keep squeezing until something drips out, preferably the name of the people who had recently acquired such stuff. It had to be common knowledge within political circles.

Ned stared at the pig's head for a long time. It was on a platter in his room which he had taken at the Ballygojingle Retreat, a popular local hotel. The station book was laying on the floor on a piece of plastic sheeting. He went to the door and called in a plain clothes porker.

"Take that up to Johns Road and give it a good going over, Pious."

"Yes, sir."

"And take this disgusting outrage with you, Pious." Ned pointed to the pig's head. The lips were curled back in a grotesque sneer. The garda cap had been slashed and the pig's ears pulled through. It looked very well.

"Yes, sir", replied Pious. He was a bit frightened of the pig's head.

"I want a full forensic report. The shit might be a rare type. If it is I'll knock a sample out of every damn crook in the country."

"Yes, sir", said Pious, brightening up at the prospect. He wrapped up the station book and put the pig's head in a plastic bag. He was wan and shaking.

"I know how you feel lad", said Ned. He put his arm around Pious in a fatherly way. "It's a form of evil mental illness we are dealing with. These people must be locked away and I, for one, don't care how it's done Pious. It's a pig's head today, it will be a bullock tomorrow and then?" Ned pointed to a framed coloured print of John Paul hung on the wall.

Pious gasped. He snapped out, "Evil sir. The lads are bulling to tackle them, sir, and be gob now, I would not give much for their chances if we get them".

This was very true. The porkers had drafted into Ballygojingle over two hundred heavily armed porkers. They also had two full companies of Free State Infantry as back up, plus air cover, just in case the blaggers started to shoot back.

The brave young porkers scoured the area of Ballygojingle, in Task Force groups of fifty, eager to do battle and when the cowardly blaggers did not oblige the porkers fell back on the old reliable and arrested all the local 'subversives' under the Offences Against the State Act.

The 'subversives' were ferried to obscure gardai stations and interrogated at length as to their recent attempts to undermine the democratic organs of the Free State, alias, the Irish Republic. (Depending on who was in power.)

"I do not know what you are talking about, Inspector."

"I know all habout you and your filty politics, mister."

"I don't know what..."

"Who was it shot de pig? Eh? Only a dirty communist would do dat."

"I must insist on having my solicitor present."

"He is one too, wise guy."

"A pig? Surely not."

"A subversive. Dat's what! Trying to get you out of it wid chicanery."

"I am chairman of the local Labour Party. You are mistaken."

"A big fish. You are a big fish."

"I must insist on having my solicitor present."

"Bullshit. We don't come hall de way from Dublin for small fry. Sign de confession and I'll see what I can do for your wife and children."

"Why have you arrested my wife and children? What have they done? What have I done?"

"Sign dis and you'll know soon enough."

"What is it?"

"You are full of questions. Eh? It's a confession outlining your part in the Ballygojingle job. A confession to the murders of Councillor Clutch and Granny Gormless. Sign and I'll forget about the dog. Is it a deal?"

"I did not do any of those things. Do you understand me?"

"Who else would do it but a communist? Do ye think the gardai have ye in here for nothing?"

"Yes. I most certainly do."

"Sign it and stop fuck acting about. Sign it now!"

"I will never sign it. Never. I am innocent. Completely innocent."

"You leave me no choice but to give ye a good beating. Murphy and Egan beat the shite out of him. Oh aye, keep a bit for the forensic boys."

"What happened to the Chairman of the Labour Party, Inspector?"

"He fell down de stairs and toppled out de window. Ah sure the poor man den rolled under a creamery lorry. God bless, wasn't he terrible unfortunate?"

"Next."

"Next."

And so the arrests under Section 30 of the Offences Against the State Act continued unabated in the environs of Ballygojingle. Many were taken into custody though none found out what offence against the State they were suspected of having committed. Cynical agitators, passive supporters of the subversives in our midst, believed the gardai were using emergency legislation to take away citizens' rights. They believed the gardai were arresting and detaining people for the Ballygojingle blag and then interrogating those detained as to their political activity.

These foul accusations were treated with disdain by the man and woman in the street, (those not arrested) and the allegations of unlawful arrest and brutality against people held in gardai custody were so patently false our democratic press refused to print them.

Roadblocks were established every few miles throughout the entire State and irate motorists were advised to take their anger out on the Ballygojingle murderers by red-faced gardai who were working all hours of the day and night.

The newspapers demanded that the Government of the day should reintroduce capital punishment, whipping, flogging, birching, heavier sentences in tiny rock-breaking jails, no remission and life imprisonment for stealing a wide variety of petty items.

The blaggers were denounced from the pulpit and the faithful were urged to grass them up.

All this had the desired effect of making life extremely difficult for the Movement. They were not pleased with Mickey and Matt. They decided therefore not only to shoot the Belfast men but also the other members of the gang when they found out who they were. They despatched an intelligence unit to Ballygojingle and began to tap their sources within the Government. Training camps were disrupted, dumps were lost to the porkers, men were lost to the porkers, munitions could not be moved to the war zone and Movement business was very seriously disrupted.

When O'Stitch judged that the general public had been properly conditioned and the Movement had been squeezed sufficiently hard, he relented his grip and permitted life to go back to normal. Ned knew well the blaggers had no intention of moving a finger until all was cool but he could not tell the Minister to give the Task Force a week's holiday until the blaggers arrived back in Dublin. There were other political considerations. A duality of purposes. While the Task Force and Army were down there, they had to get stuck into someone. It was impossible for them to remain idle. They got stuck into the Old Reliables. In America it was Reds under the bed, in England it was Moles in the palace lawn, every country had their own paranoia. In Ireland the Old Reliables were those engaged in resisting the military occupation of the national territory. Please do not ask the author to elaborate in a sequel. It is beyond his limited faculties to deal with this unique phenomenon.

The Firm stayed in the bunkers for ten days after the stroke. This was three days longer than the roadblocks had been up. It was boring but the time was not wasted. Bonkie was thoroughly grilled and tutored what he could expect when he got a pull back in Dublin. He was given a cover story. It was certain he would be lifted because he was not lifted in the first raids. The porkers would want to check him out. He would also be lifted because the porkers would know who sprang him. Bonkie was to tell Sally a plausible story and, more importantly plant a couple of confusing rumours within earshot of his local grassers. It was essential to get the law off their backs before they hit the Big Grey Jug.

Bonkie was dropped off at Inchicore from the back of a lorry. It was nine o'clock at night. He wore brand new denim jeans, jacket and shirt. Denim did not leave traceable fibres. His sandals could not leave Wellington boot prints. He met Sally in the Black Lion and had most of his pint drunk when the heavy porkers stormed in and dragged him out by the hair.

"Leave him. Leave him alone youse dirty bastards", screamed Sally after the porker cars. She felt terrible. The porkers must have followed her to the pub. And all day she had been looking forward to Bonkie coming back from Cork. She sat on the pavement, head in her lap, weeping. He had told her on the phone he could not get back because of the Ballygojingle job. He had told her he had been unable to work because of it. She prayed he was telling the truth. Ballygojingle was a heavy stroke. If he went down for it they were both finished. Only she really loved him or she would have gone off a long time ago. But she rallied and went in and rang a solicitor and asked him to find out where he was. She had to go back to the pub to get her handbag. Everyone stared at her and the bollox behind the bar told her to get out.

"Bleeding culchie", spat Sally at him and marched out, her head held high in the room full of chickens.

The porkers sat on Bonkie in the car as it was driven, hee haw screaming, blue light flashing, through the quiet streets. One porker, not content with sitting on him, began to pluck the hairs out of his leg.

"Fuck you", muttered Bonkie and sank his teeth into the porker's fat ass. He screamed and lurched forward. Bonkie struggled among the two heavy porkers and managed to get his hand onto the steering wheel. He tried to steer the car into a wall. The driver slammed on the brakes and the car behind almost ran up his ass. Pandemonium broke loose. The cars had both slowed to a stop. The porkers in the escorting car surrounded the car Bonkie was in and pointed their Uzis at it.

"Shoot, shoot, shoot you bottleless assholes", roared Bonkie.

The porkers were confused. Then one had an idea! He went over to the car.

"What's going on in dere?" he asked.

"They are sitting on me in the back of the car", explained Bonkie.

The porker smashed him in the face with an Uzi a couple of times and busted his mouth. The porkers dragged him out of the car and beat him unconscious.

The taking into custody restarted. Bonkie was thrown into the back of the Renault I8. The porkers sat back in on top of him. The escorts got back into their car. The blue lights began to twirl and the hee haw began its horrible wailing. The porker car straightened up and they took off at speed for the Bridewell.

"And I must warn you", continued the porker to the unconscious Bonkie, "that anything you may say will be taken down and may be used in evidence".

"I'm a witness he was cautioned, Sergeant", declared the driver.

The other heavy porker in the back continued to pluck hairs out of Bonkie's leg.

It was good to be back home.

Chapter 12

THE porkers pulled Bonkie out of the car by the feet and dragged him into the Bridewell interrogation centre. His shirt was in tatters and his face and chest splattered with blood. The hair-plucking porker kicked his head playfully every time it hopped off the ground. Bonkie never made a sound. Bonkie was pulled onto his feet by the hair in the reception area. He was surrounded in a hostile sea of big, red, vicious faces, all of them looking at him hungrily.

"What's your name?" demanded the station porker.

Bonkie ignored the bollox. He knew well who he was. Connolly cuffed Bonkie behind the head for impoliteness. Bonkie spat a dollop of blood onto the desk.

"What's your name?" the station porker tried to act tough in front of the heavies.

Bonkie remained silent. The porker wrote Bonkie's name into the big book.

"Where do you live Byrne? That's if you are alive."

Bonkie ignored the bollox.

"What's he in for?" the station porker asked heavy porker Connolly.

"Section 30. Bonkie's ha bit hoff an IRA man." The heavies had a jeer.

The station porkers logged Bonkie into the kip and gave him a leaflet which outlined the legal rights of men and women in Gardai custody.

"Take it away", sneered the station porker. The heavies lurched forward.

"Just a bleeding minute", protested Bonkie. "I want ter ring Jimmy Apple and I want ter phone a doctor." He held up the leaflet. "I'm entitled ter do that and I want recorded that I have been assaulted, not fallen down the bleeding stairs."

The station porker's eyes narrowed in distrust. He couldn't possibly write such things in his book. He went off for a piss.

"You cheeky dirty bastard", shouted heavy porker Connolly, "you can talk when hit suits you". He snatched the leaflet and threw it on the floor. "Can't you?"

Bonkie sucked out the blood from his loose teeth and split gums. If the fun and games were going ter be on he'd get off ter a good start. He spat the disgusting liquid into the heavy porker's face. Pandemonium broke out instantly. Bonkie locked onto the nearest heavy porker and tried to strangle him, trying at the same time to use the porker as a shield. The heavy porkers were wound up like devils over Ballygojingle. They scratched and kicked each other in their efforts to batter Bonkie. Bonkie went down under the swinging fists and stomping boots. The station porkers drew their batons just in case.

"Stop", roared a voice that could have belonged to a bishop. "Stop at once."

The porkers sidled away from Bonkie and left him in a small ball on the green tiled floor.

"Get that man into a cell, Sergeant", ordered the station inspector, "and get him a doctor".

"And a bleeding solicitor", gasped Bonkie. He held up the leaflet. "Like it says in paragraph three."

"You", the station inspector pointed at the head heavy porker, "get your action men out of here. I will not be a party to unlawful behaviour. And do not come back to this station until they cool down".

The head heavy porker went very sullen. He knew what the station porker was at. Trying to get a confession with his appeals to the gurrier's conscience. Might as well appeal to a fox not to be eating chickens. "Let's go lads."

"Sergeant I want this man cleaned up. Get him some food and a hot cup of tea." He looked down at Bonkie. "Have you cigarettes my good man?"

Bonkie was in the horrors in case the porker was going to mount him. He was in no condition to resist.

"Get him a packet of cigarettes Sergeant. And clean up this mess. I won't have it in my station." And with that he marched out head held high.

The station sergeant hated the inspector. He was a religious maniac. He really believed that crooks had the benefit of an immortal soul. Redemption. It was a great pity, often thought the sergeant, that he had not joined the missioners and gone off to darkest Africa with his funny notions.

Bonkie was carried up the stairs to the cells above. The porkers stripped him of his clothes, (the heavies wanted them for forensic purposes) and left him on a bed.

The cell clanged shut. Bonkie thought he was back up in the Joy. His head hurt, his ribs ached, his balls ached, and his mouth was in a bad mess. He felt with his tongue. His teeth were still there. He tried to smile. A pain shot through his head. The door opened again. A porker came in with an orange plastic basin, full of steaming water, a towel and soap. He laid it on the floor. There was no table in the cell.

"Clean yourself up", he ordered. "I'm getting you a set of clothes."

"Go and bollox you dirty asshole", replied Bonkie.

The porker made an instinctive go to attack Bonkie. He drew back. The cell door clanged shut.

Bonkie got up painfully. He only had his underpants on. Already he was a mass of welts and bruises. The hot water and soap were irresistible. He stuck the pain and washed himself down. The water turned as red as blood. The porker returned and threw a set of civilian clothing into the cell. The door clanged shut. Bonkie dressed in the clothes, which were brand new, and lay upon the bed. He pulled the hard, coarse, smelly grey blankets up around him and tried to forget the pain.

So far everything had gone as he had expected. He now held the advantage even if it were a painful one. He had forced the heavy porkers to do what they wanted to do anyway. Bonkie intended to attack the heavy porkers at every opportunity. It would be better to spend six months in hospital than twenty years in jail. There was more than that. He hated the porkers intensely. All the rules were stripped away. They were porkers and he was a blagger. Fire and water. Fuck them. He was getting stuck in. There were going to be no verbals from alleged conversations with friendly porkers in the wee hours when one's conscience comes to the fore. He heard the porker coming along the landing outside. A key was shoved into the lock. Bonkie tensed and got ready to do battle. The door opened.

In came the drunken-driver doctor. He staggered up to the bed. He had a strong smell of spirits on him. The station inspector was with him.

"The doctor wants to have a look at you, Byrne", said the inspector.

The quack was competent enough regarding medical matters. He treated Bonkie, washed his wounds and stitched him up here and there.

"Nothing broken. Rest. He must have rest", said the quack to the porker. He avoided Bonkie's eyes. He knew Bonkie had been badly beaten but he could not put that into his report. He had a good number and he knew it. Bonkie didn't mind. That was his stroke, his number in life. "He must have rest." The quack gave Bonkie a couple of painkillers and a sleeping tablet. "I'll call tomorrow", he said to the inspector as if the porker was Bonkie's daddy.

Bonkie watched all this with wry amusement. The quack was out of his head with drink, way out in some private practice. Bonkie made no reply.

"Goodnight, Mr Hayzes." The quack waddled out of the cell. The inspector sat on the end of Bonkie's bed. He offered Bonkie a smoke. Bonkie ignored him. "You might have heard of me. I'm Inspector Garrett Goodly."

Silence.

"Well, you will, if you haven't. I know what the boys on the street say about me. That I'm soft. That I'm too soft. But I believe that there is good in every man. Even a wicked person such as yourself."

Silence.

"Oh, I don't mind you not talking to me. Some of the boys can be a bit exuberant at times. Over zealous with the job that's in it. You know trying to get bank robbers and murderers such as yourself to confess."

A pronounced silence.

"We are all entitled to salvation, Bonkie, but to be saved a person must first be in a state of grace. Which you are most definitely not. What do you need to be in a state of grace?" The porker started at Bonkie. "All you have to do is be genuinely contrite. To repent your evil ways. To say you are sorry." The porker leaned close to Bonkie and gripped him by the shoulder. "All you have to do is confess. Do you confess, Bonkie?"

There was a silence so thick you would trip over it.

"Oh, I don't mind you not talking to me. But you know if I get one in ten to confess then I believe it is a job well done. You are heading on for forty. If you go down on the Ballygojingle murders you will come out of jail, if you ever do, an old, old, man. I can help you there. If you come clean and give us the names of your accomplices I'd say, but I will not promise, you would be eligible for parole in ten years."

Silence.

"A lot of men I meet like you are terrified of making a statement. They think, 'oh, if I sign that I'm gone' but once they do make the statement, once they confess, they feel an awful lot better for it."

Yeah, thought Bonkie, that's because they stop twisting your balls.

"It's like going to the dentist with a very painful tooth. The tooth is rotten, bad to the core, like you and your kind, and it has to come. It has to come. Eventually, after putting it off and off and off, it has to come out in desperation. Out it comes and the relief, the peace of mind, the tranquillity, is enormous. That's what happens to tough guys like you. The badness builds up and up and, believe me, I know what I'm talking about, you will tell someone in the end. You will confess. That's certain. Why not do it now and save your family further anguish? At least your dear old mother will know you repented. She will be able to read, to have a copy, of your confession. Then, when she goes shopping, or to mass, people will not be able to say – 'oh, look, there is the Ballygojingle murderer's mammy'."

Bonkie couldn't believe his ears. He spluttered.

"Yes?" enquired the preaching porker. He whipped out his notebook and pencil. (Always a pencil so mistakes can be erased and corrected.) "What is it?"

The same silence. The blaggopause.

"Oh, I know you feel threatened. You think we all hate you. That we are only trying to lock you away for life. I can understand that, Bonkie. But even you will admit, if the rot has not gone too far, that you have put a burden on someone who does love you dearly. It's a heavy load for your mother to shoulder. But just think man. If she had a nice framed copy of your confession above the mantelpiece she could stand up with pride and tell the neighbours that you had repented and, er, grassed up all the others. The older, more sinister men who led you astray."

Bonkie had let the laughter out at that. His mother, Bess Byrne, was dead eight years. She had driven an XJ 12 into a bridge support, at over one hundred miles per hour, over on the M1 in England. Bonkie had been given five days parole from the jail to go to her funeral. She had been one cool auld one.

The preaching porker adopted a very prim expression. He started up again in his Kerry brogue.

"Laughter before tears. Laughter before tears mister Byrne. That's it now." He began pacing the cell like an agitated prisoner doing a bad whack.

"You have been in and out of prison all your life", he began on a new tack, "and your real marriage, the sacrament, is in ruins. You deserted your lawful wife and five children. Two of the boys do not attend school and are potential criminals. They will end up behind bars surely. You made another young woman bear you a bastard daughter. You co-habit with this woman in sin, in my society. You exist in state housing. You draw social security which comes from my taxes. You were the lowest form of life in this state. And now you are a murderer who raided and looted a shrine town. You are intolerable, yet you have a soul. Confess I tell you and cleanse that precious gift the Lord has given you. Make a statement Byrne!"

Bonkie groaned into an upright position. He swung off the bed and lifted up the basin of bloody water. He flung it over the preaching porker.

"Fuck off and bore someone else", yelled Bonkie.

The preaching porker screamed like a scalded cat. The porker with the keys, who had been skulking outside the door as a witness, jumped into the cell. He ran at Bonkie.

"Leave him guard", said the preaching porker wearily. He turned to face Bonkie wiping the dirty water off his face with a spotless white handkerchief.

"You will do two whacks, Byrne. You will do a big whack up in the Joy and you will do natural life in hell. Remember that, Byrne. Hell, now and after."

The preaching porker went to leave the cell.

"Inspector", said Bonkie.

"Yes?" replied the preaching porker expectantly.

"I pissed in that basin before you came in."

The door slammed loudly behind the porkers.

Bonkie lay back down on the lumpy bed. He was exhausted. Some of the things the preaching porker had said had gone to the centre of his heart. His 'real' wife was happily shacked up with a straight guy who went off to work in the morning and came back home at night. He was there seven days a week to be nagged or whatever. It was a great pity there was no divorce. His ex-wife and her fella could remarry and he could propose to Sally. Bonkie loved Sally beyond words. They had both decided to have a child and when she was born Bonkie felt a deep emotional stirring inside him. It was much different to when his other five kids were born, and he did not know why. He reckoned himself it was because he loved Sally so much. They had called her Saorise. Freedom. Wee Saorise. If Bonkie loved Sally he adored his daughter. He had had great difficulty restraining himself when the preaching porker had been trying to upset him by referring to her as a bastard. Bonkie did not like that. It sent him into the moodies to have to live in such a vicious society. He looked at the painkillers he had been given. They seemed to be OK. Bonkie swallowed them in his spit and hoped they got to work soon. He was in bits. He lay looking at the dismal cell. Cells are all alike. There is a smell, a feel, a rotten atmosphere in them that only a person who has been inside can relate to. The boredom is written, scratched or scraped all over the walls. The hopes – 'John Dornan, Bail Application, High Court'. The despair – 'JD shot down'. The whack – 'JD five years'. Hatred and degradation – 'Fuck The Law' smeared in excreta. Violence – blood, black and curdled, stuck on the walls. Love – 'Mary Purcell loves baby Jossie and Paddywhack too'. Death – 'Martin Brady fell off this bed and died of multiple injuries received thereof'. Humour – 'Sleep on the bleeding floor'.

It was the written life set down in felt markers, biros, pencils, lipstick, eyebrow pencils, nail files, anything that would leave a record. Grim graffiti. It was all stuck together and hung on the walls by a prison paste that went yellow, brittle and dank with the passing of the years. Bonkie could remember the smell of his first cell and what was written on the walls. He got up off the bed and hobbled over to the toilet bowl cemented into the wall and had a piss. His urine was flecked with bright streaks of blood. He reached down and searched behind the bowl. He found a packet and opened it up. Two and a half tipped cigarettes. In the bottom of the packet were a few matches. He lit up and silently thanked the prisoner who had left them behind. The painkillers began to bite. Bonkie relaxed as best he could, reserving his strength to do battle with the heavy porkers. He psyched himself up by reminding himself that he would never see Sally or Saorise again if he broke. But he knew. He was Bonkie. The Law would not break him. All they could do was stitch him up, if he gave them the slightest opening.

He had been dozing. The rattle of the door woke him. Taunted his anxiety. He was waiting on them coming. The porker came in silently and handed him a brown bag. It contained cigarettes, fish and chips, chocolate, and a couple of paperbacks. The door slammed shut. He rubbed his eyes and opened the books. One was about the life of the

English hangman Pierpoint and the other was a book from the flat, Papillon. Love, Sally. She had written that on both. She was an intelligent woman was Sally. The books made their point. Bonkie brightened up. If Sally knew he was here then she must have contacted a solicitor who, no doubt, would be on his way over. He lit up a fresh smoke. Saorise was getting up to school age. She had written da in the paperbacks and made a few spidery children's drawings. He shook his head at Sally's choice of books. Papillon's epic struggle to gain his freedom and the wretched end Pierpoint gave to the poor unfortunates who were convicted of murder. The devil or the deep blue sea. Bonkie needed no reminding of what was facing him. He settled down and began to read of the heroic exploits of Albert Pierpoint when he was the No 1 hangman. It seemed to Bonkie that hanging was a family business over there and the assistant hangmen constantly hoped the No 1 hangman would do a botched execution so they could get his job. He was getting drowsy. The print danced before his eyes below the weak naked bulb set high up on the wall. The door opened.

"Dere his ha solicitor to see you, Byrne."

Bonkie got up and walked downstairs with the porker to the small room beside the station sergeant's desk.

"What has happened to my client?" roared Jimmy Apple when he saw the state of Bonkie.

"Ask him yourself", said the porker. "He doesn't talk to the likes of us." The porker slammed the door.

"What time is it, Jimmy?" asked Bonkie.

"A quarter past twelve, Bonkie. I got over as fast as I could. Who beat you up?"

"Ah, the heavy porkers. You know the score yourself. They have me down for a heavy bleeding stroke." Bonkie knew the room was bugged.

"Right", said Jimmy. He got out his note pad to take the details. "What are you in for?"

"I don't know. They said for being a member of an organisation but I think they have arrested me because of the Ballygojingle stroke. I don't know what they are talking about on either case."

"Section 30 Bonkie. You are supposed to be taken in on a Scheduled Offence, which incidentally does not incude bank robbery – or murder. So they take you in and log it as suspected membership."

"Then I'm in illegal detention. Wrongful arrest."

"Technically you may be. The reality is that the gardai are entitled to suspect anyone they please of being a member of the IRA or any other organisation and bring them in for questioning."

"Even a robber? Or, a granny in a bleeding wheelchair?"

"Yes. That is the law. And, they can then question one as to non-scheduled offences such as bank robbery and the shooting down of grannies in the street."

"You bleeding listen to me", snarled Bonkie, "I am a car robber and a housebreaker. If yer don't believe me look at my record or, if yer like, I'll go up and screw your gaff but I don't know nothing about this Ballygojingle. I was far away when it went off. Understand?"

"Did you give your alibi to the gardai?"

"Are you codding me?"

"I suppose if you did they will go down and grill the witnesses."

"What bleeding witnesses? What do you mean?"

"They are likely to charge you." Jimmy tapped his ear and pulled a face. "With Ballygojingle and the shooting of the Councillor. It's political now."

"Good", declared Bonkie. "I am glad they are going ter charge someone."

That put a spanner in Jimmy's head. It rattled a bit and then he asked.

"Why is it good Bonkie? I'm lost. Fill me in on your thinking."

I'd love to fill yer in Jimmy, up in the mountains in a six foot hole. Dirty rat.

"They must have evidence to charge someone. That leaves me out of it."

"I don't follow you."

"The evidence will prove it was another bleeding crook. Not me. I told yer, I wasn't bleeding there. Do yer have me now, Jimmy?"

"Of course, Bonkie. It's not me you have to convince. You are, we are denying these scurrilous allegations. Disgraceful. Unwarranted and so on."

"Good man Jimmy. I knew you would understand me. I'm in nothing either."

"Well. Even the gardai know that. They can, now that you are here, take your fingerprints, your weight and height, swabs for firearms residue, a hair sample and all your clothing for forensic examination."

"Are they taking all these things to prove membership?"

"No."

"What are the forensics for? To prove buggery."

"Don't talk ridiculous Bonkie." Jimmy was getting peeved.

"You don't talk shite Jimmy. I'm arrested on membership and I will be interrogated, fingerprinted, tested for a different charge. Why didn't they arrest me on bank robbery and murder? It sounds fishy, bleeding poxy ter me."

"If you were taken in on murder they would be obliged to bring you to the next available court and charge you."

"I have yer now. And no two days of questioning. No two days of collecting so-called evidence to make a case. It's called fabricating evidence, Jimmy. I am in illegal custody and yer know it too."

"There is nothing you can do about it. That's the way it works."

"I want yer, Jimmy, to go immediately and put me in a Habeo in front of a High Court judge at his gaff. I want yer to knock the beak up. O'Dailigh."

"Not a chance. Ridiculous talk Bonkie. He would throw me into jail. You want me to attack the most potent weapon in the gardai armoury? Not me Bonkie. I am an officer of the court. You must realise – very few people are questioned for the offence on which they are taken in, on which they are allegedly arrested. Section 30 is used by the gardai to circumvent the common law. It lets them have an opportunity to question a person for 48 hours during which time the gardai endeavour, shall we say, to eliminate the suspect from their enquiries."

"You mean they try to get confessions out of people. I'm having none of it."

"You are obliged to give an account of your movements if you are asked for it. If you refuse you can get six months."

"Big bleeding deal. I'm giving nothing to no one. The whole thing is twisted, the law is stood on its ass. The only organisation I was ever in was the ITGWU and that was only for three weeks. I tried ter get a job as a security man and when I was sacked they wouldn't back me up. I am not co-operating with this charade. I'm not going ter be stitched up."

"Calm down Bonkie." Jimmy changed tack again. "If you have nothing to do with this, as you say, then there is no problem. Is there?"

"That all depends if you were dragged out of a boozer by the hair and taken down here with a baby hippo sitting on yer. Doesn't it? It all depends on how much of a beating the heavy porkers have yet ter give me. Doesn't it?"

"Now, now, Bonkie. I shall have that stopped. They shall not mistreat my client. Not Jimmy Apple's client by God. Er, tell me this. Where were you on that Tuesday? It shall go no further than I. Be assured of this, Bonkie."

"I was down", Bonkie dropped his voice, "I was down the sticks getting a bit of stuff together, antiques, sil..., I was down in Cork".

"Getting together a bit of silver?" Jimmy wriggled his eyebrows.

"Yeah, but nothing bleeding illegal Jimmy. All straight and above board."

"Oh, of course." Jimmy said this like yer would placate a madman with an axe.

"It took me a few days to put it all together. To dig it up. I mean out. Out of the warehouse. I was waiting for the buyers to come when all this came on top. Roadblocks everywhere. Not a good time for a robber to be bringing home his poke. Porkers at roads, railway stations, bus stations, everywhere. So I put me few bob away and I laid low and came back when I thought it was cool."

Jimmy stared at Bonkie as he spoke. The solicitor knew he was telling the truth. Bonkie wasn't up to the Ballygojingle stroke. No way. He was protecting his few bob.

"Bonkie, why didn't you tell the gardai you were down the sticks? You don't want this on your back."

"Don't talk shite Jimmy. I'm telling the porkers nothing. Nothing. Not now. Not ever."

"Alright", Jimmy backed off. "I'm only looking at this in the long term. Even if you are released Bonkie you don't want them to suspect you of this. There is going to be big trouble about this stroke. I can tell you. It was the taking over of the Garda Station. All sorts of citizens rang in to say the bank was being robbed. One of the gang was answering the phone giving them bad advice and, in some cases, vile abuse. Public confidence in the Law and all that."

"I don't bleeding know what yer mean, Jimmy."

"There is going to be a lot of heat, Bonkie. Someone is going, someone has to go down on this one. God help them. That's all I can say."

"Well Jimmy. It's like this. I have not one but I'd say a hundred good witnesses that I was in Cork on the day that bank was robbed. So, like I say, I don't give a bollox."

That stopped Jimmy in full snoop and shocked the porker listening in. You couldn't stitch someone with a hundred alibi witnesses.

"A hundred witnesses, Bonkie? But where?"

Bonkie assumed a smug position and tapped the side of his head slyly. He was delighted. He knew he had wrecked the porkers' heads. One alibi witness put them in a frenzy. One hundred? Massive paranoia.

"It isn't too hard to work out, Jimmy, but it's between me and the jury so to speak."

"There are no juries in the Special Criminal Court, Bonkie. Just three Judges."

"Three bleeding monkeys, see no evil, hear no evil, speak no evil. Jimmy I'm falling off my feet. The quack said I was to be given rest. So you tell the porker out there I am to be let sleep. I am telling yer now, and I want yer to draw it up in writing. I have no intention of making any form of statement or incriminating remarks for a crime I know nothing about. Give a copy of it to the desk porker. Yer see I don't talk to them. Kind of a breakdown in communication."

Jimmy scribbled away.

"I want yer to tell them any more heavy gang tactics and we go to court on an assault action for damages. I'll let things stand if they leave it off. Fix that. Tell them I'm giving fuck all. No prints or hair. Nothing. I want yer to call here tomorrow with a barrister and a doctor before nine o'clock."

"What do you want the barrister for?" asked Jimmy.

"Habeas Corpus. Illegal arrest, illegal detention, assault, violation of Constitutional Rights. I'm not bleeding having this heavy scene."

Jimmy sighed.

"Alright Bonkie. We will go to court if that's what you want but it will cost you."

"Five hundred pounds is all I can afford Jimmy. Just for the motion. You can get a junior for that can't yer?"

"It may not be necessary Bonkie. I'll have a stern talk to the man in charge of the case. I don't think you will be assaulted again." He looked at his watch. "Time flies Bonkie. I'll let you go to bed. Do you need anything?"

"No thanks Jimmy. Just draw up the anti-verbal and I'll sign it." He yawned.

Jimmy wrote out a short statement stating his client did not wish to make any statement, either in writing or verbally, with regard to the offence for which he was being questioned. He had been advised of this by his solicitor. Jimmy added his signature and the time. Bonkie signed it.

"If yer think we don't need the barrister Jimmy yer can hang onto the five hundred. Just get them off my back."

"Oh, I think that will cover my fees adequately, Mr Byrne." Jimmy smiled.

If I was getting five hundred punts a touch, thought Bonkie, I'd bleeding consider going straight. Adequate.

"Rest assured that you will not be at any legal disadvantage, Mr Byrne. I for one am quite certain of your innocence in this grave affair. Never shall it be said that Jimmy Apple and Company did not do battle for their clients. Er, about the fees, do you have them at hand?"

"I only had fifty punts on me when I was lifted Jimmy but..."

"No matter. That shall be a sufficient deposit. You can give me the balance when you get released." Jimmy stood up and rumbled towards the door. He banged it. It opened at once.

"Give this to the desk sergeant, guard", ordered Jimmy. He handed the porker Bonkie's written intention not to make any statement. Jimmy turned to Bonkie. "You go on up and have a sleep, Bonkie. I'll make a bit of a fuss down here."

Bonkie got up from the dingy table.

"I am finished with Mr Byrne, for the moment", called Jimmy to the porker.

"Are you right now?" asked the porker of Bonkie.

Bonkie walked out of the interview room with the jailer. He walked into a wall of hatred. There was a bunch of heavy, sports-jacketed, tie-wearing, square-headed guardians of the fragile democracy, standing between the stairway to the cells above and the interview room. Bonkie had to walk through them.

"Murderer", hissed a porker. He smelt of beer. He had big hands, full of red freckles and prominent veins.

Bonkie shouldered his way through the heavies.

"Come on lads. Out of de way now", pleaded the jailer porker. Then he confided. "His solicitor is in the interview room."

Indeed he was. Jimmy came out of the interview room like a bull. He roared and snorted and berated the heavy porkers. He threatened the station porkers with every conceivable legal penalty. Bonkie could still hear him roaring as he was locked back in his cell.

Bonkie relaxed in the cell. He knew Jimmy believed him and would tell Ned O'Stitch Bonkie had nothing to do with it. Jimmy was now putting on a bit of a show to get his five hundred pounds. He was welcome to it. Bonkie climbed, fully clothed, under the blankets and popped the sleeping tablet. He was fast asleep within a couple of minutes.

Down below in the reception area the squad of heavy porkers, who had come for an all night session with Bonkie, left the station enraged. They muttered dire threats against the legal profession and resolved to have the current 'Special' legislation made more to the liking of the gardai. It was utterly impossible for the gardai to do their job if murderers and bank robbers were put to bed at ten o'clock and were not to be disturbed.

"Dey will be calling dis de Hilton next", spat an enormous heavy porker at the station porkers as he left.

The station porkers locked the gates and started a poker game.

Jimmy Apple rang Ned O'Stitch and assured him Bonkie had nothing to do with the Ballygojingle stroke.

"Are you positive?" asked Ned.

"Almost. Let me say I am fairly sure he had nothing to do with it. It's not within his capabilities, Ned. He is strictly small time. He says he has not one, but a hundred alibi witnesses."

"Where?"

"I can't say, Ned. He is keeping them up his sleeve."

"I'm sure he is, Jimmy. The thing is would Mr Byrne be pulling your leg and mine?"

"Definitely not. He doesn't know what good friends we are. I am positive of that. He was recovering some property he had buried and was in process of selling it. He could not get back with the activity after Ballygojingle."

"Jimmy, find out all the details if you can. In particular see if he can give you any leads on two Belfast men. I want their names."

"OK Ned. In the meantime tell Sullivan not to beat up Byrne."

"Is he badly beaten?"

"Yes. And it will serve no purpose only to cloud the issue. Byrne will most certainly give no co-operation to anyone. Especially if he is beaten."

"I'll have that stopped Jimmy. You find out what's going on there Jimmy. If he wasn't on the stroke he knows something about it. Find out what he knows Jimmy."

Ned hung up the phone. He thought the matter over for a few minutes. It was obvious that Byrne was not needed by MacGregor's gang to hit the bank. He wasn't a specialist in any way. The Firm had their pick of fifty top operators if they were short of a soldier for a stroke. He was now uncertain as to Byrne's involvement. Maybe he was sprung to do some deal about stolen property. Hmmmm. Ned picked up the phone and ordered the heavy porkers not to be beating Bonkie further. He had to have the bloody names. The correct names. Otherwise he could not move. Imagine putting together a book of evidence for a man who has a watertight alibi? Someone who was in London or having dinner with the Bishop. Ned was in a bit of a pickle. The Ballygojingle job had escalated. It had been raised at Cabinet level. The press was still frothing at the mouth. Jimmy Apple was his best prospect otherwise he would have to trade with the Special Branch and he didn't want that. The Special Branch might dig up the Northern Ireland mens' names for him but what else would they dig up in the process? Ned would have to show his hand. Leave himself vulnerable and when he got down to it what he was up to was downright illegal. He was a one man show. Had to be. He sighed and went outside for a walk in the cool night air. It was beautiful out here in the countryside. His new home was top class. He could settle here with no problems at all. Ten pounds a week. The place was worth sixty at least. He walked through the well-tended gardens, fragrant with flowering shrubs and blossoms. Ned breathed deeply through his squashed snout. There was no trace of the nearby city out here. It was ideal too for his dogs. He thought about the Ballygojingle job. If he solved the case he could leave the Force with a very big reputation and much influence. He would be welcomed into SS Security with open arms and a salary commensurate with his status. He had to be extra careful. Keep his forensic records close to his chest.

Ned went in and made himself a hot whiskey. He played a little martial music then went to bed with MacGregor's gang on his mind.

In the Bridewell Bonkie tossed and turned fitfully in the dirty, lumpy bed. He was in a big city where all the people were porkers. He was running, always running, but there was nowhere to go. Every building was a porker's shop. He was running here and there and the porkers opened up their big square jaws and laughed and laughed. There was nowhere to rob! There was nothing to steal! Gangland was up in Glasnevin. There was no crime of any description! No citizens, only porkers who spied on each other. No courts, no prisons, no solicitors, no barristers, no screws. Bonkie was the last robber in existence and he had no bleeding place to rob. The porker men and women gathered him in O'Connell Street and jeered him. They all had the smell of the slop out in the Joy on them. He tried to leg it but they made a little jail for him with their bodies. A little square for him to walk anxiously around in. Sally was shouting 'it's only a dream' most of the time, 'it's only a dream'.

Bonkie woke as the grey dawn was filtering through the bars. He felt so bad he refused to process the complaints from his aching body. He was sweating and his mouth was stuck with dried blood. "That's all I bleeding need", he muttered, "a poxy fucking nightmare". He turned over and tried to doze off. The sleeping dope was still in his blood and he managed to nod off. That horrible prison sound came to him. The insertion of the first key of the day into the lock on the door. It is a sound known to all prisoners. It cuts across all prison classes and brings to all people in prisons everywhere the reality of their captivity. Illusion is shattered. Pretence destroyed. Barriers swept aside with a contemptuous turn of a key. The key turned once then twice. It was eight o'clock in the morning. The door was flung open.

"Here's your breakfast", said the jailer porker. He placed beside Bonkie's bed a small, much used, plastic cup, half full of tepid tea, and one slice of thin white bread thickly spread with margarine. "And the doctor left these for you", he held out two painkillers.

Bonkie took the painkillers. He put them in his mouth and washed them down with the tea. It was sickly sweet. He threw the rest against the wall and the piece of bread into the jakes bowl. There was no point in complaining about the breakfast. It would just be a waste of effort. He sat up and lit a smoke. Bonkie hated being in the Bridewell. It was a terrible kip. He stood up and paced the cell to get a bit of circulation going. He didn't feel too bad. He ate last night's chocolate and began to bang the door. The peephole slid to one side.

"What's the racket habout?" asked a porker.

"I want out to have a wash."

"We'll see habout it."

"Let me out for a wash or I'll kick the bleeding door down."

Five minutes later the door opened.

"Are you looking for a wash?" enquired the porker.

Bonkie ignored the stupid question and walked out onto the landing. He went to the sink and ran the tap. Hot water. He looked in the mirror. His face was a mess. One eye was closed over and he had a few stitches in his lip. He looked as if he had gone the distance with Mohammad Ali. After he had washed and shaved Bonkie started to walk back to his cell.

"How are yer, Bonkie?" shouted someone.

He looked around and walked over to the big cell the voice was coming out of. It was Paul Doyle, a stroker Bonkie knew.

"How are yer Paul?" asked Bonkie. He was glad to see a friendly bit of a face.

"No talking dere", ordered the porker.

"What are yer in for?" asked Bonkie ignoring the porker.

"I was lifted on a bleeding warrant. I'm off up ter the Joy for six months. I thought I had paid the bleeding fine last time."

"How much?"

"Two hundred and fifty quid, Bonkie . . ."

"Get away from that door, Byrne", order the porker.

"Go and bollox", replied Bonkie. He turned back to the cell door, "I'll see if I can get that for yer Paul. Here's a few smokes." He put a few smokes into the peephole and matches.

"Tanks Bonkie. There is a few of us in here. I'll see yer up in the Joy."

I hope not thought Bonkie to himself. The porker beside him was hopping as if he was going to piss himself.

"They are all entitled to their smokes", said Bonkie to the porker. "They are only on remand."

"Dey might set fire to de cell, Mr Know All. People hin here are entitled to nothing."

Bonkie ignored the porker and walked back into his cell. The porker slammed the door more loudly than usual. Bonkie spat at the door and gave the porker his two fingers. If they could get away with it they would hang yer from the wall in chains. Paul Doyle was always in the Joy for having no insurance. He couldn't get it anywhere. Bonkie was considering paying his fine when the heavy porkers came for him. He took a deep breath and went down to the interview room.

Behind the porkers' table sat two very heavy porkers. Bonkie sat down without being asked. If the porkers had asked him to sit down he would have been obliged to stand up during the interrogation. He intended to do the opposite of anything the porkers told him.

"Name and address?" demanded the younger of the two heavy porkers. He was a half intelligent looking brat. The other porker, a fit looking, grey haired man, sporting a Pioneer pin, watched Bonkie's reactions keenly.

Silence.

"I asked you for your name and address. You are obliged to give them to me by law. Now, name and address?" There was an air of menace in his questioning.

Silence.

The porker jumped to his feet and kicked back his chair.

"When I ask you a question you will reply. Do you understand that?" He pointed his finger at Bonkie. "You will answer my questions. Give me your name and address."

Silence. Bonkie began to pick his nose. This brat of a porker was going to be very easily wound up. The porker's eye began to twitch in a nervous tic.

"All the same Bonkie", began the elder porker, "Sgt King is entitled to hear you speak, for you to tell him your name. Sure, he might want to send you home."

Silence.

"Sure wouldn't the Sergeant be the right eejit if he sent home the wrong man? Ha, ha, ha, ha." The elder porker took out a packet of Polo mints and offered one to the Sergeant. The Sergeant took one, staring at Bonkie with great hostility. Bonkie ignored the proffered mints.

"You ignorant pig", shouted the younger porker. His mint shot out and shattered.

Bonkie smiled to himself at the very idea of the porker calling him a pig.

"I am Inspector Sullivan, Bonkie. I want you to give me an account of your movements on the day the Bank of Ireland in Ballygojingle was robbed, when the Gardai Station was overrun..." – both of the porkers' faces clouded over at the recollection of this outrage – "... and when two innocent citizens were murdered on the street going about their lawful occasions". The elder porker let the import of his words wash over Bonkie who, it must be said, continued to pick his nose.

"I want you to give me a complete account of your movements on that day so that we may eliminate you from our enquiries. Let me make myself clear, Bonkie. You must give me this account of your movements by law. I must warn you that failure to do so will result in your being brought before the Special Criminal Court and charged with failure to give the said account."

Silence.

"What were you doing on that day? Were you on the street? I don't believe so. You wouldn't know one end of an RPG7 from another. Were you in the Gardai Station? No. That was a Cork man. Where were you Bonkie? I want to know."

"He was in the bank, Inspector. He was the bag man."

Bonkie kept a straight face. He looked at a crack in the green flaky wall.

"Dublin man, your build, Bonkie. It's possible. The man with the shotgun. Any old fucking idiot can use a shotgun, Bonkie. Eh? Things went wrong, Bonkie. If you were on this job you are gone and the key will be thrown away. If you were not involved in this job you stop your hard man act, your big time nonsense, and you prove, you PROVE to me mister that you were not there." The elder porker spoke very clearly, crisply. He meant every word he said. "If you do not prove to my satisfaction that you were somewhere else at the time then I shall believe you were there. And I'll prove, one way or another, your guilt."

Silence.

"He is your man, Inspector. The guilt is written all over the rat. He is scared shitless. Look at him. You bastard Byrne. You are not so tough without your shotgun and your hood are you?" The younger porker sneered at Bonkie.

"I've dealt with all the blaggers in this town, Bonkie. None, not one has refused to give an account of his movements for this stroke. Some took your stupid attitude until they saw sense." He must have hit a button or something. The door opened and at least twenty heavy porkers came into the interview room. They were all carrying Uzis and barely controlled hatred. Before they could start their freaking out Bonkie rose up and gave one a beautiful kick in the testicles.

"Leave him, leave him", screamed the elder porker. He and the younger porker dragged Bonkie back into his chair. "Out, out, out lads", urged the elder porker.

The heavy porkers stood in a semi-circle around Bonkie, all pointing their Uzis at him. They withdrew carrying out the porker with the sore groin.

"You don't pull a stupid move like that again, Byrne", gasped out the elder porker. "Those lads are just waiting for a chance to leave you like a tea strainer. You are in big trouble man! Don't you see that? We know you didn't fire the rocket launcher. Me, me here, I am the only person in the country who can do you a good turn. Did you get your breakfast, Bonkie?"

Silence.

"Sergeant, go out and bring in Mrs Houlihon."

The younger porker went to the door.

"You can tell me anything in confidence", whispered the elder porker. "It will go no further than you and me."

A long thin woman dressed in a tweed suit, came into the room. She pointed her finger at Bonkie and trembled.

"That's him, that's him", she screamed. "He's the one that had the bag full of money. I'd know these eyes anywhere. Murderer, murderer", she panted, and then fainted.

"You", pointed out the elder porker, "are done, Bonkie. Take that poor woman away".

She wasn't a bad auld actress that one thought Bonkie. He had seen worse on RTE. The younger porker helped her to her feet.

"Are you alright mam?" he enquired solicitously.

"Oh, poor Mrs Gormeless. A harmless creature all her days. Be the Lord God isn't that a terrible wicked man ye have there now." She was led out muttering.

"Get a statement from her as soon as she is well enough", ordered the elder porker. "The eyes Bonkie, the shape of the face through the hood, the build, the accent, a hair here and there. Don't be a fucking eejit, as they say, someone is going down on this. You are all we have. Do I make myself clear? You better tell me you did not do this and then prove it to me. Start talking, it's seven o'clock on the morning of the job. Where are you?"

Silence.

"I know where he was", butted in the younger porker, "he was getting tooled up. He was moving into position from a safe place. In the mountains I'd say. He was sleeping in the van Inspector. Holed up ready to come down, to rob and kill. To destroy. To pillage. To desecrate. He is keeping his mouth shut because he cannot open it. He was there. He is the bag man. Why give him a chance to clear himself? Stitch the dirty piece of scum up. Put him down".

"Seven o'clock in the morning. Where were you? Talk. Talk now while you get the chance." The younger porker came back over and sat facing Bonkie. The door opened again. A station porker came over to the Inspector and whispered in his ear and left.

"There is a solicitor to see you, Bonkie. He can come in here." The porkers lifted up their pads and went to the door. "You are going to need all the legal help you can get."

The younger porker drew his finger across his throat and pointed to Bonkie.

Fat Jimmy Apple rushed into the interview room. He was breathless.

"You are late", observed Bonkie.

"Sorry. Couldn't get here sooner. Pressure of business. What did Sullivan want?"

"He said he wanted to help me out. Don't yer know yerself but, I have this feeling, maybe I am paranoid, that he really wants to lock me away for life."

"OK Bonkie I get the picture. Now I have made certain representations on your behalf. You will not be maltreated again. I have a simple proposition for you. Tell ME your alibi and if it sounds reasonable I'll vouch for you."

"And they won't put me down for this stroke?"

"That's correct."

"There is a problem, Jimmy. I wasn't down the sticks organising a jumble sale for the Irish Countrymens Association."

"I know that. That's why I am intervening in this way. I know you cannot give the gardai your alibi because of your business. When I say I will vouch for you, I mean, I shall tell them I am satisfied, as an officer of the court that you had no part in this terrible crime."

"That sounds reasonable enough, Jimmy." Bonkie pretended to think about it.

"Of course, if I do not believe you or if you give me a pack of lies I'll do nothing. Either way."

"Alright Jimmy I'll tell yer where I was."

Jimmy switched on the recorder in his briefcase and ostentatiously put away his pen and folded his arms.

"Shoot Bonkie." He wriggled his eyebrows.

I'd love to shoot you Jimmy, thought Bonkie.

"Do yer remember when Menten the Nazi was robbed? When his gaff was done down the sticks?"

"Yes, I remember it very well. He was in Holland at the time."

"That's right, Jimmy. Well I screwed the place. Tied the bleeding auld one up. The place was empty. The sly old bollox had moved out all the really good gear. The old masters and the fine antiques. I got two sets of silver. A set of some type of French silver, er, Louis bleeding somebody. The American geezer said it was exquisite. I think he was gay. Anyway, the other stuff was the gear. A set, a complete dinner set, knives, forks, spoons, cruet sets, platters, everything, of very fine Georgian. They were very pleased with it."

"Who?"

"I can't tell yer that, Jimmy. The geezers who were setting up the deal. When I done the gaff I had all the silver in the boot and I buried it in a wood beside Cork. I dumped the jammer and came home by train. I brought a bit of silver from each set to see if I could get a buyer. I got nicked and when things began to come my way I was up in the Joy for a desperation stroke. Some friends of mine had a big buyer."

"And that's where you were – down digging up this stuff and selling it?"

"Well I only dug it up. I didn't have much to do with the selling."

Jimmy Apple was in bits. The idiot in front of him had given away a fortune, probably for buttons, to MacGregor's gang. Who would bring such a dope with them to rob a bank?

"What did you do after you gave them the silver?"

"I waited around in Cork until they gave me my money. I was hanging around for a couple of days having a few drinks. Enjoying myself and then the Ballygojingle job blew up. I stayed where I was."

"Did you get a good deal, Bonkie?"

"Bleeding great. I got a couple of grand clear."

Jimmy Apple nearly cried his eyes out.

"Where were you Bonkie on the day of the stroke?"

"I was in Cork. That's all I'm telling yer Jimmy and I can prove it too."

"That's not very much for me to go on, Bonkie. Tell me, was there a Belfast man there? I heard there is a big fence who comes down from Belfast for good stuff. I, er, would like to meet him."

"I didn't meet him but I could find out for yer. Is there a few bob in it somewhere Jimmy?"

"There might be Bonkie. Did you meet any Northern men at all?"

"No Jimmy it were all – no, I met no Northerners."

"Ah, sure it doesn't matter Bonkie. I'm only making enquiries for a client of mine. A very delicate business." Jimmy winked his eye.

Bonkie winked back and nodded his head. A nod is as good as a wink. Don't say any more Jimmy, sure, isn't the whole country bent, even those up in the Castle?

"Did yer get the doctor for me, Jimmy? asked Bonkie.

"Bonkie, let it lie. If I bring in an independent doctor they will charge you with assault and bring you before the Special Criminal Court."

"And if I don't get the family quack?"

"They will drop it and no more physical abuse."

"Alright."

"Did the gardai ask you for an account of your movements?"

"They did."

"Did you give them it?"

"No, I did not. And I'm not going to either. The thing is I am not refusing. I just cannot remember."

"Did you tell them you cannot remember?"

"No, I did not. And I'm not going to either."

"Very interesting, Bonkie. From a legal point of view. You are not refusing. You cannot remember. And there is no legal obligation for you to say you cannot remember because you have the right to remain silent under caution. It's a most interesting point. Who gave you that piece of advice?"

"I came by that at the Mountjoy Bar, Jimmy. Sometimes we

jailhouse lawyers do come up with a legal point that is very good before they change the law. Bonkie allowed himself a laugh. Then he changed tactics again. "Jimmy the law had a mad auld one in here throwing herself on the floor. Letting on to faint. A big skinny one with a hooked nose. A horror picture. She bleeding said she recognised me through a hood. Said she recognised me by me eyes."

"Was it a proper ID parade?"

"Never mind that. She could not have recognised me because I was not there. It's a load of nonsense. What's going on?"

Jimmy knew exactly what was going on. The porkers were trying to freak his client out. To jolt him into making mistakes. To watch his reactions. Guilty men, people with things to hide are very defensive. All they were looking for in this particular instance was to find out if Bonkie was involved. To see if he was one of the Firm of blaggers. And had used Ban Garda Mary Russell from the shoplifting squad as a prop. He had known at once who it was. Hooked nose and horrible. Bonkie was behaving as an innocent man would behave – to a certain extent. He was behaving with the confidence of a crook who knew he was not involved in this stroke.

"Bonkie, the courts are accepting all manner of evidence that would have been regarded as inadmissible a few years ago. It's the 'Special' legislation. Gradually more and more and more safeguards are shorn away for pragmatic reasons until people can be virtually sent away on the word of one person. You are entitled to a proper ID parade but there is nothing to stop the gardai from asking a witness to have a look at a suspect. Whatever credence the Special Court will put upon such an occurrence as evidential value cannot be judged. The court shall always, where it can, come down in favour of the gardai. I'll try and find out who this woman is. It doesn't sound good. The gardai will claim to the DPP that they have a positive identification."

"I told yer that is impossible."

"Oh, I know you were not there. It's just this Bonkie. We have to take everything they do as serious and think the absolute worst. It is not unknown for an innocent man to swing. Men have fallen to their death on the scaffold protesting their innocence, unfair trial, false evidence. It was no comfort for them to know they were innocent, was it?"

Bonkie lit up a smoke. His head was light. There was a foul taste in his mouth.

The Firm had warned him of the antics of this treacherous bastard sitting in front of him pretending to be acting in his interests. He, had Bonkie not known of his deviousness, would have put much more pressure on him, would have been much more dangerous than the porkers. Bonkie gave his hand a twitch or two. He knew how scapegoats were made. They were manufactured to appease some self-righteous bollox higher up the porker scale of values. Bonkie knew the fainting auld one, the bogus witness, was a Ban Garda. He began to pity anyone brought in here on a heavy stroke who was anyway green or fucked up in the head with smack or emotional problems. The porkers would have them eating out of their hands.

"I'm telling yer Jimmy. I have a perfect alibi. The auld one is making a mistake."

"Hmmm. Will your witnesses go to court for you?"

"What do you mean? I won't be bleeding charged with this."

"Famous last words Bonkie. How many times have we heard that?"

Bonkie almost lost his self control. He wanted to get up and tear into the foul, fat, rat. He had an urge to bite his nose off. He made up his mind to do the solicitor a nasty stroke. Burn down his gaff, preferably, when he was in it. Or, get the General to make him a sticky bomb to put under Jimmy's Bentley. Bonkie's anger was real when he rose up and gripped Jimmy. The fat man's chins quivered.

"I told yer, Jimmy. This is not my stroke. I have a perfect alibi. It would not be perfect if I could not get the witnesses to go to court. Would it? It wouldn't be worth protecting would it?"

"Calm down for God's sake. I'm only putting the other side's case across. Sit down Bonkie."

Bonkie sat down reluctantly. He squashed out his smoke and lit up another right away.

"I'll vouch for you, Bonkie. But remember this. You owe me a big favour and for your own sake you had better not be fucking spoofing me."

"OK Jimmy, I owe yer one. Why should I spoof yer Jimmy? You are the only bleeding one that's looking after me."

Jimmy beamed with pride. He liked to look after his clients well in so far as was possible in these difficult times.

"I'll have to go now Bonkie. I'm in court at eleven thirty. I imagine you will be interrogated with some vigour most of the day. There is nothing I can do about that." Jimmy pressed his finger and thumb to his lips silently telling Bonkie to keep his mouth shut.

"Don't worry Jimmy", blabbed Bonkie slightly maliciously, "I'll keep me mouth shut".

"Yes, you are not obliged to say anything Mr Byrne." He stood up and shook hands with Bonkie. His palms were sweaty. "I'll get back to you." He walked to the door. "If I can. You will certainly be kept for the full 48 hours." He kicked the door. It opened and his fat arse disappeared after him.

Sullivan came into the room with the younger porker King. He finished his coffee and threw the plastic cup on the floor. He sat down wearily, with a sigh, in the chair that Jimmy Apple had just vacated. The younger porker stood directly behind Bonkie breathing down his neck.

"It's seven o'clock in the morning on the day of the Ballygojingle job. Where are you exactly?" The elder porker made a doodle on his empty sketch pad.

Silence.

"He said, 'I was in Ballygojingle but you will never prove it'. That's what he said sir, I heard him." The younger porker shouted this into Bonkie's ear.

Silence.

The elder porker wrote it down in his notebook.

"Yes. I heard him say that too, Sergeant." Sullivan grinned at Bonkie. It was a silly game that could turn serious in an instant. Blaggology warfare. "You are not denying you said this, are you?"

Silence.

Chapter 13

O'HANLON the Grocer was blindfolded in the back of his shop van and he wished dearly that the hijackers had plugged his ears as well. The hijackers' language was atrocious. That was bad enough but they had decided to have a sing song on their way to wherever they were taking him and his van. The singing was brutal and O'Hanlon suspected the gang was under the influence of strong drink. One of the hijackers was standing astride him in the swaying van, rummaging in the biscuit shelves. The van, a big Mercedes diesel, was being driven faster than he had ever taken it.

"Here they are lads", shouted the rummager, "fig rolls".

The gang cheered and hooted.

"Here you", one of the gang addressed the bound grocer. He prodded the inert man with the barrel of his rifle. "How do they get the figs into the fig rolls?"

"I have not an idea, boy", replied the grocer. He heard the rummager opening up his biscuits and passing them around.

"You are selling fig rolls and yer trying to tell me yer don't know how it's done?" The rummager prodded the grocer again.

"I swear te God boy. I have not a notion or I'd tell ye for sure. Me father, God rest him, fought the Black and Tans. I'm the son of an old IRA man. I'm sure ye knew that when ye were waiting on me van. Me livelihood. 'tis all I have in the world boys. Thanks be te God."

The Firm roared laughing at the sleeved grocer. They had had their eyes on his van for a couple of months. Over nine grands worth of wheels, paid for by diddling the poor people who could not get to a decent shop. All the prices hiked up to the limit. The grocer had a regular shop-cum-post office in his village, a tidy bungalow, a farm and was also the undertaker for the county. On top of all that he was a leading supporter of the more nasty of the two main political parties.

Mickey was sitting up beside the driver. He began singing again.

"Rudolf the red nosed reindeer had a very shiny nose", all joined in, "and if you ever saw him, you might even say it glows ..."

The Firm were having a bit of relaxation after the Ballygojingle stroke. A working holiday. None of them were going to show their faces until Bonkie had been through the Bridewell. They all had great faith in him. He had been a good man on the Ballygojingle stroke. Keen. Efficient and hard. They had given him a good start to his ordeal by briefing him about the tactics used by the heavy porkers. It was a totally different scene to anything he would have experienced previously. The 'working holiday' was also going to show even more confusion about Bonkie.

He was going to have the best possible alibi for this stroke.

"... underneath the mistletoe last night,
oh, what a laugh it would have been, if daddy had only seen,
mammy kissing Santa Claus last night."

"Why aren't you bleeding singing?" asked the rummager to the grocer.

"Sure it isn't Christmas boys", replied the hooded man.

The rummager prodded the grocer viciously in the ribs with his rifle.

"It's always bleeding Christmas in gangland."

"Leave the asshole alone, number three. It's almost time. Alright get ready lads. The cross is coming up."

The Firm cocked their weapons and a hush came on the van. The nonsense of the previous half hour evaporated in the pre-stroke atmosphere. One of the Firm came down to the grocer and tied a rope around the man's waist.

The van pulled in by the side of the road beside the crossroads. It was as silent as the grave.

"Listen to me carefully", explained a hooded man to the grocer. "I'm putting you out on the road. There is a rope tied around your waist as you know. I will be holding the other end. If you try and run away, if you try and undo the rope, you will be shot. Do you understand that?"

"I do indeed, sor", replied the grocer. He was very sincere.

"Good man. Now, when the travelling bank comes down the road I want you to wave it down. Do you understand that?"

"I do, sor. It'll stop for me. Sure they know me well, I does a lot of business with them." He was very helpful.

"Good man yerself", jeered the blagger. "Now, when this operation is over and the porkers are dragging you around gardai stations asking you to identify people what will you tell them?"

"Sure and how could I identify anyone and they all wearing masks? Ah, don't worry about me boys. Me father slept with the auld crowd."

"Sure boys", shouted the blagger, "isn't the grocer one of our own?"

The Firm gave him a bit of a cheer. It's nice to have the support of the plain people when one is blagging.

"Just one more thing. What will you tell the porkers when they ask you what way we spoke?"

"Ah sure boys didn't everyone of ye have a pure Donegal brogue as thick as a Killibegs fishwife?"

"Isn't that the decentest man we have met this side of the border lads?"

"It is. It's to men like him and his father before him we owe our freedom."

"Begob now. I think we should bring him on de attack wid us."

"Do ye think he'd be awilling?" jeered yet another blagger.

"Ah lads, sure it's me poor auld heart. It's only be the good grace of God and the intercession of his Holy Mother I'm able to drive this van for a bit of a living. It's all I have in the world lads."

"Tell me this and tell me no more", whispered a blagger to the grocer, "would ye throw a bomb for the cause now?"

"Throw a bomb? Me? I..I couldn't. Me heart wouldn't stand fer it boys. Throw a bomb at who?"

"At the papists of course", roared Mickey in a well known clerical voice.

"In the name of God who are ye?"

Mac took the blindfold off the grocer.

The grocer looked up at the men standing in the back of the van. He was very frightened. The men were all dressed in navy boiler suits, black balaclavas and Wellington boots. All were armed to the teeth. One individual had two hand guns, crisscrossed bandoliers of cartridges, a shotgun and four grenades on his chest.

"Alright the joking is at an end. The lads were only having a bit of fun with you. Stand up".

The grocer stood up and Mac put him out the side door and kept hold of the rope. Mac gave the grocer a green bag full of paper (they had already robbed the grocer of his poke on principle) to wave at the travelling jug.

A Granada station wagon came down the road facing the spot where the grocery van was laying up. It beeped its horn three times, flicked the lights, and turned to park out of sight at the cross.

"Get ready lads. The bank is coming, grocer", shouted Mac to the roped man, "just wave it down nice and natural."

The travelling jug came trundling along the road. It stopped for the grocer, pulling into the side of the road. The grocer was yanked back into his van. Three men went around the side of the travelling jug. They surprised the clerk at the side door opening up. He had been travelling up front with the driver.

"Open the door and take it easy." The blagger put a pistol to the clerk's head. The clerk opened the door.

The Granada had pulled up behind the travelling jug. The blagger in that went and took the driver out of the cab. He brought him over to the grocery van. The driver and the grocer were trussed up and put at the side of the road. It only took about three minutes to collect the poke out of the travelling jug. The lads in the jug brought the clerk over beside the other two trussed men and he was similarly tied up lest he come to harm. They were all moved about twenty yards from the two vehicles so they would not be caught in the flames.

The Granada was moved up front onto the route. One vehicle was doused with a few gallons when the porkers turned the corner. They appeared as if by magic.

"Porkers", came a cry from the blaggers. It was a uniformed car, a little two door Escort.

Mickey shot the front tyres off it without even thinking. Someone put a couple of rounds into the Rad for good measure. A shotgun blast took off the blue light.

Mac started up the grocer's van and put it across the road blocking it. It stank of petrol. He saw the porker car reverse on wobbly flat front tyres. He breathed a sigh of relief. They were pulling away. He jumped out of the cab and in the next instant all the glass in the Merc van disintegrated. Rounds cracked and spat past him. The cab of the Merc was like a sieve. He took all this in at once. Someone had emptied the magazine of a sub into the cab.

"Douse the jug", screamed Mac. It was already being done. Mac raised up his M16 and slipped off the safety. He could see the mutton head with the Uzi. The porker was trying to hide behind the open door of the Escort. He could not have hid a head like his behind a barn door. Mickey crawled up beside Mac.

"Will I take him out?" asked Mickey.

"For fucks sake no, Mickey. Keep his head down until we fire the vans. OK?"

"No problem." Mickey snapped two quick shots that kicked up the dust at the porker's knees.

The porker replied by breaking cover, standing up, and firing a whole magazine at the van. Mickey had great difficulty not shooting the asshole through the thick head. He pinged two rounds very close to the porker's head. The porker then went to ground behind the Escort door. You are dead mister, thought Mickey idly. He thought the porker had been watching too many westerns. Mickey noticed the two uniformed porkers slide away along the ditch towards the cross. Sensible men. They had been driving the squad car and the porker with the sub had been hiding in the back. Nasty. Very sneaky. Blagger goes up to take the unarmed porkers and is left like a hamburger on the boreen. The armed porker tried to wriggle into a better firing position. Matt laid down a blistering fire on the other side of the squad car. Someone blew in the windscreen with a shotgun. Mickey pinged another few rounds close to the porker's head. There was silence. That seems to have taught the idiot a bit of sense, thought Mickey.

"This is the gardai. Throw down your weapons and come out wid your hands in the air. De game is hup."

Mickey could not take it in. The tears rolled down his hood. He jerked with laughter.

"Alright, now, me buckos. Yews had your chance, now yews can take the medicine." The porker fired off another wildly inaccurate burst at the van.

Mac crawled up to Mickey. He had a petrol-soaked rag in his hands. "I'm going to do the van, Mickey. Pull over to the jug. The Granada is parked about fifty yards up the road. If the porker comes through the fire take his leg off. Put him out of action. Hurt the bastard, Mickey."

"No problem."

Mac lit the rag. "Move", he yelled at the lads and flung it into the grocer's van. Nothing happened for a moment. Then the van was an inferno. Ten gallons of the best.

The grocer roared his eyes out in the ditch. Why burn the new van?

As Mac ran from the blazing grocery van Georgie fired the travelling jug. It too caught first time. The Firm ran towards the Granada parked up the road. They passed three cars full of interested locals who could not get past the road block. They had already started to reverse when the van flared up.

There were two sharp cracks. A roar and a bellow. Mickey came running, last man along the road.

"I whacked the bastard, one in each leg", he gasped out and sat into the back seat. The Granada took off smoothly and quickly.

"He came through the flames then?" asked Mac.

"Did ye expect any different?" said Mickey and then, "aye, the thick pig burst through, no problem to him. He had two mags, one taped to the other for quick change".

"He was trying to catch us in the getaway car. They are getting sneakier, Mickey", observed Mac. "Two years ago there were only ten porkers to do this entire area. None of them had a gun."

The Firm contemplated the result of taking a mag of an Uzi into the Granada. They were sitting blaggers. Squashed up like hooded sardines. The logical conclusion was to kill the porker but, then? They had only lifted about eight grand from the travelling jug. Whacked out it was about a grand per man after expenses. A scream for a dead porker for a grand a man? There were damn easier ways of making money.

"Is the porker bad Mickey?" asked Alfie. He was driving, twisting and turning around boreens and rutted cart tracks, cutting across roads, weaving along his route that was etched into his memory.

"Well put it like this, Alfie. He could not get up. He was physically incapable of running or walking. I hit him in the bone alright."

"The bleeding luck we are having", spoke up Georgie, "the bollox is liable to kick off. It's come on top of our last two strokes".

"Naw, yew are wrong there Georgie. There was plenty of life in the porker. I saw the rage in him. He was hit hard but not dead hard. He was crawling forward with his weapon. He'll live. But I'll tell yew this now lads. The sooner we hit this Big Grey Jug the better."

"Aye", agreed Bob. "We have been lucky too. The thing is boys the risk, the whack, is the same for ten punts or ten million if it's down to killing porkers."

"Well anyway lads", said Mac, "this should take the heat off Bonkie and scramble the porkers' tiny minds. Do you think they will ask him to account for his movements for this one?"

The crack brought a bit of a laugh but the Firm were subdued. The country would soon be unworkable if porkers with Uzis and two big balls began popping up in obscure crossroads guarding a lousy few grand.

"How far to the first change, Matt?"

Matt checked his route card and his Omega. He was Alfie's navigator in case the driver went off the route, which would be very serious. It might take precious minutes to get back onto it.

"Eleven minutes, Mac."

"Do you want me to push it Mac?" asked Alfie.

"No Alfie, just get us there nice and safe. We are in good time. They cannot get a whirly bird up until another half hour at least."

The Firm made their first change without incident in the ruins of an old monastery. They changed into a Transit, fitted out as a camper, and fired the Granada. No one saw them change.

In the camper George looked at the small bag of poke. There was less than eight grand in the bag. It was a disgraceful day's pay. They had lifted over a grand off the grocer too. Together it would not pay for the petrol for firing cars and vans. The camper slowed down, after fifteen miles, on a bend. It stopped and four of the Firm jumped out with the money and the gear to make their way to yet another poxy hole in the ground.

Mac and Georgie drove the last lap, abandoned the van, fired as per normal, and took off into the hills on the Bultacos.

Everyone in the Firm knew they could not last like this indefinitely.

Chapter 14

THE younger and elder porker harassed Bonkie the rest of the morning about verballing him up. Bonkie ignored them as much as possible and was as silently disagreeable as he could be. He discovered that the four corners of the ceiling had spiders' webs strung across them of great grace and style. Bonkie liked spiders. It was a curious thing but most prisoners did like spiders. Maybe it was the way they could run up the walls and then spin a silken rope and fall safely over the other side; always a very attractive skill to a man locked away. They were very independent too. Bonkie used to pull the wings off flies and throw them into the webs in his cell but the spiders never ate them. Maybe it was because they had no wings. Maybe it was akin to a butcher trying to sell you a pig with no legs.

In the exercise yard after a shower of rain the webs on the barbed wire sometimes caught the sun and became patterned rainbows. Glistening hues and contours and all with a very natural symmetry that was quite staggering if one considered the wee spider had no brain. How could it construct such little masterpieces?

"At one time in this country people like you were brought up the mountains, Byrne, and shot. No fuss. No one cared. It saved a lot of bother all round." The elder porker was getting ugly because his homespun tricky-dicky questions were falling on deaf ears. "What are you bloody looking at?" he shouted and thumped the desk.

Silence.

"He's looking at the spiders' webs, Inspector. Maybe he thinks he is a fly man."

"Byrne, we have a positive ID against you. We have a verbal admission against you. There is no doubt we will have forensic evidence too", the elder porker managed a grin, "and, before I am finished with you we will know all the details". He looked at his watch. "What you got last night was only a taste. I'm sending you back to your cell to think the whole thing over. We are going to get rough with you, Byrne. I'll give you such a hard time we won't be able to stop you talking."

Silence.

"Go and get the desk sergeant", the elder porker ordered King. He had a last go at Bonkie, "if a man's wise, Bonkie, he always buys a bit of insurance. Think about it. I'm in a position to do a lot for you".

The desk sergeant came in.

"Take this ignorant lout back to his cell. He has a lot to think about."

Bonkie was of the opinion that the heavy porkers were away over to the Legal Eagle for their lunch and that he was being sent to his cell to partake of the Bridewell lunch which is renowned for its meagreness and unfailing ability to curdle even the most hardened stomachs.

The cell door banged behind him. He sagged a little. It seemed sometimes that he had been born in a cell. The door got to even the most hardened men. The sound. The bang. The clang. The echo. It was sound, just on its own, that sometimes made men howl with frustration and fury. He had never understood why the old lags used to say 'banged up' instead of locked up. Now he knew. It was a whole series of bangs and weird prison noises that were violent manifestations of the penal system. Like the tapping of a fascist with his whip on his jackboots. The rattle of a baton on riot shields. The scream of the dive bomber. The ringing of the screws' shodded boots as they marched in step outside the cells in the early hours. The banging on the walls and bars with hammers looking for holes and cut bars.

It was all a great symphony of state violence, institutional music, conducted by faceless little men and women from the comfort of suburbia. It was in their material interests to keep prisoners in permanent confrontation within their precious 'democracy'. Prisoners were a commodity like tonnage. They had put all manner of marks and labels on men, women and children. Imprisonment was big business now. It was flourishing when most civilised, Christian countries were questioning its very concept. Some people believed that the nature of imprisonment was intrinsically immoral and incompatible with love for fellow man.

Bonkie just thought it was poxy. Everyone knew it didn't work. If they were honest they would admit it was just a place to dump in the unwanted and a place of punishment for all.

Why, he wondered, was he thinking about the Joy? He knew the law had nothing on him. Still, it was there. He didn't want to go back to jail. There was a time when such thoughts never entered his head. They were bottless nagging thoughts. If one listened to them nothing would get blagged. One thing was certain. He would rather be dead than sent down for life. That was without doubt. He had twenty grand. Not enough to get completely out, but a start. The only thing was, what did the boys really want him to do?

The porker came in with the dinner. A small tin plate with a bit of mash, a few cold peas and a slice of cold meat. A cup of the same breakfast liquid, it could not be called tea. The porker laid the dinner on the floor. Bonkie ignored it and him. The door slammed. He gritted his teeth. He kicked the slop into a corner and lit up his umpteenth smoke. There was no doubt he was under pressure, not physically, but upstairs. Rationally he knew the porkers would be unable to stitch him up.

The fact remained if enough pressure was put on them they could get him charged and remanded in custody.

Bonkie lay on the bed and tried to get a bit of kip before the afternoon session. He knew he was going to be interrogated until twelve o'clock that night and possibly longer. And the same again tomorrow until the 48 hours ended. But after that he would have a few drinks, take Sally out, and relax. Maybe plan how to spend his poke. Slamming doors, creaking musty beds, horsehair ticks, slops, shitty grey blankets, green paint. An unreal underworld peopled by giant, square-headed men, dedicated to keeping lesser mortals in their place. Prison, jail, nick, detention, imprisonment, penal servitude, the Joy, Pats, the Bog, remand, parole, Loughlan House, Shelton Abbey, Limerick Jail, Cork Gaol.

Even as he napped fitfully Bonkie alternated between his dreams and his nightmares.

He was brought down at three o'clock to a deserted Bridewell.

"In dere, Byrne", said the porker. He held open the interview room door.

Bonkie went into the room and froze. He stared at the evil-looking porker sitting behind the desk. Bonkie knew this was the man who would put him away.

"Sit down, Mr Byrne. I am Superintendent O'Stitch. I have

something to say to you." Ned extended his hand to the empty chair.

Bonkie did not move or speak.

"Very well. What I have to say will not take long. The gardai are almost convinced that you were not involved in the Ballygojingle murders. I myself have an open mind on the matter. I am sure, convinced, that you know some of the members of the gang who carried out this raid.

"I wish to proposition you, accordingly.

"Here is my proposition to you. Get for me the names of the two Northern Ireland men who operate with MacGregor and company and I will look after you in the event of you getting into any serious trouble. I can assure you of bail and, depending on what you do for me, I can get you anything from a very light sentence to immunity from prosecution.

"I want MacGregor's gang and I am prepared to pay very well to have them. If you have the balls to put them away properly, and I mean set them up on a stroke, it is worth twenty-five thousand punts to you. Cash. If you deal, you deal with me direct. I assure you of complete confidentiality. When you want to contact me call the Castle and ask for me. I will ring you back and give you a number and come to meet you.

"If you repeat this conversation to anyone I'll make it my business to put you away for a long time."

Bonkie stirred a little. He contemplated attacking O'Stitch.

"You will remember this conversation Bonkie. It is the most important one you will ever have in your life I assure you. I expect you to ring me within the week." He slid Bonkie a slip of paper across the table with the grass number on it. Bonkie stared at it with loathing. Ned lifted up the blackjack he had been swinging below the table. Bonkie would have run into trouble there and he was in no state to fight. One whack of the blackjack would have burst him wide open. His face was bad enough.

"You are either exceptionally clever, Mr Byrne, or a petty criminal who is batting out of his league. I note", said Ned hitting his palm with the blackjack, "you had enough sense not to attack me just now. Astuteness or fear of authority? Well, only time will tell. I am banking on you being a petty crook so we can get down to some serious business".

Bonkie stared at the porker with loathing.

"You see, Mr Byrne, I can see no conceivable reason why MacGregor's gang should buy you out of jail? Except you were to do them some considerable criminal favour. What did you do? I will know that in due course. My instinct, my experience tells me you are not of the calibre for robbing banks."

Bonkie managed to hang his head in mock shame. It was the hardest thing he had ever done. He was boiling. O'Stitch mistook the redness of Bonkie's face for the flush of embarrassment and not the rage of a degraded man.

Ned bashed the desk with his blackjack. The sergeant came in.

"Throw this fucking eejit out", he pointed at Bonkie. "Give him his stuff and release him."

Bonkie walked out of the interview room. He clenched his hands to stop them shaking. He breathed in deeply and out slowly. Get a grip of yourself. This porker has wound you up like a spring in five minutes. Do not react. Think. Use your head. Think the worst. They are going to hit you with a murder charge outside the gate. Keep cool. Nothing to say. No. Say, I am completely innocent.

"Sign here, Byrne", said the desk sergeant. He handed Bonkie an envelope containing his possessions. His fifty quid was missing. There was a receipt there from Jimmy Apple. He signed.

"Your missus is here, Byrne."

Bonkie turned around at Ned O'Stitch's voice. The porker was searching for Bonkie's soft spot. Sally was standing by the barred gate with wee Saorise. They were beautiful. Logically Bonkie should have given Sally a dose of abuse to show he didn't care but he couldn't. He went over to the gate.

"Open it up if yer releasing me otherwise let me back to the cell."

The porker opened the gate. Bonkie stepped through. He picked up his kid.

"How did yer get down here? I mean how did yer know I was being released?" he asked Sally.

"I drove her down Mr Byrne." Ned winked at him through the gate. He turned to Sally. "If he ever gets in trouble, Mrs Byrne, you let me know and I'll see what I can do."

Sally knew Bonkie was on the verge of throwing a whizzer. When he lost control there was no stopping him.

"Come on Bonkie", she tugged him away. Saorise began to cry. Bonkie patted the child's hair. He turned like a man made of ice and walked along the tunnel to the world outside.

"I'll bleeding blow that bastard's head off, I swear I will." They were outside the tax offices. "What were you doing?"

"You better listen to me good Bonkie. That policeman arrested me and the child. He's winding you up and he's doing a good job. Now cool it. Don't start fighting with me. Please." She looked pale and drawn, ready to weep.

"Did you fall, daddy?" asked Saorise. She touched his swollen face with her tiny hand.

"You, you are in bits Bonkie. I, I thought", Sally got her handkerchief and dabbed her eyes.

"Yes, little chicken", said Bonkie to the child, "I fell down the stairs". He pulled Sally close to him with his other arm and whispered to her, "I'm sorry, Sal. That porker was trying to get me to be a grass. Don't cry now. Yer know it breaks me heart ter see yer cry." He nibbled her ear.

Sally felt him stiffen again. She looked around. Ned O'Stitch's car crawled past. Ned was staring at Bonkie and his family. Bonkie felt there was something obscene the way the porker was weighing him up.

"Are you going to give me a kiss too?" asked the small girl.

The child had a calming, stabilising effect on Bonkie. She brought a bit of sweetness into a hard world. He gave her a gooser on the cheek.

"Yer know Sal she must get her looks from you. She is a little beauty."

Sally and small Saorise both were pleased at Bonkie's compliment. They went into Hughes' pub.

"Have yer any bread, Sally?" She handed him a tenner.

"That's our lot. You got no labour this week. Are you going to sign on?"

"No, I got a few bob." He gave her a conspiratorial wink. "Give us a pint, a packet of crisps and a lemonade." The barman went off. "What do yer want Sal?"

"A pint of harp."

"And a pint of harp", he called to the barman. They sat down.

Sally let him get a couple of pints into him before she told him.

"The gaff is in a bit of a mess, Bonkie."

"Tell me now and get it bleeding over with Sal." He knew she was stalling.

"Early this morning the door came in on top us. A gang of men carrying weapons. I didn't know who they were. They said they had a search warrant but I never saw it."

"Have you been", said Bonkie interrupting, "in the porker's shop all that time?"

"They took me to Fitzgibbon Street. I had to take Saorise with me. There was no one to look after her. They were screaming about yer. Really bad stuff. They said they were going ter do yer. I'm frightened Bonkie. They locked us in a cell for a couple of hours then that nice man came and made them take us out."

"What bleeding nice man?"

"The one who let yer go. I told him yer never done the Ballygojingle thing. He said he believed me. He said no one understood yer and yer never had a proper start in life."

"Jesus Christ. Young fella bring us a pint of harp and a large rum. Go on Sal." There was the beginning of a grin on Bonkie.

"He gave the men who wrecked the gaff an awful telling off. Then he drove us over ter get yer out. He thought Saorise was a lovely child."

"Jesus Christ. Sal, see that fat frog O'Stitch he would frame his bleeding auld one. He's the dirtiest bollox in Dublin Castle. He, HE sent the porkers to do the gaff. Don't yer understand? HE had yer lifted. Yer should never, never, believe a bleeding porker. How many times have I to tell yer?"

"But he seemed to be – he gave the child sweets."

"Where are they?"

Sally pulled out a big tube of smarties from her bag. The child made a go for them.

"Poison, they are poisoned." Bonkie snatched the tube of smarties. There were a lot of people in the pub who knew Bonkie well. They stared at him. Hughes' did most of the District Court trade. The child began to cry for the sweets.

"Jesus Christ." He gave them to the child. A paper boy came in with the early press. Sally bought one off him. The raid on the travelling jug was banner headlines. **GARDA SHOT IN RAID.**

"Give me the paper Sal." Bonkie scanned the article quickly. He knew at once it was the lads. He turned the pages. "Where is the pictures page?"

"I'll get it. You'll knock over the drinks." Sally went to the entertainments.

"I'll clean up Sal and we will take in a picture. What do yer say?" He went close up and snuggled into her and they studied the pictures. The child was pleased to see them touch and laugh.

The sneaky porker who had followed Bonkie into the pub saw nothing unusual in the reading of the paper. He was a skinny looking auld fella rescued from retirement because of his non-porker like features. He could have been anyone's poor old grandpa.

"I think we won't be able ter go until the middle of the week, Bonkie. We have to clean up the gaff and we are broke. That's our last tenner."

"Is the gaff bad?"

"It was when I left and they were only starting."

Vandalism to cover up the bugging of the gaff. Bonkie reflected on the expertise of the Firm. They had pulled a stroke to take the heat off him. The very least he could do was obey their instructions. To grow bleeding up and not let a bit of a hiding and a bollox of a porker be freaking him out.

"Alright little chicken, let's go home", Bonkie lifted up the child. "Are you right Sal?"

Bonkie carried the child out of the pub on his shoulders. Outside on the way past the markets he began to play aeroplanes with Saorise. The child loved it. Swishing and dipping towards the ground. It was scary but she felt secure in her daddy's strong arms. Her giggles rang out along the street.

"Again, again, daddy."

The surveillance porkers, trained by no other than the pig mecca, Scotland Yard, scratched their heads and wondered what in gangland was going on?

The flat was in terrible condition before the porkers had a go at it. It was officially listed as condemned, unfit for human habitation. It was in such bad nick and in such a bad area that the Corporation refused to accept rent for it and had no interest in having Bonkie and Sally evicted for squatting. Bonkie had fixed it up as best he could. He had replastered the walls, replaced the corrugated iron shutters with windows. He had re-plumbed the entire place, connected up the electricity and killed off all the rats and mice. Well, all the ones with tails. It was a good thing that Bonkie had done this because they may have mistaken John Paul for the pied piper when his cavalcade drove past the building and scurried after the entourage of venerable dignitaries. Directly across from the slum building was the local church soaring high into the sky. Bonkie had once screwed the safe out in the back offices but there was so much uproar, auld ones putting curses on whoever done it and such like, he had never gone back. It had been a handy touch.

Gurrier came barking out from behind the pile of broken furniture strewn in the room. There was only one room really, a tiny kitchen and an equally small jakes. The gaff looked even more dismal and dilapidated than when Bonkie had first jemmied in the door. Gurrier waved his stumpy tail. He was the best ratter in the tenements. Bonkie scratched the Jack Russell between the ears. The dog was glad to see them.

"Take her up to Old Ma Tin, Sally, and let her play." Bonkie pointed to Saorise. The child stared at the remnants of what, until then, had been for her a happy and secure place.

"Come on, Saorise", Sally took her hand, "your granny wants to see you".

"I want to stay with me daddy." The child clung to Bonkie's trousers.

"Go up and see your Granny sweetheart. I'll come up and get you. You can bring Gurrier up to bite her poxy auld cat."

Sally shook her head. "You are terrible." The child was anxious to go up and huss the dog on the cat. Sally took her up to the eccentric old woman who had refused, defied everyone, to have her shifted into an old age cubicle. The tenement she lived in was run down but she did not see it in its sordid condition. She saw it as the happy place it was, full of life, spilling over with laughter and tears. This was where she reared her family. This was where she had come as a virgin bride with her man. All her existence was within the four walls. How do you write a nostalgic reply on an impertinent form that threatens an old woman with jail if she tells a lie? How do you relate the strength of memory, the comfort in old familiar things? They called her Old Ma Tin because she had thrown the sheets of corrugated iron off the roof when the Corporation men had knocked off for the day. The district, what was left of it, had wakened to the sound of falling iron. Old Ma Tin was seen on the flat roof hurling down the sheets, roaring to the four winds about the

Corporation and their tin sheets.

They left her alone after that secure in the knowledge she would just peter out or become senile and have to be shifted by the doctor. But Old Ma Tin was over ninety and was still going very strong. Eventually everyone had forgotten about her. Weeds sprang up around the slum and it sank into the state of irreversible decay. The building gave up the ghost and began to die along with the rest of the inner city.

The vultures perched on their high speculators' stools and bided their time until the people had been transported out to the new slums. They waited patiently, but with confidence, for the places of habitation to fall empty one by one until a wasteland had been created. Until the buildings were only fit for the bulldozer and out of the rubble would rise the towering office blocks, the new city-centre shops and hotels, the penthouse suites, the pay off for the faithful. When that time came Old Ma Tin and the squatter, Bonkie, would be dragged from their slums by the porkers and flung onto the side of the road. They called it the Forcible Entry and Occupation Act or a Court Order that the flat was condemned. During the evictions of old, the Bailiff's men used to nail a bit of paper onto the cottage door before they smashed it to pieces and evicted the peasants.

For the time that was left before development Bonkie, Old Ma Tin and the like were left to exist without any harassment. The mohair suit gang did not want any undue adverse publicity.

Sally came down from the old woman's place. Saorise got on great with the old lady. She had considered bringing her up there earlier on that morning. As she looked at the mess she was glad she had not. The old woman had a lot of old nick-nacks up there. The spacers who had broken up her flat would surely have done the same to the old woman's stuff. Whoever had broken up the flat had gone berserk. There were gouge marks in the walls. The ceiling had been punctured with hammer blows. Crazy stuff. Bonkie was in the middle of the heap of furniture. He was sorting out the bedding. It was in a mess, Corn Flakes, milk, the contents of the fridge flung about the heap.

"That's yer nice man for yer, Sally." Bonkie put his finger to his ear to show her the place was bugged. Sally copped on. Bonkie went into the tiny jakes. He ran the water in the sink. He waved Sally into the jakes. Bonkie sat on the bowl and Sally sat in his lap. Her softness, just her closeness, put him on a happy buzz. She felt him growing. At a time like this, too. Bonkie got very close to her ear. "The place is bugged", he whispered. "If I talk nonsense just go along with me, OK?"

Sally nodded. More bleeding hassle. She was sick of it. She went to get up, to draw away from him.

"I have enough, Sal, to buy us a gaff." He said this very softly.

She looked at him sharply. Neither of them spoke for a couple of seconds. The water gurgled away and put the bug out of action. He wasn't lying. She knew him, he wasn't that cruel. Not to her.

Bonkie silently crossed his heart and hoped to die if he told his sweetheart a lie.

She saw the sparks of hope, real hope, in his eyes. She saw in him the pride of bringing home the prize. It would be cruel to deny him the bit of praise he was due. He expected it. Sometimes he really was a small boy the way he got on about things. She gave in and pushed away the heavy weight that was eating away inside her. Sally straddled him, grinding her bum into his hard groin, and rubbing him with her breasts. It was a game to them, a sexual game. She kissed her fingers and put a kiss on his lips. The sink was overflowing. Sally jumped up and turned it off.

"Bleeding hell, Sal", protested Bonkie.

"Later Bonkie. Don't yer think we should have a bed?"

The place wasn't as bad as it seemed. They put the bed up on books. Saorise slept in a big cradle which was not broken, only upturned. The TV they didn't care about. Bonkie could always nick another one. Likewise with the stereo. It took them about an hour to get the gaff into a livable condition. Bonkie went up and thanked Old Ma Tin. Saorise was fast asleep and he carried her down the foul, damp, dark, rat infested stairs. Gurrier scurried behind and skipped into the flat.

"One bleeding day sunshine", whispered Bonkie to his sleeping daughter, "you'll have yer own gaff in the sticks with yer own garden and I'll make yer a swing".

The child smiled in her sleep and put her arm around his neck. Bonkie carried her into the swathe of yellow light that cut into the blackness.

The heavy door to his flat slammed shut and plunged the stairway into slum black. The rats came out of their holes and ran up and down the steps, in and out of boarded-up flats, sniffing here and there, scavenging, shitting and pissing, leaving infection and disease as they went.

The bolts slammed home and Gurrier took up guard at the door. Bonkie was locked in for the night.

Chapter 15

CRINION held a do at his elegant home to celebrate his son being called to the Bar. He used the opportunity to introduce O'Stitch to the O'Mally-Smyths. It was almost the end of May but Crinion did not have the good weather he had expected. The rain fell heavily and constantly all that Sunday and the marquee on the lawn was a bit of a damp squib. Crinion employed a firm of caterers to the aspiring domestic gentry and they laid out on the long, linen-clad trestles, a first class buffet. The centre piece of the buffet was a roasted suckling pig. It had two olives for eyes and an apple stuck in its mouth.

The many porkers Crinion had invited thought the pig was a cute little fellow and none had the heart to eat him.

O'Stitch stared at the stuck pig with his inscrutable frogs eyes. He had no appetite for anything. It was almost six weeks now since the Ballygojingle job and the burning of the mobile bank at Ballygobackwards and he still had not a notion as to who the Belfast men were. MacGregor's gang had shown up one by one, in obscure places, and had surrendered themselves to the local gardai with their lawyers and barristers. Of course they had kept their mouths shut, who wouldn't? And had walked out again free to rob and plunder again.

O'Stitch contemplated on the effectiveness of the interrogation methods used by certain Latin-American states. The criminal did not keep his mouth shut over there and laugh at the law. Bonkie Byrne had proved to be a washout, as big a washout as the driving rain that rattled off the tent. Ned downed his brandy. A white-jacketed waiter brought him another. Byrne had not even given his name on the two occasions Ned had ordered him picked up. Ned had, in desperation, threatened Jimmy Apple with removal of his licence to practise law if he did not produce the names of the men he wanted. Jimmy Apple burst into tears at Ned's threats. He was a spineless, pathetic degenerate.

O'Stitch was under bad pressure not only from the interfering politicos, but now also under fire from within the Force itself. After the shooting of the garda at Ballygobackwards the backstabbing had began in earnest. And after all the subversives and blaggers he had put away. It was a national characteristic never to say a good word about another Irishman. Ned had been able, due to his spectacular success in the forensic fields, to monopolise the best resources of the Force. This had caused resentment and petty jealousy by the more conservative officers whose thunder Ned had stolen.

If he lost his place at the top of the porker ladder SS might well decide to patronise someone else. Ned had been able, after a gigantic porker battle up in the Phoenix Park, to persuade the Commissioner to give all SS vans round the clock armed protection. This decision amounted to millions of punts.

The immediate result, after a couple of very nasty surprises, was that gangland blanked all SS vans. The blaggers would not touch them with an M60. The money harvesters soon copped on and gave their business to SS. Two major security firms went out of business. They could not compete. SS gobbled them up. Only the shoestring companies were left operating and all they had were the leavings, guarding building sites and corporation houses. Virtually all poke in the country was being shifted by SS.

O'Stitch stared out across the lawn. The tall elms along the driveway bent over in the wind. It was more like a November day than the beginning of June. A foul day whatever. A day to match his mood.

"Ned, there you are." The voice came from behind the porker. "Here are some people I want you to meet." Crinion's voice had taken on a different accent.

Ned turned. The woman he looked at was stunning. Much, much, more than beautiful. Fair hair fell naturally from her slim neck to spill around her leopard skin stole. She was cold in the damp tent. Her green eyes appraised Ned. The porker detected in the look a grab for life. A zest. The woman had a very sensual aura about her. Ned was struck by the immediate notion that he would be very pleased to have her suck his cock. He brushed aside the ridiculous thought, knowing she would not even look at him sexually, and remembered his good manners. He managed a bit of a smile.

"This is Patrick and Delores O'Mally-Smyth, Ned." Crinion was flushed with success. A bit of life had warmed up his grey foldy flesh. And then as if he were introducing the sea lions at Duffy's Circus he pointed to Ned and announced, "and this is Superintendent Edward O'Stitch, our own Sherlock Holmes".

Ned almost swallowed his glass. He coughed up his brandy. Crinion was well jarred.

Delores extended her hand to Ned, "I am most pleased to meet you, I'm sure".

"Pleased to meet you Superintendent", Patrick shook with the porker.

"Ah, call me Ned, please. Everyone else does even the lads up in the Joy."

"Patrick", confided Crinion, "works at the Central Bank".

Ned noted that. He was aware that Crinion was introducing him for a reason.

"Very interesting", replied Ned inanely.

The woman burst out giggling. Patrick shot her a sharp glance. She had promised to be good today. It wasn't much to ask her to keep up bloody appearances.

Ned had a feeling he had seen the banker before somewhere. He had definitely seen this man before but he could not remember when. He brushed the thought aside. Delores had contrived to lower her stole a little and expose her bosom. She was one classy lady. She was pissed off with the prim hypocritical party. All it lacked were a couple of Bishops to liven it up. The wives were atrocious altogether and the men with their sneaky 'I'd love to fuck you' looks behind their backs. She had been propositioned twice in the first half hour by some very persistent pillars.

Ned stared at Delores quite frankly. He was curious as to why she was embarrassing her husband. Was she an exhibitionist? Delores wanted to run along the buffet and do a striptease. She wanted to do the most outrageous things possible in this damp tent full of dead, pious, forelock touching, zombies. She wanted to interrupt the knots of porkers' and bankers' wives and tell them that tomorrow she would be leaving Dublin for two weeks in Rome with the Minister. Two weeks of art galleries, the opera, good music, good food, drugs, plenty of sex and rock and roll. She began to titter at the very thought. Could you imagine their faces?

"Delores", chided Patrick. He was blushing.

"It is a party you know, Pat, not a board meeting. I have to powder my nose I'm afraid." She looked out at the small pink mansion.

"I'll get you an umbrella, Delores", said the host, "bloody rain".

"Perhaps the Superintendent will escort me across the lawn. I shall feel safe in the arms of the law."

"My pleasure mam", replied Ned. He was quite enjoying himself.

"There are brollies by the flap, Ned." Crinion and O'Mally-Smyth went to mingle with the crowd of revellers.

Ned held the golf brolly into the wind. Delores hung onto his thick arm. O'Stitch was the ugliest man there. She had been quite pleased, for whatever perverse reason, to walk out of the tent with him. The wives' heads swivelled as if they were on rollers.

"What do you think of the party, Ned?"

"It's going very well I thought."

"Liar", she looked up into his face. He exuded power this ugly man.

"I am not under oath, fortunately. You are very observant young lady. The party is a f, er, a."

"A fuck up. The party is a fuck up." Delores staggered a little.

"I am twenty eight years old, you know", she added. "I am over the age of consent." She didn't know why she had said that. It just came out. They were at the back door of the mansion. Delores went in and shook her hair. Ned took down the brolly and stepped into the large kitchen.

"I'll only be a tick, Ned. Be a dear and wait for me. There's booze up there", she pointed to a shelf.

Ned smiled and waved her away. He was exceedingly curious about Mrs O'Mally-Smyth. She had aroused his interest as well as his desire. He had not had feelings such as these since he was a young courting lad all those years ago.

Delores shook out a tiny piece of coke onto the side of the marble bath. Very carefully she chopped it up with a razor blade. It was really good coke. She had bought an ounce of it in the States. The coke fuelled her zest, her appetite for life. Delores wanted to cram as much living into her time as possible. She rolled up a ten pound note and sniffed up the two thin lines, one for each nostril. She curled and stretched. She licked her painted lips. She looked at herself in the full length mirror. She lifted up her dress and wriggled out of her pants and made a series of poses. She knelt on the ground and watched herself masturbate climaxing very quickly, very sweetly, very strong. It was not enough. She opened the door softly.

"Ned, will you come here for a moment please?"

O'Stitch walked along the small corridor. The door was ajar. He knocked.

"Come in", she said. The coke had taken away her inhibitions.

O'Stitch stepped through the door. It closed behind him. He turned and the blood in him soared. Delores stood by the door subconsciously barring his exit. Her pants were around her high shoes. She said nothing but slid to her knees and ran her hands up and down Ned's legs searching, urgently groping for his cock. She opened his fly and unbuckled his thick belt. His long stiff cock sprang out pointed up towards her face. It could not be harder. She started at the bottom of his shaft gently nibbling then making long sweeping licks with her tongue. Delores gripped the shaft in her hands and gently pulled Ned's cock back and forth, back and forth. She sank her lips over the end of his cock and sucked in time to her pulling faster and faster and faster. Ned strained and his hot seed filled her mouth and she swallowed it greedily. She climaxed again herself, this time flinging up her dress exposing herself, showing the ugly man her fingers and her pussy. Ned's cock stayed where it was. She licked him clean. His cock was as hard as when he started.

Delores stood up abruptly and pulled up her knickers. She turned to the mirror and began to smooth herself down. Ned stood gasping. His senses were still reeling. Delores opened the door and walked out.

Ned put his cock away. He had been used and discarded. The porker washed his face and hands to cool down. He went out into the kitchen. She was there waiting for him.

"Shall we go, Superintendent?" Her eyes were mocking him, as if to say, what did you expect? A biddy to lay on her back and open her legs for you?

Ned took her arm and opened up the brolly. The pair walked sedately across the lawn. It had stopped raining.

Sgt Potter, Special Branch, stepped out of the small pantry room off the kitchen and beside the jakes. His hand was shaking as he opened his notebook. On reflection he closed it up. This was dynamite. He had been detailed by Chief Superintendent MacIntrigue to watch Ned at the party to see what was cooking so to speak. He had casually followed the pair across the lawn and had entered by another door. When Ned had gone into the jakes he had followed. The gasping and heavy breathing was very plain. He did not know what the Boss was going to make of this. And your woman looked so la de da. So God Almighty snooty. What was the country coming to? Between senior policemen fornicating in toilets with other men's wives and robbers attacking holy places with rockets, it seemed at times as if they all lived in a big green banana republic. He went in and checked the jakes and found traces of the coke. The Branchman was deeply worried. He put the couple of grains into an envelope and returned to the tent. The party was in full swing. He was just in time to see O'Stitch leaving. He stayed on. Officially he was there to snoop on Crinion, who had invited him as an old friend, but he had known what the Boss had meant and had snooped anyone who talked to Crinion. The Branchman decided to have a drink for fate, he had been drinking tonic water, because the information could either make him or break him, all depending on how it was used.

Bonkie began to get a bit paranoid after the Firm had not contacted him for a couple of weeks. He began to get notions they had fucked off with his poke. What could he do? He had been told to go about his normal business with one important proviso – he was not to stroke. Nothing. Things were getting tight. The culchie bitch at the labour had made things hard for him asking him weird stuff about his first wife and where was he on such and such a date. He couldn't tell her he was on a blag, could he? The bitch had looked at his battered up head and insulted him. Just like a porker. Tried to degrade him. Maybe she heard I done this place a couple of times. Or was it three? He had left the labour empty handed and went back to the gaff. He liked living in Sean MacDermott Street. It was handy to all the best strokes. Sally had turned the place into a decent kip in no time. She was a good woman. Too good for the likes of him, well, so her auld one kept screaming. She was mad to get Sally and Saorise to go and live with her. Turn the kid into a nun or something with her mumbo-jumbo. Bonkie had told Sally not to be taking bread off the auld one, it came with a lecture on hard work and frugality, but he knew she did when Saorise needed gear. He could not object if he couldn't get it for her. Bonkie held up the bag of mixed corn and shook it at the child. He had got it on credit in the pet shop in Parnell Street.

"Are we going to feed the pigeons, daddy?" yelled the child. She ran to him.

"Yer come on." He lifted her up. Sal wasn't saying too much. Bonkie thought it was because he hadn't produced the poke. Maybe he was spoofing her. "I'm just going to feed the birds Sal."

"I'll have yer dinner when yer get down. Don't you get mucky young lady."

"Oh, I won't mammy. And my daddy will wash his hands too. Won't you daddy?"

She patted the child and gave Bonkie a peck on the cheek.

"Are yer in the big D, Sal?"

"Just in me moodies that's all. Push off Bonkie and you miss Muffet. I'll be fine." She closed the door on him. What could she say to him? That he was not providing for them? That he was eating the kid's clothes? He would scream out and pull the first move at hand. That's the way they had him wound up. Nothing could be discussed rationally. It was all the manipulation of conditioned emotions. Her ma was putting on the pressure to move out to Finglas. Where, said Bonkie? That's in bleeding China! The people around here did not accept her either especially when he was inside. Very clannish and sometimes very petty. The wrecking of the flat such as it was. Bonkie's arrest. If he had the money to buy a gaff he must have pulled the Ballygojingle job. It was alright if he robbed a few banks as far as she was concerned but the murder hunt, the heavies and the hysteria were a different scene. And Bonkie was behaving very secretly too. Hiding things from her. He said it was to protect her. Protect her from what? Him? She stared out the window. Saorise could not live here not with the condition of the place. The worry gnawed away at her guts. She would have to go and see the doctor and get something to make her sleep. She couldn't sleep in a place that she knew people were listening into. What was she going to tell the doctor? She had better get something for her nerves while she was going.

Bonkie had a fine loft on the roof. If the building had not been condemned the Corporation would have made him pull it down. Back to front nonsense. When he was inside an old boy from the flats across the way looked after the birds for him. Sally did not like going onto the roof and scraping out pigeon shit. He could not fault her for that. Either you liked pigeons or yer didn't.

The child loved it up on the roof. Bonkie kept the roof spotless like his loft and Saorise played happily up there. He had carried up enough soil and bags of peat to make a roof garden. It was a bright oasis in a bland concrete desert. The birds cooed happily at his approach. They knew him well. Bonkie dropped his bag of corn and dashed to the loft. Someone had been there. He had left the top bar on to stop the kids getting in. It was undone. For one horrible moment he thought that some rotten kids had thrown a cat in, or, got into the loft and wrung his birds. He was through the door very quickly. The birds were fine. He sat Saorise down. The child went and sat on an old chair in the corner not to disturb the feeding of the birds. She was a bright child remembering the agreement Bonkie had made with her when she was really tiny. Bonkie began to refill the water containers and sprinkle corn into the nesting boxes and feeding trays. He went past his rows of paired birds. In the last nesting box in the red clay breeding bowl was a bundle of twenty pound notes and a message. Bonkie opened the cage and lifted the poke out. The note said, 'see you soon – grow a beard'. He counted the poke. One thousand pounds exactly.

"Did the pigeons lay the pound notes daddy?" asked Saorise.

"No, no that was a hen and the golden bleeding egg." His head was whirling, plotting. The Firm must be OK. He knew they would not let him down. One more stroke like this and he was out.

"But sure we haven't got a hen daddy. Only pigeons. We only have pigeons."

Bonkie shoved his poke down his underpants. He went over and lifted up his kid. Women were always watching, always on the alert. He could imagine the kid telling her sweet little friends at the creche her daddy's pigeons laid pound notes. The loft would be torn to bleeding bits before she got back home.

"And there was the nutter tree that grew a golden pear. And what else? Let me see, oh yeah, the pig that laid golden handcuffs, and the screw that laid the golden key..."

"But what's a screw daddy?"

"It's a scary monster that takes little boys and girls into its den and makes them eat lumpy porridge with salt in it, that's what." He tickled the child with her hair.

"Oooooooh", she pretended to be frightened.

"And it makes them wash all day long and it won't let them out to play or go home for their dinner."

"Oooooh daddy what will we do?"

"Well, I suppose we shall have to make a magic spell or something. I know. Close your eyes. I'll ask Hungry Horace and he'll tell us a magic spell. Now no peeking. Promise?"

"Oh I promise." The child covered her eyes and peeked through her fingers.

Bonkie lifted out a bull checker of no distinction save it had a mighty appetite for corn. It was a big bully of a cock bird. He spoke to the pigeon and answered himself in a squeaky voice.

"Hungry Horace tell us a spell. What shall we do to keep the screw from taking us into its den?"

"Eat plenty of ice-cream and fruit", squeaked the pigeon.

"Ugh, we will not do that. I don't like ice-cream and fruit."

"But I do, daddy", whispered Saorise, "I do".

"And yer have to buy a little girl a new doll and call it Shaky Shovelling Shimmering Sloppy Sammy", squeaked the pigeon.

"Go way outta that wid yer", said Bonkie to Hungry Horace, "or I'll pluck yer and roast yer in the oven. No one wants a doll". He put the bird back into his cage.

"Yes there is daddy", whispered Saorise.

"Who?" whispered Bonkie looking around.

"Me", whispered the little girl.

"Alright but first yer have to help me let these birds out for a bit of exercise. Open those cages and let them fly."

The child opened the bottom cages and Bonkie did the top. The birds on the perches sensed he was going to open the trap. The trap was opened and they shooed out the birds. The loft emptied. Bonkie went outside with the child and they watched for a while as the birds circled the roof until they had gained enough height to fly above the highest building. They looked well. The dove, the lark, freedom. The birds took off. He didn't know where to. It was their choice if they chose to come back. He locked the loft and left the trap open.

"What is it Sal?"

"Coddle. Are yer ready for it?"

"Turn it off and save it for tomorrow. Coddles always better after it sits for a while."

"What are we going to eat?"

"Ice-cream mammy. Hungry Horace said so."

"What are you telling her, Bonkie? Whose Hungry Horace? I don't know."

"Come on Sal. I'll treat yer to ray and chips? What do yer say?"

"Don't ask me twice Bonkie. I haven't been out of here these nine months."

"Go and get changed, Saorise."

They didn't go to the chipper but to the Chinese and had a nice meal. Saorise had ice-cream and fruit. Bonkie slipped the poke to Sal under the table.

"There's a few bob for yer, Sal. I couldn't get it sooner. Slip out and put it in the Building Society before it closes."

"How much is there?" she asked.

"Seven hundred and fifty. I have another two hundred here for the housekeeping, off yer go now."

Sally slipped across the road and put the poke away nice and safe. Bonkie watched her from the window of the restaurant. He was glad to see her return safely. This area was full of snatchers. She had not been followed either.

Jimmy Apple came up with an answer to his problem after a restless night's sleep. He scurried along to a public house where members of a well-known organisation were known to carouse. He made discreet enquiries of a deaf, one-legged barman, and was told to wait. Presently a greasy man, who wore the checkered headdress of the Palestinian freedom fighter as a scarf, viewed him from the bar. The greasy man looked at Jimmy suspiciously and drank a pint of stout without taking it from his lips. He wiped his lips on the headdress then waved Jimmy up to the bar. Jimmy waddled up.

"Are you?" asked Jimmy not daring to mention it.

The greasy man rolled his eyes in his head then pointed firmly to his empty pint glass.

Jimmy, not wanting the man to believe him devious or indeed unpatriotic, bought him a pint. "I want to see..."

The greasy man tapped his ear with one hand, lowered down the pint with his other hand, yet still communicated to Jimmy that he dare not say anything. With a series of rolling eye movements he made known his desire for another pint. The deaf, one-legged barman brought the pint of stout without consulting Jimmy. He berated Jimmy until he was paid.

"I want to see the Chief of Staff", blurted Jimmy.

The greasy man went deathly pale. He drank the pint smoothly, slammed the pint down onto the table, then tore around the empty public house. He checked it all out including the ladies' jakes just in case there were a bunch of Brits in drag hiding in there. It was all clear. There was a fresh pint waiting for the greasy man at the counter. He gripped it like an Armalite and put it away. He slunk over to the door, looked outside, up and down South William Street, then waved Jimmy outside.

Jimmy sat into the car. He was surprised when the greasy man sat in beside him and the car pulled off. It was being driven away with no one in the driver's seat.

"What's going on?" screamed Jimmy.

"We'll ask the questions", came a voice from the front seat.

Jimmy looked over the seat and saw the smallest man ever to drive a car. The midget was wearing a leprechaun mask. "I didn't know you had the little people working for you", said Jimmy. He slumped back into the seat.

"Funny bastard", came a squeaky voice from the front seat.

Jimmy remembered thinking 'how does his wee feet reach the pedals?' before the greasy man put a foul smelling hood over his head and shoved a revolver into Jimmy's rumbling guts.

"You never mind who works for us", the greasy man burped and Jimmy smelt the Guinness he had just bought the lout, "now why do ye want to see the CS?"

"I'm making enquiries about two Belfast men. They may have been involved in the Ballygojingle job. I have", said Jimmy, "a proposal which the Movement may consider to their advantage".

"Don't shoot him whatever you do, Brendan", shouted the midget. The car lurched forward in a burst of speed.

How did he see over the dash?

"Oh, we won't shoot him yet." The greasy man poked Jimmy a bit with his gun then relented. He had been decent enough to buy a few jars. He couldn't be bad.

"Me father slept with the auld crowd", screamed Jimmy.

"Ah sure did you hear him", mocked the greasy man to the midget, "isn't he one of our own?"

Chapter 16

THE money that Bonkie gave to Sally relieved a lot of the immediate pressures on the gaff. It was good for her to be able to buy whatever she needed especially for Saorise. Bonkie was astounded at the price of children's requisites. He had never really bought much before, always preferring to get what he needed through the more traditional methods.

Bonkie settled down and was relaxed and happy and, what surprised Sally, he was not out at all hours screwing and snatching. She attributed this to the secret novenas she had been saying for the domestication of her impulsive lover. If Bonkie knew she was over in the chapel lighting candles for him he would go off his head. Sally had no moral qualms about taking blagged poke. The way she had it all sussed out, life was all one big rip off and everybody sucked everybody else's blood to survive. And, yer have to live. The Commandments were not written to keep the poor down. If they were used as a cynical code to legitimise exploitation then the whole thing was rotten from the top. Bonkie refused to discuss the whole thing. They had an argument once and he got pissed and gone and thrown empty stout bottles through the windows of the PP's new house. She never discussed religion with him after that. She thanked God that they had found a little happiness.

One day he came back and started strengthening the door with a steel plate. He cut a bolt hole in the kitchen floor into the rotten, bricked up, basements.

"Let's go out for a bit of air, Sal." He put the gun down his pants.

"What's going on, Bonkie?" They were away from the accursed bugs.

"There is a bit of aggro, that's all. If anyone knocks at the door, never open it if I'm not there, Sal. If they try and get in we can escape into the basement."

"Who for God's sake? What have yer bloody done?" She was shaking.

"I can't tell yer" He hugged her. "Ah, Sal, I was looking at a small gaff that might just suit us. I'll have me poke soon and then..."

She knew he was appeasing her. She saw Alfie in the distance sitting on the wall beside the North Wall Road. Even this walk in the park with her and his kid was a ruse. They were his cover.

"Bonkie why don't yer give it all up now? If yer have the money why not open a small business. A little shop. That's what yer always wanted. We could buy a gaff straight in a few years. Saorise is starting school soon."

"There is only one more stroke Sal. Just one and then..."

She didn't even listen to him. How many times had she listened to the blaggers' dream? El Dorado. The Crock of Gold. Treasure Island. Cuckoo Land. Walter Mitty. He was talking small boy adventure and was up at the slightest noise from the dog to blow away anyone who came to the door. They were trapped in a rat infested slum, waiting for men to come and shoot them. It was too much. And they could not even fight about it. The place was supposed to be bugged. She walked off.

"Sal, hang on there a minute." He was looking at Alfie waving urgently at him.

She ignored him and walked off with the child. She was going to collect up the kid's stuff and her own and go to her mother's. The child began to scream for her da. He didn't follow them and hold them and say he was sorry and that he would stop while he was free and able to love them. That's all they wanted. When he didn't do it she began to cry too. A woman and a child sobbing their way along the North Strand.

When she reached the flat her sorrow had turned to anger. She left a note. 'Gone to China to the Boxer', (he said her mother looked like a boxer dog) 'if yer want us back – wise up, and get a gaff. Love, Sally'. She knew the note would wreck his head but he was better doing the rest of his few months than ending up as a stiff. She left him the dog for company.

He hadn't got time to run after moody bleeding women. He jogged over towards Alfie. Opening a bleeding sweety shop, my bollox. Little dolls' houses.

Alfie handed him a motorcycle helmet. Bonkie put it on and they were off on the big Honda speeding out along the Northside, opening up the big machine along the Malahide Road. Alfie twisted and turned taking a route that only another bike could take. No other bike followed them. They ended up at the back of the mobile home at Portmarnock. The Firm were all there.

"How are yer, Bonkie?" called Georgie.

"Nice to see yew", said young Matt.

"You are looking well boy."

Bonkie was welcomed back into the fold. He had proved to be a sound man. He detected the grim atmosphere. There were bad vibes here. They were all tooled up too.

"What's the score lads? Are we blagging?" They had told him there was going to be a big stroke coming up and to watch the door. They had given him the 357 Magnum to protect the gaff. No problems. He had done that, now here he was ready to work. Ready to get it over with.

"The question is Bonkie, are you ready to blag?" said Mac. He looked depressed.

"What do yer mean? There's nothing wrong with my bleeding bottle, Mac."

"That's not what I mean, Bonkie. The big stroke we were looking at. It's all down to you. You are the only bloke who can pull it off."

"And that's why yer sprung me?"

"That's right."

"I thought as much. I knew yer didn't do it because yer fancied me. Let's have it. If it can be done I'm bleeding game." Bonkie was eager. He reflected. "How much is the stroke worth?"

"More than yew can imagine, Bonkie", replied Mickey.

He received a few hostile looks. Bonkie wondered what stunt he had pulled.

"That's an awful lot of poke, Mickey. I mean I can bleeding imagine a hundred, no, two bleeding hundred grand. I can see it sitting there on the floor."

"Bonkie", Mac broke in gently, "can you imagine this mobile home crammed full of twenty pound notes?"

"There's nowhere in Ireland with so much..." Bonkie's eyes lit up, "only the Central Bank. You're not going to blag the Big Grey Jug? You are crazy. Where are yer bringing the poke back to? The Bridewell? We will ring up and reserve a few cells".

"It's the big stroke, Bonkie. The real big one. Yer know that." Georgie had the same blaggers' look in his eye.

"So is Fort bleeding Knox, Georgie. So is the Bank of England. Are yer going to tunnel it out?"

"No Bonkie", Mac held up O'Mally-Smyth's photograph, "you", he pointed to the banker, "are going to go in and sign it out for us".

"You are codding me."

"Can yew hear anybody laughing, kid?" remarked Mickey.

"You shut fucking up, Mickey", Mac turned to the Belfast man. "If this stroke doesn't get off the ground it's because of you. You fucking spacer."

"Why is that, Mac?" asked Bonkie. "Who is that?" he pointed to the photograph. "What's going on here?"

"Mickey here has the Movement on our backs. If they find out we are operating with him we are all well and truly bolloxed."

"Yew knew what the score was before Ballygojingle", defended Mickey.

"You never told us about old man Gill. Did you?" Mac filled Bonkie in "... and that's why we told yer to fix the gaff to repel gunmen and gave you the short. It'll be alright – I don't believe the Movement know we are Mickey's comrades". He sneered the word comrades at Mickey.

"And yer want me to go into the Jug and take the manager's place?"

"That's right. And we pull up in a security van and you have us loaded up."

"The risky bit is getting bleeding in. If they cop me on I'm gone. I presume you will have the real geezer kidnapped and held somewhere safe?"

"Naturally. We can't let him wait down at the pub."

"I know that Mac, but still it's a very heavy stroke. Kidnapping. Trying to do their biggest jug. I'd say I'd get a very long whack on this one. The risks are very big."

"The rewards are bigger again, Bonkie. A million pounds is nothing to that place. Look, the thing may not be practical at all. We won't know what the system inside is until we scoop the man. All we know is he signs out all the poke."

"Is he really that much alike, Georgie? Did yer see him yerself?" Bonkie respected Georgie's judgement.

"Bonkie you are him. Not alike. Not similar. Identical. Like Siamese twins. I mean identical twins." The Firm laughed at the idea of Bonkie being moulded to the banker.

"I wouldn't have a clue what ter do in there. I suppose if I bluffed it in I could smash a bleeding window and throw out a few bags of poke and scream off on a bike."

"You're willing to take on the stroke then?" asked Mac.

The Firm held their breaths.

"If it can be done I'll bleeding do it. Am I willing? Whose going ter stop me? If its blaggable at all I'll, we'll, bleeding blag it." The Firm were buoyed up by Bonkie's cheerful bottle. He had been to a certain extent isolated from the strain and stress. And he had not been heavy blagging as long as they had.

"You are going to have to change, Bonkie. You are going to take over this man's identity completely. It will take time. We will have to study him. Know everything about him."

"How am I going to do that? I don't bleeding know him from Adam. I'll need to hear him speak. I'll need to hear him whistle, everything, Mac." Bonkie was caught up in the stroke now. It appealed to the actor in him, the performer. It really was the big stroke. The Big Grey Jug. It attracted Bonkie's ego like a horseshoe magnet does a lucky nail. "Do yer know where this geezer lives?"

"We have a good deal of intelligence on him, boy", said Bob. "We will take the gaff, lift him, interrogate him. We will put the security van together and if necessary we will blag again to finance. We will carry out all intelligence operations on the mark."

"And what will I be doing?"

"We have a nice gaff for you and yer missus, Bonkie. Yews can stay there getting into yer role. It's nice and quiet and dead straight too. And it's not too far away from the city." Georgie said to Mac. "Have you the keys?"

"I have", he threw them to Georgie. "Disappear Bonkie. Collect the wife and child and we will move yer in. The story will be you have moved to England."

"When do I move lads?"

"Tonight. As soon as possible, Bonkie. We have to start the stroke secure. That means fixing you up properly. Will your missus mind?" asked Mac. Then he added, "it's a very nice place. A modern cottage, nice garden, not far from here".

"No, she will be delighted I'd say. Anyway she will do what she is bleeding told. What about my whack? Me poke? I'll need me poke."

Mac handed him two books. One was a building society book, in his own name, and twenty thousand pounds clear deposited in it. The other book was a bank book for Mr and Mrs Smyth. There was six thousand seven hundred and fifty punts in it.

"The twenty grand is your own whack. The other few grand is operating money for you and the new gaff. There is a form in the book for specimen signatures. When you move drop into the manager and sign them. The poke was deposited on your behalf by a solicitor from a legacy. It's all above board." He gave Bonkie a set of car keys. "Your jammer is English Rego as is all your ID. It's all dead cool and authentic, Bonkie. It can stand a pull no problems. You are an exile returned. Put on a bit of a Brit accent. One thing, Bonkie. Bury the Building Society book with the straight name. It will take a couple of months to get your money out."

Bonkie gave him back the books. "Give em back out at the gaff, Mac. What do I tell me missus if anything?"

"As much of the truth as is safe. Tell her yer going to do a big stroke. Tell her we are calling. She will have ter know, Bonkie."

Georgie had met Sally at Bonkie's getting out do. He had liked her. She would be cool if she was treated with a bit of common sense.

"Will you and Matt be calling, Mickey?" asked Bonkie.

"Only if necessary, Bonkie but I don't think so. Myself and Matt are doing the surveillance. Why, is there a problem?" Mickey lit a Parkdrive and gave an impression that if there were a problem he'd soon blow it away.

"Sally will be fine if there won't be a heavy scene. Yer know shooters and all that. Will we use the gaff for briefings and that?"

"No, Bonkie. At the back of the gaff is a big old barn. It's about a hundred yards away and can be got at by a dirt track without going near the cottage. The barn will be used for meetings. It's just she might see us about the place and if she doesn't think it's all straight it could ruin the stroke. There won't be any gear about the place except your own. It's perfect", ended Mac.

"When do we go ter work, Mac?" asked Bonkie.

"I'd say around Christmas. After Christmas when all the old money is in. That will give you a bit of time to get into your role. One thing", asked Mac, "what happens if your missus doesn't want ter move? What are you going to do?"

"I said when do we go ter work Mac?"

The Firm all stood in line and shook Bonkie's hand. He was a genuine blagger heart and soul.

Sally's auld fella Johnny was delighted to see his daughter and his grandchild. He had great time for them both and secretly for Bonkie too. But he was forbidden to speak favourably of 'that dirtbox' in his wife Gracie's presence.

"Ah, I knew you'd see sense one day. Ah, sure I knew didn't I Johnny", rambled on Gracie. She was laying out her table for a cup of tea. Like she had seen the nobs do on the box.

"You know nothing you foul, insidious, ignoramus", said Johnny and not in a whisper but in a soft voice. He was carrying out experiments on his theory that his wife never listened to anything he said.

"Ah yes, your father knew I was right but he couldn't say. Could yer, Johnny? Not when the 'dirtbox' was driving him to the pub in a big new Ford motorcar?" This was a jibe back to the time Bonkie, in an effort to impress Sal's parents, had taken Johnny for a few pints. He had driven him down in the new Cortina his company had supplied him with. Bonkie was a travelling salesman. They had got on great down in the pub and Johnny was well impressed with a prospective son-in-law who came across so many free samples. Whiskey, watches, vacuum cleaners, everything you could think of that was in a gaff. They had been driving home when the gardai started chasing them. Bonkie wouldn't pull over. He slowed down, jammed on the brakes and shoved the Cortina into reverse and crunched into the front of the squad car. Bonkie pulled away with half the squad car hanging onto his rear bumper. He pulled up at a cul-de-sac in Finglas West and jumped out of the jammer.

"Goodnight Johnny", he had said to him, "I'm just going for a piss." He had ran off over the back gardens and poor Johnny had ended up in the District Court.

Bonkie had gone to Court and cleared the auld fella's name but the damage was done. His name was in the paper. Auld Johnny was pleased. People believed him to be a hen-pecked scrap of a man. He was delighted that Gracie was 'mortified'. And then Sally had been made pregnant and went to live with him.

"Why can't yer get married?" the ma had screamed.

"Because he's already married that's why. And he has five kids."

The auld one had waged a constant battle since that time to have her rescued from the 'dirtbox'. "Ah, yes. Johnny knew I was right. I said to him, what firm is it gives yer a new car every three days? And, says I, what kind of firm is it that he doesn't work days? But who would listen to me?"

"No one can avoid listening to yer", said Johnny by the fire. "It's just no one takes any notice of yer. Yer dirty louser. You'd scare a crocodile."

Gracie ranted on regardless. Johnny believed he would soon be able to insult her in a normal voice. He believed she was totally obsessed with hating Bonkie. She told the gardai everything she ever heard about him and prayed he would get a big whack.

"Ma, I only want to stay for a while. A few days. Maybe a few weeks until we get a gaff to stay in." Sally drank the tea gratefully.

"I'll get yer some sugar from Mrs Puff. I'll have ter go to the supermarket tonight. Oh, my child is back. Thanks be to God." Gracie ran out the back door and up to prayer leader Puff's sanctimonious residence.

"Come here, Saorise and give yer Grandpa a kiss." The little girl went and sat on Johnny's knee. "She has gone to spread the good news, Sally. Bonkie isn't maltreating yer, is he?"

"Ah no, da. He never raises his hand to me. It's the gaff and the area. It's getting me down. I need a bit of a rest that's all."

"Go on up before she gets back. Your room is always ready for yer."

Sally and Saorise went up into her old bedroom. All her teenage things were here. It was a comforting familiar room. John Lennon smiled down at her, his sad, compassionate eyes squinting as if he had just seen her again. Her hurling sticks and her trophies all neat and tidy, the shields and medals, glinting. Over in the corner was the picture of the very wise, very holy, old man with the grey beard and the visionary look of paradise radiating out from him. She looked at him. "Hello Padre Pio." She waved to him. The wardrobe was lying open. All her old clothes were in there. They didn't fit her. Why did she keep them? Her auld one was really freaked out over Bonkie and why? Everybody had to kick off. Why spend your life freaked out about someone else's affairs? Sally changed and lay on the cool, clean bed and rocked Saorise asleep.

"Padro Pio you understand, I know", she whispered to the holy man she confided in. "Please make Bonkie see sense. If he is doing just one more stroke please let it be his last. Oh yes, and ask the Lord to give us a gaff." Sally too fell asleep. It seemed only a few minutes before she was awakened by a tapping on the window.

"Let me in Sal", said Bonkie. "I'm hanging onto the sill."

Sally looked at the lunatic. What could she do with him? She went over to the window. "What do yer want, Bonkie?"

"Let me in will yer, I can't hang on here. I'll break me neck if I fall."

"Why can't yer use the door like everyone else?" she opened the window and he climbed in.

"If I rapped your door the Boxer would pour boiling oil on me, Sal. Yer know she's not right upstairs."

"My mother's not right? Yer have a cheek Bonkie yer know. She has reasons ter be upset. Don't think yer can come up here..."

"Before she comes up and bites me listen will yer..."

"And don't interrupt me, Bonkie. There are no bleeding James Bond bugs up here..."

Bonkie only knew one way to shut Sal up when she was working up into a temper and that was to kiss and tickle her. He grabbed her and gave her a gooser on the lips. She resisted but she could not make noise because of the ma. Bonkie tipped her onto the floor and began to tickle the soles of her feet. Sally had to bite her nightie to stop from laughing. The giggles got too much and they came out as a high pitched whine. In the struggle Sally's nightdress came off. All she had on was her knickers. She never wore a bra. She tickled Bonkie back under his weak spot. She dug her fingers into his arm pits and wriggled.

Bonkie had to let go. Sal rolled on top of him and straddled him.

"Sal, Sal, don't – I give in. Sal I have a gaff for us."

She stopped. Her eyes went serious.

"I swear. On the child's life. Yer know I wouldn't do that. It's ready an all for us. Yer don't need nothing either. We are buying all new stuff."

"Now? But where? Oh, Bonkie what's it like? Is it a flat? How did yer do it?"

"Sal listen, it's a lovely gaff. A cottage just outside the city, with gardens, and we have a jammer and plenty of poke. We are bleeding rich. Sal that's not why I came here."

"Why did yer come then?"

"I wanted yer to know I love you."

Sally melted and wrapped herself around him. She would go anywhere with him and he knew it.

"And", said the Boxer opening the door, "our prayers were answered Mrs Puff".

The Boxer, Mrs Puff and Mrs Praise looked into the bedroom. Sally was undulating on top of the prostrate Bonkie.

"Bleeding hell", yelped Bonkie. Sally jumped off him. Her firm breasts, nipples high and hard, greeted the sympathetic delegation up to welcome back the prodigal daughter.

The Boxer saw red. She lifted up one of Sally's hurling sticks and set about Bonkie. He didn't mind but she started lashing out at Sal who was trying to slip on her jeans. The Boxer was hysterical. Bonkie chinned her and knocked her cold.

"Come on Sal or we'll miss the boat." The two snoops were still staring into the room. "Are yer bleeding looking fer something?" Bonkie put his hand on his fly. They fled screaming.

"What's going on here", demanded Johnny. He went to the wife.

"She fainted Johnny. Come on fer Christ sake, Sal."

Saorise watched all this from the bed. Adults were weird. Really weird. Bonkie was over at the window. Housebreakers always leg it out windows when it comes on top. Sally ran over to her da. She kissed his bald head. "We got a gaff da. I'm off." She lifted up the child. "The door Bonkie. Use the door."

"Oh yer. The door." He was eyeing the Boxer warily. She was coming to. He fled past her and legged it down the stairs.

"Don't forget ter write", shouted the auld fella after her. She and the child went down after Bonkie.

"Water, water", groaned the Boxer.

"I wouldn't give yer a drink in the desert yer poxy auld bag of shite", replied Johnny.

"Get me a priest. Ah get me a priest."

"It's a Bishop and a shorthand typist yer need. If yer going ter go hurry up. I'm going down ter play a game of darts."

The Boxer jumped up and beat Johnny around the bedroom with the hurl. Johnny didn't give a bollox, at least it was better than being nagged. He hid under the bed. The Boxer ran out into the street waving the hurl, flinging obscenities after Bonkie and Sally.

Bonkie made rude signs to her through the back window.

"That's a crazy auld one there", said the taxi man.

"Oh absolutely", replied Bonkie in his poshest accent, "I do tink it's the area. It's very downhill I do tink".

The taxi man laughed to get his tip. They were all bleeding crazy. Yer man's bird was only wearing a pair of jeans and a tiny top. No shoes. The kid was still half asleep and in it's night clothes. Yer man was a nut too. He climbed in the window and came out the door. Said he lost his key. "Where to now?"

"The back airport road."

"Where abouts? It's a big road."

"I'll tell yer when I get there." Bonkie handed him a tenner to shut him up.

Chapter 17

GEORGIE picked up Bonkie, Sally and Saorise walking along the Airport Road. Sally wasn't too pleased to see him.

"How are yer going on, Sally?" he asked looking at her in his mirror. She was a lovely chick.

"Alright. Where are we going Georgie?" her tone was a bit frosty.

"To yer new gaff. Didn't Bonkie explain it to yer?"

"We had a bit of trouble with the auld one. Had ter leave in a bit of a hurry", Bonkie explained as he eyed Sally fondly. "I'll explain everything to yer at the gaff, sunshine."

She said nothing and looked out at the passing scenery. He always said sunshine when he was feeling guilty. She knew all the rotten bastard's ways. They cut across around to the back of Howth. The sea breeze came into the car and stirred Sally's interest. She was bursting with curiosity but she would not display it in case she was disappointed again. They passed through Howth village. Saorise was excited at her first sight of the sea and the fishing boats. It seemed out here in the air and seascape as if the world of the City had split open and revealed a new brighter place. Georgie turned down a narrow country lane for about half a mile. They were a couple of miles from the village. He slowed down and slipped into a gap between a privet hedge bigger than a man.

The cottage greeted them dramatically. It sprang into their view. One moment driving along a small boreen and the next staring at the most quaint of places. Georgie killed the engine. He knew the gaff would hit them like that. He had deliberately refused to talk about it or describe it. "You'll see."

It had at one time indeed been a cottage but it had been lovingly restored, renovated, extended at the back and maintained. The walls were constructed of brown granite blocks that had taken on a subtle hue with age. The walls were thick and secure keeping out the cold and heat. It was a two storey cottage and the small upper windows, curved Georgian panes and frames, sat back into the deep dark yellow thatch. In the bottom windows resting on the thick sills grew a variety of flowering house plants. The gaff was a quality place. It was select, and very, very, private.

Sally and the child got out in a dream. They stepped into the fragrant garden, a tiny bit overrun but full of flowers and buzzing bees from the hives at the back of the gaff.

"Are we going to live here, Mammy?" asked the child.

"Bonkie?" asked Sally.

"Ah yeah, Sal. No problem. Do yer like it?" Bonkie felt very pleased.

"Sally the gaff is only out on rent", said Georgie bluntly. "At the very least yer can have it to Christmas. I don't know what the score is after that."

Sally set the child down. The little girl ran off to explore her new home.

"Don't go on the road", called Sally.

"I have never seen another car up this road Sally", said Georgie smiling, "it's kind of a half private road. Wait till yer see the gaff". He gave Sally the keys. Bonkie took them off her and opened the big oaken door.

"I might as well do this right." He lifted up Sally and carried her over the threshold.

"Put me down Bonkie, yer nut." She was blushing a bit. Sally was in the main room. The furniture was all old Irish from various periods. In the corner by the big open fireplace, with crane and kettle on the hob, was a full sized Irish harp. By the window was a very old Harpsichord. The walls were covered with paintings and prints. Bonkie spotted three Salvador Dali prints immediately. He done a bit of painting up in the Joy and was very much impressed by the ideas of the surrealists if not all of their art. Georgie saw him look at the works. "There is a small studio out the back, Bonkie. There's everything yer need if yer want to do a bit."

Sally called Saorise in. She wanted the child to share the good vibes of their first look at this gaff. To the child it was a fairyland. To Sally it was a dream. To Bonkie it was many things. A place to hide out and plan strokes, a manifestation of what poke could do, but, his first thought had been that this was a very rich and easy gaff to screw. The kitchen out the back was good enough to prepare and cook the best of grub. The freezer and fridge were full. The wine, spirits and liqueurs were all the best quality, all chosen with care and skill.

"Bonkie, Bonkie come in here", cried Sally.

Bonkie went into the bathroom. Whoever had done up the gaff had sunk a Roman type bath into the floor. It was big enough to take five or six adults and had a little shelf running around it so one could sit down. The place was tiled and mosaicked depicting some very lewd scenes of young ladies, Greek gays and satyrs. The place spoke of discreet sexual pleasures in times past. Saorise had climbed into the bath. Only her eyes were visible.

"There's a hole in the ground." She pointed to the plug hole. Bonkie lifted her out. He wasn't prepared for a place like this. Sally took his hand. The vibes in this place were exhilarating.

"Ah don't be worrying Bonkie. I know it's only for a while. We'll have the best of a summer you wait and see."

"Sal, there's a reason for the gaff. The lads will..."

She put her finger to his lips to stop him speaking. "I'm not stupid Bonkie. I know something's going on. As long as I'm out of the other place it's cool."

"Really Sal?"

"Truth of God on it. This is a, it's paradise compared to it and me ma's." She saw his frown. "Why have yer such a jaw on yer?"

"Me pigeons. Who's going ter look after me pigeons? The dog. We left Gurrier behind Sal." He ran into Georgie. "I have ter go home. I have ter get Gurrier."

"What do yer mean? This is yer home now, Bonkie or should I say Patrick? Yer don't have a Jack Russell named Gurrier. Middle class, English made, Irish exiles have woolly sheepdogs or bleeding Corgis like her. You will never set foot in Sean Macker again."

"You tell him Georgie. He wants ter go and get his pigeons." Sally liked this scheme whatever it was they were cooking up. Ordering Bonkie to live in a marvellous gaff and doing away with his shitty pigeons. He had her tortured when he was up in the Joy about their welfare. "The auld fella across the road will look after them. He always does."

"I reared that dog ever since I nicked him as a pup. He'll bleeding die without me I'm telling yer."

"You wise up. You are on the boat ter bleeding Manchester, where you will disappear into the great grey crowd of Paddies. I'll make sure the dog and pigeons are alright. Relax." Georgie was going to throw it in the Liffey tied into a rock-filled sack. He'd kill every bleeding dog in the RDS to protect this stroke.

"Give him to somebody that will be kind to him, Georgie."

"Oh, I will Bonkie." He reached over and touched his arm. "Yer can depend on me Bonkie. Yer know that."

"Yer a good mate ter have, Georgie." Bonkie settled down in the sofa.

"Sally there a few things yer should know."

"Don't be spoiling me now, Georgie." She fluttered her eyes at Georgie and was rewarded to see Bonkie pull a moody head.

"We are pulling one stroke. Just the one. If it bleeding works, we are out of the game. Permanent and for good. There is enough poke involved to make us all rich for life. Yer could do, or buy, anything yer wanted."

Sally looked around at the gaff.

"That's right Sally. You can have a nice piece of life like this, only, this would be yer country gaff to get away from it all. It's cool isn't it?"

Sally nodded. This was something she could understand. Something real she could believe in.

"And the only bloke who can pull this stroke is Bonkie."

Bonkie preened himself and stuck out his chest a bit.

"We are all depending on him and you too Sally. And that's about all I can tell yer about the stroke except there won't be any shooters used on it."

"No guns? How are yer depending on me?"

"Bonkie has to play a role, a part, like an actor. The better he is at it the more chance he has of pulling it off. He has to change his ID, his habits, his way of talking, he has to assume another man's ways of going on. Do yer get me?"

"And yer want me to play along? To help him be this other bloke?"

"That's right Sally. Are yer willing to go along with it?"

"I'd do anything fer Bonkie. He knows that. I'll do whatever it takes. Who is he to be?" Sally liked the sound of this. It was a lot different to hurling a brick through a window and running off with the gear with half of Dublin chasing him. She was intrigued too.

"All you will be given is a name, Patrick. From now on his name is Patrick. Your first job is ter stop Bonkie saying – bleeding. Call him Patrick and stop him bleeding this and that. That's yer first job."

"Is that all?" asked Sally. "What about him biting his nails? Oh yer and he ..."

"Knock it off Sal. Bleeding hell ..."

"Now, now Patrick." Sally waved her finger at Bonkie. "No more of yer bleeding talk."

"Perfect Sal." Georgie was very pleased. Now yer are Mr and Mrs Patrick Smyth. All yer ID is in that drawer. Your history is in that drawer. It's very short and it's only for the local porker if he should show up, which he won't. Your bank account is in the Balbriggan Bank. Come out here Patrick and I'll show you and Delores yer jammer."

"Delores? Me?"

"Come on dearest. Delores", Bonkie chuckled, "I thought I was ble, bl, bad with Paddy".

Around the back of the house was a Cortina 1600 a few months old. It was a nondescript car with English plates. It was fitted with a towbar and beside the car on its trailer was a clinker-built sixteen foot sea boat with small cabin and powerful outboard.

"Yer can use the boat whenever you like Patrick, only don't go out without checking the weather. She is fully equipped with radio and an inflatable. Have yer ever been out to sea before?"

"Only on the B&I going ter Holyhead."

"I'll get Bob ter give yer a few lessons. It's his boat really."

"Did it cost a lot?" asked Sally.

"Not really. A coat of paint or two and changed the appearance. He nicked it on a group of anglers down in Kinsale or somewhere. It's cool. It's been laying up in storage this four years except for the odd trip. She's a good boat."

"Fishing tackle?" enquired Bonkie. He always fancied a bit of fishing.

"In the shed over there. Sally there is a big auld barn over at the back of the trees there. It's very dangerous. Don't let the child into it and don't go into it yerself, please."

"Delores. Call me Delores." Sally was liking this scene more and more. She'd have six months with Bonkie in ideal conditions. If they had to pay for all this it would cost hundreds of pounds a week. She hopped into the boat and showed the child the little cabin.

"We'll be back in about twenty minutes Sal, fuck it. Delores." Bonkie and Georgie went off towards the barn.

"Yer are going ter have ter stop cursing Patrick. It's not a game. It's real. One slip and yer bolloxed. One slip and we're all bolloxed. I'll show yer the van and gear." They walked down behind the garden to the barn. The side door opened for them. Mac was in there. He was wearing overalls and welding goggles.

"Come in lads."

The double wheel base Transit was stripped down to the chassis. Stacked neatly against the wall were sheets of steel to make up the body and the angle iron for the frame. It was a brand new van. There was a welding plant and a compressor with spraying equipment.

"This will be the van to take out the poke, Patrick." Mac addressed him in his new name.

"No problem, Mac." Bonkie fell into his new role.

"How did Delores take it Patrick?" asked Mac.

"She believes it to be a very good idea." Bonkie had cut away all his Dublin twang.

"Say that again." Georgie was agog. The voice bit was going to be the main thing.

"She believes it to be a first class idea." Bonkie grinned. He had secret talents.

"Well I'll be bolloxed", said Georgie. "All the years I have know yer Bon, er, Patrick and yer can speak posh."

"Such language George. It's a bra bric moon lit nic the noo. 'ave yer got yer knickers in yer 'andbag luv? Get hup hout ha dat wid ya." Bonkie was enjoying himself. He had always been good at taking the mickey out of people.

"That's very good, Patrick", commented Mac. "It may not be the marks but I'd say you'll get it. What does she think of the gaff?"

"She is delighted with it, Mac. And to tell you the truth so am I. I could do with a bit of a break. When do I go to work?"

"You are working now, Patrick. Shave off the beard. Put on the gear in the wardrobe. Do yerself up like the man in the photograph. Burn all yer old gear and Delores' too. Do whatever it is you do to relax. Paint, fish, screw, play postman's knock. Try and forget everything. Everything except what you have to do Patrick." MacGregor's eyes burned into Bonkie. He could see the poke in there.

"I'll do it, Mac. I'll do it."

"Right Patrick. The first thing is you have to lose half a stone in weight. That means you stick to the diet. You can have the best of food and wine but in moderation. You need above all to be sharp and fit. Run along the beach every day, at least four miles building up to ten, and no dope Monday to Friday."

"What do yer mean?" Bonkie didn't like the sound of the restrictions.

"We are all under the same orders, Patrick. When we are on duty we get no booze at all. We need every bit of wit we can get."

"No problem. Can I drive around?"

"Keep as much to the gaff as possible. You are going to be very busy anyway but under no circumstances are you to go near gangland. If yer blow this through stupidity I'll personally blow off yer head."

Bonkie jumped at Mac who pulled out a short. Georgie got in between. Bonkie had gone very ugly.

"Cool it, cool it, for fuck's sake", he pinned Bonkie by the arms. "It's not a personal threat. He's not bleeding attacking yer. It applies to us all. It is cool enough." He shouted at Mac. "Have yer no sense? Why didn't yer explain it?"

"The only way ter say it is straight. It was my job ter say and I said it to his face. If anyone fucks up the stroke they are dead as doornails." Mac put the pistol back into his pocket.

"Yer didn't say anyone, yer said me." Bonkie relaxed. Georgie released him. No one saw where the blade came from but Bonkie had it flicked out in a flash. He held the stiletto point to Mac's jugular vein. "If you, if you fuck up Mac I'll cut your throat." Bonkie released Mac and walked out the door back to the gaff.

"Why did you do that, Mac?" Georgie was furious.

"It had to be done. I inferred he was stupid. I insulted him. It will drive him along I'm telling yer."

"Yer may have caused bad blood."

"I don't care if he hates me until my dying day Georgie. All I want is to get the poke. He can call me all the bloody names he wants. After the stroke I'll tell him I'm sorry and he can kick the bollox off me but until then, he needs discipline. That's the best way to give it ter him. Self motivation. He hates me. He'll prove me wrong. Good. If it's any consolation to yer I think he's a great bloke. Now fuck off out of here I've work ter do." Mac picked up the welding gear and pulled down the welding mask. Georgie walked towards the door.

"Georgie, now that it's done leave it be."

"Aye, aye, sir", replied Georgie bitterly.

"One more thing. See if yer can persuade Patrick to part with the push button. I thought I was gone then, yer can show him the shotguns."

Georgie smiled and left. Mac had turned a queer colour when Bonkie pulled the blade. He was very fast. Rapid. He went back to the gaff.

"Patrick, me auld flower. Come here till yer see these." Bonkie was pacing the floor like he was in his cell, in the Joy. Restless. Caged. Brooding.

"What is it, Georgie?" He was away somewhere else formulating replies to Mac. Telling him where to get off. Imagining confrontations to come. How he should have handled things just then. Treating him like a bleeding halfwit.

Georgie opened the slim cabinet by the front door and took out the shotguns and the .22/50. Two small pump shotguns and the .22/50 was a Manlicher with scope. "These are yours Patrick. The licences are in the locker. If yer go shooting take them with you."

"You mean they are straight?" Bonkie was over sharpish. He hefted the pump.

"What's that?" he nodded at the Manlicher.

"It's a .22/50."

"What use is a .22 Georgie? A pop gun would be better. Beat the porkers with the butt."

Georgie lifted up one of the rifle rounds. It was as big as an Armalite round. Centrefire with almost as much punch. "It's only the head is .22 Patrick, the case, the charge is full size."

Bonkie handled the round. "I never saw a .22 like that before."

"Where is the missus?"

"She is running the bath and getting Saorise ready for bed. Why?"

"Come on and we'll fire off a few rounds. Oh yer. Here." He handed Bonkie the .357 he was carrying in Sean MacDermott Street. "Mac said yer can have it as a personal."

"Is he trying to apologise or something?" Bonkie took the revolver.

"No, he's not. He's the boss. It's his job to say unpleasant things. He's dead straight."

"There was no need."

"Just drop it Bonkie. This stroke is bigger than us all. There is no room for personal emotions. We are all pros. If I fuck up through bad stupidity I'll get one in the dome. So what do I do?"

"What do yer do?"

"I make sure I do my job and I don't fuck up. Come on I'll show yer where yer can have a shoot off any time yer want."

Sally bathed the child in the sunken bath and put her to bed in the room above the sitting room. The window overlooked the sea. She told the child a story and answered her questions about the ocean and then tucked her into the bed. It was the first time she had a room to herself. Sally stayed until she had Saorise fast asleep then went down and soaked in the hot perfumed water. This was the life. She lifted up her martini and sipped. Hmmm. Yes. She could get used to this no problem, and, Bonkie was telling the truth. One big stroke!

Chapter 18

O'MALLY-SMYTH'S routine was easily established. It was regular as clockwork. He rose at seven fifteen Monday to Friday and jogged around the area for a half hour. He returned to the house, entering by the back door which was left open, showered, shaved, had a light breakfast and left for the Bank in his Merc at ten minutes past eight, arriving there usually before half past. He made his own breakfast while his beloved slept the morning away in her own bedroom, that is, if she were there, for Delores was more often away funning herself than in the house.

Delores had been away for a few days and Mickey and Matt had gone into the house when the banker was out jogging and made wax impressions of all his keys. It was an easy matter then to wire the house at their leisure, to wire the car, and they even wired the garden shed. Mickey had lain in the big back garden in the early hours with his box of bugs. The banker followed his routine and left for work. Matt took up position in case the wife should return unexpected and the da rose up out of the garden and went in by the back door. No one saw him enter or leave three hours later.

Mickey had time to wire up all his bugs to direct current which eliminated the need for batteries and he also had time to conceal them well. He was well pleased with his morning's work. He put a receiver in O'Mally-Smyth's roof space to collect the conversations and phone calls and wired the receiver to a small but powerful transmitter which sent the signals to the other receiver he and Matt had installed in a rented house less than a mile away. Here, under the cover of respectable businessmen the two Belfast men listened to every word spoken in the O'Mally-Smyth household and from their safe gaff followed the banker to and from work, to and from the golf club, and checked out all the intelligence they gleaned from their bugging. O'Mally-Smyth was perfect to scoop. All the lads had to do was go up and open his front door and walk in on top of him, or, wait on him coming back from his run, or, scoop him as he ran along the road trying to get the sleep out of his eyes. There was no gardai surveillance on the banker of any kind. Nobody ringing up with code words, no sneaky porkers about the area or following him into work. That was perfect for scooping him but it indicated that there was one very secure system down at the Big Grey Jug.

Mickey and Matt had everything they needed to know about the Banker in a week. He went to work, came home, didn't go out much, lounged about the house studying Arabic and economics, worked on his business and played golf every Sunday with the Chief Security Officer, Maxwell. He was a man who relished his privacy and there were no callers at the house except for tradespeople. Mickey and Matt collected together the day's intelligence, taped it, typed it up and Alfie collected it and brought it to Bonkie.

Bonkie was adapting to the role of the Banker very well. He had mastered the speech and undoubtedly, dressed in the suit and tie, his hair trimmed and shaved back at the front a little (O'Mally-Smyth was receding at the front) he could pass for the Banker. The thing was that was not good enough. The Firm were stuck as to what went on inside the jug and the information was not to be had by surveillance. But, the Firm had realised right from the beginning that the real information would only come when they scooped and interrogated the Banker. In the meantime every bit of information they uncovered about his affairs was all to their advantage while Bonkie shaped up for the role. Things were shaping up very well.

Two weeks after Bonkie moved out to the cottage Georgie was shot dead as he left a public house in the City.

Bonkie had been woken by the phone ringing at the side of the bed. He reached over Sally and lifted it off the hook.

"Yes?"

"Sorry to disturb you Pat", Alfie's voice was full of tension, "I was just checking you were there. I'll be out right away. OK?"

"I'll expect you." Bonkie put up the phone and swung out of bed.

"Who's that?" muttered Sally sleepily.

"Nothing. I'm getting up for a while." He slipped on his trousers and went down to wait. In the sitting room Bonkie lifted up the stone in the fireplace and took out the magnum. He loaded it and went and got out the pump. It was always loaded. Bonkie sat in the dark by the window waiting for the coffee to heat up. There was something serious up. The phone was only to be used in emergencies. He heard the bike. Alfie turned into the cottage and parked the Honda.

"What's wrong, Alfie?" he closed the door behind him. They went into the back room. Alfie sat up on the bar-type stool.

"Georgie was shot dead at around twelve."

"Dead?" Bonkie's stomach heaved then he became very angry. "Who did it?"

"We don't know yet. They tried to pull him into a van. Georgie put up a struggle. They shot him. With a sub. He was sprayed with a sub."

"It wasn't gangland. Who would want to shoot Georgie?" Bonkie was shocked. "Do yer want a cup of coffee?"

"Thanks Pat. They wanted him for information. To grill him. Mac is getting Bob and himself offside." He sipped the coffee.

"Jesus Christ. You are all on the run then?" Bonkie considered that. There was going to be no arrest and trial. A few days in a hood and thankfully someone to blow out your brains. No funeral. A shallow grave and a spit on yer corpse. "They know then about us and Mickey." It was a statement of fact.

"Yes. I'd say that's the way of it. They were after Mickey and Matt's place and us. Georgie knew that."

"But why did they shoot him? There's no info in a corpse."

"Panic? Lost their head when he got stuck in. We are all sentenced to death."

"Dirty bastards." It was incomprehensible to Bonkie that anyone would shoot another human being for robbing a jug. It was back to front. Yer shoot the ones who prevented yer robbing the jug – not the bleeding ones who robbed it.

"We all have to go, Pat." Alfie was feeling blue and down.

"I'll tell you something. I intend to die, if I have to die, rich. I'm pulling this stroke and I don't care if I'm to be hung, drawn and quartered."

Alfie drank the last of his coffee. He took the Browning out of his pocket and began to strip and clean it.

"If anyone tries to lift me, Pat, I'll blow them away."

"Are we going to do anything about this?"

"What can we do? Attack them? We haven't a bleeding chance. Yer might kill someone, but who? If yer want ter find out who done Georgie it's down to scooping and torturing people."

"What are we going to do?"

"I don't know." Alfie put the Browning back up. He cocked it and tested the mechanism. "Hit the Jug as planned. What else can we do?" He slid in the mag, put a round up the spout and put on the safety. "This is only a tool ter me. When I put it on it's ter make bleeding poke." He put the pistol away.

"Shusssh," Bonkie put his finger to his lips. "I can hear a car." He went to the front of the house with the pump.

"It'll be Mac and them", whispered Alfie but he drew the Browning anyway.

Mac and the lads came to the front door. It was dodgy enough with the four of them travelling through the city in the early hours of the morning. Bonkie let them in. They were all carrying gear. "Into the back lads."

Sally heard the car pull up. She went down to see what the score was. The men in the kitchen looked at her with barely concealed irritation. But there was more to it than that. They all had a killing look about them and there were weapons everywhere. Machine guns and heavy rifles. "What's going on?"

"Georgie has been shot", replied Bonkie. "He's dead." He glared at her.

"Dead? Georgie?" Sally panned out and hit the floor with a thud.

Bonkie lifted her and carried her into the front room. He lay her on the sofa. Mac brought in a glass of water. "Here Pat."

Bonkie was embarrassed. He got a little water between Sally's lips. She came to slowly. "Are you alright love?" he asked.

"I think I'm pregnant." She began to cry disconsolately.

"We'll see yer down at the barn, Patrick", said Mac. "I'm sorry if we upset yer missus. I'm sorry love." Mac turned and walked out of the sitting room.

Bonkie carried Sally up to bed. He had the crazy thought that the baby she was conceiving might have Georgie's spirit. He had read once up in the Joy that when a person dies their spirit is given to a newborn baby. It worked out fine mathematically. Oh yeah and those who got no spirit were the nasties. He put Sally to bed.

"Will I get the doctor for you?" He went to comfort her. She turned from him.

"No."

"Can I get you anything?"

She just lay there staring straight ahead and wouldn't answer him. He mumbled to her.

"Have to go and see the lads." He left the room. The dawn was breaking over the sea.

The midget led Jimmy Apple into the man who lived at the top of the tower block by the hand. Jimmy was in a dark, stuffy, confined world of hooded terror.

"Someone here asking questions about our two friends", squeaked the midget.

"Sit down", commanded the man who lived in the tower.

Jimmy sat and fell on his fat arse. There was no chair for him. Only ropes for his hands and feet. His shirt was torn off and his flabby belly and fat chest exposed. "What are you doing?" he whinged. "My father slept with the old crowd."

"So did Cromwell", whispered the greasy man to Jimmy as he put the smoothing iron onto the solicitor's chest.

"Ooooo", wriggled Jimmy, "what is that?" He imagined it to be a stethoscope or some other such instrument. Until it began to heat up.

"What do you have to tell us?" asked the man who lived in the tower.

"A, ahhhhh. It's ahhhhhhh", screamed Jimmy. He banged his head on the floor and howled.

"It's what?" asked the midget hoping to elicit some great paramilitary secret.

"It's painful, it's fucking painful ooooooh", Jimmy writhed and tried to shake off the hot iron but the midget stood on the solicitor's chest, dug in combat boots for leverage, and pressed down on the iron with all his might. The midget took off the iron and looked at the burn mark. It was a perfect impression. The midget examined it minutely. They always fascinated him. They looked so odd. Like a valentine heart that springs out of yer card. The porkers were baffled by them.

"I'm going to ask you some questions, Mr Apple. If you tell me lies I'll have the little fella take the iron to your balls. Now, what are you up to?"

For the first time in his life the solicitor told the truth. It was hard but he achieved it first time. They didn't even have to burn him again. Jimmy was given Mickey and Matt's names. It suited the man who lived in the tower. He gave orders for the Firm to be picked up. They were all, naturally, sentenced to death.

Georgie used head, fists and boots in an effort to escape as the ASU tried to pull him into the van. He almost made it. He was five yards clear from the van when the first heavy, hollow nose bullets from the Thompson tore through his back punching big holes out through his chest. One round hit his heart and as he lay dying the midget poured the rest of his magazine into his head.

The man in the tower threw the midget out the window. The little bastard screamed all the way down. I aimed for his legs indeed! It was suicide. Midgets were always committing suicide in a noisy, irksome way, jumping under buses in the rush hour, setting fire to themselves at cup finals, blowing themselves up on aeroplanes along with all the big people. The little bastard had no business being with the ASU. He had bluffed his way onto it to prove his manliness. To prove he was one of the boys. Well he wasn't. He was a poxy midget. You'd think he would have went out like the man he wanted to be and not be wheeeeeeeing all the way down.

Jimmy Apple was obliged to report to the man who lived in the tower twice weekly and had to carry out a number of different functions for him such as telling O'Stitch misleading information about certain Movement matters. O'Stitch would not be pleased by this, knew Jimmy, but what could he do? He didn't fancy having his balls ironed out and then jumping off the tower. No. That didn't appeal to him at all.

Ned O'Stitch was delighted to get Mickey and Matt's names from Jimmy. He started at once to put his finale into action. This was going to be the best stitch-up anyone could dream up. The fact that he had no evidence against the Firm did not daunt him in the slightest. He'd soon put that right. Ned put in a discreet call to the Black Porkers up above and got down the two Belfast men's records. He had photographs, fingerprints, ages, characteristics, methods of operation. Ned opened up his Forensic Cabinet and took out his file on MacGregor's gang. He added the Belfast men's names to the gang and sighed. He was happy as a pig in shit. He took Bonkie's file out and threw away his stand-by evidence. No use collecting evidence for a man that wasn't in the country and who had a hundred alibi witnesses. It was ideal that he was out of the way. Ned intended to insert another man into Bonkie's alleged role in the Ballygojingle job. Joe Snatchel. Ned had his lengthy statement before him. Joe had confessed to being involved in the Ballygojingle job (in a minor capacity) and was willing to give evidence against the Firm in court. In return for this brave stand Ned gave in writing to Joe's solicitor (Jimmy Apple) a guarantee Joe would not be prosecuted for the rape and killing of two hitchhikers. Ned had Joe's confession to these and a host of other sex-related offences nice and safe in his filing cabinet. Joe was being held up in the Joy in isolation where he was treated with every consideration even to the extent of having a few pints while he read up on his pornographic studies. A few hairs here and there, a bit of verbal and MacGregor's gang were gone. Ned put on his cap and overcoat and headed for the DPP's office with his statement to have the Firm charged with murder. Murder and bank robbery.

The man he left in charge of the office worked for the Branch. MacIntrigue had been astounded at what the Branchman had put in his report, verbally, to him. He had ordered O'Stitch to be watched discreetly. The Branchman sat behind Ned's desk. He saw the file in the secret waste. ATTENTION! THIS WASTE MUST BE DESTROYED BY FIRE! The Branchman pulled out the file. The undated forensic evidence against Bonkie fell on the floor. He pocketed it and rang for the clerk to empty the waste bin.

"Make sure you burn that, garda."

"Right Sergeant."

The Branchman was baffled. It was a queer assignment watching the country's top man but it was a damn sight queerer to find him throwing away what appeared to be forensic evidence from a case. And that was odd too. The evidence although preserved for court had no date, no case on it. He noticed though that the spaces were blank. Ready to be filled in.

"Brady", he called to one of his men.

"Yes Sergeant?"

"Take over here. I'm wanted below." The Branchman walked across the courtyard and knocked on MacIntrigue's door.

The Firm sat disconsolately around the completed SS Security van. It was a first class job needing only the registration plates to complete it. Bonkie came in after leaving Sally. He carried the pump which did not suit him at all well now he fit the banker's part. Bonkie had worked really hard on his part.

"How is the missus?" asked Mac.

"Fine. I took care of it." His reply was curt. He was still a bit cool with Mac.

"I have something for yew", put in Mickey. He gave Bonkie a photostat print of O'Mally-Smyth's driving licence. The banker's signature was firm and clear. It would not be too hard to forge. Mickey behaved as per normal. It was obvious he was saying the stroke is going ahead regardless.

"That's perfect, Mickey. I reckon I'll have no problems with this." Bonkie put the sheet of paper in his inside pocket.

"What are we going ter do, Mac?" asked Alfie. He was Georgie's best mate.

Mac sat up on the workbench. He was shook up and in a murderous mood. There was nothing they could do about Georgie. He was gone. Dead. Blown away. And, the Big Grey Jug was still there. He had ter hold this stroke together. It was more than the big one now: it was the difference between life and death. They all needed enough to pull out of the country.

"The stroke goes ahead. That's our first priority. Georgie still gets his full whack. We'll give it ter his auld ones. Any objections to that?" Mac looked around fiercely daring anyone to protest.

"I'll go and see the auld one, Mac. See if she needs anything. What about the funeral? Are we going?" Alfie meant are you going with me.

The Cork man spoke softly but with emotion. He too had been very close to Georgie. "Alfie, boy, it's bad news this day. It's shocking, boy, but if Georgie were here now, and it were one of us down, he'd expect the stroke to go ahead."

"What are yer getting at?" Alfie sounded weary. He rubbed his eyes.

"That you represent us at the funeral."

"You mean yer not going because of the poxy stroke?"

"You go Alfie", continued Bob determined not to become emotional, "but take precautions. We can wake him after we have our business concluded boy. You know that makes sense".

"Sense be bolloxed", exploded Alfie, "it doesn't make any sense to be ripped to bits after coming out of the boozer after a few pints. I'm going ter his funeral and no one is going ter stop me".

"No one is trying ter stop you", said Mac smoothly, "are they? We are asking yer to represent us all. To represent the Firm. Yer know all gangland will be there and we have ter make a show. We have to show our face but what's the sense of getting nutted? We can't go tooled up because the porkers will search us all. Whatever happens that's a certainty. But the Movement can have men and gear anywhere. What do yer want us ter do?"

"I know all that, Mac."

"Georgie will laugh in his coffin when we pull this, Alfie." Bob clenched his fist. "And when we pull it I'll find out who done this and I'll do him a bad one when he's not expecting it. I swear ter God I will boy."

"He's dead right", Bonkie placated Alfie, "if we try anything it's just plain stupid. Georgie protected this stroke with his life. He knew what would have happened to him if they had got him inter the van. If he went down for the stroke the least we can do is not throw it away."

"It's agreed then, lads", asked Mac, "do we carry on with the stroke?" And the answer being so obvious he carried on, "out there we are dead men. We won't even have that risk on the stroke so let's get down, for Georgie's sake, and behave like the professional he was. We owe him that". Mac whipped up morale but there was no need really. Their position was very clear. Without the poke they were dead men, hunted rats. The stroke was everything. The only question to be answered now was – when do we go ter work?

Alfie went to the funeral in the same car as Georgie's parents. He conceded to the Firm not to carry a pistol. He got out of the car and saw Georgie's wife, the one he abandoned, by the cemetery gates with all her relations. They were all dressed in black and the wife was crying even though she hadn't seen Georgie in years. Alfie reckoned it was weird but to be expected in a bleeding country that forbade divorce. The wife was keening and being consoled by the priest just as if Georgie had been the model husband.

Ned O'Stitch and his gang of heavy porkers stepped out from behind the mourning in-laws. Alfie thought it was cool. They were going ter frisk him.

"You go on Mrs Beak", he said ter the auld one. The auld one and the wife hugged each other and the grief of Georgie's death united them for a brief minute.

Alfie never did get ter see his old mate laid ter rest. He was spread eagled against the cemetery wall and searched. O'Stitch stepped forward and charged Alfie with murder and bank robbery. Alfie was bundled into a porker car and driven off to the Special Court.

The press who had haunted the funeral flew after the porker cars, misery vultures, hopping red lights, breaking the speed limits, in their urge to bring the good news to the plain people.

In the Court O'Stitch objected to bail on the grounds he had confidential information that Alfie and his gang were going to murder the witness.

"What bleeding witness?" shouted Alfie from the dock. He was led below.

To be stitched up or shot? Which was it to be? Is there an alternative? Yes. Go flat out. Do the Big Grey Jug now. While they were still alive. Set the date Mac. The sooner the better.

This weekend.

Chapter 19

HE longed for the end of the week. The job in Cash Control was utterly boring. It was a job that could be performed by a senile robot. His main function was to sign hundreds of forms of every type endlessly. There was no banking involved at all. He hated having to descend into the bowels of Dublin each day but O'Mally-Smyth had one big consolation. He was rich and getting richer as SS expanded and became more and more profitable. In a few years he would be so financially powerful in the Bank, in his own right, that he hoped to delegate the job to a subordinate. Already he had begun the process of replacing old staff and putting in his own men. They did things his way and cut through the red tape that strangles so much of our enterprise and initiative. He turned into the drive of his house. Delores was away, as usual, for the weekend which for her started on Wednesday or Thursday. Her white Rolls was parked at the side of the house. He was glad she was not there. The thin veneer of the happily married couple that was presented so painstakingly by him to the banking public, and his bosses, was abandoned in the house. A state of mutual contempt was in existence, neither of the pair caring in the least what the other did. They ignored each other as much as possible but beneath the ignorance the bad feeling lay poised, ready to spring and strike like a coiled angry cobra. They hated each other and were it not for the money involved would have lived as far away from each other as possible. Yes, he was glad she was not there walking naked past him when he was studying. Trying like an immature schoolgirl to tease him, to show him too what it was the Minister craved. He buried himself in his Arabic and steeled his will. For some perverse reason she resented this. It had become a game for her when she was bored, which was most of the time, to titillate him, to bend over before him on some pretext exposing her buttocks and neat trim pussy. She'd pick up her bag then leave in the Rolls. His wife driving around the city in a Rolls wearing no knickers. He shuddered to imagine, indeed he could not imagine, what she got up to. He hoped she would not cause a scandal and ruin everything. The bitch owned ten per cent of the company. He resented that bitterly.

He parked the Merc and opened the front door. Here he could plan his future, here was where he did his real work, slogging away towards the day when he would own his own bank. He was a banker and no one, not even a degenerate and greedy wife, was going to deflect him from his goal.

O'Mally-Smyth was grabbed from behind by a pair of powerful arms. A cold metal object was shoved into his neck.

"If yew make a sound", snarled the first hooded man who appeared in front of him, "I'll cut your throat". The man put a fighting knife to his chest, while the man who was holding him had his hand over the banker's mouth. "Understand?"

O'Mally-Smyth nodded. He understood very well. The men bound and gagged him expertly before he had time to even be shocked. He was strapped to one of the dining chairs. His interrogation began almost at once.

"Who lives here with you?" asked a hooded man. He took off the gag. The banker was not going to go hysterical.

"My wife. Look there is no money..." O'Mally-Smyth was slapped across the mouth by the man. The hooded man's dark eyes bored into the banker.

"No one asked yew for money mister. Just answer the questions and nothing else. Who else besides your wife?" He shouted in his ear. "Who fucking else?"

"Only my wife. We have no children", he apologised.

"Where is she? When is she due back?" Mickey already knew where she was. Down in Galway having a session.

"I don't know. I mean she won't be back until Monday. She doesn't usually come back until Monday or Tuesday sometimes." He knew it didn't sound right.

"And yew don't know where she is?" asked the hooded man.

"No, I don't."

The hooded man gave the banker a mild going over then gagged him and put a hood on him.

"The bitch isn't here", he heard the man say, "and he has no kids".

Had they intended to kidnap the wife and kids and hold them for ransom? The banker chewed over that information. They could not be too bright if they did not have those details.

"Who are you expecting to call at the house?" The hood and gag were again removed. This was a different gunman. He had some kind of a machine gun and was in combat gear.

"No one. I spend the weekend working alone."

"Do you go out at all? What do you do on Sunday?"

"Nothing much. I go to mass and have a few jars at the local."

"Hmmmm", said the gunman, "that's very interesting". He took out a pair of pliers and pulled out O'Mally-Smyth's front tooth. "If you", said the gunman softly, holding up the bloody tooth in the pliers, "tell me anymore lies I'll pull out every tooth in yer head and then start on yer fingernails".

The banker was in a bad state. When he tried to speak blood blubbered all down the front of his suit and shirt. "Don't, for God's sake. What is it you want?"

"Information. Accurate and detailed information. We know a great deal about yer already. If yer lie yer get tortured and shot. If yer tell the truth yer get well treated and we will leave yer alive. We are not robbing you."

"What information is it you want?"

"Don't pretend now, Patrick. You are Cash Control Manager. We want the cash. You are going to tell us how we can get it. Yer life depends on it."

"Then I am a dead man", muttered the banker. "It's impossible to get any cash out of the vaults. Impossible."

"Oh yeah? Tell me all about it. Start at the beginning, from when yer go inter work." The gunman reached over and wiped the blood off the banker's chin. "Tell me everything Patrick. And don't try and fool me now." He tapped the banker playfully with the pliers. The banker winced. "You never go ter mass of a Sunday. Yer up playing bleeding golf with the American Imperialist Maxwell." Mac was enjoying freaking out the banker.

"Imperialist? No, he works at the bank ..."

The gunman with the dark eyes grabbed him and shook him so violently the chair almost toppled over. "American Imperialist", he insisted, "as if yer didn't know. The fucking CIA man".

The banker's head was well and truly confused. He put all thoughts of resistance out of his head. It wasn't his money they were after, if indeed, it was money they were looking for. "I'll tell you anything you wish to know", Jesus his mouth hurt like hell, "but no heavy stuff".

"Untie his hands", ordered one of the gunmen. When this was done, "do you want a drink?"

"There are painkillers up in the bathroom and some cotton wool." The banker felt his mouth. Great as his shock and fear at the gunmen in his house, greater still was his worry. No one could get money out of the bank. What was going to happen to him when they realised this was the case? What would happen to him if they tried to rob the bank regardless? He was handed a large glass of whiskey. O'Mally-Smyth managed to get it down without hitting the wounds in his mouth.

"Another?" The gunman held the decanter.

"No, thank you. You must realise from the very beginning that I am not responsible for the security arrangements in the bank. I cannot bring any money, not a penny, in or out of the vaults. No one is allowed to bring money of any description, in or out."

"How is the money taken in and distributed?"

"By the security companies or by special courier."

"Tell me about it. Tell me about it. Smoke?"

The interrogation went on all Friday night until Saturday morning.

The Firm moved O'Mally-Smyth to Mickey's rented gaff, driving through the early morning traffic. Mickey removed all his bugs from the house. O'Mally-Smyth was given a cup of tea laced with sleeping tablets and he was put to bed under guard. The Firm were all in the big D. It was no problem the banker filling out an order for cash, up to any amount, and for him to arrange a van to have it collected. The problem was the gardai were obliged to be notified of all monetary shipments so they could provide armed protection. This included an escort of Free State Troops.

The armed escort was not in itself an insurmountable problem. The Firm could turn the van off sharpish onto a side road and give the escort the slip. Blow down a few trees in their path. Open up on the soldiers while the money van swings onto a route. The big problem was that the gardai would want notification of where the money was going to and always rang up to verify and make arrangements at the other end. This was done by Maxwell's security office which had instant contact with all parties to the shipments and at a fingertip all relevant information. Any odd or peculiar shipment would have to be cleared by them. Bonkie could get into the jug alright and give all sorts of orders but it was looking bad to get any poke out of there. Mac explained it all to Bonkie.

"The old money, the stuff to be burnt is shredded up and stuffed in big mail bags. It's taken to another place, up to Ballsbridge, to be put into the furnace. That's how tight it is. Even the rubbish, as they call it, is shredded before it is burnt."

"Anything to stop a man earning a shilling", observed Bonkie bitterly. "Who collects the rubbish?"

Bob looked at his neat notes of the interrogation. "Security. It's an old practice. From the time they used to bring them up unshredded. Every Tuesday after lunch. Two men, usually a Transit, but it could be a lorry depending on the amount of rubbish. It takes genuine rubbish too, boy."

"Any escort with it?" asked Bonkie, a faint hope rising in his heart.

"I never asked him, boy." He leapt up and ran upstairs with the rest of the Firm. Matt was sitting at the end of the bed. He jumped up. "What's wrong?"

"Wake up, wake up you lazy bastard." Bob shook the banker. "Coffee, get the man coffee for God's sake boys." O'Mally-Smyth was dragged down the stairs and sat by the fire. He was groggy and exhausted. The hooded men were all staring at him. They were restless, agitated. The coffee put a bit of life into him.

"What do you want for Christ's sake? I've told you everything." He was dejected.

"The rubbish van. I want you to think about the rubbish van. Did it ever have an escort?"

O'Mally-Smyth was cross with such stupid questions. "Yes. I told you."

The Firm were shattered.

"But not now. Not after we got the shredder. It only carries, shredded, you know, useless, shredded. Like a cabbage. Shredded like a cabbage." He began to weep.

The hooded men began to cheer and dance around the room waving their machine guns and pistols at the ceiling. One of them put his arm around his shoulders. "Don't be crying, mister. Yew are only letting yourself down. It's alright. It'll be all over soon. Just a few more wee questions. You can answer them can't you?"

"Yes." He sniffed. "What do you wish to know?"

Bonkie listened carefully to the banker's voice. It was a bland neutral accent, false and affected to begin with. He could do it easily.

"And if the rubbish van, as you call it, was to call on a Monday, or a Thursday, instead of a Tuesday, what would happen? Would it be let in?"

"Yes, after the Chief Security Officer checked it out. It would come up on the computer you see."

"Do you have to sign any documents for it such as you do for consignments of money?"

"No. They just come down and the rubbish is handed out to them."

"In those big distinctive sacks with the red stripes painted across them. Are these sacks passed out along the roller through the wire mesh?"

"Yes. The very same as the sacks of money."

"Is the office rubbish sent out in the same sacks?"

"Yes, we shred all the Bank's confidential documents. It all has to be burned."

"How many sacks go out each week?"

"It varies", O'Mally-Smyth yawned. He could barely keep his eyes open. This was ludicrous. Questioning him about bags of rubbish. "The rubbish must go out each week. It's a fire risk. Obviously we cannot have a fire at the Central Bank."

"Do you have fire practices?" Bonkie used his own accent.

"Fire drill? Yes we do –"

"Who authorises them?" Bonkie's nose was on the scent.

"I do of course."

"How long do they last?"

"It varies." He'd love to see the bastard asking him these stupid things swinging on the end of a rope. "Half an hour maybe more."

"Could you remain in the building while the rest of your staff went on fire drill? Could you stay at your desk?"

"Of course. I am the boss."

"You would be down there all on your own then? For at least half an hour?"

"Yes that's correct."

"And no one watching you?"

"Watching me? No, but there are closed circuit television

cameras. They are on sweep all the time. All the time."

"Show me on the map here exactly where the shredder is located and tell me who is the man in charge of it."

O'Mally-Smyth needed no aid in going to sleep after these sessions were at an end. He fell into a deep, deep sleep hoping the gunmen got whatever it was they wanted.

Bonkie rang Maxwell from O'Mally-Smyth's gaff on Sunday morning. He told the American to call and collect him because his car had broken down.

"Sure thing Patrick. I'll be there about nine thirty. You can stand me breakfast. Do we have a deal?"

"How do you like your flapjacks Maxie?" Bonkie was cool as ice.

"With eggs, sunny side up, and tay not coffee. OK?" Maxie was in great humour. Patrick had assured him of the renewal of his contract.

His wife was thrilled.

"Nine thirty it is." Bonkie put down the phone. He looked at the three lads, "fifteen minutes lads".

Maxwell pulled up in the street in a mustard coloured Volvo. He walked sprightly up to the O'Mally-Smyth's door. Patrick was standing there with the door ajar.

"Hi ya, Paddy boy." He walked past Bonkie.

"Hi ya Maxie", Bonkie turned and walked in behind him. He closed the door.

"Don't shoot", said the American calmly, "I'm an American citizen." He raised his hands high above his head. Bonkie came walking into the room. "What the fucking hell is going on Patrick?"

"They have kidnapped my wife, Maxie. Do what they say for God's sake."

"Alright, alright man. Anything you say."

The American was tied to a chair and the interrogation began. Maxie told the same things as the banker. Neither was lying. At lunchtime one of the gunmen handed the American the phone. He placed a pistol to the man's head. "Do it."

"Hello dear. How are ya keeping? Oh fine just fine. Listen, honey, I have to go off on a bit of business with Paddy." There was a pause. "Listen will ya, his car has broken down. We have to meet some people about business. Yes, the business. It's urgent."

"When will you be back?"

"Monday afternoon at the latest. I'll make it up to you honey." The phone slammed down at the other end.

"How did she take it?"

"Fine. Just fine. She's just a mite peeved that's all."

Maxie was moved out at dusk and placed in the same place as O'Mally-Smyth. He was in a different room and didn't know the banker was there.

The Firm shook hands with Bonkie out at the Banker's house. He was on his own now. There was nothing else they could do. It was all down to Bonkie now. He closed the door and went into O'Mally-Smyth's study. It was almost eleven o'clock.

Bonkie poured himself a glass of whiskey, it would be his only drink, and he tried to get a bit of relaxation. Well tomorrow he'd be in or out, up or down. In a way he didn't give a bollox. He wasn't scared and that, to him, was the main thing. At least he would go out with a bit of honour and a bit of respect. He dozed a bit by the fire and never heard the front door open. When he opened his eyes there was a really sexy chick sitting in the chair opposite him. She was out of her head on something. It was Delores of course.

"Did you have a thrilling weekend? How was the interest rate, hmmmmm?" She poked out a pert tongue at Bonkie and made licking motions with her lips. She slipped out of her coat and threw it on the rug.

"Alright", said Bonkie. He was uneasy. He hadn't expected this. He couldn't help looking at her.

"Alright", she mocked him in a high pitched laugh. Then she noticed the look.

"How long is it since you had a fuck? Can you still get it on, Patrick?" Then she spread her long lovely legs wide one over each arm of the sofa. She put her head in her hand and looked at him quizzically. She flicked her tongue in and out of her mouth rapidly.

Bonkie had an enormous erection on. He stepped across and slapped her on the mouth. He turned her around and tore off her pants. She was surprised. She shoved her buttocks in the air. Bonkie tried to ram into her. He was floundering. A hand came between her legs and gripped his cock. She guided him into her hot warmth. "Oh you're so big, so hard, it's so big", she moaned and wriggled on his hard cock working herself up and down it. Holding it half way down only letting half of it enter her. She climaxed rapidly and tried to climb off Bonkie before, just before, he ejaculated. Bonkie gripped her tightly around the waist and began to pound into her, harder and harder, faster and faster. She let go of him, urgently responding to each of his thrusts taking all of him deep into her. She moaned and moaned scratching the rug with her nails. Bonkie flung himself into her and his orgasm was a series of violent spasms. Delores gasped for breath. Bonkie kept going pulling her back and forward back and forward until he was riding along on a wave of sensual pleasure. Delores settled down to a passive role as Bonkie fucked her from the rear. He was superb. He was unstoppable. The thought came to him that if he could fuck the banker's wife then he should have no problems screwing the Big Grey Jug. He quickened, quickened, until he strained and filled her again. She put her hand around again and gently massaged his testicles, touching, feeling, gripping the thickness of him. He was so hard, so broad, Patrick was never like this. Bonkie began to go limp. He pulled out his cock and quickly pulled up his trousers. She wanted to suck him.

"No", he said primly.

She put on a very petulant face. Fierce anger was on her face. She stomped off up to bed.

How could he let her suck his cock? When he was seventeen he had, with two other Dublin tearaways, gone into a tattooist's in London and all had the same job done – 'All for you' tattooed on their cocks. He couldn't really let her see that. He was famous up in the Joy for his decorated penis. The first time Sally had seen it she was fascinated. She liked to see the letters get bigger as it went erect.

Bonkie went up and went to bed. He had sorted out that hot bitch. She wouldn't show her face before he was away to work in the morning. Bleeding slag she was. He set the alarm and tried to get a few hours sleep. Tomorrow was the big day.

Bonkie left the house quietly with his briefcase and his overcoat under his arm. It was a lovely fresh morning. He breathed in deeply. Was this his last taste of freedom? The weeks of preparing for the stroke were at an end. He was like a prizefighter going for the title after all the rigorous training. All he could do was his best. He sat into the Merc and pulled the heavy door closed. The car started first time. He put the lever to drive, released the handbrake and pulled out into the street. Everything was relaxed and calm. The middle classes were sending out their breadwinners into the market place. Strangers, to Bonkie, and to each other, all performed the same ritual as he. Up, into the car – a different one for different status – out into the street and away into the city. In the solid well-maintained investments formidable matrons roused and grilled their offspring into the day's training schedule. The brats were trained in the pursuit of wealth and status and were prepared after the lifelong indoctrination to make sure they succeeded at any cost. To fail, not to be successful, was unthinkable. This fear banded them together as a class of select exploiters who talked and acted differently to their fellow citizens. They called us the Labour Pool which, to Bonkie, sounded just as bad as the cesspool. It denoted something that could be filled up or drained off, something that could be pissed in, something to sail battleships on, something that could be sucked out, something that could be poisoned, something that could be bottled, something that was contained by boundaries. He had never heard of the Labour Pool breaking its banks and swirling off to rush and roar along the streets depositing gold and silver in its turbulent wake. It was an insipid grey pool of depressed, sedated, drunken, but above all duped, fools. Fuck them thought Bonkie. If they take it, it's their own business.

Down in Sean Macker kids were waking up wondering where in God's name they were going ter get their next fix. Up in the Joy, Jimmy the Murderer was turning in his barbed wire cocoon as the screw turned the first master lock off. Another day ter get through. The second lock went off at eight thirty and the door opened for another day's whack. Ah well, at least he hadn't got a bleeding mortgage hung around his life sentence like a millstone. In the estates and schemes the robots were finishing their rushed cup of tay and off scurrying to catch the bus. Musn't be late or I'll get the boot. They don't like slaves that are not punctual. It breeds irregularity, slovenliness, bad work practice, contempt for the employers, and loss of profits. That's all for being five minutes late on a Monday morning: what must be in their heads when a blag, a decent blag, goes off? Some moron with a shotgun gets enough in five minutes (so it seemed) to buy a gaff? That had to cause unease at the top. It had ter stick in the managerial craw. What will happen to production they screamed if they, pointing out at the asbestos-breathing, dermatitis-covered, drooping drones, all start it? Who will cut his neighbour's throat for a hundred pounds a week? Less tax.

Whatever they bleeding do with it all.

If Paddy Murphy takes it into his head to go a blagging instead of to his lawful employment, driving a getaway car instead of a bus, the bleeding managers and the middle classes will have to go on the labour and yer can't have that, can yer? Anarchy. Subversion. Alien ideology.

Bring out the FCA. Give the porkers two machine guns each in case one breaks down. Stop them at any cost.

But what was the cost? It ran into countless millions to try and stop a few blaggers.

Economically it would pay the Minister for Justice to give every bona fide blagger, a man who had at least five proper jugs, a town and country house, a cabin cruiser, fifty grand capital and a pension of two hundred and fifty a week. No one would blag in such circumstances. Yet, to even suggest such a scheme would warrant certification that one was criminally insane. The masses would go berserk. Suburbia would put up the barricades. The churches would start issuing out AK47s. Civil servants would form subversive organisations to topple the government. It wouldn't be hard as they had it by the short and curlies anyway. So had the porkers and priests. If people from space, alien economists, studied the proposal to subsidise blaggers not to rob, a type of redundancy or severance pay, then the whole thing would make perfect sense. It was no use. They would put the space people into quarantine and deport them on the next rocket home. It wasn't good counting to spend, say, one hundred million to stop one million going astray.

Security was a business. It was as essential as the arms race and the dole.

Confrontation within society, between nations was essential.

He stretched in the Merc. He put on a tape. Bonkie didn't mind a little Mozart. He felt refreshed and vital.

Just out of perversity, or curiosity, he drove around Sean Macker before going to the bank. The next time I come around the street it will be in me own Merc and kids will say – look there's Bonkie. He used ter live here I'm telling yer. Yer a dirty liar, Weasel. And the kid would run over and shout. How are ya, Bonkie. Can I mind yer car? He'd get out and go in ter Murray's and have a few pints and the locals would say – that's Bonkie. He made it ter the very top.

He'd come out and drive off, give the young fella a fiver or a tenner – it all depended how rich he was, just as he was driving now towards the Big Grey Jug.

Sally lay with the child cradled in her arms. She hadn't been able to sleep and when she did the same nightmare came. Bonkie was lying in a shallow grave with the front of his face blow away. She had the nightmare the first night she moved into the cottage. But he'd been there beside her in the bed, strong, solid beside her. It had only been a nightmare and when Georgie had been shot dead it had come to her that it was true. She had second sight they called it. She could see things sometimes. Once she had seen Geraldine Fitzpatrick squashed and flattened on the road in a dream. Five days later she had been killed by a coal lorry. She had the dreams on and off. Some happened some didn't, but this one was so vivid, so clear and real. She saw him kneeling and the bullets tearing into the back of his head, taking away his face. And then he slowly fell forward into the grave and twisted around with dead sightless eyes looking up bewildered at his killers. How could she tell him that? She hated him going off on a stroke and thinking she was a moody bitch. The wind caught the door and slammed it shut. She startled and hugged the child closer and buried herself under the blankets.

Mrs Maxwell received a call from her husband. He sounded cheerful. He would be back home for his meal that evening. He would be phoning the bank to let them know he would not be there until after lunch. I'll phone for you offered the wife. The gunman with the magnum to his head thought this a good idea. He nodded to the security man. That's terrific honey. Thank you. He was bound and gagged again.

Superintendent O'Stitch drove along the dual carriageway from Swords towards the city. Mike Murphy had put on Mario Lanza singing 'O What A Beautiful Morning'. The porker reached over and turned up the sound. It reflected his mood most exactly. He had dispensed with his driver collecting him in the mornings. They did not know at the Castle of his deserting the wife or of his new bungalow and it would surely be imprudent for them to find out before he resigned. He had to collect up the rest of the Firm first. That should take a few months during which time he could take it easy and plan his retirement. Get down to a serious bit of greyhound breeding and racing. MacMahon had turned out to be the best of a trainer, the best. Life was good. Thanks be to God, said Ned and made the sign of the cross on his forehead for luck.

Delores O'Mally-Smyth heard her husband going out to work. Had he really done that to her last night? She resolved to leave off the coke for a while and the booze. It was burning her up. The sexual performance of Patrick the night before didn't fit into her head. It wasn't him. But of course it was. She was confused, depressed and hung over. She had rowed with the Minister at Galway and had gone off in the huffs. She put the pillow over her head and shut out the world.

Up in the remand wing of the Joy Alfie said a prayer and then some more that the lads pulled it off. Fuck up the trial with a few tame barristers and get him bail in the High Court. Ned hadn't charged him for nothing. He had a one hundred per cent track record. Everyone he had ever charged had gone down the Swanee for a long time. He didn't get up for the porridge. He had bacon, egg, sausages and strong aromatic coffee in Bewely's the day before. He turned over in the bed. He wouldn't be able to eat today anyway if they were serving up Christmas Pudding and had bunny girls carrying it around the cells. His prayers changed to a chant so low not even a spider could hear him – come on Bonkie, come on Bonkie, come on Bonkie ... He looked at his watch. He should be there now.

Bob and Mac, decked out as dickheads, relaxed in the barn beside the cottage. They had perfect ID and the van was registered up to an SS van that was in the security company garage with the engine and gear box out of it and up on the bench.

"Mac, what time is it now boy?" Bob had asked the time a few minutes before.

"It's a few seconds to half past –" The phone rang at half past. Mac picked it up. "Bank of Ireland, Inchicore", he spoke into the phone.

"Sorry. Wrong number." Bonkie put back the radio phone in its socket and stepped out of the Merc. The flunkey saluted him. "Good morning, Dennis", said Bonkie and sailed past him.

"He's going in now, Bob". Mac bit his nails.

"Relax Mac. It's going to be a long morning boy."

The phone rang again a few moments later. Mac lifted it up. "Bank of Ireland, Inchicore."

"This is Mr O'Mally-Smyth speaking".

"And how are things? How is our contract?"

"Piece of cake old boy." Bonkie put the phone back on his desk. He pressed his intercom. "Send me in Mr Dockrell please."

"What did he say" asked Bob.

"He said that it's a piece of cake." Mac smiled.

"A what, boy?"

"A piece of bleeding cake. Wee buns. He's in. He's in Bob."

Mr Dockrell came into O'Mally-Smyth's office. He was a pleasant easy going man. Very eager to please.

"I have to do a fire drill this morning Michael. I have to check everything myself. I want you to take over all my duties for the day. Can you do that?"

The assistant manager looked a little surprised. It was no secret however that the Boss detested the form filling. "Yes, that should be no problem, sir."

Bonkie had intended to make some excuse about having a sore throat to cover up any defect in his manner of talking but he saw no necessity to do so. The man in front of him was behaving perfectly. "Good man. Divert everything off me this morning will you?"

"When will the fire drill take place, sir?"

"Just before lunch. Bloody things. Keep it to yourself. I want you to take all calls for me, deal with anyone who may call, just as if I were not here. Let my secretary know on the way out. All right." Bonkie reached for a sheaf of papers.

"There are some documents that must have your signature, sir."

"I'll do them all after lunch. This fire drill business. It's", he lowered his voice, "it's coming from the very top. I think the whole bank will be out. Insurance assessors."

"I have you, sir. And we are not supposed to know, snap inspection to test our competence." The assistant manager wanted to be in the know too.

"Keep it quiet."

The assistant manager rose to go. "Thank you, sir."

"But", said Bonkie taking off his glasses for emphasis, "make sure you are ready."

"You can rely on me, sir." Dockrell winked and left the office.

I bleeding hope so, thought Bonkie otherwise I'm in trouble. I haven't a clue about banking, well, not the straight end of it anyway.

He got himself a millboard and clipped onto it a few sheets of print and a sheet of blank paper. Armed with these mysterious items he wished himself luck and stepped out into the poke cavern. He had tried to visualise, from the banker's descriptions and diagrams, what it would be like in the vaults. His conception of all that poke was as a penny is to a chest of treasure. At first he didn't know what it was the workers were carrying, pushing and pulling on little carts, around the place. It was money of every denomination. Blocks and blocks of it stacked on racks as high as the ceiling, so much money they shifted it around on truck trolleys and in one corner for the gold and silver was a forklift. Bonkie had easily carried the Ballygojingle poke with one hand. It was only a pittance. This was just the same as the warehouse department in any big factory he reminded himself. Relax. His legs were trembling.

"Good morning sir", greeted a worker. He was carrying two huge sacks of twenty pound notes. One in each hand. They were so big, so swollen with poke they dragged along the ground.

"Morning", Bonkie looked at the sprinkler above him as if preoccupied. He didn't know who the lick was but he wouldn't good morning him carrying that poke if he were up above. He walked along the racks checking the fire points at the end of each. Fire extinguishers, axe, buckets of water and sand, fire hoses and a sprinkler system screwed into the roof above the poke. Couldn't have the poke going up in smoke so to speak. He read the instructions that had to be obeyed in case of fire. Everyone had to assemble up in the courtyard above, or, in practice the canteen. Great. They could all have an early lunch.

There was a camera at the end of every row of racks where the poke was stored. Its sneaky little metal head turned this way and that always trying to catch someone out. They were well out of hand-reach, about ten foot up the wall. They were going to be a problem. They had a view of everything. He hoped there was a blind spot in by the shredder.

There was every type of money down here. Not just Irish money but foreign money too. All neatly stacked and marked. There was new money, reissue money and money condemned to the shredder. The serial numbers of the new money were pinned up on the rack. Bonkie noticed there were no lists of serial numbers against the reissue of foreign currency. It didn't look like money. It was all wrapped up in white paper packages like cartons of cigarettes. He opened the door to the porkers' department.

It would take a hundred blaggers to screw this place in a blag. At huge long tables sat over fifty girls flicking through, counting money, at professional speed. The money blurred below their nimble fingers. Bundles flicked into open-mouthed voracious bags. Hundreds and hundreds of bags all waiting to be fed. How could anyone work in here? They would have a nervous breakdown. In the middle of the tables were stacked ones, fives, tens, twenties, fifties, and hundreds. All the way along to the end of the table. The girls worked either side of the mounds of poke. They pressed buzzers and young lads brought them new bundlies when they ran low.

"One hundred in twenties", they shouted at him.

"Two hundred in twenties", this was said as if they were ordering buttons for shirts. Two hundred grand in twenty punt notes. No problem. The young fella had them up in a flash.

"Fifty in tens."

"Two hundred and fifty in twenties".

The girls took no notice of Bonkie. They were too busy. He walked through the packing room, checked it all out and back out again.

"What's he doing?" asked the security man up in the office above.

"Checking the fire equipment", he peered into his screens.

"Oh, good luck. Another Rocking Horse".

"A Rocking Horse? I don't think we were told about it", observed the man who monitored the vaults. "Get on and ask him."

"Right."

"Excuse me, sir. You are wanted on the phone."

"Who is it?" he asked the young fella.

"Security, sir."

Bonkie's stomach turned to ice. Not from fear but the horrors the stroke was going to be fucked up. He went to an extension.

"O'Mally-Smyth here. What is it?"

"A little birdie told us you were going to have a Rocking Horse maybe."

"So?" Bonkie didn't know what he was talking about.

"Ah come on now, sir. You know the drill. We like to know to maintain our schedules and so forth. What time do you think it is at?"

"I don't know what you mean. What Rocking Horse?" Bonkie was sweating.

"You don't know?" the voice hardened.

"Put Maxie on for me."

"Ah, that's it. He's not here. He won't be back until after lunch I'm told but we know the drill up here. We have to be ready for it too."

"The fire practice?" Bonkie copped on. "I told the boss you see."

"Ah!" exclaimed the security man, "that's it. And he never came in. That's the way of it so".

"Just before lunch. Twenty past twelve. Sorry about the confusion. It's really meant to be a snap drill, like the real thing. Keep this quiet. We will be watched today. I want everyone out. Thank you for calling. You are very observant thanks be to God." He managed to put a bit of lightness into his voice.

"Ah, sure you know us, sir. We miss nothing up here. Good luck." Security hung up. "It's a big one, Eddie. At twenty past twelve. Maxie knew all about it."

Eddie punched out a code on the computer. "It's not programmed to take place. It's not like him not to feed that in."

The other man laughed. "Sure it's not like him not to come to work of a Monday morning either."

Bonkie was drenched in sweat. He pulled out his handkerchief and mopped his face. Inside his suit the sweat ran in rivulets from his arm pits and soaked his shirt. He was certain he would stink to the high heavens. It was only a quarter to ten. He walked on into the room where the money brought to the jug was checked and sorted out. It was organised along the same lines as the packer's room. The only difference was that when the girls came across ragged, worn or torn notes they threw them into a basket at their feet. When they filled a man came along and emptied them into a big mail sack at the end of the tables. It had a red three inch band painted horizontally and vertically on it to distinguish that it contained rubbish. With so much poke about it would be easy to drop in good poke and it would not do to burn good, clean, money. If it were burnt or stolen or lost it was all the same. When the sack was full it was taken to the shredder.

Bonkie was really sick in the shredder room. He watched hundreds of thousands of punts being gobbled up and spat back out as worthless pulp. The old money was checked off, condemned, then tipped into a big hopper on top of the machine. The machine gobbled it into its blades and chopped it up finer than one could cut paper with a pair of sharp scissors. The destroyed poke came out compressed in thick bundles to fall into the big sacks. As each filled up, the sack was tied and dragged over to the area beside the wire fence where the bags of poke were issued out to the armoured cars. The compressed bundles of shredded money were rectangular brickettes with hundreds and thousands of poke symbols in each brick. All the colours of the poke range were in the bricks. Some made from old pound notes were predominately green, others were bright red full of shredded old twenties. They were heavy and one man could just manage a sack full of the money brickettes. This place was really tight. Bonkie looked at a van being loaded up. Directly in front of him, beyond the two wire mesh fences, was the lift gates. The van came down in the lift and backed up to the fence. Its load was waiting on it. The despatcher put the money bags on the roller that ran between the fences and rolled them out. The dickheads from the van collected them and loaded up. They drove back into the lift and up into Dame Street but they were forbidden to move off without their escort. It was all very calm and relaxed. Business like. In and out. There were vans to be loaded and unloaded. Another van came in to unload. The back door was flung wide open. It was stacked with bags of poke. The dickheads flung them out onto the rollers as if they were bags of spuds. Inside, the receivers dropped them into big plastic baskets on wheels and took the incoming poke to the checkers. It was extremely efficient. The door beside Bonkie opened and a big man walked out.

"Just a minute there", said the heavy porker. He was carrying an Uzi. Worse, he was one of the heavy gang that had booted him around the Bridewell. Bonkie had spat into his face.

Bonkie got ready to leg it. Leg it to where he thought? I'm in a bleeding cave. A tomb. A catacomb. Bonkie in the porkers' den.

The heavy porker raised up his Uzi.

Chapter 20

BONKIE turned as slowly as possible from the heavy porker. His name was Connolly from the Task Force.

"Excuse me, sir", said the porker. Bonkie turned back. The porker put his Uzi under his sports jacket. Bonkie took the initiative. He was under pressure. "Do you have to carry those things about the vaults?"

"I can't leave it houta me hand. Regulations, sir." The porker was cool.

"Oh, it's not me sergeant. It's the bloody unions. Always complaining."

"If a gang of thugs came into de place you wouldn't hear much houta de unions den. Dey'd all be a hiding in de canteen."

"I never hear much out of the unions, except complaints, at the best of times. However. Are you looking for something?"

"Dere's no milk for de tay hand we are not hallowed to leave our post."

Bonkie collared a worker and sent him for milk. "What are your orders in the event of a fire drill?" It seemed incredible that Connolly didn't recognise him.

"We stay as we are. We stay down in the vaults no matter what happens. Hit's honly ha practice."

"Perhaps. But that's not according to the book. The manual states that I must have my department cleared of **ALL** personnel. Are you in charge down here?"

"I am. I'm on duty until ten o'clock tonight. We know habout de regulations but dey are disregarded hin de hinterest of security. I take hit dere's going to be a Rocking Horse today?"

A girl came and gave the porker two pints of milk. He never paid for it.

"And I know all about security, sergeant. The point is everyone is legally obliged, for insurance reasons, to go up to the assembly points in the event of a Rocking Horse. That puts me in a bit of a dilemma, doesn't it now? We don't want you to leave the vaults. How many men have you here?"

"Six. Dere's six of us. Our orders are not to leave unless hit his cleared by security. Our own security."

"I certainly don't want you to leave the vaults, sergeant. But listen here now, I do have a job to do, a department to run. This fire drill today is a big thing, it's an insurance assessment. I cannot have anyone moving around down here so I want you to stay in your room. Can you do that?"

"We do hit all day long hanyway, sir. You don't want us to be seen? His dat hit?"

"I have to make a report that the Department was cleared of **ALL** personnel. We are responsible for your safety too you see. The assessors will use any excuse to push up the premiums. Inefficiency – six men left behind. Six casualties. Our fire practices are dangerous etc", Bonkie waved his hands in the air, "have you any idea how much insurance costs?"

"Indeed I do not, sor. As dey say I haven't a bull's notion to be sure. How much?" The porker was mightily impressed.

Bonkie hadn't a clue. He pursed his lips and sucked air through them as he had seen culchies do when he asked them the price of a bunch of scallions. He shook his head.

"As much as dat", declared the porker. And he thought isn't it no wonder de interest rates are so high? And the amount of tax he has to pay. "What habout the half-hour patrols? We walk around de place every half-hour. You know, one or two of us."

"I'll confide in you sergeant. The alarm will go at twenty past twelve. The staff will assemble upstairs in the canteen until I call the all clear. I want no one moving down here between twenty past twelve and half past one. Otherwise I'll get onto the Commissioner and have you moved upstairs."

"Ah, dere's no need for dat."

"When the Chairman and the Board of Assessors come around I don't want them to find you here so what are you going to do?"

"I haven't a bull's notion."

"Lock your door, sergeant. Lock your door."

"Hand hif dey knock we don't hanswer. His dat hit?"

"Splendid. Now give me your men's orders for lunch and I'll have them sent down on the bank."

"Dat's very good of you. Tank you, sor."
"We can afford it I think. I'll arrange that with the kitchen. Well that's all. Nice talking to you sergeant."
"Hit was my pleasure sor. My pleasure."
I wish I could say the same thought Bonkie. You mutton-headed bollox. Bonkie went up and called in on Dockrell. "Everything alright, Michael?" he asked.
"Fine sir."
"No problems?"
"None."
"Good man. If anyone is looking for me I'm up above with the General Manager. Don't work too hard."
"I won't."
Bonkie liked Michael Dockrell. He was polite and efficient. He went into his office and buzzed his secretary. "I don't want any calls. If anyone is looking for me I'm up above in the bank."
"Yes sir."
Bonkie lay back in the big swivel chair. It was a plush office. Tastefully decorated and the absence of windows was compensated to some extent by a very big landscape that took up most of one wall. It was an original, as far as Bonkie could tell, of the Canadian Rockies. Signed by a French-Canadian. It captured the sweep and height of the wild mountains but not, thought Bonkie, the grandeur. It would be alright for a few weeks but he thought one could soon get to find it boring which was the difference to him between good art and bad. He always got the same punch when he looked at a good piece of art no matter how many times he saw it. What he really liked was a piece that slammed into you, that screamed at you, that tried to choke you with outrage or love, or passion, or joy, or beauty or ugliness. And then after yer got over the first visual assault yer had ter say what's this person at? Why is he attacking me with his palette? What did I bleeding do to her or him? There was a small still-life – a bowl of fruit done in oils in the corner. It was painted in Belfast during the Second World War when fruit, the bananas and oranges in the picture, was scarce. As scarce as the jewels the painter had made them out to be? He thought about that. It was very good but he didn't think so. They were not as good as Renoir's strawberries. He looked at his watch. Half past eleven. Jesus. Another hour to go. What am I going to do? What does a banker do? He has a gin and

tonic and does the crossword. The gin and tonic was fine but he couldn't do the poxy crossword. It was getting on for time. Quarter past twelve. Bonkie slipped on his gloves and carefully wiped everything in the office he had touched. He lifted up a stack of pink paper money bags and a few dozen elastic bands and put them in his pocket. It was twelve seventeen. He picked up the phone and dialled an outside number.

Mac picked up the phone. "Bank of Ireland, Inchicore", he said.

"I have that contract ready for you. Call in and collect it."

"And how are things at the bank?" asked Mac.

"Flourishing. Couldn't be better." Bonkie put down the phone. Apart from the detachment of heavy porkers, he reflected. No point worrying the lads about them.

"What did he say, boy?" asked Bob. He was eager to go.

"He said things were flourishing." Bob climbed into the security van and started it up. Mac opened up the gates and climbed into the back of the van. The van pulled away towards Dublin. The lads were on their way.

Bonkie went to the fire alarm box. He opened it with his special key and pressed the red button. The bells started clanging immediately in the vaults. He walked out to where the staff were filing quickly but orderly through the gates to the staff lifts. He watched them benevolently and looked at his watch as O'Mally-Smyth had shown him. He clapped his hands to hurry them along. The vaults emptied in four minutes. Bonkie went back to his office and rang security.

"We have a fire drill practice down here", he informed the watchers.

"Yes sir. We have the area sealed off."

"The practice ends in thirty minutes. Let the staff have an early lunch. They were very good."

"Right ho, sir."

Bonkie walked out into the empty vaults. He collected a small step ladder and hugging close to the wall facing the racks of money he climbed up and grabbed the spy camera. He stuck a pink paper coin bag on its snooping eye and secured it on with an elastic band. Bonkie did the three cameras along the wall in the same way. He walked as quickly as possible into the shredding room and bagged the camera there. The sweat poured off him. He was fever hot. Bonkie flung four of the big rubbish sacks into a trolley and pulled the trolley up to the racks of money.

The dollars were the first things he took. They were small in volume and could be passed anywhere. He filled up one sack with all the dollars from one shelf. They were all fifties and hundreds. He neatly tied the sack closed. He filled another sack with used fifty punt notes and the other two with reissue twenties. It took all his strength to heave them into the trolley. He looked at his watch. It was almost one o'clock. He could just pull the overloaded trolley and no more.

"Look at this", said the monitor up in the security office to the Boss.

The Boss looked at the screens. They were all showing up a pinky red colour.

"I never saw them do that before." He flicked a switch and the porkers' room came into view. They were eating and drinking away. He flicked another switch. The three porkers in the entrance cubicles at the bottom of the staff elevator were sound. He gave them a buzz. "How are things?"

"Fine."

He rang the porkers inside the vaults, "How are things?"

"A 1", replied Connolly, "why?"

"A couple of the cameras have gone on the blink. It's alright I'll call maintenance and get them down before the staff return."

It was unfortunate that security used the words 'on the blink' for it conjured up in the porker's tiny mind a flickering television screen. If they had said – the screens are showing pastel pink or rose madder then the porker's capacity for suspicion at strange and unknown things would not have been impaired and they may have investigated. Such is the penalty for the usurpation of the native tongue and the adoption of alien descriptive prose.

"Right ho", said Connolly and waved a chicken bone at the camera in his room.

Security rang maintenance and told them to get a technician down there right away.

As he passed each camera Bonkie climbed up and pulled the paper bag off its snout. It was slow and cost precious minutes but it was essential it be done. The urge to go as fast as possible to the shredding room was fierce but what use was him in the shredding room with the poke and someone comes and sees the hooded cameras? As it was now no one could see what he had in the rubbish sacks so he might stand a pull on them. And the sooner he put the cameras back on, security would not be aroused. He reached up and took off the bag on the fourth camera overlooking the money racks. The technician came into the vaults.

Bonkie saw him. He made a superhuman effort and pulled the trolley with one hand dragging the step ladder in his other into the shredding room. Once through the doors he sprinted over to the last camera, put up the ladder and pulled off the bag. He jumped off the ladder out of its range, and kicked the ladder down as he fell. The doors opened.

Bonkie pretended he was tying his lace. He stood up and walked over to the technician. He stood beside the trolley full of poke.

"Excuse me, but there is a report the cameras are not working. I have to check them out." The technician's walkie talkie beeped. "Maintenance", he spoke into it. The radio told him all cameras were functioning as per normal.

"They seem to be alright now", he said to Bonkie as if Bonkie could not understand transmitted English. He turned and went off.

Bonkie walked as quickly as possible to his office. He rang Mickey. Mickey got on the radio to Mac and Bob who were parked up around the corner from the jug in Parliament Street. He told them to go in. Bonkie rang security. It was only fifteen minutes before the staff were due back.

"Security."

"The CSO there? This is O'Mally-Smyth."

"No. He won't be back until this afternoon. After lunch."

"Did he order a van to collect the rubbish? To collect it today?"

"Just a minute, sir." The security man consulted the computer. "No. He didn't."

"This isn't good enough. I have a department full of inflammable material at the best of times without a room full of bloody rubbish. It has to be cleared. This isn't good enough."

"Sorry sir."

"You phone me the moment he gets in." Bonkie slammed down the phone. He sat down for a moment. He was bone weary. He forced himself to his feet. The phone rang again. He picked it up. "Yes? O'Mally-Smyth here."

"There's a security van here to pick up the rubbish."

"Good. Send it down."

"We can't do that sir. It's not scheduled until tomorrow. I don't have that authorisation."

"For God's sake send the bloody van down to collect the rubbish. I'm authorising it."

"The only person who can do that is the CSO, sir. I'm sorry."

Bob was sitting in the driver's seat. He was looking at a big square-headed moron who paced up and down beside the van. They got through the first gate and were waiting to be admitted into the lift that went down into the vaults. In the back of the van Mac boiled up like a lobster in a pot. The heat was fierce. They had been unable to fit out the van with air conditioning. He looked through the darkened windows. Directly across from them was a GPMG emplacement and at the entrance to the lift shaft was a sandbagged position. On the building to his right was another army position on the roof. They had no chance at all if it came on top. He looked at his watch. Seventeen minutes past. They were gone surely. The staff all came back at one thirty. The van started up and Bob put her into gear.

Mickey held his fighting knife to Maxwell's throat. He had explained it all to the security man. The American rang his office.

"CSO here. How are things?"

Mickey listened to the security man enquire about the unscheduled van.

"I'm authorising you now to let that van in. I'll be there around three."

The security man began to protest. He had to have it in writing.

"Dennis stop the bullshit. Let the van down. It's there on my instructions. I'll sign when I get to work. Do it. That's an order. It's only collecting rubbish for God's sake."

"Alright. It's your neck sir."

"Quite", replied Maxwell. He glanced at the dagger at his throat. "If my wife rings tell her to call me at three o'clock. Put me onto O'Mally-Smyth."

The security staff eavesdropped on the CSO's convervation with the banker. They were discussing some deal or other. Something about the contract being secured. They sent down orders to let the van into the vaults.

Bob and Mac descended into darkness.

Bonkie waited with heart pounding. His fear and fatigue of the previous few hours gave way slowly to the view that they were going to pull it off. The lift opened and the van reversed out. It was twenty-five past one. Five minutes. When the staff came back the scream would be heard as far away as Australia. The checkers, the men in charge of the money racks, could tell at a glance if so much as one small bundle was missing from their particular area. The van stopped beside the roller and the driver hopped out. He banged the back door like a mulchie and the man in the back opened up. The porkers opened up their door and looked out.

"Everything alright sir?" asked Connolly.

Bonkie knew it was too late. He hadn't enough time. He walked up to the porker.

"I need this rubbish out, sergeant. Can you give me a helping hand?"

Mac and Bob saw the five big porkers come out of the room on the other side of the wire fences. What could they do but stand there? They watched in awe as the porkers gripped the big sacks and flung them down the roller to them. They gripped the sacks as they fell beside the van and flung them into the back.

"And these four here lads", said Bonkie pointing out the four sacks of poke.

The porkers gripped them and flung them out along the rollers. The last four sacks landed at Mac and Bob's feet. The staff started to come out of the lifts.

Up in the security office the staff laughed at the idea of O'Mally-Smyth getting the gardai to go to work for him. There was no doubt he was going places.

"Staff, staff", cried O'Mally-Smyth as he stood between the staff and the vaults. "Just hold it there a moment please." The incoming staff stood like sheep wondering what the hell was going on. "I won't keep you a moment. I have an announcement to make." He called over Dockrell. "Just keep them there a moment please. Don't let anyone into the vaults."

Bonkie went back through the swing doors and looked over at the despatch area. The gates to the left were closed and the van was on its way. He had to give them a bit of time. How? Not another one. He had no alternative. He went into his office and unlocked the fire alarm. He pressed the button. The bells went off.

"Fire drill, please staff", he shouted at the assembled bank staff. They were like sheep. They just turned and walked back to the security elevators. Bonkie waited until the last had filed through the security cubicles. He followed.

"What is going on, sir?" asked the porker in his hutch. He looked at Bonkie in a very odd way. He was suspicious as hell.

"I wish I knew", replied Bonkie sharply. He knew he must look, hot, dishevelled, his cool was gone. He saw the porker pick up the phone. The door opened before him and he walked to the elevator. It took a long time coming down. He stepped in like a drunk man. Like a shipwrecked man climbing into the lifeboat. The doors opened.

"What's going on down there?" demanded a heavy porker. There were three security men with him.

"That's what I'm going to find out. How the hell can I run a department like this?" Bonkie stormed out along the corridor. The security men got into the elevator. It seemed to Bonkie the game was up. He turned at the first chance and slipped out the door into the car park. The flunkey waved him out into the traffic. In front of him he saw the van being escorted by a motorcycle porker.

Bob had driven out the jug with no problems. He didn't even need a pass. He was only carrying rubbish. Things were looking good. As he pulled out into the street past the long row of SS vans a motorcycle porker raised his hand. They were bolloxed he thought and not a bit of gear between them. The porker fell in to give them a clear ride through the traffic.

Bonkie watched the motorcycle porker return Bob's salute. He sat astride his Honda in the middle of the road holding up the traffic to let the van through. A big solid figure of authority. It was the first time Bonkie had ever seen a porker do anything useful. The van needed every minute it could get.

In the back of the van Mac's bangers were at crisis point. The porker's big beetroot head with the white helmet stuck onto it frightened him with its friendly grin. If it was chasing him it would be cool. He could try and burst it or something. The porker got smaller and smaller and then he saw the Gresham on his left.

Bonkie followed the van when the lights changed to green. The Speedy U turned and drove off on his track. Bonkie caught up with the van at Whitehall. He overtook, giving the lads a beep. Bob waved to him as he passed. The VW van was parked up in the Crofton Airport Hotel carpark. Bonkie set the triple incendiary in the Merc, wiped the car again, and drove away in the VW. The security van was waiting for him at the switch.

Bonkie pulled out his four sacks and checked each one by slitting it with a stanley blade and having a look inside.

"Four?" asked Mac incredulously. Bonkie nodded and took the wheel of the VW. Bob set the incendiaries in the van and left ten gallons among the sacks to make a good blaze.

"Right Bonkie", said Mac, "that's it". He slammed shut the side door. The van pulled away down the side road, leaving the security van locked and hidden in the leafy layby.

In the back of the VW the lads changed out of the dickhead uniforms and pulled out two M16s in the very remote chance they came across porkers. No one was getting this poke back. The lads switched on the porker radio they had taken with them in the security van.

"Anything?" asked Bonkie.

"Not a squeak or a squeal outta them", said Mac. "Bonkie, how did yer do it?" He touched the big sacks of poke. "What was it like?"

"Mac, I've been wanting to say this all day. It was a bleeding piece of cake."

"How did you get the porkers to throw out the bags boy?" asked Bob.

"Ah sure aren't they big strapping culchies? I wouldn't 'ha been able except for the likes of that I'll tell ye."

"All units, all units", screamed the radio. Mac turned it up. "All Sierra and Task Force Units operation Griptight. All units, all units, operation Griptight."

"The scream is on, lads", said Mac. He cocked his M16 and edged over to the back door of the van. Bob loaded up and took position at the side door ready to pounce out on any unsuspecting porker.

"All units are to be on full alert for a Mercedes saloon motor vehicle, silver grey in colour, registration number NDI 230. The occupant is to be detained and Sierra summoned."

"It's a scream surely boys. Griptight is sealing off the entire city I'd say. How far are we off base Bonkie?" asked Bob.

"Ah it's cool. Another five minutes or so. We are well outside the ring. There won't be any roadblocks on this road." He looked at O'Mally-Smyth's watch. "I'd say they will find the Merc soon. It went up a couple of minutes ago."

"It doesn't sound as if they are onto the security van yet", mused Mac.

A squad car blue light flashing, hee-haw screaming, screamed past them going for the city. The lads in the back held their breath.

"It's cool", said Bonkie. "That's the Howth squad cars. They must have ordered them into the city. It's cool. There will be no one out at the Base."

"All units, crackle, crackle, all units be on the lookout for SS Security van registration RZJ 557. Detain occupants who may be masquerading as employees of the company."

"I bleeding love it, I bleeding love it", enthused Mac. The porkers' heads would be very addled and cross indeed.

The VW passed through Howth before the radio spoke again. "... abandon search for Mercedes vehicle. Forensic units go to Crofton Airport Hotel. A vehicle answering the description of that sort is reported to be there. A unit of the fire brigade is on its way ..."

"They will be dragging dickheads out of vans and law abiding assholes off aeroplanes up in the departure lounge. It's a good one boys." The Cork man was exceptionally pleased.

"Turning in for home lads", said Bonkie. He drove up into the barn. Bob locked the doors and Mac dragged out the bags of poke.

It was a lovely sunny afternoon. Bonkie ran through the fields to the cottage. Sally was pushing Saorise in the swing in the back garden. Bonkie sneaked up on her. He grabbed her. "Guess who?" he yelled tickling her.

"I seen ye coming but I never told her", said the child.

"Oh, thanks be to God he's back", cried Sally.

"What's bleeding God got ter do with it, he wasn't on the stroke was he?"

"Bonkie don't say such things." She was outraged at such blasphemy. "Did yer do it?"

"Did I what? It was a piece of bleeding cake. Just one ...", he stopped and gave her a long warm kiss. "Sal it's over. For good. I done it", he could hardly believe it himself now. He sat on the old bench. "I pulled off the big one."

"No more robbing?"

"No more robbing, no more poxy jail, no more poxy anything. Right! I just came up to let yer know I was safe. I want yer to burn every bit of paper in the gaff and all this clobber. I'm going down ter count me poke."

"How much did yer rob?"

"I don't bleeding know. So much I don't bleeding know. Whoever said such a ting before Sal? A few people in history I'd say."

She raised an eyebrow at him saying aren't you exaggerating a wee bit?

"I swear Sal, so much I don't bleeding know." He changed into his denims and ran on a cloud back to the barn.

Mac and Bob had cleared the workbench top and were stacking the bundles of twenty pound notes onto it from one sack. There were ninety-seven bundles in the first sack. Bob was calculating it all up on his pocket calculator.

"One million, nine hundred and forty thousand punts."

"That's only one sack", croaked Mac.

Bonkie had a paranoid feeling that the white paper-wrapped bundles contained blank papers. He tore a few open. It was the poke all right.

"All units, all units, abandon search for SS Security van. Van found abandoned and in flames at Turnapin Lane, Airport Road. Come in Sierra Six. Come in Sierra Six ..."

"They found the van too boy", chuckled Bob.

Bonkie slit open the second sack of twenty pound notes. It contained one hundred and three bundles.

"How much was in that one, Bob?" Bonkie gazed at the steadily increasing stacks of poke.

"Two million and sixty thousand punts. Total so far is exactly four million punts. Four milliion punts." He lifted up a few sheets of paper that were laying in the bottom of the sack. "What are these?"

"Oh yer. Serial numbers of the fifty punt notes. I took them just in case but I think they are only off the new ones that were there like. Those ones", he pointed to the sack, "are used fifties".

"Fifties", said Mac, "and what's in the other one?"

"Dollars", replied Bonkie proudly. "I took all the fifty and hundred dollar bills that were there."

There was three million six hundred thousand in fifty punt notes. The dollars totalled nine million odd. Altogether over seven and a half million in punts and the nine million dollars. The Firm were stunned. Each blagger was now a punt and a dollar millionaire. They were outta the game. It was only down to getting their poke into a jug nice and clean. The thought struck Mac.

"I'm not putting my poke into the Bank of Ireland", he put on a posh accent, "place isn't damn secure".

"You're wrong there Mac", said Bonkie, "the security there is bleeding deadly. We were poxed lucky ter pull this off". He filled the lads in how tight things had been down there. "... and I'll tell yer I'd be very pleased to deposit my poke in there. I'd kinda feel better in me mansion, don't yer know, knowing that the heavy porkers were looking after me interests."

They had a good malicious jeer at the porkers' expense.

"If they ever find out we pulled this one boys", observed Bob, "I'd say we will be found up the mountains with our balls in our mouths."

"It won't be down to us? Will it?" put in Mac.

"Who will it be down to?" asked Bonkie innocently.

"O'Mally-Smyth. Who else?"

"What about when he turns up screaming about his two front teeth not ter mention being kidnapped?"

"Because he's not going to turn up anywhere."

"Is there something I don't know Mac?"

"The banker is on the run boy with all the money he robbed from the bank. Him and his accomplice are missing ..."

"Presumed dead, I suppose." Bonkie was quiet. They should have told him.

"Mickey is looking after them", explained Mac. "He wants to earn his few bob."

"Both of them? The American as well?" Bonkie was going to rear up but what's the use crying over spilt blood?

"You had enough of it to do the ringer Bonkie. Yer have ter realise if it ever got out we pulled this we would be under threat for the rest of our life. It has ter be this way. It'll be the great bleeding Irish mystery. The press won't mind one of their own making off with all the poke and an American friend to help. They will love it. But if it's a blagger. A Paddy with a gun and a hood they will scream endlessly for yer head on a spike. Mickey found out all sorts of information when he bugged the gaff. Yer man's wife is having an affair with a bleeding government Minister. That's political scandal for the opposition. The whole thing is going ter blow up in the porkers' faces. Hopefully."

"Do yer mean ter say", said Bonkie pointing to the poke, "this is all going ter be down ter the banker?"

"It's looking that way", said Mac.

"We would be dead cool", enthused Bonkie, "lie low. Give us time ter get the poke safe inter a jug".

"And the banker", Bob explained, "had a finger in SS Security company".

The chief dickhead up there was on the phone to O'Mally-Smyth a few times."

"Fuck him", declared Bonkie. "I don't give a bollox about him. He lied ter us about the fire practice anyway. The porkers never left the place. Let's whack out the poke."

Ten dollars and the punts were whacked out into seven equal piles. Each man, including the dead Georgie, came out of the stroke with one million and eighty-five thousands punts and slightly over one and a quarter million dollars.

Bonkie's whack fitted comfortably into the mail sacks. It felt good.

Later that night Mickey and Matt arrived when he was up in the cottage with Sal, and took away their poke. Matt called up to see him. He and his da were off to the Middle East. They were going to purchase SAM missiles to shoot down the Queen's aeroplane whenever they got the chance.

"Yeah, well good luck ter yer", said Bonkie shaking hands with the young fella. He was going to advise him ter open up a chain of massage parlours or a couple of classy brothels but he was afraid the da would hang around and stiff him. What could he say? "Make sure yer fire it at the right aeroplane." He resolved always to travel by boat. The banker and the American were never mentioned. The richest virgin in Ireland. Bonkie shook his head. It was a crazy bleeding country.

The stroke was finished. They were all finished with stroking and each other. That night when he went down to the barn, only his poke was left. He put it into big plastic airtight containers and buried the poke in two separate holes in the sand below the waterline at low tide. Not only was the poke buried but it was under water most of the time too. No one knew where it was but himself. He buried one hundred grand to filter into a few banks immediately and showed Sal the dump in case anything happened to him in the interim.

When he came back to the cottage there was only Sal and the child there. The VW had gone. The Firm would never be back. He went to bed and wrapped himself around Sal and fell into an exhausted sleep.

Sally's nightmare never came back and every time she tried to tell it to Bonkie he went moody and refused to listen.

Chapter 21

FIVE days after the big stroke Bonkie was nicked getting off the ferry at Dun Laohire. He was coming from Hollyhead. Bonkie had left Sally and Saorise behind in a rented chalet on the Isle of Man. It was cool out there for them and she could relax a bit and look after the small bit of life that fluttered inside her. The Met Office forecast a good summer too. What odds? Summers were all alike up in the Joy.

It was impossible to miss Bonkie as he staggered down the gangplank. There wasn't a hair on his head. He had shaved the lot. His bald skull was criss-crossed and pluckered with scars from old wounds. On each ear he had an earring tattooed and for good measure, a big gold earring in the right ear. He had 'love' tattooed on his right hand, on the fingers, and 'hate' tattooed on the other. To complement his bizarre appearance he was dressed in rocker gear: studded leather jacket and tight leather jeans.

The passengers on the ferry looked at the drunken, loudmouthed, middle-aged fool with shame and disgust. One could understand, if not condone, teenagers behaving in such a way, but a man of that age? They were glad when the gardai gripped him at the bottom of the gangplank. He didn't put up much of a show then. Off he went as quiet as a mouse.

The porkers had a warrant for his arrest. The bailswoman had withdrawn her surety at the Appeal Court on the grounds that Bonkie had fled the jurisdiction. After the court had withdrawn the bail the auld one whispered to the gardai she had heard that he was coming back for a few days. She was frightened in case Bonkie attacked her for lifting the bail.

The porkers understood her fears perfectly. Bonkie was taken straight up to the Joy. The place was still humming with the impact of the big stroke. When Bonkie was sorted out and in his cell it seemed to the prisoners that he had never been away. His appearance did not look in the least peculiar up in the Joy. Prisoners often shaved their heads for various reasons and anyway, Bonkie was a well known eccentric. Alfie was in the remand wing. Bonkie sent word to him to see him on doctor's parade the next morning.

"Back hagain, Byrne?" jeered Creeping Jesus. His faith in humanity and the overall righteousness of his position was re-established. The happiness, the sense of conviction that he was right, oozed out of the screw. "People like you never learn. Do dey?"

Bonkie ignored the idiot. The Joy was as cool a place as any ter lay low until the heat died down about the big stroke. Ballygojingle had faded into insignificance. Bonkie walked up the corridor to the exercise yard. Creeping Jesus followed him breathing his fetid bacon and cabbage breath down Bonkie's neck. "One haway for exercise", screamed Creeping Jesus to the screw on the gate. "One haway." The screw opened the gate and Bonkie stepped into the yard. Creeping Jesus was staring through the bars at Bonkie. There was a tiny bead of moisture on his lip. Bonkie wondered idly what it was the screw was at. He was turned on. Bonkie went over to the jakes and threw up his guts. He washed in the cold water and dried his face with jakes paper.

"How are yer, Bonkie?" asked Dessie O'Hare. He was a kite man.

"I'm in bleeding bits, Dessie. I was nicked coming off the bleeding boat ..." Bonkie walked around the yard with the small timers talking shite.

Delores sat in her front room. She was pale and drawn. The gardai were all over the house searching it. They said they were looking for firearms.

"... and you are sure your husband was at home last night?" The big man in front of her gave the impression he did not believe anything she said.

"Yes. I told you several times."

"And he left for the bank this morning as per usual. What time was that?"

"I have already told you that. What is going on?"

"We thought you might be able to tell us. Was your husband in any kind of debt? Was he involved in gambling or..."

"Now this is far enough", exploded Delores. "How dare you. I demand an explanation of what is going on."

"Inspector", called a Ban Garda from the hallway, "can high see ye fer ha moment?"

The inspector returned in a few moments. He put the small vial of coke on the table.

"You are demanding nothing Mrs O'Mally-Smyth. Possession of a hard drug is a serious offence. Get yourself dressed."

"Why?"

"I'm arresting you under section 30 of the Offences Against the State Act."

Delores began to scream the walls down for the Minister's assistance.

Ned O'Stitch was taken into custody by MacIntrigue and his Branchmen.

"You better have a good reason for this", the Commissioner told MacIntrigue.

"I have."

"Go ahead."

Ned roared like a caged bull. He threatened MacIntrigue with everything including death. In the next cell to him was Crinion. They were all in the Bridewell under section 30. Ned had, naturally, denied any knowledge of any wrong doing and elected to exercise his right to remain silent when asked his relationship with the banker, his lovely wife, Crinion and SS Security. Ned began to get worried when the Branch began to ask him about moving, and leaving the wife, and not notifying anyone, and about the greyhounds. Ned still remained silent. He stayed as quiet as could be until the Branch dumped over one hundred thousand punts, in twenty punt notes on the table, and one hundred thousand dollars.

"This money was found at the back of your new bungalow Superintendent. Under the dog kennels. How did it get there?"

O'Stitch began to scream, "I'm being framed. I'm being stitched up".

Even the Branchmen laughed at that.

Orders were given to open Ned's filing cabinet in his office. Ironically this is what saved him from prosecution. Everyone knew for certain what he had been at. To expose him would bring the law into disrepute and disgrace. The plain people would lose confidence in the law enforcement process. His forensic gathering processes and his advanced system of putting together evidence before a crime went off was overlooked as a zealous preventative measure. Let the blaggers do their whacks.

Joe Snatchel's statements were found relating to the sex murders. The gardai insisted in the interests of justice these should now be offered to the DPP and Snatchel tried for the murder of the two girls.

Shortly after Snatchel heard the news he hung himself in his cell.

"How did things go Bonkie?" asked Alfie. They were standing on sick parade outside the doctor's surgery.

"Bleeding great Alfie. We fixed the case agin yer. Mac says they will enter a Nolle at your next appearance. Snatchel was giving false evidence agin yer in return for immunity from prosecution."

"The dirty bollox." Alfie's voice went down to the merest whisper. "How much did we take out of it?" There had been wild speculation in the media.

"Your whack is over one million in punts and one and a quarter million in dollars. Mac has it buried for yer and Georgie's whack too."

Alfie went a bit pale. It was hard ter take it in. He looked at Bonkie's scarred head. His auld one had often told him. 'Never judge a book, son, by its cover.' He wanted to throw his arms around Bonkie and run screaming and whooping along the landing.

"I'm", Alfie sniffed back a tear, "I'm bleeding choked Bonkie".

"Well this will unblock yer. We stitched up Ned with the odd few bob. Buried it out the back of his offside gaff. He's on permanent suspension. Listen Alfie, I have ter go. It's best that we don't be seen speaking together."

"Byrne", called the medical screw.

Bonkie disappeared into the doctor's surgery.

A blagger pulled in beside Alfie. "Do yer know yer man, Alfie?"

"No not really. He was asking me did I want a bit of work."

The blagger was mortified. "Have fuck all ter do with him. Nothing I'm telling yer." The blagger was indignant.

"Why is that Tonto? Is he dodgy?"

"Naw nothing like that Alfie. It's just he's a fucking eejit."

THE QUARE FELLOW

The chaplin will rub God salt
upon my cracked soul
this blessed day
and I shall shuffle
bound – but blissed
so they say
to stand upon
the trapdoor of paradise.
Supernatural gracelined walls
insulate the scaffold bay
I am sorry
beyond words
to go this way
and my feet have turned to clay.
I have not confessed
as yet
and therefore will give no tribute
to an indifferent God.
Will the entity
of all love – hear?
when they snap me as a twig
I can hear two shovels
softly scraping
for me a secret grave to dig.
Human hands
from the strands of life
they have twisted me a rope
a line turned and twisted tight
and my mother writes of hope
The screws are coming now
with the hangman
and a priest for good measure
I'll face the person I killed anon
Isn't life a dead mans pleasure?

Seamus O'Mulgreavey